DEATH AT THE SEASIDE

by

Frances Brody

Magna Large Print Books
Long Preston, North Yorkshire,
BD23 4ND, England.

British Library Cataloguing in Publication Data.

A catalogue record of this book is
available from the British Library

ISBN   978-0-7505-4471-9

First published in Great Britain in 2016 by Piatkus

Published in Large Print 2017 by arrangement with
Little, Brown Book Group

Magna Large Print is an imprint of Library Magna Books Ltd.

Printed and bound in Great Britain by
T.J. (International) Ltd., Cornwall, PL28 8RW

To Ralph and Mary Lindley

One

On the eve of her sixteenth birthday, Felicity Turner made a plan. From then on, everything fed into The Plan, Felicity's Plan. On her birthday, a guinea postal order arrived from her godmother and a Scottish five pound note from her father. She put the money in her savings bank book. Added to the existing balance of two shillings and ninepence, this gave her six pounds, three shillings and ninepence towards The Plan.

When the weather turned fine, something else happened. Brendan Webb – they had been courting since Christmas – began to work on that boat in his spare time: the *Doram,* owned by the jeweller. Felicity walked up to Sandsend to watch and to help a bit when it came to painting. It was a fine boat, bigger than most of the fishermen's cobles, and it had an engine as well as sails.

The jeweller, Mr Philips, said that Brendan could take the boat out when she was seaworthy.

The two things came together: Felicity's Plan and the boat. She would go find her dad. Brendan said he would help her.

Her dad's first picture postcard had arrived before Felicity learned to read joined-up writing. The looping large lines on the stamp side of the card looked like scribbles. When she asked her mother to read the card again, and again, and again, her mother turned snappy. 'I'm here. He isn't.'

Felicity knew the truth. 'You sent him away.'

Eventually, she learned to read her father's untidy scrawl. She saw now, looking back, that Walter Turner had never taken account of her age. In a way, that pleased her. On two cards he forgot to write Dad. He signed himself Walter. Three times he signed W Turner.

The cards, which she kept in a chocolate box, came from the Flowery Island of Madeira; the Jewel of Portugal's Coast; Glorious Cape Town; Boston (no adjectives) and Dublin's Fair City. When the more recent postcards came, starting two years ago, she saw that Walter Turner's travels had finally brought him within reach. He might come home.

He did not come home, but remained within reach.

Felicity had never forgotten how the sun changed the colour of her dad's hair as she rode on his shoulders. She remembered his looming shape when he kissed her goodnight, the smell of shaving soap and the silky touch of his blue cravat. Her favourite thing was the leather case that held brushes and comb along with a silver-plated box for a tablet of Imperial Leather soap, a shaving stick and a strop to sharpen the razor – the razor not to be touched. Her dad often laughed. Once he told her that life could be so amusing you just had to laugh.

She kept two photographs in the chocolate box along with the postcards. One photograph showed the three of them, taken in the photographer's studio, Dad sitting on the chair with Felicity, age three, on his lap, Mam standing beside them, her hand on his shoulder. Felicity saw now that he was old, even then he was old, and her mother young. The other photo was just Felicity and her dad. She was about six, and scowling. They were by the harbour, with a ship in the background. She used to believe he had gone away because she scowled.

He had come back three times since then, in the night. Each time, her mother told her that she had been asleep and dreamed his visit. That wasn't so. He kissed her forehead. He kissed her cheek. He slipped away like a shadow, like a ghost.

It was time to find him and bring him home, especially since her mother had become too friendly with the jeweller. She acted as if Felicity's dad would never come back.

Two

There's a moment when one realises that the horizon is no longer a joining of sky and land. It's the sea. The first glimpse of the sea always lifts my spirits as if suddenly I've returned to more carefree times. I had no distinct notion of which road I should take to find my way to the Royal Hotel, but by following my nose and some sliver of memory, I found myself on Whitby's West Cliff – just where I needed to be.

I stopped the car outside the hotel, taking off my motoring goggles and blinking into the light of a glorious day. Sun glinted on the North Sea that shone almost blue as it reflected the summer sky.

Leaving the car, I crossed the road and walked a few yards south, for a good view of the River Esk as it flowed into the sea between the two piers. Red-roofed houses climbed the cliffside. The ruined abbey stood proudly defiant. Beside it, the older still St Mary's church gave off an air of dignified sympathy. Whitby. Some irresistible attraction had drawn so many people to this end-of-the-world town hemmed in by the sea at its front and the wild moors behind. This was a lucky place for me, where I met my husband Gerald. We were young and had no notion that a war would come, and part us forever. We had walked together along the cliffs and on the shore, fell in love, chose my engagement and wedding rings. Captain Cook still surveyed his domain, his statue placed so that he looks out not to sea but towards the estuary.

Black's Guide to Yorkshire will tell you that Whitby is a town of much antiquity but little historical importance and that it owes its origin to the abbey founded in the seventh century by Oswy, King of Northumbria. For me Whitby is a place of happy memories. That's what I might recapture: the carelessness of being young, of having a future so vague and amorphous that it seemed like a dream, or a tale from some long-ago story. I had toppled into love. More miraculous still, the toppling was mutual.

Feeling fragile after recent events which need not concern us here, it seemed to me just the spot for recuperation. In Whitby, one can be alone and yet feel connected to the whole world. Once, whaling ships docked here. Now, fishing boats bobbed on the horizon, as they had for centuries.

On the beach below, children played in the sand and took splashing steps into the waves. Bathing tents formed a line across the shore, some white, others gaily striped. I took out binoculars for a closer look. A woman, baby in her arms, sat on a chair made of solidly packed sand, her parasol wedged into the arm of the sand-chair.

I felt suddenly lighter, and ready for anything, as I turned and walked across to the imposing, white-painted clifftop Royal Hotel that would be my haven for the next two weeks. The elderly doorman greeted me, took my car keys and said he would fetch in hand luggage and hatbox. My trunk had come ahead of me, by rail.

The place really did have an atmosphere of quiet refinement, just as advertised. The spacious entrance, high, ornate ceiling supported by grand pillars and a sense of hushed efficiency was just as I remembered. An immediate difference between now and back then was apparent at the reception desk. The man on duty was instantly recognisable as a former soldier, his face lined and pinched. The empty left sleeve of his jacket was neatly tucked into the pocket – one more living reminder of what we had experienced. It was brave and perhaps wise of the hotel management to put him on show. It's over. We've come through.

'Hello. I'm Mrs Shackleton and I'm booked here for a fortnight.' Just saying the words lifted my spirits.

A month ago, Mr Sykes, Mrs Sugden and I held a confab. We agreed that nothing ever happens in August and we might as well shut up shop and go away. Like the Wakes Week, when mills and factories and whole towns have a complete shutdown. It so happened that we all decided on the east coast for our well-earned rest. Mrs Sugden would pay a visit to her cousin in Scarborough. Mr Sykes and his family are in the habit of staying in Robin Hood's Bay, a fishing village a few miles south of Whitby.

The receptionist gave his best attempt at a smile. 'Welcome to the Royal, Mrs Shackleton. Have you stayed with us before?'

'Yes, but a long time ago.'

He looked for my name on his list. As he did so, I read the discreet notices boasting of the grand concert to be given by Frank Gomez and the Municipal Orchestra, and the Saturday dance with Howard Jones's Dance Band in 'the only ballroom in Whitby with a spring floor'. A spring floor. I imagined green linoleum strewn with buttercups and daisies.

He followed my gaze. 'We have dancing partners for both ladies and gentlemen. The dances are very popular. Everyone enjoys them.'

I wondered if the 'everyone' included himself. Probably not. He seemed a kind man and I guessed he might make an effort to make widows, spinsters and old soldiers especially welcome. I would no longer let myself think that thought: Did you ever meet Gerald Shackleton? Did you serve with him?

As he reached for my key, I asked, 'Have you a telegram form?'

'Yes and we can send it for you.' He took out a form from the drawer. 'Would you like to write it in the library?'

14

'It's very short. I'll do it here if I may.'
'Of course.' He handed me a pen.
'Thank you.'
My promised message to Mother was brief:

Arrived safely Kate

She had worried, advising me to travel by train and not drive through the wild moors. I reminded her that people further north than Wakefield long ago stopped painting themselves with woad, and that I would drive by way of York and Malton, all very civilised. Besides, driving is part of the enjoyment.

I handed the telegram to the receptionist.

'It'll go within the half hour.' He turned to the cubby holes that lined the wall. 'And this letter was left for you earlier.'

I recognised the handwriting. It was from my school friend, Alma, who lives in Whitby. I am godmother to her daughter, Felicity.

The receptionist tapped the bell for a porter. When the porter did not straight away appear, he said, 'Let me take you up, Mrs Shackleton. You've a lovely room on the first floor, with a sea view.'

He stepped from behind the counter and with his one good hand picked up both my valise and hat box. 'This way!'

We climbed to the first floor. I unlocked the door on a large airy room. I was clumsy in getting to my purse and he waved away my attempt to tip him. 'I hope you enjoy your stay.' He smiled and was gone.

What is it about the seaside that one must look

15

out to sea? I immediately went to the bay window. Watching the waves felt so soothing. I had come to the right place and looked forward to exploring. Even the weather looked set fair.

A young chambermaid tapped on the door, asking might she help me unpack. Normally I like to do for myself, but she had a nice smile and a willing air. Perhaps she needed the tip. I said yes, and asked her name.

She unfastened the trunk. 'Hilda, madam.'

'Are you named for St Hilda of the abbey?'

She laughed. 'If I am, it was a big mistake according to my mam, and I wished I wasn't, because who wants to be named for a saint?'

'Hilda's a nice name.'

She lifted out my pleated silk Delphos robe and gave it a shake. 'Aye well, could be worse. At least I'm not named after one who succeeded Lady Hilda, Edelfled Saxon Princess.'

Hilda's turn of phrase reminded me of Whitby people's tendency to disdain the definite article. 'Edelfled became a ghost, you know.' She placed the robe on a hanger, changed her mind because of its length and folded it carefully.

I love the rich colours of the Delphos tunic, turquoise, purple and orange, and have the habit of bringing it on holiday, even when there may be no opportunity to wear it. It was bought in Paris in 1908 by my mother's sister, Aunt Bertha, and carries its colourful history in every fibre.

Being here alone I would dine in the hotel each evening, starting with a cocktail so as to appear devil-may-care, not minding that I am solitary and looking forward only to a stroll on the pier and a good read after supper, though I had not brought a good book – only a couple of detective novels. But perhaps Gilbert K Chesterton was right to say that next to authentic goodness in a book – and that alas! we never find – we desire a rich badness.

As Hilda hung up coats and dresses and I unpacked toiletries, we chatted. She is from a seafaring family and lives in a cottage in one of the yards across the river.

'You should take a look about there, madam. To me real Whitby is east side.'

'I'm looking forward to exploring, so I'll take your tip.'

'Do you want a cup of tea fetching?'

'No, thank you. I'm going to stretch my legs and find a café.'

I changed into my voile dress and coat, the colour of sky and sand. Hilda retrieved my hat with its matching band. I left her to continue unpacking, giving her a shilling tip, which pleased her mightily.

I made my way back downstairs and went into the library to read the note from Alma. As I remembered, this room had an entirely different feel to any other room in the hotel. It held a deep sense of calm that would quiet the most agitated spirit. There was no one in there. Books and jigsaw puzzles remained undisturbed. I sat in a comfortable chair, looking out onto the narrow balcony and across to the sea.

Even though I have the incomparable Mrs Sugden as housekeeper, as long as one is at home there is always some domestic niggle; a bill to pay, a letter to answer, a neighbour or friend to speak to, a favour to return. Being on holiday is a great release from obligations.

The rather breathless note was a postscript to the letter from Alma that had arrived a couple of days ago.

Dear Kate, I forgot to say – when you are settled, come to the pier that is where you'll find me. Steel yourself for a surprise. Here is a clue: halfway along – pepper pot!!
  Your affectionate friend,
  Alma

The silly note made me smile. Did Alma think we were still schoolgirls? It would be good to meet up with her again. Most of all I looked forward to seeing my lovely goddaughter. Over the past ten years, she had spent regular holidays with me in 'the big city', with lots of outings. Alma had put her on the train in Scarborough and I had met her in Leeds. Now that she was working for her living, I would not see so much of her. Felicity is very special to me and has been since I held her in my arms on the day of her christening.

Three

The North Sea took on a terrible blackness, so dark as to be nothingness, the white foam showed grey on the lip of the waves. Only the lighthouse beam and the distant twinkle of far-off ships gave

Felicity a sense of this stretch of beach being the same place, the familiar daytime place.

Her boots squelched as she walked in wet sand, avoiding the rock pools that teemed with life. She had walked here so often, barefoot, sand between her toes. They had found fossils, shells and lucky pebbles, explored rock pools, watching the little crabs, marvelling at the sea anemones. She would tie her laces together and give the plimsolls to Mam to carry. Those days were gone.

Now she was grown up, had been working for two years, and nothing marvellous had happened – except Brendan.

Every birthday for ten years she expected Dad to come back and surprise her. Now she knew that would not happen. Time to strike out. If she didn't make a move, no one else would. She lengthened her stride. This voyage would change everything. Her father would be so glad. It's time to come home, she would tell him. Mam wants you home. Deep down, she knew that must be true. Before she presented him to her mother, she would say, Here is someone who has wanted to come back for so long, and now here he is. She would leave them together.

She was old enough to know there must have been fault on both sides. That was what she heard women say when she earwigged as she served in the café. 'Fault on both sides.'

The steady rhythm of the waves lulled her thoughts. She could not imagine how it would be to see him again. Her plan had not stretched that far. Was that a human sound? She turned. No one, only the relentless waves as the tide ebbed. At her

19

back, the moon hung low behind the skeleton of the abbey, high on the steep West Cliff.

Felicity wished she and Brendan had arranged to walk along the shore together. Brendan had gone earlier, so as to load supplies.

They hadn't told a soul. Her mother would know when she read the note. Brendan's mother would know when his aunt said, 'He's not with me.'

Mr Philips had decided to trust Brendan with the *Doram*. The man would have a blue fit if he found out how far they intended to sail. He didn't question them, and Brendan let him assume they would go to somewhere nearby, Lindisfarne at the very farthest.

Felicity began to hurry. The thump of the waves took on a sinister sound in the darkness. Don't be silly, she told herself. The tide won't change its direction to come and get you, wet you, wash you away.

As she walked, the blue serge trousers itched her legs. She had never before worn such clothes, trousers clumsily sewn by herself from a remnant bought on Church Street market. She wore two vests, a blouse, the bulky Aran knit cardigan, a borrowed muffler and to top that the yellow oil-skin frock. What a sight she would be in daytime. When she put the outfit together, it seemed as if she was doing it for someone else – like helping with costumes for the amateur dramatics.

In her knapsack she carried extra socks, under-wear, a flask of cocoa, sandwiches, hard boiled eggs and lemon buns brought from the café where she would never work again because Miss Botham blew a gale about her leaving in the middle of the season, August being the busiest month.

In the forty minutes it had taken her to walk from Whitby to the cove at Sandsend, the tide had ebbed further. The moonlight picked him out, tall and thin. Brendan waved both arms and hurried to meet her.

She'd always known him, seen him about. But it was only since December she realised he was the best dancer in the Spa ballroom. She hadn't let him meet Mam because he was from the east side and Mam would want to know this and that and all about him. His mam would be the same, only in reverse.

Felicity's mother was full of warnings, worries and dire prophecies when it came to Felicity and boys. She would say Felicity was too young to be so serious about a lad. Not that she had room to talk. Felicity had seen her own birth certificate alongside her mam and dad's marriage lines.

By moonlight, Brendan's dark-red hair looked black. She hadn't loved him the first time they danced together. She liked him then. He was a good mover and he made her laugh. He had a certain way of smiling, tilting his head as if to build up to it and then giving a big smile. She'd fallen for him when he was walking her home from the New Year's Eve dance. She got a stone in her shoe. He bent down, took off her shoe, shook out the little stone and then put her shoe back on. 'It fits, Princess Charming. You must be my bride.'

They had both laughed, but they knew he meant it, and that it would come true.

He kissed her and he wasn't smiling. 'Have you

21

changed your mind?'

'Would I be wearing these daft trousers if I'd changed my mind?'

'Only I been looking at maps and charts again. It's a longer way than you think.'

'We're going to do it, Brendan. We said so.'

'And I don't know why I didn't think of this, but us names'll be mud. People will talk.'

'If they've mucky minds, that's their lookout.'

'They'll blame me. Your mother'll put a curse on me.'

'My dad will come back with us. Everything will be all right.'

He took her knapsack from her and put it on his back. 'Did you tell anyone we're going?'

'No.'

'Somebody knows.'

'Well I didn't tell anyone.'

'In't concealed bulkhead, there's a packet with your dad's name on it. It wasn't there this morning. Somebody's onto us.'

'I can't think who, but they won't stop us.'

The *Doram* bobbed on the tide. They splodged out to meet her. In this lack of light it was impossible to see that the boat was a good size, painted blue and yellow. She looked grey and small. She was twenty years old and had hardly been out to sea. What if she wasn't up to it? Felicity was superstitious enough that she didn't want the *Doram* to feel her sudden mistrust. You're a good sturdy boat, Felicity said in her head. We'll take care of you if you take care of us.

But perhaps there was a good reason why the *Doram* had lain neglected for so many years.

Four

The wind suddenly gave a fresh gust as if to puff my sails as I left the hotel. Gulls squawked their derision as I debated which way to go, not remembering my way down higgledy-piggledy streets. I would keep to the main thoroughfares, if the streets of Whitby could be called that.

Reluctantly turning my back on the sea, I took a turning that would lead me into town, passing large dwellings, many kept as boarding houses and with most of their signs stating 'No Vacancies'.

As I walked onto Skinner Street, I paused to look in shop windows. Some were familiar from years ago. There was the post office, and when I saw that I remembered. This was the street where Gerald bought my rings. The thought should not have had such a powerful effect on me but it did. Putting off the moment when I would be drawn to the jewellers window, I went into Dowzells newsagents shop next door. Here I would buy postcards and a copy of the local paper for Dad. My father is superintendent of the West Riding Constabulary and whenever he goes away he likes to have a local paper, to see what preoccupies people in areas outside his own patch. I picked up a slab of butter toffee, remembering that Felicity liked it.

The woman at the counter tilted her head and gave a smile, almost as if greeting an old friend. She looked so happy, as if she had just come on holiday herself.

She was a little taller than me, and a little older, chestnut hair streaked with grey, shining eyes that appeared flecked with sunlight. She wore a cotton frock, patterned with geraniums. While I chose postcards, she stocked a shelf with chocolate bars, and then served boiled sweets to an old lady.

As I paid for the postcards, *Whitby Gazette* and toffee, I exchanged a few words with the assistant about the fine weather and number of holiday-makers coming to Whitby this year.

'Have you just arrived?'

'Yes. I'm off to hunt down a cup of tea and a bun.'

'Walk along the shore to Sandsend when the tide is out,' she suggested. 'There's a nice little café there.'

I paid her and she offered to make space for me to write my postcards on the counter.

'Thanks, but I'd be here an hour. It takes me ages to think what to say on a postcard.'

She laughed. 'I'm just the same. Sometimes it's the simplest things take the longest time. Where are you staying?'

'At the Royal.'

'How lovely, and do you have a view?'

'I do.'

There was a small poster taped to the counter, advertising a fund raising Bazaar, Sale of Work and Concert at the Seamans Mission the next day, Sunday.

She saw me read it. 'It's in aid of the Mission, as we all call it. I do hope you'll come along. It should be an enjoyable afternoon, and for a good cause.'

'Yes, I'd love to.'

'Excellent! I have some tickets if you'd like to get yours now.'

'I'll take three tickets then, no – four.'

Alma and Felicity might want to come and Felicity would be bound to have a friend.

As I left the shop, a tall, rotund man strode in, dapper and lively in striped suit and heavy watch and chain. He went behind the counter, saying to the assistant, 'I expect you want a break.'

I smiled to myself as I heard her say, 'Then you expect right.'

As I left the shop, a river of holidaymakers flowed downhill towards the town. I turned to join them, and then suddenly there was the jewellers shop. J Philips, High Class Jeweller.

I stopped so abruptly that someone bumped into me. We both apologised, though the fault was mine for coming to such a sudden halt.

It had been my intention to walk past, without looking, without thinking about that day so long ago. Yet look I must. Suddenly, nothing else mattered. There was the window display, hardly changed. The sensation gave me a slight shudder. As I stood in the here and now, my other self from years ago also looked into the window. I was here, alone, and also standing beside Gerald as we rather self-consciously looked at rings. Our fingers touch. The memory of that moment was so strong that all that has happened since fell away.

Perhaps the wind did not entirely drop to nothing, and the gulls continued their cry, but I was trapped in the past so intensely that I could not catch my breath and could not shift my gaze from the tray of rings.

For a moment, I did not realise that someone was speaking to me. Bringing myself back into the present with a little shake, I saw that the man who had entered the newsagents, the owner I supposed, now straightened papers in the rack outside. He looked at me in an odd way. He was waiting for an answer, having said something – but I did not know what.

He covered the awkwardness. 'Are you all right, madam?'

'Yes. Thank you.'

He straightened his cuffs and his gold cufflinks shone in the sunlight. 'Nice display, eh?'

'Very nice.'

The man's voice and my inane reply had broken the spell. The window was no longer completely dominated by rings. There were china ornaments, bangles, brooches and earrings. There was even a bracelet that would go perfectly with the black and white dress I had bought in Schofields for my goddaughter, Felicity.

The writer of a syndicated fashion column that appeared in our local paper gave her opinion that a black and white frock was very useful to a girl in mourning, or not in mourning. The sleeves could be either black or white. The columnist also suggested buying under-slips in both black and white. This particular frock had kilt pleats at the front, which seem to be coming in again. Not that Felicity is in mourning – that I know of – but it will be useful as well as pretty, just in case. Besides, someone is always dying.

This bracelet would definitely chime with the

dress. It had a delicate gold chain set with stones, alternating tiny pearls with jet beads – the jet Queen Victoria made famous and desirable when she chose it as her mourning jewellery after Prince Albert died.

It amused me to see that Victoria's favourite gemstone, readily found along this coast by fossil hunters, was now being sold in long necklaces for young flappers.

Step into the shop. That's what I must do. Otherwise, each time I came along this street I would be stopped in my tracks, caught in another time, and it would not do. After a different purchase, I would be able to walk by the shop with only the smallest pang of sadness and nostalgia, and not be overwhelmed. Besides, the bracelet would be perfect.

Would the jeweller be the same man? The name scrolled in gilt across the window was the same: J Philips, High Class Jeweller. I remembered him as tall and thin with bright red hair, but he was not so very old and that was before the war. Perhaps, like Gerald, he had not come back.

The clapper sounded as I entered the jewellers shop. A glass cabinet on the opposite wall contained dainty and elegant clocks. One in particular caught my eye and asked to be taken home. It was a pretty thing, with an embossed tulip design. Sorry, clock, but I have one similar to you already.

The long glass-topped counter was divided into sections for watches, bracelets and rings. I looked at the bracelets under the glass of the counter but didn't see one I liked half as much as the one in the window.

I waited. No one came. I pressed the counter

27

bell, and waited. A grandmother clock ticked. The minute hand moved. One minute, two, three. A shop with such valuable goods should not be un-attended. Whitby must indeed be an honest town.

Now that I was in the shop, sealed off from the world outside, the memories returned, but not painfully. We had chosen my ring from the window. Mr Philips had checked my ring size. He was a charming man. His ginger hair had a natural wave. His skin was a pale pink shell colour. He would need to keep out of the sun so as not to burn.

One of the clocks chimed.

Another minute ticked by.

Some quality in the tick-tock quiet of the place made me uneasy. Perhaps that was why I went behind the counter and tapped on the door that connected to the room at the back. I called out, knocking as I did so, 'Hello. Anyone there?'

The room beyond was dimly lit, the curtains closed. Yet I sensed that there was someone there and was drawn into the room.

I glanced about. The figure – the shape – I did not straight away realise it was a body, lay face down in the centre of the faded square rug that covered much of the stone floor.

'Mr Philips?'

But no, what little there was of this man's hair was grey. For a few seconds I froze. Why had I hovered in the shop when I might have come in sooner and given him first aid?

He lay on his front, his head turned, arms bent at the elbow as if he had tried to break his fall. I knelt beside him and took his hand, saying his name, whether he was Mr Philips or not. I felt for a pulse on his wrist. Nothing. I felt for a pulse at his throat. Nothing. This *was* the same man who had measured me for a ring. His moustache had kept its colour. I heard myself say his name again, Mr Philips, as if to rouse him. Impossible. He was no longer able to answer to his name. I stared, transfixed, at the neat white cuff, the diamond cufflink, the slender hand with its shapely nails. Something on the floor near his leg caught my eye. It was a bead of Whitby jet. Having noticed that one bead, I saw more strewn about the floor, enough for a whole necklace. Had some thief made off with whatever he, or she, could carry?

He was too well-dressed to be a corpse, in a suit of good quality wool, with a narrow grey stripe. Even in death he was handsome, cleanly shaven with his neatly clipped moustache. Yet his hair was not so sleek. Where his skull curved down there was a dark damp patch. The unmistakable sweet and sickly smell rose to greet me: blood. Yet there was barely a gash at the back of his poor head. The mark was slight enough to have been made by a comb. Here was a man who had taken great care with his appearance and only that morning started his day expecting it to end in the usual way, and to begin again tomorrow. Something made me stroke his delicate hand, not that such a gesture could comfort him now. A neat blot of blood had trickled and marked the rug.

Mr Philips would sell no more engagement rings to romantic young men for their starry-eyed sweethearts.

I looked about the room. It was used as a sitting

room, with a sofa and chair. There was a small kitchen table and a couple of straight-back chairs. A safe on the wall stood open. Below it, leaning against the wall, was a painting that must have concealed the safe. It was a seascape, a storm, a small boat being tossed on the waves. The picture had been set down carefully against the skirting board.

More beads were strewn across the floor. A necklace had snapped.

The door to the yard outside was closed. Under the window was a sink, draining board and gas ring. An inner door must lead upstairs. I stared at it, half expecting someone to materialise. No one did. The house held a deathly hush, but all the same there might be someone in an upper room. If so, might that person be the killer? I looked about for a telephone but saw none. Neither could I spot a set of keys that would enable me to lock the shop and go for help. I must go for help. Call the police.

No one else must enter, but how was I to ensure that?

Trying not to look, I bobbed down beside Mr Philips's body and felt in his pockets for keys. There were no keys, only a hanky, a wallet and a ticket.

I wanted to be out, away from there – yet hated to turn my back on him and make for the door. I felt a ridiculous tingle of guilt at leaving him, as though someone should sit and hold his hand, tell him that life had done its worst and to have no more fears.

Back in the shop, I checked for keys behind the

counter. Nothing.

Fortunately one of the locks was a Yale. I dropped the latch.

The busy-ness of the street outside felt strange. The harsh light of day sent me dizzy. I steadied myself in the porch of the shop, and glanced about. My first thought was to stop the very next stranger who walked by, but I quickly dismissed that idea. Once on the pavement, I could not think what to do. The flow of people had ebbed. A telephone. I must find a telephone.

I went back into the newsagents and waited. The woman assistant was not there, only the owner who had spoken to me earlier and who now weighed out two ounces of cough drops for a stooped old man whose fox terrier sniffed my shoes. The shopkeeper poured the cough drops into a paper cone, handed them over and took the money.

The customer left and the shopkeeper, Mr Dowzell I presumed, stared at me. I suddenly became aware that I must look as if I had seen a ghost.

'Do you have a telephone?'

'We've no telephone here.' He frowned as if mention of a telephone was a lewd suggestion.

I couldn't think what to say next and was on the point of telling him what had happened when he leaned forward eagerly. 'Is something wrong? What's the matter?'

The need for care and discretion stopped my mouth. He might be the town gossip. Not that men gossip. They simply pass the time of day with laconic enthusiasm. He wouldn't believe me that I had found a body. He would want to look

31

for himself, and trample all over. If it had been the friendly female assistant, I might have felt differently. I turned to go. 'It doesn't matter.'

He called after me. 'I think by your look it does. Trust me. I'm an ex officio JP.'

Never trusting people who say 'Trust me', I lied, muttering something about needing to report a missing purse.

I left the shop before he had time to offer more credentials.

I retraced my steps. One can always rely on a post office having a telephone and the post office was nearby.

A queue snaked from the counter to the door. This was a busy time, coming up to Saturday half-day closing. I ignored the queue and walked to the counter. The queue did not ignore me. Murmurs of disapproval followed my progress.

I waited until an elderly woman who wore a man's brown trilby had completed her purchase of a tuppeny stamp.

'Excuse me, but may I have a word with the postmaster or mistress. I need to use the telephone urgently.'

'I am the postmistress.' She placed her hands flat on the counter and leaned forward. 'The telephone is for post office business only.' She looked me up and down to assess my worth and wrote me off as a toff who feels entitled to push in. 'They may let you use the telephone in the Royal Hotel.'

I lowered my voice. 'I need to call the police.'

'The police?' Her voice was loud enough to raise a response from the queue. 'Then I must make the call. On what matter?'

Was I to announce the jeweller's death to every-one in the post office, and by extension to the whole of Whitby? No.

'Never mind. I'll go to the station.'

'As you please.' Disappointment and triumph fought for supremacy in her face. Disappointment that she was not to be privy to some 'incident', triumph that she had put me in my place.

'Where is the police station?'

'Spring Hill, by the railway, behind the Coli-seum.'

Several people who waited their turn gave me a good stare as I left, probably feeling considerable satisfaction that my attempt at queue-jumping had failed miserably.

I did not run but did that Girl Guide walk where you almost race for thirty paces and then walk normally. Suddenly, I lost my bearings and came to a stop, until I saw the churches and knew that I must be close to the main road. Behind the Coliseum, she had said.

Never had I been so glad to see a police station. Yet one of those moments of uncertainty came over me. Had I really just walked into a shop and found a body? Why me? Why today? A black and white dress was a perfectly satisfactory gift without my having to add a bracelet. I needn't have stepped across the threshold of J Philips, High Class Jeweller. For all I knew, Felicity wouldn't want a bracelet. Bracelets could be annoying. Did you push it up your arm or let it dangle? I tried to picture the bracelet, so that I would not have to see the man, with his neat attire, his bloodied head and the paleness of his skin. How long had he lain dead? Certainly, he was as cold as any stone. But see him I did, in the glow of a long-ago afternoon, behind his counter, with his red hair and his understated manner. And then in the cold light of his back room, lying so still and pale, and forever.

An officer came to the desk. He was in his middle thirties, pleasant-looking and ready to smile.

His face changed as I told him why I had come. My news merited the revelation of his name. 'I'm Sergeant Garvin.'

He made a few quick notes: my name, where I was staying, when and why I had gone into the shop. Not letting me out of his sight, he stepped towards a back room and spoke to someone.

A young constable emerged.

'Take over the desk. I'm going with this lady to Philips's jewellers.' He picked up his cap, its white metal badge embossed with the Yorkshire rose, lifted the hinged counter shelf and came to my side of the desk.

'I dropped the latch on the shop door,' I said as we left the station and walked out onto Spring Hill. 'We may not be able to get in.'

'You did the right thing, madam. I'll gain entry all right.'

As we walked back, a different way to the way I had come, we drew some interested glances from people who stepped aside to let us pass on the narrow pavement in Silver Street. The sergeant led us through yards, up steep steps, round back ways until I began to wonder where on earth we were going. All the while, he was surreptitiously looking about him, as if expecting to spot the jeweller's assailant hiding somewhere.

We came out on another narrow street and approached a back yard where he told me to wait by the gate. As I did so, he tried the door, without explaining that this was the back of the shop but I guessed that it must be. He looked at the sash window, which was barred and latched. We then walked up and by a roundabout way found ourselves back on Skinner Street.

In the jewellers doorway, Sergeant Garvin fiddled with keys and the lock. In no time at all the door swung open and the clapper rang. 'I'm sorry to ask you, Mrs Shackleton, but step inside please.'

I did as he asked, understanding that he did not want to let me out of his sight. Surely he did not imagine that after going to the trouble of reporting the crime I would run away.

He went round the counter and into the back room, but not for long.

He sighed. 'It's as you say.'

We left the shop. This time, he dropped the latch. I glanced about, wondering whether some person from the post office queue might be on Skinner Street and now think, 'Ah, that person really did want to make an important telephone call. She wasn't just jumping the queue.'

A deluge of holidaymakers flooded the street, gawping into windows and discussing where to go for fish and chips. The day had become strangely unreal.

The sergeant spoke quietly. 'I'll walk you back to your hotel, Mrs Shackleton.'

I guessed why and so did not object. He would need to contact his superiors. He was escorting me to the Royal because he wanted to be sure that I really was staying there. The man was thorough, good at his job.

As we walked, Sergeant Garvin sympathised with me for having a poor start to my holiday. I appreciated his remarks as I have a liking for people who are given to understatement. For some unaccountable reason, I had only just now begun to shake and to feel very uncertain on my pins. He gave me a quick glance and I believe would have taken my arm but under the circumstances that would have looked uncannily like an arrest. We drew curious looks from passers-by. Who was the woman in the voile dress and coat being escorted by the local bobby?

Back at the hotel, we waited for the revolving door to come to a stop. Sergeant Garvin waved me in and followed, of which I was glad, feeling suddenly unable to push the door.

'Is there somewhere you'd like to sit, Mrs Shackleton, while I order a brandy for you?'

I looked about. 'There's a quiet room – the library.'

He nodded. I felt an odd mixture of both relief, and annoyance with myself. After years of nursing, the sight of a body is not new to me, but under the bizarre circumstances of today it was the unexpectedness that shook me, combined with the memories of the younger me trying on rings, feeling so shy and so happy. Now that memory would be forever overlaid.

In the peaceful library, someone had left a

36

novel on a chair arm. I sat by the window, looking out at passers-by but not seeing. Would it take the whole two weeks of my holiday to banish the sight of that poor man lying on the rug?

No. It would take forever.

The sergeant came back, at the same moment as the waiter who carried a silver tray bearing brandy, water, neat sandwiches, a slice of ginger cake and a pot of tea. When the waiter had gone, Sergeant Garvin said, 'I must ask you not to leave Whitby until you have made a signed statement.'

'I'm booked here for two weeks.' A nightmare thought came between me and the world around. Might I spend the whole fortnight tripping over dead bodies? At that moment I wanted to jump into my car and drive straight home.

He placed his cap on the chair arm. 'Tomorrow will be soon enough. I'll write up what you've told me and if you think of anything else, you can tell me.'

'Very well.'

'You are here alone, according to the register.'

'Yes.'

'Is there anyone we can contact for you? You've had a bad shock.'

'Thank you but no.'

'Do you have friends in Whitby?'

'Yes, an old school friend, Alma Turner. I'm godmother to her daughter.'

'Ah!' He leaned towards me, giving the impression that he would snaffle my sandwiches and swig the brandy. 'I know them well, Mrs Turner and Felicity. Mrs Turner has become well-liked. That is something of an achievement for an outsider.' When I had no answer for that, he continued. 'I must ask you to keep the news of Mr Philips's death to yourself for now.'

I agreed, of course, but his comments struck me as at odds with his question as to whether there was anyone he could contact for me. If I had wanted the support of some friend, then I would naturally tell them why.

He picked up his cap. 'In spite of how things looked in that room, there may be some explanation other than foul play. The truth will emerge when the investigation is underway, but until then I would not have Whitby awash with rumours.'

'Of course not.'

'Will you be seeing your friend soon?'

'This afternoon.' Alma would think it odd if I did not seek her out after she had left me a note. It would be best to do that, although hard to carry it off and act as if nothing terrible had happened.

'It may be difficult for you, but please refrain from mentioning the death, even to Mrs Turner.'

'Very well.'

'Thank you.' He pulled on his cap and turned to leave, closing the door gently behind him.

As I was left alone to sip brandy and water in the calm of the library, I sensibly told myself that I was letting my imagination run away with me in thinking there was some significance in the way he mentioned Alma Turner. It was natural enough that he would not want the death of the jeweller to be widely known before he had informed his superiors and secured the premises.

By the time I finished the brandy and had managed to swallow a few bites of sandwich, the initial

38

shock had passed. Knowing the value of something sweet for shock, I made myself eat some of the ginger cake. For the briefest of moments, the calmness of the room soothed me. I made a conscious effort to breathe in and out slowly, counting my breaths, trying to feel normal.

After such a shock, how would I manage to keep calm, meet Alma, and say nothing about this horror?

I resisted the urge to jump into my car and drive straight home. But in this state, pedestrians, other motorists and lamp posts would have to clear the way.

Be brave, I told myself. Police orders are for you to stay put. You are here on holiday, and to see Alma, and Felicity.

Only when I left the hotel, to walk to the pier, did I become uneasy at the thought of seeing Alma. The sergeant had given the impression of being curious about her. I thought again of his words. Why did it disturb me that he gave the impression of being interested in her?

I answered my own question. It was because when he said, 'please refrain from mentioning the death, even to Mrs Turner', the tone and the emphasis in his words seemed to say something different. 'Please refrain from mentioning the death, *especially* to Mrs Turner.'

My mind raced. Surely the sergeant could not imagine that Alma had some connection with the jeweller's death?

Five

Brendan brought the engine to life, there being no wind. As the boat chug-chugged out of the bay, Felicity sat beside Brendan at the tiller. She emptied her boot of water.

There was a knack to climbing into a bobbing boat. Tonight everything was awkward and difficult. She had felt like a galumphing double-humped camel, swaying as she hauled herself aboard, a wave breaking over her sea-boots and sending an icy burst of water down her leg.

'It'll be a losing battle,' Brendan said as she put her damp boot back on.

She looked back at the cliffs of Whitby, taking her last glimpse of the moonlit abbey.

When imagining this journey, she hadn't seen darkness. In her mind's eye, the sky was blue and the sea smooth.

Brendan gave her a nudge. 'Go look at that packet with your dad's name. See if you recognise the writing.'

The first time she discovered that the boat had a false bulkhead, a secret space for storage, she had been delighted. She slid off the partition and stowed her knapsack alongside Brendan's bag.

As her eyes adjusted to the darkness, she saw the brown paper packet, neatly wrapped and tied with string. She could make out her father's name but struck a match so as to read what else was written. The writing was neat, a good hand, block printed. Whoever wrote it was polite as it was addressed to 'Walter Turner, Esquire'. The address was wrong. He lived in Elgin. She struck another match. Under the name were the words 'now at Harbour Street, Hopeman – first house'.

Nothing else was written on the outside. Might someone be trying to mislead her, make her think she had the wrong address and must turn back? Well they could forget that. She undid the knot and unfolded the brown paper. Something was wrapped in oilskin. The oilskin turned out to be a money belt, with snap fasteners.

She didn't need much light to recognise big white five pound notes. Plenty of them. The only other item was a plain postcard. In the same block print as her dad's name, someone had written 'Business as usual'.

Six

After the horror of finding the jeweller's body, every nerve jangled. I had the odd sensation of feeling entirely lost. Yet the lay-out of the town was coming back to me as I neared the bottom of Flowergate. There are two piers in Whitby, almost parallel with each other. The East Pier is bare except for its benches and lighthouse. The West Pier believes itself to be the centre of the universe with shops, fish market and streets that lead to the top of the town.

41

Passing the cockle stalls and the stores displaying their buckets and spades, I looked around, and peered into café windows. Alma had told me to look out for the pepper pot but I could see no place of that name.

As I continued to the bend in the pier, near the Marine pub, I saw a small white building with a sloping roof that came to a point. It was near enough the shape of a pepper pot to be called by that name. The door of the building was decorated with moons, sun and stars on a blue and green background and the painted figure of a woman in flowing robes and turban with a single startling red jewel at its centre. On closer inspection, I saw that the painted face with slightly protruding eyes and translucent skin that gave off a kind of unearthly glow reminded me of someone: Alma. Whoever painted it had captured her beautifully. The turban did not hide the widow's peak that made Alma a curiosity at the age of twelve when we first met and when we could not have imagined that widowhood would be visited on so many of us. As far as I knew, Alma's widow's peak was not prophetic. Her much older husband, Walter, had simply stepped from the scene. She rarely spoke of him except in a vague way, saying he had moved to warmer climes for his health.

Flowing script on a painted sandwich board announced the name of the pepper pot's occupant, and of services on offer.

Madam Alma
Fortunes

This was a surprise. But then, Alma was full of surprises.

It had surprised me when she asked me to be her bridesmaid, and then godmother to Felicity. We were not particularly close at school. There were other, closer friends with whom I've entirely lost touch. Alma was a strange and sensitive girl, with an unfortunate habit of fainting. One of the girls, I forget which, knew that certain goats fainted to avoid danger, a breed by the name of Tennessee Fainting Goat. Apparently, if something alarming happened, the goats would play dead. Our unkind nickname for Alma became Alma the Fainting Goat. She had an intense way of recounting stories that would hold everyone in the dorm rapt. I felt a stirring of guilt about that cruel nickname. It persisted until a particular fainting fit, following the visit of a boys' choir, led to a hysterical reaction throughout the entire school. Girls were fainting all over the place. Only after the doctor arrived and his nurse administered rather unpleasant medicine did the business come to a full stop. Being one of the few who did not faint, I was inadvisably made head girl.

Alma and I were once regular correspondents. Our letters became infrequent during the war, and just after. Two years running, she absent-mindedly sent Christmas cards with the message, 'We have moved,' but not giving an address. It was little Felicity who became my correspondent, sending thank you letters for Christmas and birthday gifts and, when older, coming to stay with me.

In recent years, Alma had sent me mimeographed flyers advertising her books for sale. I bought them out of loyalty, although I had no desire to learn *How to make Amusing Objects out of Newspaper* or to gather *Yuletide Decorations from the Natural World*.

Her latest book, or rather pamphlet, is *Prophetic Tellings* by Madam Alma. Mrs Sugden, usually the most sceptical of women, read this offering cover to cover and thought that in future years it might come to rank alongside the writings of Old Mother Shipton of Knaresborough.

After I had dawdled on the pier for about ten minutes and was some yards away from the pepper pot, a woman in her late thirties emerged. The woman walked in my direction, a smile on her face. She must be a satisfied customer, recipient of a favourable fortune. I approached cautiously, not wanting to take up Alma's precious time during working hours. She must need the money and another seeker or two might be loitering nearby, waiting their turn. At some point, Alma would emerge for a cup of tea, unless she had a spirit lamp kettle in there.

Perhaps Alma divined my presence, or spotted me. The door was left ajar after the departing customer. Alma appeared, ready to whip away the Engaged sign from the doorknob. She wore an unusual swirling dress in different greens, sewn from panels of cotton, chiffon and cambric. Her dark-red turban was decorated with a stone of Whitby jet, rather than the ruby in the picture on the door. She smiled, her pale skin slightly

44

tissue paper-lined around the eyes. Reaching out her hand, she drew me inside. 'Kate, how lovely to see you and a thousand welcomes.'

If she were indeed a fortune teller, she ought to sense that I had just had a terrible shock. Perhaps I am a good actress, or have seen too much death. Alma showed no sign of divining that anything was amiss, though she frowned.

'Are you tired from the journey?'

'A little. You look well, Alma.'

'Don't say that! People always say a woman looks well when she is beginning to show her age.'

'Well you do look well, and when you said you would be on the pier, I never expected this.'

Her pebble-grey eyes sparkled with satisfaction. 'My own abode, my workplace, my inspiration. Sit awhile. I've done enough predicting for one day. And I might be looking well, but you're looking peaky.' She frowned. 'Is everything all right?'

Everything was far from all right but under orders from the sergeant I had little choice but to pretend otherwise. 'It was a long drive.'

There were just two chairs in the small space, on either side of a round table that was draped with a maroon chenille cloth and set with Tarot cards. I sat in the customer's chair. On a shelf to Alma's right stood a crystal ball on an ivory stand. Beside it, a white porcelain hand etched with delicate lines marked Life, Love, Happiness, Money pointed a finger at the crystal ball.

Alma put the Engaged sign on the door and shut it.

'It's a little warm, but people will expect me to be private while giving a reading, and that's what they will think I'm doing.'

'Then let's meet later. I don't want to put off your prospective clients.'

'On the contrary, a closed door attracts customers.' She took her seat opposite me. As if by habit, she straightened the cards, frowning at first, and then pushing them aside. 'Always best to have one's cards on the table.'

'Do you really tell fortunes?'

'Of course!'

'Sorry.'

'Oh it's all right. I expect people ask you if you really do investigations.'

I smiled. 'When I meet people who don't know, I keep quiet about it. I only sent you my card to show off.'

She smiled back. 'I know what you mean. People can be so sceptical.' She tapped the cards. 'And sometimes the results leave such a lot to be desired. The Tarot often indicate that one should keep on keeping on. Very dull.' She picked up the cards and shuffled.

'Alma, how did you come to be telling fortunes on the pier?'

'Ah, good question. The person who was here – a genuine Romany, unlike me – moved to Scarborough. Of course that annoyed the Urban District Council no end. Madam Rosa was popular with visitors and it offended local pride that she went to work in the land of Algerinos.'

'Algerinos?'

'It's what Whitby people call Scarborough people. They dislike each other intensely. That's why Madam Rosa's departure was regarded as

46

treachery and she wasn't allowed to name a successor. Women from two rival Romany families want the job and I was asked if I'd step in, until there is some settlement, otherwise the Council lose rental income and have disappointed visitors.'

'But you're not a fortune teller.'

'Oh I don't wear a black bombazine dress and terrify or delight people with shocking prophecies, but I do have a gift. Don't you remember? I always had a gift.'

It was true that she had told fortunes at school, cast spells and was generally thought to be a little psychic. She was also a dab hand at elaborately interpreting dreams which I thought was to entertain and bid for popularity.

'How about an exchange, Kate? Let me tell your fortune and you can investigate something for me.'

'Oh, thanks Alma, but I don't want to hear about my future. Spare me the details.'

She laughed. 'Lucky you, not needing to know.' She glanced greedily at my hands, as if she might just grab one and impart something significant. I placed my hands in my lap. My life and love lines were my own affair. She must have noticed my unease because she allowed a change of subject.

I asked her about Felicity. 'How is she? I can't wait to see her.'

'She's very well and has left school, tried a little this and that. She was working in a sweet shop on Brunswick Street in the mornings and washing up at the café next door in the afternoons. Now she's fallen on her feet and has a job as a waitress in Botham's tea rooms.'

'What a lovely place to be.'

'I only hope she'll settle to it. Nothing suits her for long.' Alma sighed. 'To tell you the truth, she has taken against where we live. She ... oh, you don't want to hear, not on the first day of your holiday.'

'Of course I want to hear.' For several years, Alma's address had been Bagdale Hall, which sounded rather grand. 'Why has she taken against the place?'

Alma made a gesture as if it was all too much to explain. 'It's too big, too draughty. Her friends won't come because they say the house is haunted, that kind of nonsense. She doesn't talk to me like she used to. She might talk to you.'

'I hope she will! I'll go to Botham's for tea and surprise her. I've brought her a dress but I can give her that later.'

Alma smiled. 'That will please her. She goes dancing these days. Mind you she looks very smart in her waitress outfit.'

'I'm sure she does. Everything suits Felicity.'

Alma stood and opened the small high window. There was something she wanted to say and so I thought I had better encourage her to spit it out. She might help me shake off the image of the poor dead man. 'Alma, what's this about my investigating for you? And you said in your letter there was something you wanted to talk to me about.'

'Yes, you see I don't know how you go about finding out things, making enquiries, without alerting someone – the authorities for instance.'

'Tell me what it's about and I'll see if I can help.'

'It's regarding that husband of mine, Walter Turner.'

48

'Ah. You never mention him in your letters.'

'I wouldn't want to commit certain things to writing. Though perhaps I should have said something to you, given that you were my bridesmaid and everything, but I felt ... I don't know, embarrassed. Ashamed.'

'Why? Tell me about Walter. He was so much older than you. I don't suppose he enlisted?'

'No, he did not enlist, and yes he was older, is older.'

'How much older? I don't remember.'

'He was a young thirty-seven when we married, or so he said. Actually, he turned out to be fifty-seven.'

'Never! I didn't think he was so much older.'

'He's now in his seventies, wherever he is. The truth is, Kate, Turner turned out to be not what he seemed in more ways than lying about his age.'

'Wasn't his age on the marriage certificate?'

'It would have been if he had presented the correct documents.' She closed the cabin window, cutting us off from the slight breeze. Within a moment the cabin grew unbearably close.

'He went abroad, shortly after Felicity's sixth birthday – to Madeira. But then he sent postcards from other places. The postcards stopped, but I have a strong sensation of his being back on these British Isles of ours, somewhere or other.'

'He abandoned you?'

'Not exactly. I'm wondering whether Felicity heard on her birthday. She is always first down to collect the post, but she didn't say.'

'Has Walter helped you financially, with Felicity, and your ... well everything.' I felt a sudden rage at this man who had left Alma in the lurch. Small wonder she was on the pier telling fortunes and churning out pamphlets. I did not remember Walter very well, except for thinking that he was old enough to be Alma's father and perhaps that was what she wanted, her own parents having died when she was young.

'Walter has helped, in an arms-length indirect way, so that we have somewhere to live at least. He bought us a half share in the house – in Bagdale Hall.'

This seemed to me an evasive and mysterious answer, but I did not interrupt. She continued.

'I've kept a terrible secret, an unbearable secret. Because of it, Felicity blames me. She blames me for driving her father away. It wasn't like that at all, but I can't tell her the truth.'

'Can you tell me?'

'Yes. In fact, I've hoped for months that you would come. I've sent you astral messages every week since Felicity turned sixteen in May. Perhaps your idea of coming to Whitby is a result of my thought waves.'

I urged her to say more about what was worrying her. I sincerely hoped my decision to come to Whitby bore no relation to Alma's thought waves. Life is complicated enough at times without suspecting that one can be prey to astral messages.

'I've never told anyone what I'm going to tell you. Before I say anything bad about Walter Turner, I must say that he did me a good turn. You may not remember that I used to faint a lot as a girl.'

I tried for an expression that would convey the

difficulty of recollecting the unfortunate fainting fits. 'Well yes, now that you mention it.'

'Walter Turner practised as a hypnotist for a time. I thought hypnotism worth a try and so it was. He cured me of my fainting. That was how I met him. Later, I bumped into him in York Minster. We fell in love and married. It seemed like fate at the time, and I suppose it was.'

'How romantic.'

'Too romantic. I won't insult you by swearing you to secrecy because I know you'll be discreet. He liked women, Kate. He enjoyed falling in love. It was only afterwards I discovered that falling in love was his hobby, you might say. He did it all the time, and he meant it too. He didn't stop loving me, but when we were penniless and his roving eye led him to a wealthy foreigner of some pedigree, I told him to go. I said I would be better off without him, and so it proved.'

'You separated.'

'He would have gone with or without my permission. You see I'd found him out – or rather a previous wife had tracked him down. Falling in love wasn't his only hobby. Marrying was something of a habit.'

'He was a bigamist?'

'I've had a long time to ponder this and I've decided that he was an enthusiast for matrimony. I suppose bigamist is the unkind term. So we weren't legally married. Felicity doesn't know.'

Now was not the time to say that when I met him for the wedding, I thought she must be making a mistake but it was obvious from the voluminous dress that she had not much choice in the

51

matter. 'Oh Alma, have you kept this to yourself all these years?'

'It's not the kind of thing to issue bulletins about, is it? Most of the time, I try not to think about it. But someone has found out, I feel sure. Someone must have told the police. Sergeant Garvin has been asking me questions.'

'What kind of questions?'

'Oh, nothing I could put my finger on and swear that he suspects. I'm not called into the station. He makes no official calls. But whenever our paths cross, there's something – a comment, a query. He has asked me about Turner several times. I put him off, pretending not to follow his drift.'

I imagined Alma would do that very well. She was good at vagueness. 'Has this happened often, the sergeant's questioning?'

She took an official-looking document from the drawer in her table. 'Several times. This is my licence to tell fortunes on the pier. He came to check when he knew very well it was in order. Also, during his time off, he collects fossils as Felicity and I do. We've bumped into him several times. There's always something, some little question or comment.'

'How awkward for you, Alma. But are you being over-sensitive?'

'No. I'm sure I'm not.'

'Can you remember anything specific he's said?'

She twisted the wedding ring on her finger. 'I'm trying to remember. He puts me in such a panic that my mind goes blank.'

'Even if he does suspect, you are no longer with Walter. You were the innocent party.'

'I married innocently enough but once I found out, I didn't tell the authorities. That makes me party to the crime. Think of the shame that would come from a court case!'

'If you've kept this to yourself, who do you think may have found out?'

'I don't know. But consider Felicity, who through no fault of hers or mine would be classed as illegitimate if I do speak up. Heaven knows the poor girl feels self-conscious enough, having a fortune teller for a mother.'

'Doesn't Walter ever write, or send money for Felicity?'

'I want nothing more from him, alive or dead. If he turned up tomorrow and offered me the moon, I'd tell him to keep it. He bought us the house on Henrietta Street, and I never told you this but that was claimed by the sea one January. We had to hop out in the middle of the night and watch it slide away.'

'What a nightmare. Felicity once said something about it, but I didn't fully grasp what she was saying.'

Though it would be better to try and remain neutral, by now I had taken against Walter so thoroughly that it struck me as just the kind of thing he might do. Buy a house that would be swept into the sea. I was ready to hold him responsible for floods and freaks of nature as well as bigamy and abandonment.

'Was the property insured?'

'Good heavens, no. Everybody knew where the house was heading, except Walter and I.'

'And you now live at Bagdale Hall.'

'Yes, my half share, thanks to Walter again, and that wouldn't have been my choice.'

'Then how did it happen and who has the other half?'

'Walter went in with Percival Cricklethorpe, a local artist. He painted the pictures on the pepper pot door, the moons, sun, stars and me. The house is in our joint names. We each have a floor and share the ground floor – the kitchen and the public rooms.'

'That sounds an interesting arrangement.'

'Walter's idea and since he put up the money I didn't say no. It could be worse. I was supposed to be delighted with it.'

'But you're not?'

Alma sighed. 'I wouldn't go as far as that. You'll meet Cricklethorpe. He's a good artist and a sweet man but sharing with him puts me in an awkward situation too. My whole life feels so very temporary.' She looked glumly into her crystal ball. 'That's why I used a post office address sometimes. I expected to move on, and I never have.'

'How long have you been in Bagdale Hall?'

'Five years.'

'That's a long time to feel temporary.'

'Oh Kate, I've felt temporary all my life. I do tell people's fortunes and see their futures, I really do, but my own evades me entirely.'

'How old would Walter be now?'

'Seventy-three.'

'Say he had died, would you hear?'

She clutched the end of her shawl and gave it a good twist. 'Possibly not. He didn't always go under the same name. Crickly is more likely to

54

hear than I. I believe he and Walter are in touch now and again.'

'This might sound callous, Alma, but if you don't know whether he's alive...'

She finished my sentence. 'The grim reaper may have solved the problem for me.'

'And then no one need ever know that you weren't legally married.' I banished from my mind the image of a funeral with a dozen mourning women around a single grave.

'I don't want to make enquiries myself, Kate. I want to know but I dread the answer.'

'How hard for you and for Felicity, not knowing whether he's alive or dead.'

'It would be useful to be thought a widow, but I would hate to deceive Felicity, or upset her.'

'Do you bear Walter no malice?'

She sighed and opened her palms, in an accepting manner. 'He was a bounder and a charlatan, but charming. He cured my fainting fits. I had a cut-price wedding and a bouncing baby. Things could have been worse.'

'Does Felicity ask questions?'

'She stopped talking about her father ages ago. It's just this business with Sergeant Garvin. As if he's probing on someone else's behalf.'

'If this Mr Cricklethorpe, your co-owner of the property, is in contact, I suppose he would tell you where Walter is.'

'It wouldn't be so bad if Sergeant Garvin would let the matter drop. He misses nothing. He sees it as his duty to ensure all in Whitby is above board. This can be a tut-tutting sort of town. I'm sure if I served in a shop or attended church on Sundays no one would dream of questioning my background.' She picked up a copy of her prophecies from a pile on the ledge beside her, and began to fan herself. 'We might think of something, some way of you coming into contact with Sergeant Garvin. If you cross paths with him, you might slip in the fact that you were witness at my wedding, and how we are good friends, mention Walter Turner and perhaps hint that he is dead.'

'You know I'll help you if I can, Alma, but I'm not sure that would work.' I could not quite think how I would manage to hint that Walter Turner was dead, and that the news had come to me but by-passed Alma. Also, I could not tell Alma that I had already met Sergeant Garvin under rather unfortunate circumstances. I cast about for something to say, while she looked at me expectantly.

I'm sorry to say, I merely stated the obvious. 'You've made the best of things under difficult circumstances.'

She looked so miserable that I picked up a couple of copies of her shilling prophecies. 'One for my neighbour, and one for my mother. They'll be very interested.'

This was my pathetic attempt at consolation. It worked, to some extent. Alma paused in fanning herself. She reached for her pen, dipped it in the inkpot and signed each pamphlet with a flourishingly illegible scrawl. 'It's what authors do these days you know, adds a personal touch.'

'Yes, I suppose it does.'

She blew the ink dry. 'I have made the best of things as you say, and I may not have developed my gifts if life had treated me more kindly.'

I put the money for the prophecies on the table. 'There is that. I certainly wouldn't have been investigating if Gerald had come home.'

'But he didn't, and you are, and very good at it. I'm sure you'll be able to think of something for me. You trace people, don't you? Trace Turner. I know the obvious move would be for me to tackle Crickly but that would be so humiliating.'

It would be a waste of time for me to start investigating something when Alma would be well able to find out for herself. I tried to put her off. 'Perhaps you're worrying too much. If Sergeant Garvin knew something, he would act on it. There's no question of your admitting to being in a bigamous marriage. All you have to do is keep quiet.'

'I would like people to think I'm a widow. After all, I'm not properly married.'

'But why now, Alma?'

'It's only fair that I should tell you. A gentleman is interested in me.'

'Tell me more. Who is he?'

'I'll tell you how it happened. I did my own Tarot reading and for once, surprisingly, my romantic prospects were most definite. There was no mistake. That very afternoon, I met the gentleman in town. We were acquainted of course – everyone in Whitby is. He asked me to tea. Since then, he has shown great kindness to me, and to Felicity.'

'Oh that's nice. Who is he?'

'You won't believe my good fortune when I tell you. Finally, something in my life has gone right. He's well-placed, a bachelor, still handsome. Heaven knows how he's stayed free so long.'

Something came back to me, from an article I

had read. 'I'm sure there's a legal way around your difficulty, if you think this new friendship might lead to something. Say you hadn't heard from Walter for seven years, he might be presumed dead without your having to say a word about the marriage being bigamous.'

She sighed. 'I can't do that, because of Felicity. It's impossible. She'd want proof. She's never forgotten him.'

We were silent for a moment in the face of this impenetrable difficulty. 'Well, this man, might you simply ... you know ... people do.'

'He's far too respectable for that.'

'Who is he? What's his name?'

'His name is Jack Philips. He has the jewellers on Skinner Street.'

I am usually good at not revealing an over-reaction but I was suddenly aware that my mouth had opened wide enough to swallow the crystal ball. Alma had set her sights on Jack Philips. This could be the reason Sergeant Garvin told me not to mention the death to her. Did the sergeant suspect my friend of murder?

Seven

The heat in Alma's fortune-telling pepper pot was now unbearable. I felt slightly sick.

She leaned forward, full of concern. 'Kate, you've gone green. Is it something I said?'

Of course it was something she'd said. She had

pinned romantic aspirations to a man who lay dead on a worn rug in the back of a shop brimming with diamonds. I couldn't find the words.

'I'm so sorry. Here I am, rattling on, and you've had a long journey and probably no lunch.' She stood. 'I must shut up shop and we'll go for tea at once.'

'Stay here, Alma. You may have other customers. I'll walk along to Botham's and surprise Felicity.' I needed time alone, to gather my thoughts and try and stay calm, and keep quiet about what I had seen. Before she could stop me, I picked up my bag and made for the door.

She was behind me. 'I'll close now. I've told enough fortunes for one day.'

'No! Don't let me stop you having your palm crossed with silver. We'll have plenty of time to catch up.'

'You always were the best, Kate.' Her voice became slightly tremulous. 'I know you liked our school, but I hated it, except for you. You never once called me by that beastly name. I think it was Pauline Bennett who started it. Do you remember her?'

'Yes I do.' She was a jolly girl who excelled at games.

A movement near the door of the hut caught our attention. We both realised that someone was there, and that a consultation might be required. Here was my escape opportunity, before the heat baked me to a crisp.

'I'll see you at Botham's, Alma. Don't worry if you can't make it. I might just go back to the hotel and have a rest.' I had begun to hope she wouldn't make it. I hated the thought of keeping my secret about the murder.

Going to the door, I spoke in a louder voice for the benefit of the person outside, waiting her turn. 'Thank you so much for the consultation, Madam Alma.'

She saw me to the door, saying in a stage whisper, 'Don't go to the Baxtergate Botham's. Felicity's in the Skinner Street tea rooms.'

Skinner Street. The last place I wanted to go, passing the jewellers, which might now be under police guard.

As I left Alma's domain, I glanced at the waiting client. She returned my look and smiled. 'Hello, Mrs Shackleton.' It was the chambermaid from the Royal.

'Hello, Hilda.'

By this evening, it would be all round the hotel. The new guest made the fortune teller her first call. 'She's a widow, you know, probably enquiring after her marriage prospects. And did you know she was escorted back by the police this afternoon?'

The gulls, perched on cliff ledges, guffawed at life in general and me in particular. The sea had become rather choppy. The sun slid behind a cloud.

Alma had said that Pauline Bennett had started the name-calling. Pauline was captain of the hockey team and always chose me first. In return, I had amused her with a little tale about the Tennessee Fainting Goats. Now it all came back to me. The taunting of Alma Bartholomew was entirely my fault. It is not often that life offers an opportunity to make amends, but here was mine.

It was only to be hoped that Alma had not fallen in love with the unfortunate jeweller. How horrible it would be if she had already built castles in the air, and was soon to find out that the man of her dreams had been murdered and that her former bridesmaid and old friend had known and not told her.

I dismissed my earlier mad thought that Alma might be a suspect. Was she right in thinking the local sergeant knew something about Walter Turner's bigamy, I wondered.

Better still, I might discover that Walter Turner, hypnotist and deceiver, was no more – and she would be well and truly free of him.

After a stroll along the pier to clear my head, I made my slow way to Botham's for tea, and to say hello to my goddaughter the waitress.

I braced myself to walk past Philips Jewellers shop. It appeared deceptively normal. The shop was tightly shuttered and the Closed sign displayed. Otherwise there was no outward sign of anything untoward having occurred. I deliberately kept as far away from the window as I could, walking along the edge of the pavement, passing the post office, also now closed.

It was a relief to walk through the familiar doors of Botham's, breathing the smell of freshly baked bread and sweet cakes. I walked up the stairs to the tea room, taking my time, feeling the solid banister under my hand, reassuring to the touch.

An oasis of calm with its dark polished wood, white starched table cloths and family portraits, the tea room created the feeling of life being lived

61

in the best sort of way. The most striking portrait was of the baker businesswoman who had founded this flourishing enterprise. Mary Botham died years ago but in this portrait, she looked real enough to step from the frame and inspect her own tea-shop; a woman of substance, stout, astute and every inch a grandmother and matriarch.

The place was busy, with families, couples and friends all too immersed in their own concerns to notice another customer waiting to be seated.

A young waitress smiled and asked where I would like to sit. I chose a seat by the window and ordered a pot of tea, explaining that I was waiting for a friend. There were newspapers on the table by the wall. This reminded me that somewhere along the way I had lost the *Whitby Gazette* bought for Dad. For diversion, I picked up the café's copy. The paper had not changed in years. On the first page was a photograph of two buses locked to each other on the swing bridge. The article had the caption:

Whitby and Modern Traffic Problem which must be faced

On Monday morning, two motor-buses endeavoured to pass each other on Whitby Bridge, with the result that they came into contact and stuck. It was some time before the roadway was cleared, the wheels of one of the vehicles having to be lifted onto the pavement.

The story of a murder would destroy the tone of the paper altogether. Would it ever again, after reporting the death of Mr Philips, be able to deliver, with its former innocent enthusiasm, stories about fertile ewes and healthy lambs?

I had finished my tea. The waitress had asked, once more, if I wished to order. 'Five more minutes, and if my friend doesn't come...'

Then I caught sight of Alma through the window. She wore a glorious purple and gold robe over her multi-coloured gown. Her hennaed hair, now released from its turban, was swept up into a ridge from her widow's peak to the crown and caught with combs, creating the shape of a Roman helmet. It was topped by a scrap of purple cloth. A small gaggle of bedazzled visitors parted for her to pass and enter the tea shop door. Moments later, she swept into the room, turning heads.

The waitress had already recommended the best polony sandwiches and pork pie. To that we added scones, Russian slices and gingerbread.

'Is Felicity on her break?' Alma asked as the waitress took our order.

The girl blushed. 'I don't know, madam. I don't think she's here.'

Something about her voice told us that Felicity certainly was not here.

I poured tea.

Alma tonged a couple of sugar cubes into her cup. 'I wonder if they've sent her to the Baxtergate premises today? That would be a feather in her cap. It's rather grand, you know.'

While we waited for our order to arrive, we talked about what events would be worth attending during my time here. Alma told me about the concerts, the fund-raising bazaar and sale of work at the Seamans Mission, and about the shows coming to the Coliseum. All this was just what I might have expected: to walk, to explore, and to attend whatever took my fancy. But that was before I went into the jewellers shop.

The waitress brought our food. I forced myself to eat something while we chatted about the news in the *Whitby Gazette,* which is so much more entertaining and reassuring than talking about news from *The Times* or the *Yorkshire Post.*

Alma mentioned an item with a coupon to cut out. 'The editor offers half a guinea for the fire that's been burning longest in a farmhouse kitchen in the Whitby area. To enter, a person gives their name and address and fills in the blank for the number of years the fire hasn't gone out.'

An image came into my head of the cold hearth in the jeweller's back room. How long had he lain there, I wondered. I tried to blank out the image and to listen to Alma. I asked, 'What's the record so far, for a farmhouse fire?'

'Who knows? Apparently some fires have burned for over twenty years.' Alma placed a Russian slice on her plate. 'Felicity made me laugh. She said, if someone claims their fire hasn't gone cold since Victoria came to the throne, how will the editor know that's true?'

At that moment a tall, rather handsome woman dressed in black came striding towards our table, smiling graciously – until she came upon us. Her expression then turned to one of subdued annoyance.

Alma looked up in pleased surprise. 'Miss Botham, hello.'

Miss Botham shook her head, not in denial of

her name but with some barely controlled irritation. 'Good afternoon, Mrs Turner.' She spoke very quietly, which Alma took as a hint that she should do the same.

'Is something wrong?'

'I am disappointed in Felicity.'

'Oh?'

'To give me such short notice.'

'Notice?'

'And with no explanation. We're at the height of the season. It's most inconsiderate...' Miss Botham stared at Alma. 'You do know about it...'

Alma clearly did not know about it, but raised voices and the sound of crashing crockery from the direction of the kitchen caught Miss Botham's attention and she turned away.

'What can she mean?' Alma pushed away her Russian slice. 'Felicity hasn't given in her notice. That would have to come from me. I came with her to see about the job and it was made clear. They're very proper about that kind of thing. It's in the letter of engagement that the parent or guardian must give notice.'

'We'll find out soon enough. Perhaps there's been a misunderstanding, or she's unwell.'

'I'd know if she was unwell.'

'I'll come back with you. It can't be anything too serious. Perhaps someone upset her.'

'She does take umbrage easily, and she is rather impulsive. But this is her third job this summer!'

'Don't let this spoil your tea, Alma. Eat your Russian slice.'

From the numbers of people who exchanged

'hello' or 'good day' with Alma as we walked down Skinner Street, I realised that she was well-known here, and popular, too. I was glad of that.

Alma took my arm. 'This way. We pass by Amen Corner.'

'Amen Corner?'

Alma indicated the churches. 'I call it that because there's a church on every corner.'

'Whitby folk must be very religious.'

'Seafarers and their families have good reason to be. It helps to know there's someone up there looking out for them. And I'll send up a prayer that Felicity hasn't entirely cooked her goose. I'll drag her back there to talk to Miss Botham, sort it out.'

We waited to cross Bagdale, the main thoroughfare into Whitby. I had of course seen the old house that we now approached. We waited on the pavement for a bus to pass, followed by a sanitary cart, its iron hoops rumbling noisily across the cobblestones.

When the cart had passed, I had a clear view of the fine Tudor mansion solidly built of soft-hued stone, its walls unadorned with ivy. The pointed dormers on the second floor and the tall chimneys suggested that it was built with light and warmth in mind, and gave off an air of welcome.

We crossed the street during a brief lull in traffic.

Despite looking as if they had not been cleaned in a hundred years, the small panes in the leaded lights reflected the early evening sunlight.

'How beautiful this is! You didn't tell me you live in a Tudor mansion.'

She gave a dismissive gesture. 'I live in a state of

66

deep chill, with ghosts treading the stairs half the night, mice scuttling about the kitchen and Mr Cricklethorpe dragging me into his money-spinning enterprises and complaining that there isn't sufficient light for him to paint.'

'Oh yes, you told me he's an artist.'

'Aren't we all, Kate? Artists of some sort or another. How else would we deal with life? But yes, he is a good painter. You'll meet him.'

I paused by the small paved yard in front of the building. It was surrounded by a low wall with a gate.

'We don't use that door.' Alma led the way along a narrow pavement around the side of the building.

On the wall of the house were two stone heads. 'Who are they?'

'Oh, them – search me! From their headgear, they must have been important. One of the owners had them brought from a mason's yard. They're said to be all that's left of Stockton Castle. The previous owner took a fancy to a gravestone, too, and put it in the front yard. Takes all sorts.'

'This must be the oldest house in Whitby, Alma.'

'I suppose it could be.'

An arched entrance that may once have been the main frontage of the building led to a flagged yard with a well at its centre. By the entrance to the porch I stopped to read the inscription above. 'Grow old along with me, the best is yet to be.'

Alma sighed. 'Robert Browning was such an optimist.'

'It's very romantic. Whoever built this house was in love.'

'And we all know where that leads. Now, brace yourself, Kate. A cloud-burst on the moors flooded us last year. Four feet of water tore up the parquet. We're back to stone flags, a permanent smell of damp and a piggy bank towards reinstalling electricity.'

I followed her through the porch into a large room with a wonderful fireplace of dark oak, intricately carved and with figurines on either side. A log fire burned low.

Alma paused, and stooped to add another log. 'We keep a fire in here to ward off the damp.'

'What an unusual fireplace.'

'It was made from a Dutch pulpit. There are all sorts of connections with Holland. See the Delft tiles, they were used as ballast when ships came into Whitby. I'm glad we were able to save them. Lots of people came in to help us clear up, thank goodness. Dear old Cricklethorpe is very popular. He plays the dame in the annual pantomime and for that he's heavily revered.'

'I look forward to meeting him.' I paused to read the inscriptions above the fireplace, *DEX AIE* and below that 'Stay me with flagons, comfort me with apples'. 'The owners were fond of quotations.'

'Yes. Apparently *Dex Aie* is old French for God aids us, and believe me as an occupant of this place one needs God's aid. The flagons and apples quote is biblical.'

'It's the Song of Solomon.'

'Love, all that endures, eh? In spite of everything.'

Here was my moment to ask the question, to try and find out how deeply Alma might be affected by the jeweller's death. As we stood by the fire, I asked, 'Have you fallen in love with the man you mentioned, the jeweller?'

'Why do you ask?'

'I just wondered.'

'No, not yet, but I could. I might. We'll see.' She nudged my arm. 'Come on, let's brave the kitchen, see if Felicity's there.'

We turned into a corridor and through another room. A staircase led to what must be servants' quarters. 'The house is very grand.'

'Felicity hates it. She blames me for bringing her to live in a haunted house.'

'And is it haunted?'

'We do have a room where you might catch a glimpse of an old lady nursing a baby.'

'Don't tell me, there'll be some tragic story attached.'

'Yes. The poor baby died.'

'Any others?'

'Felicity had a gallant who kissed her cheek and made his exit where there used to be a door. He was said to be kissing his wife goodbye.'

'Did Felicity mind?'

'Not at first. Would you mind if someone kissed your cheek? The poor child thought it was her father who'd come home. She was most upset the next morning.'

'Does that ghost still visit?'

'Yes, but we've changed rooms. He kisses Mr Cricklethorpe now. The story is that the poor man went off to war and never came back. There's no malice in the Bagdale ghosts, honestly. You'd be most welcome to stay.'

69

'You did say that and thank you, but I don't want to impose and I'd already booked the Royal.' Thank God, I mentally added. It would be difficult enough for me to sleep at all after what I had seen today. Ghostly company was the last thing I wanted.

I followed her through another room and along a forbiddingly dark hall. 'It's a characterful place.'

'No need to rub it in, Kate. I know you like baths and mirrors, and who blames you? I wouldn't mind a touch of that myself.' She knocked on a door before throwing it open. 'Felicity!'

I thought it odd that she knocked on the kitchen door but then she stamped and clapped and there was much scuttling. I followed her into a huge kitchen with its light odour of mice. The low-beamed room may have been unchanged for a century. A black kettle sat on the hob.

Alma added a few coals to the fire. 'Well, she's not here.' She picked up the poker and dislodged ash. 'It's costing us a fortune in coal and logs, but Crickly and I agree we need to try and dry out before the weather strikes again.'

We left the kitchen to its former occupants and walked back along the hall.

'Will Felicity be indoors on a day like this?'

'I hope so. I want to know what she's up to.' We climbed the wide oak staircase. She produced a torch to light our way. 'All the windows are in the rooms so the landings are dark. We can't see here, not since the flood destroyed the electrics.' She shone the torch about so that I could make out the doors. 'This is Crickly's floor. We have the floor above. Do you know, I can't believe Felicity was so

70

mad as to leave Botham's. I'm hoping it's not too late to do something about it or she'll really scupper her chances. Who else will employ her after this?'

I followed her up the next flight of stairs.

She shone the torch at the ceiling. 'We have such lovely chandeliers. After all this time, I still forget and want to switch on the non-existent lights.'

Alma turned a doorknob. She led the way into a high-ceilinged room. 'We've plenty of space, you see. This is my room. Hang on here, Kate. I'll see if Felicity has gone to bed and hidden herself under the eiderdown. Her room's at the end. I hope she isn't moping. She's done that a lot lately, the kind of moping best done in a gloomy room.'

I listened to her footsteps as she trod along the bare wood floor.

In Alma's room, a spectacular bed with an ornately carved headboard and footboard took up a large proportion of the wall to my left. It was the kind of bed one sees in a great country house, where someone tips a wink and tells you that George III slept here. A wardrobe, dressing table and a sofa, all from different periods and in an eclectic mix of styles, were dotted about in a somewhat haphazard way. A desk by the window was piled with papers. Perhaps Alma was writing another book.

A wash stand held bowl and jug. The mantelpiece was lined with ornaments. But the most dominant piece of furniture in the room was a floor-to-ceiling glass-fronted cabinet that held every type of fossil imaginable. I was drawn to look, crossing the room in the gust of air that blew from the leaded casement window. In the slant of light, motes of dust danced.

Before I had time to take a close look at the shells and fossils, Alma came back into the room. 'Something's amiss. She's not there and there's... I don't know ... something's wrong.'

'What do you mean?'

'There's a sense of absence. Oh dear. I wish I had my full powers.'

'What?'

'My full powers. I'll say this for Walter Turner, and give credit where it's due, he cured me of fainting but to be brutally honest I suffered a diminishment in sensitivity. I didn't mind because that can be a burden, but now there's something that I can't quite catch. Something in the room...'

Without another word she went back onto the landing. I followed. 'Might she be with friends somewhere?'

Alma lit a lamp.

Felicity's bedroom was a neat, square room with a four-poster bed only slightly attacked by woodworm. A table stood by the bed. 'Her lucky pebble isn't here. She keeps it in this dish, doesn't take it to work with her.'

I glanced about the room. A mantelshelf ran above the fireplace. On it stood an envelope, a used envelope whose address had been crossed out and the word 'Mam' written.

'Alma, could that be a note from Felicity?'

She spun round. 'Ah! You're right. I didn't see that. I wasn't looking at surfaces but sensing interiorities, the feelings under the skin.'

She picked up the note, read it and then walked

slowly back to the four-poster bed where she sat down heavily. She handed me the note, indicating that I should read it.

Mam, I have gone away for a short time. Don't worry about me. There is something I must do. I will be all right and will send you a postcard saying when I will be back. I have some money saved but have borrowed 30/- on the watch-guard so as not to be short. Sorry. I will redeem it when I come back. Here is the pawn ticket to keep in a safe place for now.
   Love, Felicity xxx
   PS I will see Auntie Kate next time.

She took a second note from the envelope, read it and handed it to me.

Dear Auntie Kate
   Sorry to miss you after I have wanted you to come for so long but I have to go somewhere and I think you once told me that you have to do a thing when the time is right. I will come and see you in the winter.
   Love, Felicity xxx

I looked across at Alma who seemed to have difficulty catching her breath. It was a moment for brandy, or hot sweet tea. I had neither but took the slab of toffee from my bag. Keeping the packet in its brown paper I gave it a tap against the casement ledge to break a piece off, at the same time managing to chip a bit of plaster off the windowsill.

'Here, something sweet. You've had a shock.'

Alma sat down heavily on the bed. 'How could she, and without a word? What is she thinking of, giving up her job for some wild goose chase, and not saying where she's gone?' Alma clenched her fists. 'I'm a patient woman, Kate. I've done everything for her. What more could I have done? This is how she says thank you. Three jobs in three months. I despair! And she knew you were coming.' Alma closed her eyes. 'I foresaw trouble, but I didn't foresee this.' She withdrew the pawn ticket from the envelope, as if to make sure it was real. 'She has pawned our single valuable, my grandfather's watch-guard, and our one resource in time of need, and who has she pawned it with?'

Alma is a little short-sighted and too vain to wear spectacles. I thought she could not make out the name but it was a rhetorical question. She handed me the ticket. The watch-guard had been pawned with J Philips, High Class Jeweller.

The next seconds were like being whooshed back in time. Alma's face grew even more translucent. A flush crept across her cheeks. Her eyes seemed to grow out of their sockets and look heavenwards. And then she collapsed in a faint.

It was fortunate that she was sitting on the bed. I caught her. For someone who appeared so slender in her flowing robes, Alma's weight threatened to break my arms.

In this absurd position, lowering her head towards her knees, I heard a tap on the open door and turned to look. Framed in the doorway was a man in britches, gaiters and a velvet frock coat – someone out of the last century. For a mad moment, I wondered was he one of the Bagdale Hall ghosts, but I don't believe that ghosts have the good manners to knock on doors.

The man nodded furiously as if the sight of us was precisely the tableau he had expected. His mouth extended into a rictus grin across the big red face decorated with enormous salt and pepper eyebrows that poked into the room like an insect's antennae.

He stroked a wispy grey beard the colour of his sparse, petrified hair. 'Hello, ladies. Pardon the intrusion. I heard voices. Don't let me interrupt your ... your ... swoon.'

By the time Mr Cricklethorpe, for that was the velvet-clad gentleman's name, returned with a carafe of water and a crystal glass containing a liberal amount of whisky, Alma had revived a little, with the help of smelling salts and soothing words.

Alma took a gulp of whisky. She looked again at Felicity's note. 'What idea can she have got into her head?'

The pawn ticket fluttered onto the bed beside her.

I picked it up. It was dated yesterday.

Felicity may have been one of the last people to see the jeweller alive.

Cricklethorpe stood like a gentleman-in-waiting, looking anxiously at Alma. 'Is there anything I can do?'

She glared at him. 'Did you have any idea what Felicity was planning? Did she say anything at all to you?'

'Good heavens, no!' Cricklethorpe reddened slightly as he spoke. His neck above the cravat began to blotch. He was lying.

Eight

You couldn't call the covered-in part of the boat a cabin. That would give too much glory to a planked-in space where they might rest or sleep.

Felicity needed to think. She struck a match and lit the lamp, filling the low space with a soft vanilla light.

She took off her oilskin frock and sat down cross-legged. She hadn't intended to look closely at the five pound notes until daylight but curiosity got the better of her. She counted the notes. One hundred notes. Fifty pounds. She had never seen so much money.

Since whoever left the money for her father had provided a money belt, she might as well use it and keep her own cash in a safe place. Six pounds three shillings and ninepence from her savings plus thirty bob from pawning the watch-guard and ten bob borrowed from the Rington's tea jar made eight pounds three and ninepence.

She lifted the Aran cardigan and fastened the belt at her waist. There was a flask of cocoa in her knapsack. Should they have some now? No. Save it. She went back to sit beside Brendan as he steered the boat by the stars. When they passed a lighthouse she was happy because it meant they were well on their way.

It made her feel nervous to have such riches strapped around her middle. She reached for

Brendan's hand. 'It's money. There was a money belt in the packet with fifty quid.'

'What?' His voice rose in amazement. 'Who put that there then? You must've told someone. Your mam.'

'No. She never speaks of Dad, and if she had fifty quid she wouldn't send it to him. There's a postcard with it.'

'Where from?'

'Not a picture postcard, just a plain card and a message, "Business as usual".'

'Oh.'

'What do you mean, oh?'

'Your mam sees the future, doesn't she?'

'She reckons to but she doesn't. And if she'd seen this future coming she'd have throttled me. And you as well.'

'I think we should turn back.'

'No!'

'If we've got someone's money, they'll be expecting summat for it.'

'Such as?'

'Some delivery.'

Felicity had a sudden inkling of what he might mean, yet it made no sense. 'I don't understand.'

'They say your dad has done a lot for Whitby and Upgang folk over the years. You know the sort of thing.'

'What, what has he done?' She wondered if Brendan was right and her father had done something for Whitby and Upgang. Did he send a donation to the Mission? Why would he when he never came back?

'You don't know?'

'If I knew I wouldn't ask.'

'They say your dad has dealings.'

'What kind of dealings?'

'And that's why you live where you live.'

She knew only the vague explanations her mother gave. 'Your father went abroad for his health', or, 'His work takes him to distant places'.

Until now, it had never occurred to Felicity that the vagueness might be deliberate holding back, keeping secrets. If it hadn't been for the postcards and the atlas, Felicity would have had no idea where her father was. He was more elusive than the Scarlet Pimpernel.

She took off her wet socks, walked barefoot across the deck and looked up at the blackness of the night, as if the multiplying stars might give her an answer.

'Are you saying my dad's a smuggler?'

'No! I don't suppose he brings anything in himself.'

But he did. Felicity knew that he did. Sometimes. That would explain why in her dreams she had felt his kiss on her forehead and her cheek. Her mother said it was imagination. Mr Cricklethorpe, Crickly, had said it was the ghost of a long-ago soldier, kissing his wife goodbye.

She knew now who had put the packet there. Like the creatures living in rock pools, they all knew what to do without being told. Cling to a rock. Clam up.

'I know whose writing that is.'

Nine

Between us, Mr Cricklethorpe and I persuaded Alma to sit by the open window, in the hope that the air would prevent another faint. He placed a cushion at her back and a shawl over her knees, tucking it round her until she said, 'Crickly, do stop fussing,' but in an affectionate way. I wondered whether he was in love with her, and then thought not. They were friends. He was looking out for her – to the extent of lying about where Felicity had gone?

After she asked him to stop fussing, Cricklethorpe turned his attention to me.

'I'm so glad you're here, Mrs Shackleton. Felicity prepared a room in the hope that you might honour this humble house with your presence.'

'And then she slung her hook,' Alma chipped in. 'Where on earth can she be?'

I thanked Mr Cricklethorpe. 'That's kind of you, but I have a room at the Royal.'

'Ah, pity. Their gain and our loss.' He hid his disappointment well, hooking his thumbs in his waistcoat and nodding vigorously, an activity that brought his broad shoulders into play. He was not a man given to small gestures or contained movement. 'You will find the Royal satisfactory, I'm sure. The view across the West Cliff will make up for the lack of history.'

Alma rose unsteadily. She handed the whisky

glass back to Cricklethorpe. 'I am better, thank you.'

'But are you fully recovered?' He moved towards her as though expecting another faint.

'This is a blow that I will never get over, Crickly. Not a word! Are you sure she didn't give any hints to you?'

'No indeed.' Cricklethorpe shook his head several times. 'In fact I am here because Felicity arranged to join me in the twalking this evening and I thought she may need a rehearsal.'

'So much for that then.' Alma looked at herself in the glass and patted her hair in place. 'I'm going to make enquiries.'

'I shall have to twalk alone.' Mr Cricklethorpe adopted a crestfallen tone and sighed loudly. 'I don't suppose, Mrs Turner, you would be up to stepping in?'

'No I would not.'

'Of course not. How insensitive of me.'

'What is a twalk?' Immediately I regretted my question because of a sudden eagerness in Cricklethorpe's glance.

'Do join our merry band. You might even step in and take Felicity's part.' He checked his watch. 'There is time for a rehearsal.'

'Leave Kate alone, Crickly. She's going to help me discover what's going on with that daughter of mine.'

Cricklethorpe gave up his claim on my services for the mysterious twalking. 'Oh you couldn't step in.' He shook his head. 'It wouldn't be fair, not at the last moment.' As if my question had only just penetrated, he gave me his full atten-

80

tion. 'The twalking is my introduction to Whitby. I meet visitors by the bridge and conduct them on a walk while at the same time talking entertainingly about all they see and much that they do not. They hear tales of whaling, smuggling, storms and tempests, ghostly doings and the arrival of Count Dracula on a stormy night, including the parts that Mr Bram Stoker left out. I take them up the one hundred and ninety-nine steps. In the ruins of the abbey I sing a song from Caedmon, the swineherd monk. My accompanist – which tonight would have been Felicity – says a prayer by St Hilda and hands round the hat.'

He gave me the look that said one volunteer would be better than ten pressed men.

I am not sufficiently versatile, intrepid and plucky that on a single day I could drive for miles, find a dead man, cope with a distraught friend and then participate in a twalk, especially the part involving passing round the hat.

As quickly as I could, I answered his look, 'You're absolutely right. That would be entirely beyond me.'

'Then I promise to look out for you as I go about my walk. Feel free to join in at any point.' Cricklethorpe gave a low bow.

As he was about to leave, annoyance overcame Alma's upset. 'If you tell anyone in the town that she's gone, I'll strangle you. And if you see her first, tell her I'm going to strangle her.' Alma smiled brightly as people sometimes do when their marbles have become wobbly.

Cricklethorpe was not a man to give up easily. 'I suppose ... might it take your mind off the business if you come on the twalk? I have the part written.'

'No, no, no!'

'Well, if you're certain. I'll go.' He walked away, turning at the door, 'Good evening then, ladies. You know where the whisky is if you come over faint.'

When he had gone, Alma moved quickly, standing up, taking out her purse, emptying silver and coppers onto the bed. She began to count sixpences and shillings. 'That's fifteen bob.' She added coppers and threepenny bits. 'And that's sixteen and six. I'm going to Skinner Street. What on earth was Jack thinking of? I wonder if Felicity gave him any hint of her plans?'

Cricklethorpe had not gone. He was hovering by the door. He came back in, producing a watch from his waistcoat. 'My dear Alma, I keep telling you that little clock of yours loses one hour in every twenty-four. It's two hours slow. Philips will have shut up shop.' He went to the mantelpiece and wound the china clock. 'I'll buy you a new clock when our ship comes in, but I wouldn't give my patronage to Jack Philips's shop if he were the only clock seller in Whitby.'

'How do you know I'm going to Philips's?' Alma asked.

'I spotted the pawn ticket while you were swooning. The man is a scoundrel. He should not have advanced money to a sixteen-year-old girl. Make him wait.' With this, he took his leave. Again. Almost.

He came back, like the Cheshire cat, appearing and disappearing. 'Don't give Jack Philips the satisfaction of seeing your concern. When I come back, we'll see. I'll have money from the twalk.'

We listened as his footsteps sounded on the stairs.

'He's gone,' Alma said.

'What does he have against Mr Philips?'

'He had nothing against him, until Jack befriended me and Felicity. Then he became most strange. He hints that Jack has a reputation as a breaker of hearts and he doesn't want me to be hurt. There are rumours about Jack and a married woman but I won't let stories of past conquests put me off. At Easter, when Jack gave Felicity and her friend chocolate eggs, Crickly went up there to ask him his intentions. I've never been so embarrassed.'

'Mr Cricklethorpe seems such a mild man.'

'Don't be deceived. He can simmer to boiling point faster than a pan of chip fat.'

Alma picked up the pawn ticket and put it in her pocket. She scooped the sixpences and shillings into a velvet drawstring bag and added the coppers and threepenny bits. 'Will you walk with me? I'll keep an eye out for any chum of Felicity's who might know something.' She went to the mantelpiece and lifted the lid on a Rington's tea jar. 'I have a ten bob note for just such an emergency, that's one pound six and six. I'll pretend to look for the three and six and he'll let me off.'

'Look, Alma, I should...'

'No, don't offer, please! I won't take it. Neither a borrower nor a lender be.' She looked in the jar and fingered out a slip of paper. 'Ah, I don't have a ten bob note. I have an IOU for ten shillings from Felicity.'

'The jewellers is closed. I passed it earlier.'

'Oh it's all right. Jack will be at the shop. He's staying there while his Sandsend house is decorated. The smell of paint gets on his chest. Jack's an amiable man. Felicity may have confided where she's going.'

'That's unlikely, if she hasn't told you.'

She began to root through a drawer. 'I once found half a crown at the back of this drawer.'

It was unlike Alma to be so single-mindedly determined. There was something manic in her actions, arising from that need to do something. Gently, I touched her shoulders. 'Come and sit down, Alma. You are going the wrong way about this. Mr Philips won't be able to help you. Felicity must have a friend that she's confided in. Who would it be?'

'I don't know and I'm not even sure exactly where her friends live, except in the vaguest way, across the bridge, up by the church, that kind of thing.'

'Let's sit down and make a plan. You probably know more than you think. Tell me her friends' names.'

She let me lead her to the window seat where we faced each other. 'I know what I'm doing, Kate. I'm sure Jack will have asked her where she was going. He wouldn't have just handed her money.'

'There is something I need to tell you regarding Mr Philips.'

She gave a groan. 'Don't tell me you've heard tittle-tattle as well, and you only here five minutes. I'm not interested in his supposedly colourful

84

past. He has behaved like a gentleman towards me.'

'It's not gossip. It's something much more serious. I shouldn't really be telling you.'

Alma stared at me. She put her hand to her heart. 'What's happened? Kate, I can't take any more shocks. Tell me.'

I took her hand. 'Calm yourself, take a deep breath.'

'Stop being head girl, Kate. Spit it out, do!'

'I went by Mr Philips's shop today, to look at a bracelet. Mr Philips is dead.'

This was shock enough. She stared at me, repeating the word. 'Dead. Dead?'

I could not bring myself to speak the word murder. Nor did I mention the injury to his head. I fudged. 'A doctor will be called. Sergeant Garvin asked me to say nothing until he reports the death.'

For a long moment she did not speak, and then said, 'You were a nurse. How did he look?'

'There was no pulse. He ... well, he was very obviously dead.'

'Do people go blue when they have a heart attack? I don't know.'

'He looked pale.'

'Was it a heart attack?'

'I can't say.'

'He has a good colour usually, not quite florid but pink.' She closed her eyes. 'Oh God help me, Kate. What else can go wrong? And I never saw this coming.'

'Well why would you?'

'It must have been there ... in the ether, on the

cards. I've been too busy reading other people's futures. It's my fault. I should have seen some sign of this.'

'Why would you?'

'Poor Jack, and he was so happy about having his house done out. Not that I saw the house, well not from inside, but I did walk along the beach one day and look through the window. It was perfect. Through every window, it was perfect, and so modern. It's only twenty years old.'

'So sad.'

She took out her handkerchief. 'I hope he didn't suffer.'

'I think perhaps he didn't.' If the jeweller had been killed by a blow to the back of his head, he would have known little about it.

Now that there was no question of going to the jewellers, she dropped the drawstring bag of money. 'Oh such a nice man, Kate, and that house. I must admit that I let myself dream.'

I felt such an upsurge of pity for her. Having made the best of a bad job with Walter, she deserved a little happiness. 'And why shouldn't you dream?'

'God forgive me for thinking like this at such a time but the bungalow is so pretty. All the lights work. There's parquet flooring. It's on higher ground than the stream and hasn't ever flooded. He even has a cat, and no mice. Poor Jack.' She blew her nose.

It wasn't the most appropriate remark, but I said it anyway. 'I wonder what will happen to the cat?'

'He has a cleaner. She'll look after it for now I

suppose. He has no living relatives. I wonder who he remembered in his will?'

It was a relief to me that Alma's regret at the passing of Jack Philips seemed mainly concerned with the shattering of her dreams for a romance that would lead to a pretty house nestling beyond the bay at Sandsend. But sad, all the same.

She stood. 'I shall have to go into mourning.' She crossed to her wardrobe. 'Not deep mourning. Nothing had been settled between us. We were close for such a short time.' She opened the door of a large wardrobe.

'Not yet, Alma,' I cautioned. 'Don't go marching out in black. I'm supposed to have told no one. The death will probably be announced from pulpits tomorrow.'

She nodded, and took out a grey dress with black panels. 'I wonder whether he said any last words to Felicity? Where is she, Kate, and how could she do this to me?'

'She won't have thought about the effect she'd have, Alma.' I picked up Felicity's notes and read them to her again. 'She's quite light-hearted about it. Whatever she's doing, it seems to her the right thing.'

'What *is* she doing?'

'Whatever it is, she thinks it will take two weeks at least.'

Alma flung the grey and black dress on the bed. 'Two weeks! How do you arrive at that conclusion?'

'Does Felicity know I'm here for a fortnight?'

'Yes.'

I re-read the sentence from the note she had

written for me. *'Sorry to miss you after I have wanted you to come for so long but I have to go somewhere and I think you once told me that you have to do a thing when the time is right. I will come and see you in the winter.* She doesn't expect to be back before I go home.'

'That's madness. She can't be away from me for two weeks. She's never been away from me, apart from her visits to you.'

'And she'll send a postcard. That's the kind of thing you say when you're going on holiday. Has Felicity mentioned anywhere she'd like to visit?'

'We went to Lindisfarne, and I know she'd like to go back. But she wouldn't do that without telling me.'

'Is she courting?'

'Not really. She goes dancing. She and her partner won the spot prize last week at the Spa ballroom. She's friends with girls who have brothers, that kind of thing.'

'When did you last see her?'

That was the question that made Alma cry. 'I should have spotted this coming.'

'Don't blame yourself. She's almost an adult.'

'You're right and I can't keep track of her these days, what with her changing jobs, moping in winter when there's no work, out all hours in summer.'

'So when did you last see her?'

'This is terrible. I'm not even sure. Not last night. I went to bed early, and she was gone this morning. So she could have left either last night or early this morning.'

'If she sends you a postcard straight away,

you'll have it tomorrow.' I wanted her to be hopeful. But we talked in circles, as one does when something like this happens.

'If I did report her missing, it would be to Sergeant Garvin. Then it would all come up again, his sly questions about her father.'

'Perhaps the sergeant is just curious. There's no reason for him to know about the bigamy, is there?'

'I don't know. People don't forget Walter Turner. He made a bit of a name for himself, buying the house that slid into the sea, and then joining in with Cricklethorpe to buy this haunted hall. Walter wasn't in Whitby long but he managed to cut a figure, and then make a fuss about how he would love to stay but needed a warmer climate, and how he was going to send for me and Felicity.'

'That's it, Alma. She's gone to find her father.'

'No. I don't think so.'

'Was he going to send for you? Did he send for you?'

'Of course not. He had his countess by then. The sending for us nonsense was so that he would be thought well of.' Now that she had given up on the idea of redeeming the watch-guard from Philips's jewellers, she dropped the coins into the Rington's tea jar.

'Do you know what, Alma?'

'What?'

'Mr Cricklethorpe is bound to know where Walter Turner is. If they knew each other well enough to go in on this house together, surely they at least kept in touch.'

She paused for a moment and then went back to sit in the window seat. 'I suppose Crickly might know. I haven't kept track of Walter since he went to Madeira.' She looked out of the window. 'I don't care where Walter has fetched up. I just want Felicity to come back.'

'Has she spoken about her father recently?'

'No. She hardly remembers him. She never speaks of him, not any more.'

'Perhaps because she believes you're still angry with Walter.'

'No I'm not.'

'Oh, I thought you were.'

'Not angry, no, just ... exceedingly annoyed about my own predicament.' She bit her lip. With what seemed an immense effort, Alma pushed herself up from her seat.

'I'm going to take a look around Felicity's room, see if I can find any clue as to where she's gone, but first let's go find Crickly's whisky.'

'Where does he keep it?'

'There's some in the kitchen cupboard. Come down with me. I hate it when this house is empty.'

She did her bashing on the door to send the mice scuttling before we went into the kitchen. There was no whisky in the kitchen cupboard. Alma went out to the yard and came back with a bottle of malt. She took a glass from the cupboard. 'Kate?'

'Not for me.'

She poured herself a generous drink. 'Now to see what clues Felicity may have left behind. I never thought I'd be asking you to help me with this.'

In Felicity's room, the chocolate box full of postcards from Walter Turner was in full view, on the chest of drawers. Alma looked through them and handed several to me. They were from Madeira, Portugal, Boston, South Africa and Dublin. I checked the postmarks and put the cards in date order. The most recent was from Dublin but it was two years old.

'He sent postcards frequently up to two years ago. Do you know if he's still in Dublin?'

'She stopped showing the postcards to me. She was always first to pick up the post.' Alma shook her head emphatically. 'Surely she wouldn't go to Walter when he never comes to us?' She opened a drawer and took out a bank book. 'She had more money than I thought, and she's withdrawn almost all of it.'

'Alma, perhaps you should report her missing.'

'No! Even if we're right, if she's gone to him, he'll have the decency to let me know and see her back safely. He's not a wicked man, Kate, just ... well, just Walter.'

'So are you just going to wait and see – wait for the promised postcard?' Felicity has a good head on her shoulders and at sixteen is bound to believe she knows everything. That was what worried me.

Alma put the bank book back in the drawer. 'I can't go running to the police.'

'Why not? Do you have a better idea?' Although even as I asked I thought it unlikely there would be spare manpower to hunt for Felicity alongside a murder enquiry.

'We don't know for sure she has gone to him.' Alma sighed. 'You'll think this is silly.'

'Try me.'

'I'm going to my pepper pot. There's a powerful bond between me and Felicity. I intend to try and contact her, or at the very least channel her whereabouts.'

'Alma, that's all well and good but I would prefer it if we had an address for Walter. I wonder if she's taken the latest postcard with her? You go to your pepper pot and channel. I'll borrow her photograph and make enquiries at the railway station.'

'No! All Whitby would be talking about her. Let me do this my way.'

Ten

Alma and I walked as far as the pier together. She felt confident of her ability to channel awareness of Felicity's location. She would go to her pepper pot and shut the door, needing to be alone and in the right frame of mind, insisting, 'I'll have something to go on if I can just sit and be still. The answers will come to me.'

This struck me as hugely impractical, not to say quite mad, but I reluctantly gave in. It may be that Alma was relying on her subconscious. She could be underhand, but she had a fragile side to her. Perhaps she could only take in so much. The thought of Felicity going away without a word would take time to absorb, as would the dashing of her romantic hopes after the death of Jack Philips.

For now I had to trust Felicity's common sense. She must have wanted her mother to know where she had gone or she wouldn't have left the post-cards where they would be seen. If Alma's subconscious did not put her on the right track very soon, I would insist on a more down-to-earth approach.

Feeling the need for air, I walked along the pier and up the winding Khyber Pass that leads to the West Cliff.

By the Captain Cook monument, I caught sight of Mr Cricklethorpe, gesturing and in full flow. A middle-aged couple, two women and an upright gentleman of military bearing formed a semi-circle around him. He was entirely absorbed in his tale and did not see me.

Back at the hotel, the old soldier was still on duty behind the reception desk. He gave a smile that lit his gaunt face and made me wonder what he would have looked like now had we not gone through that terrible war. Cheerful, perhaps. Plump, perhaps, and certainly in possession of all his limbs. 'There's a gentleman in the bar waiting for you, madam.'

'For me?' I could not imagine who this might be, unless Mr Sykes had come from Robin Hood's Bay to see whether I had arrived safely.

The receptionist saw my uncertainty. 'He's a local gentleman. Didn't ask for you by name but I knew who he meant.' He lowered his voice. 'In connection with the unfortunate incident earlier today.'

So in spite of Sergeant Garvin's best efforts, or perhaps because of them, news of the jeweller's death had spread.

'Does this local gentleman have a name?'

'He is Mr Dowzell, the newsagent.'

As if summoned by genii, the newsagent appeared. He walked towards me from the direction of the bar, fob watch bouncing against his ample girth as he approached.

'Here he is now.' The receptionist turned away to attend to another guest.

Mr Dowzell was upon me. There was an awkward moment when we shifted out of hearing of the new guest.

'Excuse this intrusion, madam. I only wanted to say how sorry I am that I was not more – I don't know – forthcoming or perceptive when you stepped into my shop earlier, so clearly distressed.'

'Think no more of it, Mr Dowzell.'

'If I'd known...' He gave an expansive wave of the hands to suggest some lost opportunity that had slipped through his nicotine-stained fingers. 'May I buy you a cup of tea or a drink and introduce myself properly? I saw Sergeant Garvin. Terrible, terrible, Mrs erm–'

'Mrs Shackleton.'

I did not want to take tea with a stranger, or have a drink bought for me. But it seemed churlish to refuse since he seemed to think it necessary to make amends for what was my decision not to confide in him after finding the jeweller's body.

He frowned. 'Perhaps you do not frequent hotel bars and my suggestion is impertinent, but the bar is very quiet at the moment.'

Curiosity overcame me. He must have something specific to say or he would not have sought me out. 'Very well.'

We walked together to the bar. He led the way to a table by the window. 'My lady wife enjoys a gin rickey here occasionally. The waiter was on the Cunard line and knows a thing or two about cocktails. But I suppose a brandy may be preferable under the circumstances.'

'A gin rickey will suit very well.' The last thing I wanted was for this man to imagine he must take care of me with a medicinal brandy.

He signalled to the waiter and by their exchange of nods I took it that they knew each other rather well and Mr Dowzell's order need not be spoken to be understood.

He turned his attention to me. 'I wish I had been the one to find the unfortunate Mr Philips, so as to spare your distress.'

'Please don't concern yourself. It's not your fault.'

'All the same, I'm a Whitby man to the marrow. Leader of our Urban District Council. We all feel a responsibility towards our visitors. If you had come into my shop and said there was no one at next door's counter, I would have gone in there myself. Being neighbouring traders we keep an eye out for each other.'

'Did you see anyone go into the jewellers shop before me?' I immediately wanted to bite off my tongue. This was not my concern. It was a police matter.

'There's the thing.' He lit a cigarette. 'I didn't see anyone else. I told that to Sergeant Garvin. He wants to keep things quiet for now, naturally.'

'Of course.'

'Were you acquainted with Mr Philips, Mrs Shackleton?'

'No.'

'So you simply went in to support our local traders. It's what we encourage. It's what we want. Trade is the lifeblood of this town.'

He made it sound as if I had intended to buy a diamond tiara. I put him right. 'Something in the window caught my eye.'

He sighed and shook his head at the unluckiness of my choice of shop. 'Jet?'

I began to take the man's measure. He thought it his duty to be nice to the poor woman who had experienced a bad shock. 'Just a little bracelet. Jet and pearl.'

'He has rather a lot of jet now that it's becoming popular with the younger generation of town girls.'

'People expect to see it here.'

He nodded. 'They do. Of course the amount Jack Philips stocked did cause a little ill-feeling with the jet workers on the east side.'

'Oh?' Was this some hint of rivalry between jewellery craftsmen that might lead to a deathly feud? I remembered the open safe and the jet beads scattered across the floor. 'Why would Mr Philips selling jet cause ill-feeling, Mr Dowzell?'

The waiter brought my gin rickey, and a pint for Dowzell. He picked up his pint. 'Well you would not expect a pork butcher to sell beef, would you?'

'I suppose not. Are you suggesting that the jet workers might have taken against Mr Philips?'

'Heavens no, not to the extent of violence.' He stroked his jaw. 'But now that you mention it, that is not such an outrageous possibility as it may sound.' He took a gulp of beer. 'So you did not know Mr Philips?'

'No.'

'Only something Sergeant Garvin said made me think you might have known him. But of course you wouldn't, being a lady visitor.'

I wondered why Sergeant Garvin would have been chatting with Mr Dowzell. My guess was that he had done no such thing. Mr Dowzell was simply fishing, out of curiosity and self-importance. I shifted the conversation. 'Does Mr Philips leave a wife and children?'

'Heavens no, not Jack. He did not encumber himself, as he would have seen it. No, no, he was fancy free. Not that I would agree with some who say he was a philanderer. One shouldn't speak ill of the dead, so we're told. And who would begrudge that poor Jack cut a fine figure on the dance floor, now that his life has been cut short?'

He finished his pint and indicated my glass. 'Another?'

I rose. 'Thank you, no. Now if you'll excuse me.'

He pushed back his chair and stood. 'Of course. You must be tired after your ordeal.'

He suddenly looked rather forlorn. It was not his fault if he had a touch of the pomposities. 'It was kind of you to come, Mr Dowzell.'

As I left the room, he was ordering another drink, this time at the bar.

I wished Dowzell had not cast aspersions on the late Mr Philips. Now that he had put the idea in my head, I could imagine that the jeweller would have been a graceful dancer. Had he lived, Jack Philips might this very night have been gliding across the ballroom's spring floor to the sounds of the Howard Jones band, with Alma in his arms. Or someone else.

I remembered from our school days how easily Alma took umbrage. Snubs and slights never remained unavenged.

And she was very good in school plays. Quite the actress. If I were investigating the murder – which of course I was not – I would need to look at Alma through the magnifying glass of suspicion.

Once back in my hotel room, I locked the door behind me, kicked off my shoes and lay on the bed. I really wanted just to lie down in a dark room but could not muster the energy to walk across to the window and close the curtains.

My head throbbed. My stomach churned. Contradictory thoughts fought in my mind. Had I advised Alma to tell the police that Felicity had pawned a watch with Jack Philips? I couldn't remember. We had gone over the subject so many times. They would find out about that soon enough from Philips's ledger. Alma had refused, saying Felicity's departure wasn't police business. Felicity would send her a postcard, and then she would know more and think what to do. Perhaps that was how we left it.

It was too preposterous to link a sixteen-year-old girl to the death of the jeweller, but my mind ranged across the worst possibilities. Alma had said Felicity went dancing every Saturday. She was bound to have a sweetheart and he may have gone with her. What if Philips had refused to take the watch-guard and the young couple wrote the ticket and took the money themselves?

Stop it, I told myself. That is more than preposterous. First you suspect poor Alma, who has had a lucky escape. Then you put your god-daughter under the spotlight.

At last, I must have drifted into sleep because it was dark when a knock on the door awakened me.

For a moment, I could not think where I was. The knocking belonged to a dream. In my dream, Whitby Abbey became a jewellers shop, its blind lancet windows lit with emeralds and rubies, its decorative arched windows hung with black eyes of Whitby jet. A little girl beckoned me in and although she had the appearance of a novice nun, I knew her to be Felicity.

As I stumbled to the door in my stockinged feet to answer the gentle knocking, the events of that afternoon and evening flooded back. The weight of Alma, fainting against my arms. Mr Crickle-thorpe's guilty look. Mr Dowzell's heavy hints about Jack Philips's past.

I rubbed my eyes and turned on the light. No doubt I looked a fright but it would serve whoever it was right for disturbing me. I turned the knob, half-expecting to see Sergeant Garvin.

It was a relief to see Hilda the chambermaid. She was so close to the door that we were almost nose to nose. Hilda took a step back. 'I'm sorry to wake you, madam.'

'What time is it?'

'Late.' She waited for some comment from me before adding, 'I'm just off duty.'

'Is something the matter?'

She looked both ways along the corridor. 'I hoped to ask you something but I see I've disturbed you, and you missed the evening meal.'

Once more she glanced about the corridor.

'You had better come in for a moment.'

She stepped into the room, and went to the window and closed the curtains. She then turned down my bed. 'I came earlier but you didn't hear my knock and when I used my key, I saw that you were sleeping.'

'It's been a long day.'

'Are you hungry?'

'Is that why you're here, to offer to bring me food?'

'I'm here because there's something I'd like to ask you.'

I poured a glass of water from the carafe by the bed, and then sat down, indicating to her to sit in the basket-weave chair. 'Ask away.' I hoped it would not be about the murder. How many people knew, I wondered. In a place such as this, grim news would spread like the Black Death.

'It's regarding Mrs Turner, or Madam Alma as she is when telling fortunes. Not that I was eavesdropping when you had your fortune told, but I saw from the way you parted that you must be acquainted.'

'Yes we are.'

She smoothed her apron. 'Felicity told me you would be visiting. She looked forward to seeing you.'

'Did she?' Then she had a funny way of showing it.

'The thing is...' Hilda spoke slowly. At this rate we would be here till morning. 'The thing is, I didn't really go to Mrs Turner for my fortune telling, but you tipped me earlier and so I came up with the good idea of going to tell Mrs Turner something, just slip it in after she'd given me her predictions. I went to see her in my break but didn't have the courage to say my piece.'

'And you've come to me because you want me to pass on whatever it is you wanted to say to Mrs Turner?'

Hilda perked up. 'That's it exactly, madam.'

'What's so hard that you can't tell her yourself?'

She pushed her hands in the pocket of her apron and pulled them out again. 'It concerns Felicity.'

'Then speak to Mrs Turner. She won't bite. She'll be glad to hear what you have to say.' Depending on what it is, I thought.

'I missed my chance when I didn't say it this afternoon. And I can't go to Bagdale Hall. It's haunted.'

My head still ached. 'Then tell me what you know.' If this was something important concerning my goddaughter, I would need to call on Alma straight away.

'She's gone off with my brother, Brendan.'

'Where have they gone?'

'I think they've gone to sea, or are going.'

I still felt a little groggy. 'Gone to see what?'

'Gone to sea, you know, in a boat.'

Like the owl and pussycat, in a beautiful pea green boat. How long would they tarry, when would they marry? 'Where have they gone?'

'I'm not sure. They were a bit secretive. She might be dressing as a boy.'

'What makes you say that?'

'I cut her hair, just as she wanted it. I'm good at cutting hair.'

'You and Felicity are friends?'

'We were at school together. Brendan is her sweetheart – or thinks he is. I don't know if she cares about him or not. She winds him round her little finger. He made a joke about her going to sea, but now I'm sure it's true. He's gone and she's gone. They must have been taken on as crew.'

'Just because she has her hair cut, that doesn't mean she is going to sea.'

'It's not just her hair. I saw her buying blue serge from a stall on the market, to make something for herself. Well no one would picture Felicity in blue serge. It's for men.'

'Why were you so reluctant to tell Mrs Turner this afternoon?'

'Oh I don't know. She gave me such a nice fortune that I didn't have heart to say it. Besides, what if Felicity's mother tells harbour master, and he sends a boat to fetch them back, and no one will ever take my brothers aboard again.'

'Brothers. Plural. Hilda, are you telling me other brothers have gone with her?'

'I think Ian might have gone as well. I hope he has. Brendan won't do it on his own, and there's the other business.'

'What business?'

She closed her lips tightly and shook her head. 'I couldn't say.'

'Sit there!' If I let her leave the room, she might disappear home and I would be left to tell Alma half a tale. At the basin, I washed my hands and face and combed my hair. Through the looking glass, I saw Hilda fidgeting and looking uncomfortable. 'It's good that you told me. We'll go together and tell Mrs Turner that Felicity may have gone on a fishing trip. She will be quite safe because...' Here I hesitated. Who was I to say a sixteen-year-old girl would be safe in a boat full of fishermen who would regard her as unlucky as a singing mermaid? 'Hilda, can you vouch for your brother? Would you say Brendan is a decent boy?'

'Oh yes, madam, no doubt about it. He means to marry Felicity.'

'Then he loves her.'

'Oh, very much.'

That sentiment might appease Alma. On the other hand, it might not.

I fastened my shoes, and put on my coat, scarf and hat. All of a sudden I felt very dry and took a long drink of water. Tiredness had fled. Perhaps Felicity was simply desperate to be away from that Gothic house and the twalking Cricklethorpe who had enlisted her as his assistant, to go round with the hat. My sympathies were with Felicity.

'Do you have any idea which boat they may have gone with, or why they went?'

'No.' Her shoulders drooped, the corners of her mouth turned down. 'They didn't tell me, didn't trust me to keep quiet.'

'Come on then. We'll go see Mrs Turner.'

At the door, I paused. When I am on a case, I usually have my satchel with me. In it is a small camera, a flashlight, a penknife and various other bits and pieces that may come in useful in a tight spot. I am sworn to secrecy regarding the source of my ill-gotten police whistle. The satchel hung in the wardrobe, hooked over a coat hanger. I opened the wardrobe door, looked at it, thought for a moment, and then picked it up. Following my brief career as a Girl Guide, I know the value of being prepared.

'Hilda, is there anything you are not telling me?'

She gave me a wide-eyed look. 'Only them things I'm not allowed to say.'

Eleven

Brendan wanted to keep going through the night. They had plenty of fuel for the motor. Felicity knew how to keep a straight course, or told herself she did. She took a turn at the tiller, confident when Brendan was beside her. It was one thing to see how something was done, be shown how to do it. Doing it yourself was a different kettle of fish altogether. When daylight came and if the wind got up, she would have a go at raising the lugsail.

Lights from distant ships twinkled on the horizon as if copying the stars. The blackness of night turned the world small and tight, and then suddenly the moon came from behind a cloud. The sound of waves seemed to enter her head, her very being, as if they were part of her and not something out there. She found herself smiling at the thought that just hours ago she was putting out willow pattern cups, saucers and plates for the customers of Botham's, taking orders for toasted teacakes, carrying a cake stand to the table.

'You were nodding off,' Brendan said. 'Go rest.'

'I might.'

She fetched the flask and poured them each a mug of cocoa. 'How long will it take us?'

'We should be in Berwick by Sunday, with a bit of luck. After that I'm not sure. Elgin's a good way off.'

'Or Hopeman, if the writing on the packet is correct.' She had looked at the charts that were laid flat in folders under the mattress. Hopeman was a small place, on the shore. By the light of the lamp she had followed the line on the chart that marked the divide between land and sea. Tiny shapes represented buoys. Broken lines spelled danger: hidden rocks.

She knew what a scaur was too. They had written about it at school when learning of the *Rohilla* disaster. A scaur was a perilous shelving of rocks that could cause heavy breakers and surf, sometimes well out to sea. The hospital ship *Rohilla* ran aground on Saltwick Nab in 1914. Thoughts of that tragedy at sea gave her the shivers.

Far off, she heard the faint hoot of a foghorn and a louder booming reply. The sound made her shudder. 'What's that?'

'The first sound is a small boat, sounding its foghorn to let a ship know that it's there. If a ship's large, they don't always see a little boat nearby. They could bump it, sink it. The second louder sound is the ship's acknowledgement.'

'Will we come close to some ship?'

'We might. I showed you how to use the fog-horn.'

'I thought it was just for fog.' What she didn't say was, This is dangerous. I should be afraid. I am afraid.

105

Suddenly she saw something quite extraordinary. The sea began to glow as waves broke at the prow of the boat. Waves turned luminous and alive with colour, blues and greens, purples and golds, tiny dots of magic. 'What's that?'

Brendan spoke softly, afraid to break the spell. 'Creatures too tiny to see by day. They put on a show.'

She could not shift her gaze from the sparkle and the dance which continued for about ten minutes.

And then it ended, as suddenly as it had begun.

Felicity suddenly felt a pang of missing her mother. She would love such a show. She had not liked to leave her mother with just a note, and she hated missing her Auntie Kate. What would they be doing now, Felicity wondered. Fast asleep in bed probably. 'We're mad,' she said.

'It's because it's night. You'll feel differently in the day. But we should put on the life jackets.'

She went to the bulkhead and fetched the life jackets. They had practised putting them on and so she did it easily enough.

'Here's yours. I'll keep us on course.'

He took off his oilskin frock.

Three buttons on his shoulder strap glinted in the darkness. If the boat sank and his body was hauled from the sea, the cable rope and ladder detail on his gansey would mark him out as from Whitby. His mother had knitted his initials into the hem. BW. Brendan Webb. Webb, the name of the captain on the matchbox. No relation. Webb, a good name for a sailor.

If they were lost at sea, her body might be washed up on some shore where people would talk about the drowned girl in the Aran cardigan. A bonnie lassie in an Aran pattern, a mystery to unravel. Or fish might nibble the buttons, and her eyes, and the cardigan would be as lost as she was herself.

Don't be silly, she told herself. We'll be all right.

And then Brendan said, 'Don't panic but I think we've come too far out. I must have nodded off while you were resting. That's why we heard that ship and foghorn so clearly.'

'What do we do now?'

'We keep going. I'll take us in closer to shore. You have a sleep if you want. I'm wide awake now.'

'I'm sitting by you. Where's that foghorn? We might need it.'

Twelve

Hilda Webb and I left the hotel by a staff door. She led us towards the town down a steep hill and through a maze of yards, steps and alleys, mercifully avoiding Skinner Street. Even so, the image of Mr Philips's dead blue eyes and the touch of his cold hand came with me as far as Bagdale.

From the opposite side of the road, Hilda and I stared at the old Tudor hall, now dark and forbidding. The gas lamp fixed on a wall bracket cast a strange shadow.

Someone had placed a lamp in an upper window. I calculated that this must be Alma's room.

We crossed the street and made our way to the

side courtyard entrance. Hilda drew back. 'Don't make me go in there. I'll have a heart attack.'

'You'll be all right. Mrs Turner will be pleased to see you and hear your news.' I shone my torch, lighting our path to the porch. 'Be brave. Knock on the door. She probably won't hear from this distance, so we'll go up if the door is unlocked.'

'I'm scared.'

'Just knock. No one's going to hurt you.'

'The ghosts...'

'The ghosts will ignore us.'

Hilda gulped. She knocked on the door suddenly, and then took a step back, bumping into me. We waited. No answer. No sound of movement from indoors. I tried the door. It opened.

'Don't!' Hilda reached out but stopped short of touching my arm. 'What if we disturb Mr Cricklethorpe?'

'He won't mind, I'm sure.' I tried the inner door. Not locked.

'I'll come back tomorrow.' Hilda turned away.

I pushed open the heavy creaking door. 'The idea of something is always worse than doing it. Come on! We'll just climb the stairs.' I spoke cheerfully to give Hilda courage. 'You can tell Mrs Turner you have some news, that Felicity isn't alone. Think about it. If you went missing and someone brought word to your mother, she'd be glad.'

We stepped inside. The fire cast an eerie light in the hall.

'Someone's here.' Hilda paused and listened. 'I can hear noises.'

'It's just the sound of the house, drying out.'

The fire gave off a reassuring crackle. Hilda was not reassured and grabbed my arm. 'I don't like it. Why would someone have a fire for an empty room, except for ghosts?'

'Well I haven't seen a ghost. It's just an old building, with a life of its own.'

We trod the flagged floor to the foot of the staircase.

It was impossible to move silently through this house. Stairs creaked and groaned objections as we climbed, creating an odd sensation of echoing footsteps.

We crossed the landing and mounted the second set of stairs.

On the second landing, Hilda, who had slipped behind, moved beside me, not wanting to be left in the rear, I guessed.

My tap on Alma's door brought no answer. A cold chill ran down my spine. What if she too lay dead? But that was ridiculous.

Gingerly, I pushed open the door and called her name. I had been right in identifying the room from the street. An oil lamp burned in the casement window. There was no sign of Alma. I could see from the doorway that the table by the window, lit by the lamp, had been tidied. Her manuscripts made one neat pile. I crossed to the table and was rewarded by the sight of a note.

Felicity, I hope you've changed your mind about going off. Stay here and I will be back soon. I am not cross.

Hilda was beside me. 'Can we go now?'

'Yes.'

She scurried from the room. By the time I reached the ground floor Hilda was standing with her back to the wall, near the door.

'One last look, Hilda. Follow me.'

'Where?' It was less a question and more a wail.

'Just think, you'll be able to tell your friends that you went into Bagdale Hall and came out in one piece. You thought you heard a noise when we arrived. I suppose Mrs Turner might be in the kitchen.'

The room that adjoined the kitchen also had a fire. Like some fascinated visitor from a different world, Hilda stopped to look. 'They must have their own coal mine and forest for this lot of fuel.'

I pushed open the kitchen door. The place was in darkness, but this time without the scuttling mice. The noise came from somewhere outside, a scraping sound across the yard.

I called, 'Hello?'

Silence. And then a crash, something breaking.

I called again, 'Alma!'

This time, there was an answering call, shortly followed by a dishevelled-looking Cricklethorpe who came in from the yard, carrying a torch. Once we had recognised each other, we directed our beams to a spot on the kitchen flags and watched them dance. Mr Cricklethorpe brought with him the unmistakable scent of whisky.

'Ah, Mrs Shackleton. You have changed your mind and wish for a room.'

'No. I was looking for Mrs Turner. She is not in her room.'

'May I give her a message?'

'Just that I'll call on her tomorrow.'

110

'Very good. Consider it done, dear lady.' He was all shifty attention, but not towards me. He glanced back at the yard, where the voices – if indeed I had heard voices – had gone silent.

Part of me wanted to push past him to see what he was up to. He might be murdering Alma or dragging Felicity's body away in a cart. He was up to something and in a hurry to get back to whatever he was doing. 'Mr Cricklethorpe, I believe you know where Felicity has gone.'

'I? What makes you think that?'

'Because earlier, in Alma's room, she asked you "Did you have any idea what Felicity was planning? Did she say anything at all to you?" You answered the second question but not the first. Felicity may not have told you what she was planning, but I believe you have a good inkling and I wish you would say.'

He crossed the kitchen and came to stand beside me. 'I am impressed, Mrs Shackleton. I see why you have taken to looking into puzzles and troubles. I really do not know where Felicity is. Now if you'll excuse me...'

Whatever was going on in that back yard had his attention. Reluctantly, I gave up on him, for now, and let him walk me back to the front door. He talked non-stop, so as not to let me get a word in. 'It's most distressing, but I have the strongest feeling that Felicity is safe and well. I walked with Mrs Turner to the Spa, in case some of Felicity's friends might have seen her.'

'And had they?'

'No, and they were surprised not to see her. Perhaps she made some other plans. Who knows?'

111

'You do, I think.'

He laughed. 'If you need to find Mrs Turner, I have a good idea where she'll be. She sometimes walks in the evenings, her constitutional. Given her line of work, she takes measures to avoid being accosted. Certain ladies of the town feel entitled to gratis predictions.'

We were now by the vestibule. Hilda had vanished.

He opened the front door for me. As I stepped outside, he said, 'I wouldn't recommend it because you don't know your way, but she's likely to be by the abbey, communing with the moon.' He nodded sagely. 'Goodnight, Mrs Shackleton. I am glad that Mrs Turner has a friend.'

'Goodnight, Mr Cricklethorpe.'

He closed the door behind me. The key turned in the lock.

Hilda hovered a few yards from the house. She was shaking. I touched her arm. 'See, that wasn't so bad, was it? It was only Mr Cricklethorpe.'

'The dame won't like people knowing his business.'

'What is his business?' I was beginning to have an inkling.

'Oh I couldn't say. We don't say.'

'Why do you call him the dame?'

'He plays the dame in the Whitby Players pantomime. People call him that.'

'Affectionately, or scornfully?'

'Oh, affectionately. He's well-liked, he stuck to the terms, people say.'

'What terms?'

'They don't say. I'm not sure anyone really

112

knows. They just say it. "The dame stuck to the terms." When I asked my mam, she wouldn't tell me. Perhaps she doesn't know.'

'Would his business have anything to do with whisky?'

'Oh I couldn't say.'

'You don't say.'

'No, we don't.'

We walked towards the harbour. 'Hilda, Mrs Turner and Mr Cricklethorpe called at the Spa earlier, to see whether any of her friends had seen Felicity.'

'I already heard neither of them was there. That's why I'm sure.'

'I want to find Mrs Turner. Where else might she have gone to talk to Felicity's friends? Is there a café or a street corner where young people congregate?'

'Not at this time of night.'

'I'm not going to tell anyone, I just want to know where Felicity's mother may have gone to look.'

'Well there's a yard by the fish and chip shop. There's a warm pipe runs along that wall. People sit on it.'

'Then let's take a look.'

As we crossed the road from the station, I could smell fried fish. It was a long time since tea in Botham's. 'I'm hungry.'

'They won't be frying now, Mrs Shackleton. It'll be closed.'

We were outside the shop and the lights were still on. 'I wish they were open. Could you eat something?'

'I can always eat a bag of chips.' Hilda peered through the window and waved. 'They know me well enough to open up.'

She was right. Moments later, we each had a bag of chips with scraps of batter and I had the luxury of a fish-cake, liberally splashed with vinegar and sprinkled with salt.

'Where's this warm pipe that your friends sit on?'

'It's down here.' Hilda led me along an alley and indicated the pipe that came down the wall and ran just a little higher than ground level. I suppose when one is more used to outside privies than the indoor sort, a sewage pipe is simply a warm pipe. I decided against identifying it for Hilda. After all, it was cast iron and a good place to sit.

We sat down to eat our banquet. 'You're still out and about, Hilda. Where would your mother think to look for you?'

'She wouldn't. She knows I'm out working and might be held back. She's always glad if I'm held back. It means I'm waiting on table or washing up and will fetch home a bigger pay packet.'

We finished our food in silence. 'Come on then, Hilda. There's nothing else we can do at this time of night. I'll walk you home.' I screwed up the newspaper wrapping.

She took the paper from me and clattered the lid of a nearby dustbin. 'There's no need. You'll want to get back to the hotel.'

'I want to be with you when you tell your mother about Brendan and Felicity. She may know whether they really have gone together.'

Hilda's mood had lightened, and why not? She

114

had passed on her worry. Now it would be my task to talk to Alma about the possibility that Felicity had boarded a boat dressed as a boy. 'I'm sure they'll be all right. Our Brendan's eighteen.'

'Felicity is missing. If we don't find out something soon, her mother will have to go to the police – if she hasn't already.'

'It's not that serious is it? They won't come to harm.'

She led the way towards the bridge that joined the west of Whitby to the east. The water gleamed in the moonlight.

Hilda chatted as we walked, about her brothers and sisters, her gran and granddad, and how lucky she was to have a job in the hotel, so much to be preferred to mending nets and selling fish. Her mam did not want the boys to go to sea, because the sea had proved unlucky for their father. She had ambitions for them to move up beyond the hills and have some land, as her own cousin did.

On the other side of the bridge, the shops and houses were mainly in darkness, with just a few upper windows showing a light through a chink in the curtains. We walked a little way beyond the bridge before turning left onto Church Street. Here the lane was too narrow for standing street lights. What little light there was came from bracket lamps attached to the walls of houses.

'The lodgers will be in the pub now so Mam will be able to speak.'

'You have lodgers?'

'Oh yes, but they're no trouble. Mam makes a pot of potatoes and a pot of cabbage. They each bring in what they want cooking, a chop or a herring or a slice of liver.' She turned into a narrow entry. 'This way. We're Clark's Yard.'

The houses were crammed closely together and seemed to lean precariously towards us and each other. 'We're in the same yard as my grandma and granddad,' Hilda said confidently. 'Our house belonged to my great-granddad and grandma.'

In daytime, this place must seem quaint, old-fashioned and even charming. The light of the moon did not reach into this confined space. It had the quality of a frightening dream, somewhere you could turn and turn and never find your way back. Houses might reach out to touch each other in order to crush any stranger who ventured too close.

'I'll just tell Mam you're here and make sure there's no earwigging lodger. If there's no bobby on the prowl, the pubs stay open long as they can.' She came to a stop by the house door. 'If Mam knows you're here she won't brain me for trying to tell Mrs Turner about Brendan and Felicity before I told her.'

She went inside. I waited, feeling self-conscious, hovering in the close-packed yard, hemmed in by the dark shapes of houses. I had escorted Hilda, and now realised that I would have to find my way back to the hotel. I became aware of my greasy fish and chip fingers and took out my hand-kerchief to wipe my hands, and then pulled my gloves back on. Murder and upset could so easily divert one from being properly dressed.

After a long moment, I heard a raised voice. 'They never have! When was I supposed to know?'

Hilda's answer was inaudible.

116

The mother spoke again. 'Well who is she?'

Hilda must have answered.

'You've brought an hotel guest here, are you mad? Do you want to be sacked on top of all else?'

Whatever Hilda said next must have done the trick. The door opened. A tall woman, surrounded by a halo of light from the lamp within, filled the doorway. 'You better step inside, madam.'

'Thank you.' I felt as reluctant to step in as she was to invite me, but choices were limited. 'I'm Mrs Shackleton, and I'm sorry to disturb you, Mrs Webb.'

The woman, perhaps in her forties, held the door for me to pass. She must have been pretty once but her face was now lined by care and weather. I entered a decent-sized room that was almost entirely taken up with a large deal table. A half-made skirt lay across the table. I had interrupted Mrs Webb's dressmaking. Stools were pushed under the table. Along the side of the lead fire range was fixed a wide shelf. On this lay a pale girl with a pinched face and red-rimmed eyes. She was wrapped in blankets, her head on a green cushion.

Mrs Webb pulled out two stools, with one between so that we should not be too close. This must be the place where lodgers ate their potatoes, cabbage and individual choice items. We sat with our backs to the sickly child. I wondered if she would be diverted by our conversation, or too poorly to care.

I thought it best to come straight to the point, in case a troop of lodgers came rolling in. 'I'm a friend of Mrs Turner. Felicity is my goddaughter.

117

I wondered if you'd seen her. She and your son Brendan are friends I think.'

'She won't be with my Brendan. He's working on pleasure boat, *Whitby Lass*.'

'Do you mind my asking when you last saw him?'

'He sometimes stops with his auntie. She has more space.'

She hadn't answered my question. If I protested, she would clam up.

'M-a-m!' Hilda had a good wailing tone. She knew her mother could say more if she wanted.

'You go measure out porridge. Leave me to talk to this lady.'

Hilda walked into the other downstairs room. I could hear her, opening a cupboard door, clattering a tin.

'And shut that door!'

She did so.

'Does Mrs Turner say her lass has gone off with my lad?'

'No. Felicity left a note but gave no details. Hilda thinks Felicity and Brendan may be on a boat.'

'I'd know if he sailed outa Whitby, so would harbour master.'

'I'm sorry. I've wasted your time. You would have let Mrs Turner know if you'd heard anything.' I pushed back the stool, and stood.

'And I'm sorry you had a wasted journey.' Mrs Webb reached for a shawl that covered the feet of the girl on the shelf. 'I'll put you on your way.'

I wished the girl on the shelf goodnight. She did not answer.

In a moment, we were in the dark yard, the

118

buildings pressing in on us. Mrs Webb asked, 'Why didn't Mrs Turner come herself?'

'She wasn't home when Hilda and I called. She must be out searching.'

We were back in Church Street, walking towards the corner. 'I'll walk you as far as bridge, madam.'

'Thank you, Mrs Webb.'

I had the feeling she was itching to say something else. She spoke when the bridge came in sight.

'Brendan wouldn't attempt to take a lassie on a boat.'

'Then perhaps Hilda is mistaken.' I hoped that this was so, hating the thought of Felicity being at sea on such a dark night. She might be afraid, cold, wet and in danger.

'Regarding you being hotel guest, and our Hilda dragging you over east...'

'Think no more about it, Mrs Webb. I wanted to see the hidden sights of Whitby, and now I have.'

'Well thank you for that.'

Our interview was at an end, or so I thought. She did not turn back but walked across the bridge with me. At the other side, she grabbed my elbow. 'I heard about Mr Philips, the jeweller.'

'Ah yes.'

'Was it you found him? They said it was a lady staying at Royal who just arrived.'

'I found him, yes.'

'Did you know him?'

'No. It was my first visit to his shop in years. My engagement and wedding ring were bought from him.'

'I see. I just wondered if you knew him.' She let

119

go of my elbow.

'I remember his kindly manner and his red hair. Did you know him yourself, Mrs Webb?'

She took a sharp breath and held herself very still. 'What business would I have with a man like him?'

'I don't know. Lots of Whitby people are acquainted with each other.'

'He was generous to Seamans Mission, I can tell you that, and I'm right sorry he's dead.'

A couple of men crossed the bridge, going separate ways and calling goodnight.

'Thanks for walking me across the bridge. I'll go back to the hotel by way of Bagdale Hall, just in case Alma, Mrs Turner, has come back.'

Mrs Webb drew her shawl more tightly round her. 'Go back to your hotel, madam. Be comfortable. If she has it in her head that Felicity has gone to sea, Mrs Turner will be up by abbey communing with moon. We all know she does it.'

That sounded like Alma. Everyone has their own way of coping with distress, though communing with the coastguard would be more useful than gazing at the moon.

'Goodnight then, Mrs Webb.'

'Goodnight. I'd see you back to hotel, but I have an errand.'

She walked off quickly, not retracing her steps across the bridge but bearing right. I wondered where she might be going at this time of night. Thinking I might also go in that direction, I hurried after her and caught up. 'Mrs Webb!'

She turned.

'If Brendan sometimes stays at his aunt's, might

we find him there, or enquire, then we'll know whether it's true or not that he has gone on a boat with Felicity.'

She shook her head. 'I'll know that tomorrow. My sister'll be asleep now and she's too far away.'

With that, she hurried on, turning a corner, disappearing out of sight.

I now had the choice of returning to my hotel or climbing to the abbey in the hope of finding Alma. Was she up there? I turned and looked up at the abbey's dark skeleton, barely discernible because the moon had slid behind a cloud.

It would be madness for Alma to be stumbling among the ruins, calling for Felicity, fainting if she caught a glimpse of some long-dead monk or abbess. Why should I go trailing up one hundred and ninety-nine steps and risk breaking my ankle? But not only Mrs Webb thought that Alma would be by the abbey. Cricklethorpe had said it too.

When I arrived in Whitby, all I'd intended to do was spend time with Alma and Felicity, go for solitary walks, hire a bathing tent and read, or examine the back of my eyelids.

Mrs Webb was right. I should go back to the comfort of my hotel. But I thought of Alma who had been through so many difficulties since the days when she was teased at school, and that dreadful nickname which had been at my instigation, though I never intended it. The Tennessee Fainting Goat. Having allowed myself to be drawn in, feeling guilty about the nickname business, I knew that unless I could see Alma safe and sound this night, I wouldn't sleep. She must be worried sick. I should have been tougher and said Go to the police. They might have made a call to the harbour master and settled the matter.

Why on earth Alma would choose to commune with the moon I couldn't fathom. But then, Alma was not one of the world's fathomable. She had appeared shocked when I told her of Jack Philips's death. But did she know more than she was letting on?

As if in answer to my question of whether I ought to climb the one hundred and ninety-nine steps, the moon came from behind a cloud.

Thirteen

It was with mixed feelings that I bowed to the inevitable and once more crossed the bridge onto Whitby's east side.

Sandgate is a bustling street by day, filled with shops and jet workshops. All were in darkness now. As I passed a public house, the door opened and a bent old man came out. I glanced inside and saw that the room within was smaller than Mrs Webb's kitchen. The landlord belatedly called 'Finish yer drinks, lads!'

I hurried along, to avoid the unsteady fellows who would shortly be turned out. There was a powerful stench of fish as I passed the marketplace and old town hall, coming back onto Church Street. It was a good move to have brought my torch, given the moon's enjoyment of hide-and-seek with a particular cloud. I approached the one hundred and ninety-nine steps that led to the church and the abbey. There was Henrietta Street, where Alma had lived when she first came to Whitby, and had the misfortune of watching her house claimed by the sea.

Were Cricklethorpe and Mrs Webb right in thinking that Alma would be walking near the abbey? Possibly. At school she went off walking for hours alone. It was one of the habits that set her apart.

Yes or no?

Yes.

I began the climb to the abbey, counting the steps, glad of the eerie moonlight that for now made my torch unnecessary. On the forty-ninth step, it struck me how unprepared I was for the task of seeking out my old school friend. First of all, she knew what she was doing. If she really was 'communing with moon' I might interrupt her at a crucial moment and destroy some psychic perception into where Felicity had gone. Perhaps I would stumble across courting couples, or sensation-seekers expecting the return of Dracula in the form of a black dog. I am not given to fancy, but I hoped there would be no big black dog sniffing about. I lost count of the steps while trying to think of a plan.

The only plan that came to mind was to simply look around the ruins for a tall slender figure in a cloak. Part of the abbey had been shelled during those dreadful days of 1914. In the darkness, I might trip over war-damaged stones and break an ankle.

This was a foolish venture. I blamed having a

nap and fishcake and chips which had left me with energy to spare, and that awful desire to Do Something that overtakes me at the most inconvenient times.

Some of the steps are extra wide with a resting place said to be for the benefit of pall-bearers carrying coffins to St Mary's churchyard for burial. Coffin rests. I did not need to rest, finding the steps easy enough to climb, but rest I did for a few moments, looking out across the sea where in the distance I saw ships moving so slowly they appeared not to be moving at all. Below me, the town looked fast asleep. Only lunatics, drunks and the ill-at-ease would wander abroad at this hour.

At school, we pupils had a whistle to warn of approaching teachers or the arrival at the back fence of chaps from the boys' school. One never forgets a whistle. Ours was two notes rising, two notes falling. I tried it. Alma would recognise the signal. More as a comfort to myself than in hope of an answer, I whistled every now and then. When I arrived at the top of the steps, I surveyed the scene.

I passed St Mary's churchyard, doubting that Alma would be there. That would be a more likely spot for courting couples, the dead telling no tales. The sight of the ruins, the dark abbey with its blind eyes, made me gulp for air. It seemed so close, so overpowering and forbidding. Well, I was here now and so began my patrol. I shone my torch on the ground, wanting to avoid the humiliation of tripping and ending up with a sprained ankle and a painful limp back to the hotel. Now I knew how Hilda had felt in Bagdale Hall. It made me shiver to be so close to the ruins, half-imagining some robed figure would appear as I turned a corner. I whistled again and let the beam of my torch explore, wider and wider. I was drawn towards the cliff edge. If Alma had come here for lunar communing she would be disappointed. The moon once again hid behind a cloud. Alma may have gone home again, perhaps walking round to Caedmon's Tread. A movement close by caught my eye. A skinny young fox stopped for a moment to stare at me, transfixed by the beam of my torch. If there were lovers here, they would think me some kind of peeping Tom. I whistled again. When my whistle was answered, I felt a small shock. So she was here, but where? And now I remembered that she could not whistle. Perhaps she had persisted and finally learned. The wind blew. I could not tell where the whistle sound came from. I whistled again.

Suddenly someone was behind me. I felt the warmth of a body close to my back.

'Nah then, what's all this?'

I froze, and then turned. Slowly.

'Mrs Shackleton. We meet again.' It was the policeman, Sergeant Garvin.

'Good evening, officer.' I tried to speak calmly as if I usually spent my nights walking about ruins, whistling. What else was one meant to do in Whitby after dark?

'Are you looking for someone, madam?'

'Not exactly.'

'Ah, then what?'

'Well, yes, in a way looking for someone.'

'It's coming in chilly,' he remarked, 'don't you find?'

125

'I suppose it is.'

'There's no one here, except you and me. Who were you expecting?'

I hesitated. Did he also know that Alma wandered the cliffs after dark? It seemed unfair to implicate her. 'I felt like a walk.'

'You were whistling.'

'I whistle to feel brave I suppose.'

'But not a tune, more of a signal, or is it a special feeling-brave whistle?'

'That's it.'

'But you were expecting an answer?'

It was time to maintain a dignified silence, or was it?

'Take a good look at the little boat, did you?' He did not move as he waited for my answer.

'What little boat?'

'I watched you signal to the boat.'

'Oh no. I was just making a circle with my torch.'

'Ah, and it just happened to be a circle that took in the unlit boat. Do you do that often?'

Well of course I didn't do it often. We don't have many boats where I live in Headingley, it being about sixty miles inland. But I did not say that. 'I was just looking out to sea, at the ship with lights. I didn't notice a boat.' Now I felt disappointed in myself for having poor powers of observation. Was there really a boat? I wanted to go and look but that did not seem a good idea. Even so I said, 'Where?'

We went to look. 'Ah,' the sergeant said. 'It's gone now, perhaps in response to a signal.'

He suspected me of being in cahoots with smugglers. My old friends in the Girl Guides

126

would be thrilled.

'I didn't see a boat, sergeant. Truly.'

In the pause that followed, he took my elbow. 'Shall we go back into the town?'

'What a good idea.'

I put my torch away, as he guided us back to the steps. 'A whistling woman bodes ill in a fishing community.'

'Yes, so I've heard. Whistling or not, women seem to bode ill in all sorts of places. I don't believe the ghosts of the abbey will mind.'

'I suppose you might have been looking for Mrs Turner, given that she sometimes comes up here in the evenings.'

'I suppose I might.'

'Did you keep the confidence, regarding Mr Philips, only half Whitby has somehow got word of Mr Philips's death and there are all manner of variations?'

'I only told Alma when I absolutely had to, and I didn't say how he died.'

'I see. And how do you think that he died?'

'By a blow to the head.'

He did not speak again until we were halfway down the steps. He shone his torch into the distance, towards the West Pier. 'There's a light on in the fortune teller's pepper pot. That's where you would have found your friend. Mrs Turner usually goes there after she's communed with the moon.'

'Oh.' It was not much of a response, but all I could think of on the spur of the moment.

'It's against the by-laws to occupy the pier premises after the hours of darkness but in a place like Whitby it's sometimes politic to turn a blind eye, though not to murder.'

'You're not suggesting that Mrs Turner is a murderer?'

'I'm not suggesting a murder has taken place. But human nature is a strange creature. If a sweet and rather unworldly lady with expectations of marriage had a good and clever friend who thought she was being taken advantage of, that person might act on her behalf. It has been known.'

Not only did Sergeant Garvin suspect me of signalling to smugglers, he now had me in the role of avenging angel, or as a policeman might put it, murderer.

This had gone far enough. Looking out at the dark waves had unnerved me. Felicity might be out there, cold and seasick.

As if he read my thoughts, Sergeant Garvin asked, 'Have you seen Felicity Turner since you arrived in Whitby?'

'No, I haven't, and I wish to report her missing.'

'That will be up to Mrs Turner. I'm sure she'll do so in her own good time if necessary.'

So he knew, but what did he know that made him so phlegmatic? The man was infuriating. Meanwhile, as I was being escorted down the one hundred and ninety-nine steps like some criminal, 'sweet and rather unworldly' Alma was cosily consulting her crystal ball.

Fourteen

For the second time that evening, Alma sought refuge in her pepper pot. In some way she could not quite grasp, she felt blamed and guilty; blamed for what and guilty of what she could not say. She lit the lamp.

Alma had a particular fondness for her wicker chair. Each time she left, she draped the chair with a colourful paisley throw. Each time she returned, she unveiled the chair and experienced an extraordinary well of affection for this unremarkable piece of furniture. In the dim light, she sat very still, palms upturned on her lap, eyes closed.

Little flecks danced before her eyes, the light behind her eyelids shifted and changed, creating shapes and colours. The sounds of the sea hummed her thoughts to stillness. She heard a solitary gull on night patrol. After a time, several minutes, or an hour, she spread her arms, raised her palms in something like supplication and waited. Then she opened her eyes, put her hands on the table in a way that meant business and looked into her crystal ball.

For a fleeting moment the swirl matched the colour and amorphousness of the dots behind her eyelids. She looked deeply into the grey mistiness edged with blues and purples reflected from her cape. The seekers who came to her sometimes thought she discerned life's signposts: people and places; couplings; the beginnings of journeys; death wearing a midnight cape and carrying a scythe, or in the guise of a prowling black dog. They might imagine she saw sweet cupid's chubby finger pointing to the one who would be forever true. It was not like that. Looking into her crystal ball was only a way of divining, such as a water diviner might feel a twitch. It could be the twitch of his palsy or it might indicate a poisoned underground spring or the elixir of life.

Felicity was safe and not far away. Alma felt that as a tingle through the soles of her feet. She always took care of her feet. On the rare occasions when she bought new shoes the assistant – if he were male – complimented her on her perfect feet. Yet in spite of the certainty from the tips of her neat toes to her pumice-stoned heel that Felicity was safe, Alma knew that all was not well.

The control and the calm Alma needed to do her work suddenly fled as her stomach knotted with anxiety. Felicity was unprotected. She was somehow just out of reach. There was movement, a feeling of nausea, such as comes to a person in a small boat, and then it was gone.

In vain, Alma tried to recreate the mood of receptiveness, her seeing time as she called it. No use. She stood and stretched her arms. Her fingertips touched the distempered walls. With the door and window shut, the place had grown stuffy and airless but to open the door would be to break the mood, to betray her trust in the beyond and the messengers who guided her.

She picked up her pack of Tarot cards, but then set them down, unable to phrase a question with sufficient clarity. Afraid that if she tried and failed the spirit of the cards would flee.

Time to try something else. She picked up her pencil and took paper from her drawer – the discarded first draft of *How to make Amusing Objects out of Newspaper* – and began to write on the back. The words came quickly. She could barely keep up as they spilled onto the page.

She shouldn't stop to read but she did.

Felicity where are you answer me show me make a picture in your thoughts and let me know you are safe and sound and are you wanting to come home I won't make you if you don't want to for God knows at sixteen I never wanted to go home but only to wait to be where I needed to be when fate would prompt the next step and sometimes to keep moving aimlessly but movement was all I never told you about when I sold flags as a girl and instead of standing in one place I walked and walked for miles thinking that the selling of flags depended on my effort on my walking and my energy but I walked somewhere where there were no people to buy flags and yet kept on walking expecting it was only natural to keep on, keep on, and that man who came from nowhere and looked around and saw me and did a bad thing, came right up and did a bad thing and then he bought a flag and walked away and I thought that selling flags was not a good idea not for me that I didn't have the knack for it. Felicity what is it you have the knack for? Where are you? Talk to me.

Alma took the pencil in her other hand. She did not want to hear herself. She wanted some other voice. The pencil wrote.

131

It's dark, and cold, am I dead, I don't think so but am lonely as the dead and all I do is wait for something how much longer perhaps forever.

This was not Felicity. Someone else was trying to reach her. Was this Walter, after all this time?

Alma took the pen in her right hand.

Tell me, tell me who you are, where you are. Show me what you see.

Alma's hands trembled. She tried to write, but her right hand shook. She held the pen in her left hand but could not hold it still. She used both hands, one holding the other steady. The words came spidering from the pencil.

It's me, Alma. Your husband Walter Turner. Turner turned cold. Turner turned old.

Every sense of Alma's being stirred and strained. She could feel her nerve ends tingling. If only there'd been a full moon, she'd have done better than this poor job. So much of her automatic writing came out as nonsense and some not decipherable, producing only a few lines that mattered.

There was a great deal of guff before she reached those lines. She had grown sick and tired of messages from the afterlife that lacked sophistication and solidity. She could scream at those messages that told her to take the teapot to the kettle and not the kettle to the teapot. It pained her to learn from the spirits matters

132

concerning the Yukon and the South China Sea, over which she had no control. She could only worry for those involved in landslides and storms.

The message for her leaped out from the dross. Her errant Turner again, telling her for sure that he was still alive, speaking of himself in the third person.

Turner expects visitors. One long-awaited, one red-haired, with money on his mind and bad intensions.

Alma felt glad she did not have to mark her spirit guides, or her other self, whoever was responsible, for spelling. 'Long-awaited', that must be Felicity. Someone was taking Felicity to him. What was it they wanted?

Further down the page – among advice about hemming a pair of trousers, information more fitting for a seamstress than for a fortune-telling mother of a missing daughter, was another line. This was a message direct from Turner.

Don't be foolish, Ally Alma. Philips doesn't want you for yourself. He wants our daughter.

'You're wrong,' she said to the walls of the pepper pot where the oil light had begun to flicker as the wick grew low. 'Where are you? How can you be so cruel, and so wrong? Don't you know the man is dead?'

Someone knocked on the door.

At first, she thought she must have summoned Felicity and that some astral wind had blown her daughter back from a far-off place, or Walter

133

Turner himself had divined that she was once more subject to fainting fits and had whirled into her inner life again, his hypnotic powers undimmed, to set her to rights.

But then she came back into the here and now. By-laws did not permit use of the pepper pot after daylight hours. The patrolling officer?

'Are you in there?'

She did not recognise the female voice. Blinking herself back into the world she took the few steps and opened the door. She stared at the woman in black with her shawl over her head and shoulders. 'I'm not working. It's after hours.'

'And I'm not here for my fortune telling. I'm Mrs Webb, Hilda's mother.' She waited. 'Are you going to let me in?'

Alma stood aside and let the woman in. She recognised her now.

Mrs Webb was tall and broad shouldered, her hair done in a loose wispy bun, her face lined with exposure to wind, weather and hard work evidenced by her rough hands. Alma felt a stab of guilt. It didn't do for a fortune teller to have workworn hands and she had cajoled Felicity into scrubbing the laundry and peeling potatoes. Forty-five, Alma thought, as she looked at the woman's tired eyes. If Mrs Webb had called for a fortune, Alma would have guessed that worry about a child brought her to the pepper pot, or the need to know whether a husband in the afterlife had something to say.

Mrs Webb's first words gave no clue to why she was here. 'This place stinks of paraffin. That lamp won't do nobody's chest no good.'

134

She was right. Alma opened the window. 'I hadn't noticed.'

Mrs Webb let her black shawl slide from her head so that it simply covered her shoulders.

'What do you notice, Mrs Turner?'

'Pardon?'

'You don't notice the stench of paraffin. Did you notice your lass was about to run off with my Brendan?'

Alma felt her shoulders stiffen. 'How do you know?'

'A little bird told me.'

Alma motioned Mrs Webb to take a seat before lowering herself carefully into the basket-weave chair. 'Felicity left me a note. It came as a surprise. She didn't mention anyone else.'

'You got a note. You're lucky.'

Alma's voice sounded strange to herself.

'Where have they gone?'

'You tell me. They must have brass. Did you give Felicity money?'

Alma would have loved to give her daughter money, to take her again to Lindisfarne, buy her a new dress, take her to tea in Botham's so that she was the one eating cakes, not serving them.

'No.' She hesitated, but there was no point in holding back. 'Felicity withdrew her savings.' She hesitated. This felt like a betrayal. 'She pawned a watch-guard and left me the ticket.'

The air became suddenly still. Staring at the woman, Alma had the impression that the wind had dropped and the waves paused, considering whether to crash.

'Who did she pawn it with?'

135

'Mr Philips, and I wish she hadn't.'

'So do I.'

Mrs Webb seemed suddenly heavier, so heavy that the floor beneath might give way. They would drop into some dark place below the pier, where dead pirates dance and a lost bell chimes.

The wind rose again. As a breeze blew through the cabin, a mad thought struck Alma: What if we both fainted, bashed heads, and were found concussed, or dead? That thought frightened her, not because she believed it would come to pass but because there had been long periods in her life when she did nothing but anticipate disasters.

The women looked at each other across the crystal ball. Wouldn't it be nice, Alma thought, if someone told me and Felicity a fortune and it was good and true and came to pass? Mrs Webb folded her hands. Alma saw the likeness to Hilda. Now she understood Hilda's real reason for coming to see her earlier, and paying a shilling for a fortune she did not want.

After a long silence, Mrs Webb spoke. 'You were walking in the town with Jack Philips, taking tea with him. I saw you together.'

'He paid me some attention.'

'So we are both sorry he is dead.'

'Yes.'

'We might be the only ones in this town who are sorry.'

'What do you mean?'

'My Brendan is Jack Philips's son. Did you find that out?'

Alma stared at Mrs Webb. Was this true? And why would Mrs Webb tell her?

She felt slightly dizzy. When she and Jack were seen together, she had been conscious of censorious glances, of clicking tongues. It was one thing to know that Jack had a past, that there were rumours. It was another thing altogether to have this worn-out woman in her old-fashioned clothes telling her that Brendan was fathered by the glowing, wealthy Jack.

When Alma did not answer, Mrs Webb continued. 'That's why Jack takes an interest in Brendan, took an interest I should say. He gave him jobs on the boat he keeps at Sandsend, the *Doram*.'

'Are you saying that Felicity and your Brendan have gone off in a boat that belonged to Jack?'

'They've gone. The boat's gone.'

They sat in silence as the lamp began its last flickers with a corresponding increase in stink.

Mrs Webb spoke first. 'Your friend, Mrs Shackleton, was out looking for you. Hilda brought her to my house.'

'Why?'

'Because Hilda guessed.'

Alma could not think straight. Felicity could not swim. This couldn't be true. She thought of the message from Walter Turner who'd come through in her automatic writing. *Turner turned cold. Turner turned old.* It came to Alma on the breeze that blew in the window and disturbed her sheets of writing that she must tell this woman what she'd learned. She anchored the pages with the crystal ball.

'Felicity has gone to find her father.'

'To tell him you were soft on Jack? Did she kill Jack because she thought he'd taken a shine to you?'

'That's ridiculous.'

Mrs Webb gave her a look that Alma could not read. Was it pity, or scorn?

'Did my lad and your lass take revenge before they left? If they were fool enough for that, they'll be found, brought back by the coastguard, charged with murder.'

'Murder?' Alma's mouth felt suddenly dry.

'Aye, murder. Whether they did it or no. That and stealing a boat. Or was it you, Mrs Turner? Did you do him in because he took you for a fool?'

Alma's mouth opened. She shook her head. 'Why do you say he was murdered?'

'Take your head out of the clouds and think what's to be done.'

Alma closed her eyes. She placed her palms flat on the table to steady herself. Why hadn't Kate told her that Jack was murdered?

She wanted this woman to go, she willed her to go. But she did not.

'Our two have Jack's money, and his boat. That's enough to put a rope around my Brendan's neck. Your Felicity's too young to hang but you'd be waving her goodbye.'

Fifteen

Near dawn, as the world grew light, Felicity could once more see the shore and felt reassured. Perhaps that's where the word reassured came from. After a long voyage, a traveller stepped

138

ashore onto dry land.

The wind had begun to blow. Brendan had turned off the engine. Both wide awake now, they raised the sail.

They had the sea to themselves with not a vessel in sight.

'We'll sail on all day.' Brendan was doing something with the ropes, tightening. 'We'll drop anchor tonight and rest. That way we'll have put a good distance between us and Whitby.'

Felicity took hard boiled eggs and bread from her supplies. 'Shouldn't we go closer inshore?'

Brendan finished what he was doing with the ropes. He began to peel the shell from his egg. 'Best not go much closer in. This coast is still mined from war. We're avoiding danger spots.'

'How do you know where to avoid?'

'Well I don't, not exactly. We put mines close in, so the Germans couldn't land. They set mines against us. No one knows where they are.'

'That's not very clever. We could be blown up.'

'We won't be.' He bit into his bread. 'We should've brought salt.'

Felicity carried two lucky pebbles in her pocket. She handed one to Brendan. 'You might need this.'

Sixteen

'This way, Mrs Shackleton.' Sergeant Garvin politely opened the door to the police station and ushered me in.

Under other circumstances, Whitby police station might be a rather pleasant place. The entrance room looked freshly painted. On a large notice board was a map showing the Whitby division of the North Riding Constabulary with its stations at Grosmont, Hinderwell, Leaholm, Lythe, Robin Hood's Bay and Staithes. North of these stations was marked the Northallerton headquarters. There were posters of a couple of villains, a warning regarding an outbreak of swine fever and a notice showing the times of tides.

Sergeant Garvin politely suggested I leave my bag and coat with the constable at the desk. He then showed me to an interview room and after asking did I take sugar in my tea, left me there for a good long while. Slowly it began it dawn on me that my first impression, when he so courteously accused me of signalling to boats and – almost as an afterthought – of murder, he meant it. If his suspicion were not so absurd, it might be amusing.

For a station in a town where a murder had taken place, there was a distinct lack of activity, an air of night-time quiet. But then, Whitby is at the end of the line, and not so very many hours had passed since I had found the jeweller's body.

After a short time that was long enough for him to have made several telephone calls, the sergeant returned. He was followed by a constable who brought two mugs of tea, left and then came back carrying my satchel. The sergeant and I faced each other across a square unvarnished table that was scorch-marked where people had set down their cigarettes. Rings from the bottoms of mugs made an abstract pattern across the surface.

His manner was so pleasant and friendly that it almost belied the fact that he had taken my satchel for examination and apologised for the fact that he might have to detain me.

'I'm sorry we don't have china cups,' he said politely as he took out his notebook and pencil.

'That's quite all right, officer.'

'I have just telephoned to the coastguard. They are always interested if people appear to be signalling, especially at night.'

'I wasn't signalling.'

'Of course not, but we can't be too careful, you see.' He tasted his tea, pulled a face, picked up a spoon and began to stir with a slow, careful movement. 'I have your details from earlier, your name, hotel, and the address on your card. When we have finished our tea, you might give me your statement.'

'It's very late, sergeant. May we do this tomorrow?'

'I took the liberty of looking in your satchel.'

'Ah.'

'Yes.' He removed the spoon and took a sip from his mug. 'Not that I am well-acquainted with ladies' bags, but the contents of yours seem rather unusual.'

'I suppose one might think that.'

'If we were at war, which thankfully we are not, then some of those items would arouse suspicion. Camera, torch, knife, hip flask, unauthorised police whistle, set of keys.' He reached into my satchel and placed each of the items on the table. 'You might explain why these items rather than a purse, comb and powder compact.' We both stared at the aforementioned items.

'I was climbing to the abbey in the dark. A powder compact would not be of much use.'

'Nor would a camera.' He spoke thoughtfully. I had the impression that he was rather pleased to have company on what otherwise might have been a dull evening. 'Perhaps you might start at the beginning and tell me why you came to Whitby.'

The tea was strong, almost red. 'I'm here on holiday.'

He listened while I explained my fondness for Whitby, my schoolgirl friendship with Alma Turner, née Bartholomew.

'And did you know her husband, Walter Turner?'

'I did.' Remembering Alma's request that I allay any suspicions he may have about Turner's bigamy, I added, 'I was their bridesmaid and a witness. I signed the register when they married in York.' That was probably overplaying my part, but at least I had done my best for Alma.

'And have you seen Mr Turner in recent times?'

'No.' I decided against enlarging on that simple answer.

'Where did you set out from this morning?'

'I did tell you earlier, officer. From Leeds.'

'And have you recently visited other places?'

'Such as?' There must be some purpose to his questioning, other than suggestions for places of interest. Was he considering where to go on holiday?

'You tell me, Mrs Shackleton. Do you get about much?'

'Yes. I suppose I do.' Perhaps he was playing some game, or the events of the day had produced a strange effect in him. I was sufficiently interested to continue the conversation. 'I was in London recently.'

'London, eh?'

'Yes.'

'How about Northern Scotland, or the inner or outer Hebrides? They can be popular among certain circles at this time of year.'

'No. Why do you ask?'

'Oh just a whim of mine, well not entirely my whim. My friend at the coastguard was interested.'

'I went to Edinburgh once.'

'It may be that a coastguard officer will wish to speak to you, regarding signalling to the boat...'

'I wasn't signalling.'

'I see.' He wrote down, *Not signalling*. 'Then why were you there?'

'I'd been told that my friend Mrs Turner might have gone up there.'

'I didn't mean at the abbey, I meant when did you visit Edinburgh?'

'1921.'

He made a note. 'And the information that took you up to the abbey tonight was from...?'

'Mr Cricklethorpe.'

He made a note.

'Did he tell you what signal to give?'

'Signal?'

'The flashing of your torch, and the whistle.'

'I wasn't signalling with the torch. It was to help me see. As to whistling, Alma Turner and I were at school together. We had a certain whistle that we used as our call to each other. I thought if she were there, she would hear and know it was me.'

'If I were to find Mrs Turner and ask her to repeat the schoolgirl whistle, would she...' he repeated my whistle. 'Would she do it?'

'Alma could never whistle.'

'Some people can't. If I whistled, would she identify the call?'

'Oh yes.'

I hoped she would. Given her inability to whistle and the miserable time she had at school, she might not. Then what would happen? I could be charged with aiding and abetting smugglers. I would have to scour the country for whistling school friends who might corroborate my story. Even then, I might be accused of having taught a party of as yet unapprehended smugglers a particular whistle.

'Mrs Shackleton, you told me earlier that you went into the jewellers shop because you spotted a bracelet that took your fancy. Is there anything else that you left out and that you wish to tell me now?'

Of course, he knew. He had looked at the jeweller's records of items pawned. Either he had already spoken to Alma regarding the pawn ticket and the watch-guard, or he would at an early opportunity.

'If you're referring to Felicity Turner having pawned a watch-guard, I didn't know about that until later, and neither did her mother.'

Something changed in him. I had taken him by surprise. 'So it was Felicity who pawned the item?'

'Yes.'

'Not Mrs Turner herself?'

'No.'

'And you told Mrs Turner that you had found Mr Philips?'

I was becoming impatient, but it would be pointless to let him think he had me rattled. 'You asked me not to. I did so only when she counted out her money and was all set to go to Skinner Street and redeem the pledge. That's when I felt obliged to tell her that Mr Philips was dead.'

'You do know that Mrs Turner was on friendly terms with the deceased?'

'She did mention that they had taken tea together.'

'Your friend, Mrs Turner ... perhaps this is too delicate, or you may feel unable to answer.'

'What about her?'

'Mr Philips had been paying her attention. Do you think she may have come to regard his attentions as less than honourable?'

'I have no reason to suppose so.'

'And her daughter, and the daughter's young man, Felicity and Brendan, did Mrs Turner confide how they may have viewed the friendship between her and Mr Philips?'

'No.' I felt suddenly cold at the thought that he may suspect Felicity or Brendan of doing away with Mr Philips. My expression betrayed me.

Sergeant Garvin took a drink of tea. 'And you?'

'I knew nothing about their friendship until Alma told me this afternoon. When I went into the shop and found Mr Philips lying there, I hadn't seen Alma.'

He made a note. 'Had she written to you about a gentleman friend?'

'No!'

'I'm jumping to no conclusions, you understand, and neither will my superintendent.'

'Well, sergeant, I am jumping to conclusions. I'm at the conclusion that you suspect me of various crimes when all I have done is attempt to be a good citizen and a good friend.'

'That's as may be, Mrs Shackleton, but tell me about Mr Philips. Did you at any time yesterday or today see him alive?'

'No I did not.'

'You were seen outside the shop in a state of some uncertainty, perhaps upset, and this was before you found Mr Philips.'

Thank you, Mr Dowzell. The man had not simply come to the hotel to buy me a drink and commiserate. He had come to see whether I looked guilty. 'My uncertainty was about whether to buy a bracelet, that is all.'

'Just one more question. How do I know you are who you say you are?'

'I gave you my card.'

'Anyone can have a name printed on a card as I'm sure you know. Is there any person in Whitby to whom I could make enquiries as to your identity, aside from your friend Mrs Turner, formerly Miss Alma Bartholomew?'

146

I wondered about his attitude to Alma. Was there some stress on the word 'formerly', as though he knew she was never legally married? And how could that possibly matter in the context of a murder investigation?

'Why do I need to prove my identity? I booked in advance at the Royal and received a letter of confirmation.'

'Just routine, madam.'

'Not a routine I've ever heard of, sergeant. I have a cheque book in my bag at the hotel, and probably some other identification if I look for it.'

'Apart from your paper identification, is there anyone who can vouch for you?'

The people closest who could vouch for me were Mrs Sugden, at her cousin's in Scarborough, and Jim Sykes in Robin Hood's Bay. A telephone call from the Whitby police, sending a Scarborough officer to see Mrs Sugden would alarm her. A call on Jim Sykes would leave him feeling entitled to gloat and rush to the rescue. Any call to anyone at this time of night would be alarming.

When I did not answer straight away, he said, 'While you're thinking, I'll just bring in my fingerprint kit. Routine, you understand, to eliminate you from enquiries.'

'My fingerprints will be on the door handles at the jewellers.'

'Yes, so we'll want to know which prints are yours, and then we'll be clear.'

He was gone.

It was a considerable time before he returned with his fingerprinting kit. He held it with the kind of pride some child might carry his Christmas gift of a John Bull Printing Set to the kitchen table.

This would be an opportunity for me to see how fingerprinting was done by an expert.

He inked my fingers. I stared in disbelief at my hands. Were they really my hands and was this happening to me? I waited until he had finished.

With great reluctance, I drew on my trump card. 'You asked if anyone can vouch for me. My father is superintendent of constabulary in the West Riding, Mr Hood.'

'Is he now?'

'He won't be on duty at this time of night, but I can give you the number.'

He took out his pencil.

I gave him the address and telephone number of the office, and my parents' home address. This felt like such a humiliation; having to call on my father.

He stood to leave the room.

'Please don't telephone my father at home at this time of night. My mother would worry.'

'I expect she would.'

'And please be discreet.'

He turned at the door. 'I'll be typing up your statement from my notes. If there is anything you want to add, tell me now.'

I had not told him about Felicity's friendship with Brendan Webb, yet he knew about it. He had referred to Brendan as Felicity's young man. Most likely he had seen them together. Perhaps the young couple might have eloped. If I repeated what Hilda told me, I might bring Brendan under suspicion of having fled after murdering Jack Philips. Given Sergeant Garvin's readiness to suspect me for being in the wrong place at the wrong time, he might construct a fabulous story concerning Felicity and Brendan. Best say as little as possible. 'There is nothing else of relevance, officer.'

'What do you know about the murder of Mr Philips and the robbery from his safe, Mrs Shackleton?'

'Nothing. It's as I told you. I saw Mr Philips's body, the open door of the safe, and the broken necklace. That's all.'

'Thank you.' He left, closing and locking the door behind him.

What was he doing, I wondered, when he had not returned after ten minutes, then fifteen minutes, and then twenty? The man was mad. Polite, but mad.

The sound of boots clattered across the stone floor. The door opened. He returned to the table and sat down. 'Wakefield constabulary confirm that Mr Hood has a daughter, Catherine, but no one there was able to provide a description or to confirm whether Catherine had come to Whitby.'

I groaned. Dad would love me for this.

'I am reluctant to telephone a superintendent at home, after midnight.'

'Yes, please don't.'

'You will understand there are now serious on-going enquiries regarding the murder.'

Suddenly, I understood. He had never in his life had to deal with such a crime and he had no training in detection. His superintendent must be away. He had consulted Northallerton. They had called in Scotland Yard. The sergeant was afraid of making some terrible blunder and being

149

thought a provincial plod who jeopardised the investigation before detectives arrived.

'Yes. I do understand. You want everything to be ship-shape for when your superintendent returns and the Metropolitan Police officer arrives.'

He ignored my comment and hid his surprise well. 'Your story about the signalling...'

'I wasn't signalling!'

'...is so odd that no one would have invented it, and your demeanour is certainly that of a lady.'

'But?'

'I must ask you to spend the night here, for your own safety.'

'Here?'

'You are our prime witness, Mrs Shackleton.'

'I'm not a witness to anything. I simply had the misfortune to enter that shop on a whim and because...'

'Because?'

'My engagement and wedding ring came from there.' It was time to appeal to his sentimental nature, if he had one. 'I met my husband in Whitby. This is where we became engaged. He didn't come back from the war.'

He spoke softly. 'There is no one else in custody. You are not in custody, but here for your own protection. We do not like visitors to come to harm. You will have a cell to yourself and I will bring you an extra blanket.'

That was supposed to make me feel better. 'Officer, I have a lovely room at the Royal, with a sea view.'

'You wouldn't see much from the window at this time of night.'

150

Seventeen

My watch had stopped. Early morning light filtered through the cell window. For a moment I could not think where I was and then the people and events of the day and evening before slowly came into focus, shadow puppets at first and then more sharply, like moving pictures: the jeweller lying dead in his beautifully tailored suit and polished shoes; Alma, discovering the note from Felicity; the beam from Sergeant Garvin's flashlight as he escorted me down the one hundred and ninety-nine steps from the abbey.

Above all these images and swirling thoughts was the thumping voice in my head telling me that Felicity was missing. Sergeant Garvin had said, or pretended, that he would need to have this reported by her mother. Wiser heads than his would see the importance of finding Felicity.

Surprisingly, my night's sleep in the cell at Whitby police station had been excellent in spite of not being able to wash, brush my teeth, or change into night clothes. I felt no aches and pains after sleeping on what was really no more than a wooden board. What did worry me was my predicament. Had no one at the hotel noticed that I failed to return? For all the night porter knew, I could have flung myself from the cliffs or been trapped by the tide. But perhaps the hotel manager had been told that their newest arrival was

151

spending the night in the clink. For several moments, I contemplated my situation, and tried to decide what line to take with whoever came on duty next.

Not having raised fierce objections to my incarceration, or demanded that the sergeant contact my father at home regardless of the hour, I had probably cast a guilty shadow across my innocent doings.

There is a disadvantage in being too ready to see another person's point of view. Last night I had understood perfectly why Garvin might treat me with some suspicion. I also felt sure this would be cleared up within five minutes. It had also occurred to me that being on good terms with the sergeant might help me towards broaching the question that Alma had asked: did the sergeant know that her marriage was to a bigamist?

In the chill light of dawn, I saw things differently. My desire to be on good terms with the sergeant for Alma's sake had prevented me from vehement protest about being detained. Embarrassment played her fiendish part, too. One feels rather silly at being caught whistling and flashing a torch on a cliff top at dead of night.

The sad truth was that being here in a cell was largely my own fault. I should have been more assertive. But Sergeant Garvin had such a friendly and courteous manner that I had stupidly expected him to see reason. I had no wish to be rude to a hard-working member of His Majesty's Constabulary.

Someone more senior would have seen how ridiculous it was to suspect me of being involved in smuggling or to be linked to a murder where I could have no possible motive.

It was time to think this matter through logically and make sense of what had occurred so far.

Jack Philips. His body was cold when I found him. He was lying on a rug but under that rug was a flagstone floor. The door, window and curtains were closed. He could have lain in that enclosed room with its cool temperature for an hour, several hours, or perhaps overnight. I forced myself back into the moment when I felt for a pulse. Rigor mortis had set in. His hand was rigid to touch. It had not occurred to me to try and observe more closely. What I realised now was that Sergeant Garvin might not have sent for a doctor sufficiently promptly for an expert examination that would allow a reasonable estimation of time of death.

Because the shop door was unlocked, that surely must have meant that Jack Philips was alive to open the shop and raise the shutters, perhaps at nine o'clock that morning, unless some other person had gained entry during the night, or earlier that morning. They would have had to raise the shutters without being noticed. The police would know whether a beat bobby had checked the door during night patrol. Since I had made the jewellers shop almost my first port of call, at about 11.30, having left home very early, it was my estimation that Jack was killed at least two hours earlier. If he had lain there overnight, then someone else had opened the shutters. Depending on Jack's time of death, and when the youngsters left Whitby, Felicity and Brendan may or may not come under suspicion. If they did, there were two possible motives: a need for money, or Felicity's resentment about her mother's friendship with the jeweller.

Might Brendan or Felicity have anything to do with the fact that Mr Philips's wall safe stood open? It was possible. I assumed that was where he placed items that he took on pledge, and that would include the watch-guard. In my shock at finding the body, I had not looked to see whether the safe was empty. It seemed likely that something had been snatched from there, because of the jet beads strewn across the floor.

Philips's window and his counter held valuables, but they appeared to have been ignored. Perhaps that was because the killer or killers – and he or she may not have intended to kill – knew what they wanted. Had Jack Philips let them into the back room willingly, or under threat?

Was the theft from the safe because taking goods from the window or the counter would have left the perpetrator open to observation? If the killer had entered through the rear of the premises, they would be less likely to be observed. Was it a case of robbery gone wrong, or was the robbery a cover for murder with another motive?

Mr Dowzell had not seen anyone leaving or entering the jewellers shop. Now I wondered about the newsagent's cheerful assistant. If Jack Philips was a man confident of his charms, might she have been one of his conquests? I dismissed the possibility that such a friendly person, busily selling tickets for the Seamans Mission sale of work, could have any connection with murder.

In spite of my earlier misgivings, I felt sure that Alma was not guilty. She had high hopes of the jeweller and was genuinely shocked to hear about the death. Yet if she had made overtures and been rebuffed – a woman scorned – she would not take it lightly. At school, I caught her sticking pins in a doll she made of Pauline Bennett. If Jack's 'interest' in her was purely imaginary on her part, or if he lost interest, she might have taken revenge.

And then there was Mr Cricklethorpe who was almost certainly involved in shady dealings, probably including tax-free whisky brought ashore in some quiet harbour. He was fond of Alma. They shared a house. Might he have acted to keep Alma from leaving him in the lurch by taking up with Jack Philips? Or perhaps he thought Alma had unwittingly given away secrets to the jeweller and he wanted to silence him?

Both Cricklethorpe and Alma were eccentrics in their different ways. This could be turned to their advantage. Perhaps Alma's reputation for communing with the moon was her cover story. She went to the cliff top to signal a warning or a welcome to boats carrying contraband. Certainly Alma and Crickly, as she called him, could not be making much of a living from prophesying, fortune telling and leading twalking sessions for visitors. Such earnings would not pay for their logs and coals.

Perhaps Garvin suspected there was a practical and secret purpose to Alma's wanderings on the cliff at night.

Sergeant Garvin would never make 'Garvin of the Yard' and yet he had a good nose for the suspicious – too good a nose in my case. He made a connection between Cricklethorpe and my presence on the West Cliff, asking did Cricklethorpe tell me 'what signal to give'.

For my own peace of mind, once I got out of here I needed to do a little investigating of my own.

There was a tap on the cell door. How ludicrous to knock on a cell door, but it made a distorted kind of sense. I might have been availing myself of the primitive facility in the corner – an enamel bucket with lid.

'Come in,' I called, as if I were in my room with sea view. Sergeant Garvin opened the door, bearing a cup of tea.

'Good morning, Mrs Shackleton.'

'Good morning, sergeant.'

He handed me the tea. 'I've had Superintendent Hood on the telephone. It seems that someone in Wakefield contacted him after I had enquired about you. He confirms that you are his daughter, holidaying in Whitby. When I told Mr Hood you were sleeping, he said to let you be. I'm so sorry.'

Was he sorry that I was a police superintendent's daughter, or for having detained me? I chose to interpret his words as the latter. 'That's quite all right.'

Why did I say that? It was not all right, but all wrong. It was galling to think that my word had counted for nothing while a brief conversation with my father led to the unlocking of the cell door.

'Superintendent Hood vouches for you. He tells me you have helped Scotland Yard on a number of occasions and won praise from Commander Greathead.' I could not tell from the sergeant's tone whether he was impressed or unconvinced.

'You were doing your job, officer. I'm sure my father realised that.'

'You did not mention that you are an investigator.'

'I'm here in a purely private capacity, as I said – on holiday.'

'We in Whitby are not used to instances of help from civilians. You see one of our concerns is dealing with contraband. We must report suspicions to the coastguard. Smuggling didn't end in the eighteenth century as novelists would have you imagine. When I saw you, looking out to sea... Well, I hope you won't take it severely amiss that I detained you.' He looked at his watch. 'I am expecting my superiors shortly. Superintendent Hood made the point rather forcibly that the less said about my detaining you – on both sides, yours and mine – the better.'

I felt inclined to dawdle, just out of awkwardness. There was a night train from King's Cross to York. If an officer from Scotland Yard had travelled on the sleeper, he would be on his way by now. I might just loiter and say good morning.

Better not.

I stood. 'Then I'll go. Thank you for the tea.'

He took the cup and saucer from me with a look of relief. What he did not say, but I could see he thought, was that he would look a bit of an ass when his bosses discovered that he had detained me, the innocent party who had discovered the body.

'Will you have a slice of bread to put you on, madam?'

'No, thank you. What time is it?'

'Almost six. I expect to be relieved soon. I shouldn't have been on nights.'

If that was an explanation of why he had detained me, it wasn't a very good one. But it might be possible to turn the situation to my advantage. 'Why shouldn't you have suspected me?' He was about to answer but I cut him short. 'I'll go quickly. If I can help you then you must let me know.'

'That's obliging of you, madam, and if you'll sign your witness statement before you leave. It's typed and ready.'

'Before I go...'

He gulped. I saw the anxiety in his eyes. Would he never see the back of me?

'Yes?'

I indicated the bucket in the corner. 'You must have some other facility?'

He cleared his throat. 'Ah, yes. We do. We are quite modern and cater for females. One moment.'

It was less than a moment. He returned with my shoes and satchel. I slipped on my shoes and followed him.

We walked along the corridor side by side. 'I hope you'll keep me abreast of events, officer.'

He looked suddenly wary, and his footsteps slowed. If he did not want to look an ass, neither did I. 'It would be a feather in your cap if you, the local man, with a little discreet help, proved your worth to Scotland Yard.'

'Your father did say you have a habit of nosing out villains.'

Dad would say that, under the circumstances. I hated to think what he would say to me when next we met.

As he pointed out the door to the lavatory, the telephone began to ring. I opened and closed the lavatory door, but tip-toed back up the corridor, wondering if this might be my father, ensuring I had been released. Worse still, it might be my mother.

It was not. By the tone of the sergeant's voice, I could tell he was answering questions regarding the events of the day before. I took the risk of going closer, and listened.

'I did say, sir, regarding Mr Philips's reputation that it might be a jealous husband, but that mark, such a small mark ... yes, sir. Well I thought it to be the kind of blow that may have been inflicted if someone had asked him to reach for something, an item of jewellery, and he bent over. I've made a note of his female acquaintances.' There was a hesitation, as if he was reluctant to say a name, but then did. 'Mrs Turner.' A pause. 'There was a Mr Turner but he is no longer in the area. She is a charming lady and I'm sure would not have seen the threat to her reputation.' Another pause. 'She does have friends, and a daughter who might take her part and who is now missing.' A longer pause. 'Yes sir, I will do that of course. There is a benefit do planned at the Mission. A concert and sale of work. It will be too late to cancel, there'd be the matter of getting word to the outlying villages and farms. I'll mingle and see what I can pick up.'

159

Another pause. 'Yes, the Scotland Yard man is on his way. I have typed up my report.' A long silence. 'That's true, sir. A husband may have cause to feel aggrieved, but what self-respecting Englishman would hit another from behind? Would such an attack not come more readily from a female, a youth or a foreigner?'

It was a fine morning. The need for air drew me towards the harbour. There were steps leading down from Spring Street. Needing to put distance between me and the police station, I walked towards the steps. As I did so, a vehicle chugged up the road.

I turned to look. A police van stopped in front of the station. The driver climbed out. At the same time, the rear door of the van opened. A bevy of uniformed constables began to alight. I counted. Ten, eleven including the driver. No wonder Sergeant Garvin had wanted rid of me. Moments later, another vehicle arrived, an Alvin. A uniformed superintendent stepped out. It was with relief that I realised whatever else I may have to do in Whitby, investigating a murder was not on my list.

Leaving Spring Street behind me, I walked down the steps. The herring gulls and kittiwakes were up before me, calling as they swooped down from the cliffs. One strutted towards me, looking for all the world as if we had some pre-arranged appointment.

'Sorry, gull.'

The tide had ebbed. Boats dotted the horizon. Others that hours ago bobbed serenely on the waves now rested slantwise in wet sand. The sea breeze gave me new energy after being cooped up in the cell. I wandered to where a lone fisherman in heavy coat and sou'wester paused to light a pipe. I wished him good morning, quietly so as not to scare off fish.

He nodded rather glumly. 'Fine morning.'

'A good day for fishing at sea I suppose.'

'All the boats that's off is gone on full tide some long while since.'

'I met the sister of one of the fishing families yesterday, Miss Webb. I think her brother Brendan might have sailed yesterday.'

'He might and he might not.'

'Do skippers often take on extra crew at this time of year?'

He took a deep pull on his pipe and turned to me. 'After a boat ride, are you? There's paddle steamer does a trip between here and Filey.'

'Well I most likely will take the trip. But I was just wondering how it works, taking on crews and all that.'

'It's families round here. Same skippers, same crews.'

'I see. Well thank you. Good luck with your fishing.'

He adjusted his sou'wester in what might have been a gesture of politeness. As I walked away, he called to me.

'Missis!'

I turned.

He cleared his throat and spat into the sea. 'If you're the friend of Mrs Turner...'

'I am.'

'And if it's her lass you're enquiring about, Brendan's dancing partner, pay no heed to the tale that she's dressed as a lad and gone to sea. She'd be laughed off deck. Folk round here know a female when they spot one. Happen they'll be more gullible in Scarborough. You could enquire there.'

He turned from me, giving all attention to his fishing rod. If he did know more, he wasn't telling. Investigator or not, I was out of my depth here. The whole of Whitby seemed more knowledgeable than I, and why wouldn't they be?

So much for Hilda's theory that Brendan and Felicity had gone to sea. It was time to let the professionals get on with their job. I could do no more for Alma, not at present. Sunday. Would she tell fortunes on Sunday, I wondered? Probably not. What might do me good, and possibly Alma too, would be to make a visit to somewhere along the railway line and leave Whitby behind, just for today. Of course, Alma might want to stay at home and wait for news of Felicity. If so, perhaps I should stay with her, but I could make the suggestion that we have a day out.

I dismissed the thought almost immediately. Neither of us would settle to making a little trip with the worry of Felicity hanging over us.

The released prisoner, I stood and took deep breaths of sea air, looking out to the far horizon. Thinking of Felicity on a boat, I imagined every terrible possibility, and all the disasters at sea that I had ever heard of. Besides, this whole stretch of the coast was still mined from the war, German mines designed to destroy our ships, British mines, laid to destroy theirs.

162

In the ridiculous hope that Felicity had returned, or that Alma might have news, I set off to walk to Bagdale Hall.

My walk took me past the railway station.

From the direction of the station entrance, someone called my name.

His voice from the past rooted me to the spot. I turned my head to look, and there he stood. Smiling.

Eighteen

The man who had called to me was Marcus Charles. He had hardly changed since I saw him last, indeed since I met him, five years ago. His hair when he raised his hat was the same light colour with its neat side parting. He was clean shaven though had perhaps shaved on the train because I noticed a slight nick on his chin. Other than that, Chief Inspector Marcus Charles of Scotland Yard looked impeccable after his night on a train.

The constable I had seen at the police station the previous day was beside him. Marcus did not turn to the policeman as he spoke but looked at me. 'Take my case to the station, constable. I want to speak to Mrs Shackleton.'

And I wanted to speak to him. Someone sane and reliable after the madness of the past hours.

The constable took the valise and was gone.

For a moment I wondered whether we would

163

stand on the pavement and stare at each other.

Marcus spoke first. 'Good to see you, Kate. You turn up in the most unlikely places.'

'You too.'

'The buffet's open. Shall we?'

'Good idea.'

Feeling scruffy, unwashed and an idiot for having put myself in the situation of spending a night in the clink, I walked beside him into the station.

Apart from a tired waitress with a grumpy manner and a woolly scarf around her throat, the station buffet was empty. We sat on either side of a table for two. Marcus ordered tea.

Surprisingly, there was no awkwardness between us. It was as if we were picking up from where we left off. Almost. He and I had become close after our encounters on previous occasions. We had respect for each other's intelligence and ability, but that wasn't what drew us together. There was an undeniable attraction. I felt it still, and so did he. The last time I saw him was when he proposed to me, and I turned him down. It was the thought of leaving Yorkshire, giving up my work and being exiled to London that had come between us. That and Marcus's overbearing chauvinism and arrogance.

Shortly after that, he went to America to work with their investigation bureau in Washington DC.

He had written to say that on board ship he met a young American woman and they were engaged to be married. I had written to wish him well, and received no reply.

His failure to answer my letter could be read either way. He was happily married and unlikely to

164

correspond with me. Or, his shipboard romance did not last.

Part of me wanted him to be happily married. It was selfish to hope he might still be free because he was a man who would be impossible to live with – at least for me.

We both spoke at once. He asked what brought me to Whitby. I asked when he had come back from America.

'I'm on holiday. I arrived yesterday.'

'And I sailed back from New York two weeks ago. It was never permanent, you know, just to exchange ideas and see what developments our American cousins were coming up with.'

The waitress slapped down two mugs of tea.

Marcus reached for the sugar bowl. 'Do you always rise so early on holiday?'

'Not usually.' He knew very well that I was not a Sunday early riser.

'But you don't usually find a body on your first day either.'

'So you've heard.'

'Yes, and I'm sorry. I wasn't given a name but the moment I saw you standing there, your usual pristine and confident self, well ... who else in Whitby would it be? I did wonder what sort of customer would walk into the back of the jewellers shop if no one came to the counter.'

'The North Riding Constabulary didn't waste much time calling you in.'

'Long enough for everyone involved to establish a seaworthy alibi. I believe the victim had something of a reputation and several husbands could be suspects.'

'The newsagent from the shop next door hinted at Mr Philips's reputation. I daresay the hearsay will be overwhelming.' I took a sip of weak tea. 'Sergeant Garvin has my statement.'

'All the same, you might tell me in your own words. I'd value that. I'm sorry you had such a bad experience yesterday. It doesn't ever become easier.'

It did not take me long to give him the bones of my story, ending with the worry about Felicity.

'I'll do what I can to find her. Let's hope she isn't involved.'

'I'm sure she's not!' I wanted to ask him about the shipboard romance. Did he now have an American wife at his house in Hampstead, and did she join him when he went sketching, and swimming in the pond on the Heath? I hoped she did. He deserved some happiness.

Perhaps it was because of having rejected him that I felt pity that he was in a town where it would be good to sketch and to bathe in the sea, but there would be no time for either.

'Where are you staying, Kate?' he asked as we walked to the door.

'The Royal.'

'Me too.'

As I walked back to the hotel, trying to think only of a bath, a change of clothes and breakfast, questions pressed against my skull. Where was Felicity? It would be wonderful if she had returned home. And what was Marcus's plan? Certainly he must already have developed a strategy and had sent for constables from local stations. Given that I had

166

counted eleven men, the van must have done a tour, collecting constables from the outlying districts.

If anyone could find Jack Philips's killer, it would be Marcus. He was good before he went to America, and would have returned keener than ever.

The advantage of having spent the night in a cell and being turned out so very early was this: I was first to the hotel bathroom, toilet bag in hand. If any of those hardy gentlemen who take cold baths at dawn were staying at the Royal, then they were, thankfully, on another floor. Slowly, the geyser cranked into life, supplying gratifyingly hot water.

I luxuriated in warm water, soaping myself, deciding against using the rather battered back brush that hung on a hook. Instead, I washed my back with my flannel, stretching my arms to reach. The hard plank of a bed had after all taken its toll. My shoulders hurt. My back felt stiff. Pity the prisoners serving hard labour.

Someone tried the bathroom door. I splashed loudly, to send that person packing.

I lay back in the bathtub, covering my face with the warm flannel, imagining the horrors of being deprived of such comforts as a bath when I wanted one, and the ability to come and go, to open and close doors. And then I suddenly felt a wave of fear – for Alma and Felicity. Either of them could so easily become suspects. Good as Marcus was, he had made mistakes in the past – mistakes that were rectified but still mistakes. It irked me to be on the side-lines, unable to do anything. Feeling helpless can be so debilitating.

Part of me wanted Marcus to come in and wave a magic wand, and then I felt annoyed with myself for being weak – that wish that someone would come along and make everything all right.

From the tone of her note, I knew that Felicity was not running away from something. I felt sure my hunch that she was going to find her father was correct. If so, why now?

According to Alma, Felicity blamed her for sending away her father. At sixteen, Felicity would almost certainly regard her mother as being beyond the age when she might attract a man. Alma showed signs of slipping into an embarrassing love affair. Felicity, acting alone or with her boyfriend, had put an end to that possibility by despatching the object of Alma's affections, and then leaving town.

Marcus would be bound to explore that possibility. He would also consider that Alma had pinned her hopes on hooking a wealthy man. Both Cricklethorpe and Dowzell made no secret of the fact that Jack Philips was not to be trusted. Alma may have found that out for herself, and hit out.

By keeping me in a cell overnight, Sergeant Garvin had done me a favour. He opened my eyes to horrible possibilities. Or perhaps I was simply feeling utterly dreadful after the events of the past hours. Juries came down hard on women who broke the rules. Alma or Felicity – horrors, perhaps both – might find themselves on trial at York Assizes. A judge would have no mercy. Alma would hang, Felicity face life in prison.

The bath grew cool. Reluctantly, I pulled the plug.

As the water glugged away, I snuggled into my dressing gown and made my way back to my room. There, I brushed my hair into shape and thought about what I might do next. I must see Alma and find out whether the prodigal daughter had returned.

Being first to the bathroom and first into the dining room gave a promising start to the day. I was early to breakfast. A young waiter brought my tea and took the order. I feasted on bacon, sausage, egg and fried bread. The freed prisoner ate a hearty breakfast.

When I returned to my room, a different chambermaid was dusting the dresser. She offered to come back later.

'Hilda not here today?' I asked.

'She wanted a change. She's on the third floor today, madam. Is there anything I can do?'

'No, it's all right. I just wondered.'

Looking out of the window at a gloomy sky, I took the precaution of picking up my raincoat, as well as my satchel. I thought about the chambermaid's words. Could Hilda's reason for wanting a change be connected to unwillingness to see me? If so, there must be a reason. I decided to find out. Instead of going down the stairs to leave the hotel, I climbed up – two more flights.

Hilda was pushing a linen trolley along the corridor. She jumped when I said her name and turned to look at me with eyes not exactly wild but certainly startled.

'Good morning, Hilda.'

'Good morning, Mrs Shackleton.'

'I'd like a word, please.'

'I'm a bit busy.' She picked up clean towels.

'It'll be a quick word. Here or...?'

She looked about. There was no one on the corridor. She opened a door to the nearest room. 'What is it?'

'You're avoiding me and I want to know why.'

She hugged the towels to her chest. 'Mam said I'd get meself into trouble talking to you.'

'That must mean you have something to say.'

'Well I have, but I haven't to say it. Mam said.'

'Then I'll call on your mother.'

'No!' She carried the towels into the room. 'Me mam would fillet me even though I told her you're a detective and you're Mrs Turner's friend and won't get us in bother.'

I followed her into the room. 'How do you know I'm a detective?'

'Felicity told me. And then this morning, the porter said you'd been out investigating all night with police, so you might know already.'

'Know what?'

'Mam thinks nobody knows.' She replaced the towels.

'If it's something important, the police will find out.'

'That's what I said. But let them find out, don't tell them.'

'I can't promise, but I'll do my best, for Felicity's sake and yours.'

She put the dirty towels on the lower shelf of the trolley. 'Mr Philips had a boat up at Sandsend. He promised it to Brendan when he finally swallowed the anchor, but who'd believe that?'

'Swallowed the anchor?'

'You know, when he died. Anyhow, boat's gone.'

'How do you know?'

'I worked it out. Last night, after Mam walked you across bridge, she was gone for ages. Her shawl was still damp this morning. So I guessed. She told me to stop guessing and keep quiet. I said if she didn't tell me, I'd go look.'

'And?'

'It looks as if *Doram's* there because someone has put a broken rowing boat in its place, covered with tarpaulin, to disguise that it's gone.'

A crashing noise from outside drew Hilda to the window, which had been left open to air the room. She turned to me. 'Mrs Shackleton, it's the police, searching bins.'

This room was at the back of the hotel and from the window we could see the yard. A uniformed policeman had emptied a bin and was sifting through the rubbish.

Marcus had wasted no time in setting the local constables to work.

Standing side by side, Hilda and I watched the search.

Hilda turned to me. 'Milkman told housekeeper that police are searching along back of Skinner Street, every yard and midden. That'll be mucky work. You don't think about police having to do such a thing.'

'No I suppose you don't, usually.'

'What do you think they're looking for?'

They would be looking for a murder weapon, but that seemed too harsh an answer. I said, 'I suppose they're looking for clues.'

A constable called out to another and pointed

to something. I took binoculars from my satchel.

Carefully, using a pair of tongs, the first constable picked up something that he had tipped from the bin onto the ground.

I raised my binoculars and began to adjust the focus.

The second constable held open a hessian bag. The constable with the tongs accidentally let slip his prize and then picked it up again but too quickly for me to see with the unfocused binoculars.

Hilda had good eyesight. 'They've found a hammer. Looks like a toffee hammer.'

Nineteen

'Don't look now but it's the coastguard.'

Felicity looked. The boat was coming directly towards them. 'Why would they be interested in us?'

Brendan stood. He did not make much of a movement but as Felicity watched him, he seemed to plant his feet so firmly on the deck that they might push through the boards and dangle in the water. 'What did you do with the money belt?'

'On my waist.'

'And the wrapping?'

'In the money bag. What are you worrying about? We haven't done anything.'

'If they ask, we're going to Elgin, to visit your family.'

'Well we are – to visit my dad.'

'What if they know who he is and what he does?'

'Then they'll know more than I do.' Felicity thought of her mother's way of dealing with difficult situations. She would simply say, 'The planets are out of alignment,' and give a shrug, as if that prevented her knowing night from day or one end of a broom from the other.

Brendan drained his cup. 'They won't search you.'

'I hope not. Should I throw the postcard overboard?' But even as she spoke she saw that one of the two men on the coastguard boat had his binoculars out and was looking at them.

The vessel came closer, close enough to see the men's faces and the familiar uniform.

'It might be about something else,' Brendan said. 'Some warning.'

The boat came close. Felicity watched Brendan tilt his head and give the coastguard officer his winning smile. One of the officers stayed at the wheel of their boat. The other politely asked permission to board, although they all knew no one could stop him.

He was a slight man with sandy hair and a neat beard. He climbed on with the ease of someone stepping across a low threshold. 'Hello. So who have we here on the *Doram* and which of you is captain?'

A joker. And he didn't talk like them. He was from somewhere else entirely, somewhere south, friendly enough but not smiling.

'I'm Brendan Webb, and this is Felicity.'

Felicity stayed where she was. She preferred to be still when the boat swayed. Brendan had not said her surname.

The officer gave an interested nod. 'Out of Whitby?'

'Aye, sir.'

'Are you any relation to the late Captain Webb?'

'He was my father.'

'Then I'm glad to meet you. You're a long way from Whitby, Mr Webb.'

'Aye, suppose we are.'

'Are you the owner?'

'No. That would be Mr Philips of Sandsend. He let us take a jaunt in the *Doram* in return for doing her up.'

Felicity noticed that the coastguard officer perked up. Perhaps he liked the idea of a boat being done up, and taken to sea. 'And what brings you north, Mr Webb?'

Brendan looked at me. 'Felicity here...'

She could tell the truth or she could tell a lie. Her tongue could not decide. If she gave the wrong answer and the coastguard officer asked another question, she might be tripped up, get Brendan into trouble, her dad into trouble and who knew what else. The money belt felt tight and bulky. It must show beneath her cardigan.

'Felicity?' the officer looked at her.

'I helped to paint the boat.'

That wasn't what he wanted to know.

'Are you a Webb too?'

'No. I'm Felicity Turner.'

'We're engaged to be married,' Brendan said quickly.

The officer smiled. 'Well congratulations, Mr Webb and Miss Turner. And where are you going?'

174

'To Holy Island,' Felicity said quickly. 'I went there when I was little and I wanted Brendan to see it.'

Brendan warmed to the story. He spoke slowly, as if it had never occurred to him to tell about this longing to see the Holy Island of Lindisfarne. 'We've taken time off to do it. My cousin has taken over from me on pleasure boat from Whitby to Scarborough.'

'What age are you?'

'Eighteen.'

'And you, miss?'

'Sixteen.' She could not leave it at that. She felt obliged to give herself a boost to show this man that she knew what was what and wouldn't stand for being turned back. 'I've been working two years. I'm a waitress at Botham's.'

'Mind if I take a look round?'

Brendan waved his arm to take in the whole boat.

The officer looked around, touching the coiled ropes with the toe of his boot, walking from bow to stern. He then made a bee line for the false bulkhead, slid the vertical partition away and shone his torch. They had taken off their life jackets when the sun came out. The officer took them from the bulkhead. 'You should put them on.'

'We had them on, but we got warm.'

'August is an unpredictable month. Think about stopping overnight at Holy Island. There's a storm brewing.'

He tipped his cap to Felicity and climbed back into his own boat.

When he had gone, Brendan turned to Felicity. 'Why didn't you tell him truth about where we're going?'

'I was going to. But I watched his eyes when you said your name, and I watched his eyes when he learned mine. Webb, a captain. Turner, a pirate?'

'You're imagining it. That officer's not a local man.'

'There are some names he's made it his business to know.'

'What makes you say that?'

'Crickly, Mr Cricklethorpe, he said that coastguard men are clever. He's right. That's why Crickly must be clever himself. He put the packet in the bulkhead, and a money belt so that I'd wear it.'

Crickly usually paid in sovereigns. It was all making some kind of sense now. She remembered from a long time ago, seeing a box with gold sovereigns and trying to count them but there were too many.

Twenty

Sunday morning church bells rang out as I walked down Brunswick Street towards Amen Corner. A woman in black, walking just a little way ahead of me, stumbled and gave a small cry. She had twisted her foot on a loose paving stone and her shoe came off. She sat down on the low wall of the church.

176

I stopped beside her. 'Are you all right?'

She paused for a moment before answering, and put her shoe back on. 'I'm all right. Just clumsy.' She stared at her feet and then rose unsteadily.

She was pale and looked more upset than anyone would be after a stumble. She returned my gaze, but blankly, without recognition. I recognised her but said nothing. She was the assistant from Dowzells newsagents who yesterday smiled and was bright and cheerful. This morning, she looked ready to drop.

'May I help you? Would you like to take my arm?'

For a moment I thought she would, but then she shook her head. 'Thank you, no. I'll be late.'

She hurried towards the church doors.

Poor woman. I hadn't given her a second thought since buying postcards and toffee from her. Now I realised that she must have taken the death of her neighbour very hard. How shocking it must be to have a murder take place in the premises next door.

As I crossed Bagdale, I wondered how far the ripples would spread from yesterday's tragic incident. But I had someone closer to consider. Alma had suffered the double blow of Felicity's disappearance and Jack Philips's death.

Even on a sunny morning, waves of ancient damp and historic anxieties swirled to greet me as I entered Bagdale Hall. What stories and secrets the walls of this building might tell. Perhaps entering Alma's orbit made me superstitious. As I climbed the creaking stairs, I touched the solid banister for luck and reassurance. Alma was on the landing. One glance at her told me that Felicity had not returned. Pale and exhausted, she was wearing a green and yellow woolly hat topped with a pom-pom.

'I was at the window and saw you coming.'

I followed her into the room. She led me to the window seat. 'I can't keep away from the window. I've been watching the police come and go. I've never seen so many.'

The room was pleasantly warm, and the window open.

I sat down. 'Have you reported Felicity missing?'

'What good would it do? She said she'd send a postcard. I must be patient and wait for it.'

'I'm asking because I did report her missing, but really it ought to come from you, from her mother.'

'Well then I will, if you think that's best. I don't know any more.'

'Alma, why are you wearing a woolly hat? Do you have earache?'

She sighed and removed the hat.

'It's Felicity's. I knitted it for her. I thought putting it on might help me to know where she is.'

She looked wretched and must have felt utterly desperate to believe that a tea-cosy hat might help her find Felicity. 'And has it helped?'

'No.' She placed the hat on her knee and patted it. 'This morning I went to the early service. The parson led prayers for Jack Philips. He didn't say so right out but everyone knew his death was foul play. You didn't tell me that.'

'I told you that Sergeant Garvin asked me not to breathe a word.'

'You did.'

'Have you made any enquiries about Felicity, Alma?'

'Last night I went to the Spa ballroom and talked to some of her friends, pretending I'd just called in to hear the music. Nobody had seen her, and they seemed surprised that she and Brendan weren't there. She must have kept quiet about her plans.'

'You didn't go up to the abbey last night then, only Mr Cricklethorpe said you might.'

'No. I sometimes go up there but last night I was trying to find where Felicity had gone, either from her friends or from the spirits.'

'Any luck?' Now was not the moment to tell her that I had her strange habits to thank for the fact that I spent the night in a cell.

'Mrs Webb turned up at the pepper pot. She told me you'd called and were looking for me. Mrs Webb is as upset as I am. She told me something quite extraordinary.'

'What?'

'I can hardly bring myself to say it, not yet. It concerns Brendan's parentage.'

'Don't ask me to guess.'

'Do, please guess, because I never would have.'

'Then it must be someone close to you, your husband Walter, or Mr Cricklethorpe, or Jack Philips.'

'Yes.'

'Which one?'

'Not Walter, thank goodness. He's done enough damage. Not Crickly, that wouldn't be his way of going on.'

179

'Jack then.'

She made a mitten of the hat, putting her hands in it. 'Mrs Webb says they've gone off in Jack's boat, the *Doram*.'

We watched as a family of late-comers hurried towards the church whose bells had stopped pealing.

'Between you and Mrs Webb, did you come up with any ideas as to where Felicity may have gone?'

'I think you may be right, when you mentioned her father. Some little hint came to me in the pepper pot last night but it's not something I could go on. I don't know whether to go back and see if I can find out more. I can't concentrate here, too tired to think.'

'What was this little hint?'

'Something came through automatic writing. Walter Turner intervened, giving me a warning, and there was a warning for him too – about visitors, one with red hair. That could be Brendan.'

Though having no experience of automatic writing, I encouraged her to continue. Some of the thoughts she dragged from her own subconscious may turn out to be useful. But Alma does not always stay on a single topic long. She had hopped onto another thought.

'I keep thinking about Jack, how kind he was. Felicity bats her eyelashes as well as the next girl. If she handed him the watch-guard and said she was acting for me, he would have accepted it and come to the aid of the penurious party, i.e. my good-self.'

'Wherever Felicity is, at least she has money.'

180

'If she has gone to find her father, how could she have made Brendan Webb steal a boat?

'The things we do for love, Alma. You married Turner, Brendan does Felicity's bidding.'

'Surely they're not sailing to Madeira?'

'Going by the postcards, he must have left Madeira ages ago.'

'Then where? She's on the programme of the concert that follows the Mission bazaar. Well she won't be back for that, will she? It's today. And how can we even think of bazaars and concerts with poor Jack dead? And what kind of future does she have if she constantly lets people down and thinks only of her own mad schemes?'

Alma made fists of her hands. 'I want to shake her till her teeth drop out for doing this to me. I know she only had me, but I've done my best. Wouldn't you think she would have at least taken her hat? She pretended to like it. I know she always took it off the minute she turned the corner.' She scrunched up the hat. 'How could I be so blind as to have no idea what she was planning?'

'I expect all girls of her age keep secrets from their parents.'

'Well I never did. But then of course, I didn't have parents. They died when I was three. I was brought up by an old-fashioned aunt who packed me off to that dreadful school.'

Poor Alma had put up with more than most and braved the storms. I wished she didn't make me feel so impatient.

'Perhaps Turner and I deserved each other. He pretended to be a single man. I pretended to be a girl with loving parents.'

'Alma, let's try and think where Felicity has gone. This boat, the *Doram,* would it be suitable for a long voyage?'

'According to Mrs Webb it's bigger than your average coble but not for going to Madeira.'

'We've ruled out Madeira.'

'That's where his countess has a place, in the hills. It sticks in my memory and it sticks in my craw.'

She stretched her arms. 'I've been awake half the night, Kate, and going round in circles. When you told me Jack was dead, I thought it must be a heart attack. You were so evasive.'

'I had no choice.'

She stood and walked about the room, twisting a scrap of her gown round and round. 'It's almost as if there's been a curse.' For several minutes she paced the room, not speaking. She perched on the bed. 'I can't bear it, Kate. Jack befriended us both, me and Felicity. Not many men of his sort would do that. In fact, I began to think ... was that so foolish?'

'Of course not.'

'He was fond of me. He didn't ever come to the pepper pot of course but sometimes I thought he purposely bumped into me and he would chat, ask how we were.'

'And you were fond of him.'

'I'm still young, have kept myself well, have wide interests. I did a Tarot reading for myself and that was most definite. In matters of the heart I have something to look forward to in relation to a man who is close to me.' She sighed and took out her hanky. 'Fool, fool, fool.'

'No.'

'And heartless fool to be thinking of my dashed hopes when the man lies dead. But this is the third disappointment for me. There was a widower from Scarborough, but entirely under his mother's thumb, and then a retired captain from Saltburn that came to nothing.'

For a moment we sat in silence. I tried not to think about the mouse-ridden kitchen. 'Shall I make a cup of tea?'

She shook her head.

'I went looking for you last night, up by the abbey. Sergeant Garvin thought I was signalling to smugglers. I spent the night in a cell.'

'Never!'

'That's what I would have thought – never, but yes. Sergeant Garvin suspects there's something going on. Last night, when I called here with Hilda, I'm sure that Mr. Cricklethorpe was moving barrels or bottles in the yard.'

She hugged her arms around herself. 'I'm so sorry to have brought this on you, Kate, a night in the cells and everything. I don't know anything about whisky.'

'Who said it was whisky?'

'Well whatever it was.' She stood and began to walk about the room. 'I am thinking the unthinkable. If I speak my thoughts, will you tell me they are ridiculous?'

'What are your thoughts?'

'Children never want their parents to be in love. Felicity always blamed me for her father's absence. Sometimes she talked about him returning to us, coming home she would say. If she had some inkling that Mr Philips's care for me might lead me to marry him, if that proved possible, she would be upset, upset beyond all reason.'

'You think Felicity may have wanted to harm him?'

'She would not do anything terrible. But Brendan...'

'What about Brendan?'

'What if Brendan found out that Jack was his father and while Jack lived in luxury, Mrs Webb struggled and took in lodgers. It might be enough to send him into a rage.'

'Don't jump to conclusions, Alma. There'll be an explanation.'

'Do you think so? Oh, Kate, I feel lost in a fog.'

'Fog clears. This will too. Tell me more about the automatic writing.'

Alma closed her eyes. 'It was a warning from Turner. We used to communicate our thoughts to each other, when we first met, when he was my hypnotist.'

'Last night, tell me what came through from him when you were in the pepper pot.'

She frowned. 'He said ... what were the words? ... "Philips doesn't want you for yourself. He wants our daughter." But that can't have been right, can it?'

'I shouldn't think so. Not unless Philips knew that befriending Felicity was a way of being friends with Brendan.'

She looked suddenly alert. 'That must have been it. But did I allow myself to be misled by Jack? When I thanked him for taking me and Felicity to tea, he said it was his pleasure. Wouldn't that be a

184

turn of phrase that might give any woman hope?'

If she were looking for hope, then no doubt it would. Sometimes it is best to agree and that was what I did.

'What do I do now, Kate?'

'Tell the police that Felicity is missing. Give them the pawn ticket.'

'Must I?'

'Mr Philips will have entered the transaction in his ledger. It will look odd if you don't say anything about it.'

The sound of footsteps on the landing drew a sigh from Alma. There was tap-tap on the door. Alma recognised the knock.

She whispered, 'I can't be doing with him just now, Kate.'

I went to open the door, to see what Cricklethorpe wanted.

He stood there in quite normal clothes today, dark trousers, white shirt, plain tie. He held a tray with a pot of tea, two cups, a boiled egg and slices of toast.

'Good morning, Mrs Shackleton. I thought you would have had your breakfast but know Mrs Turner has not.'

'That's kind.' I took the tray from him and placed it on the table for Alma. 'Come on, Alma, this is just what you need. You must eat.'

She sighed and came across to the table.

Cricklethorpe had come into the room behind me. 'Dire news from the town, old girl,' he said to Alma. 'I know you were out earlier, so must have heard but what a shock about Jack Philips, eh? People were coming out of church in a state of utter bewilderment.'

'Yes.' Alma spoke in a whisper as if she had no more energy left.

Cricklethorpe walked across and patted her on the back. 'Eat your egg, keep your strength up.'

He left.

That was kind. I warmed towards him.

'Sit with me, Kate. He's brought an extra cup.' She poured two cups of tea.

I took it. 'Your Mr Cricklethorpe may be a smuggler, but he is a kind smuggler.'

She cracked her egg. It was done to perfection. 'You were right about the contraband,' she said quietly. 'I think the sergeant suspects. But people have to live.'

Did people have to live? That was true, up to a point – the point at which they died; the point at which they were murdered.

'Kate, did Cricklethorpe encourage Felicity to be gone, out of the way, and then kill Jack?'

'Why would he do that?'

'To keep us here.'

'Because...?'

'I don't know. He's very fond of us both, in his funny way. And we help keep the place going. No one else would live here. Local people avoid the hall because of the ghosts.'

'Try not to worry, Alma. Let the police investigate. The man from Scotland Yard has arrived and he is good.'

'How do you know?

'I saw him coming from the railway station.'

'I mean how do you know he's good?'

'Well I got to know him over the years.'

186

Alma ate her boiled egg and toasted soldiers. She began to look a little better. I once worked with a matron who swore that there was no substitute for a soft boiled egg when it came to treating invalids or a person in shock. Perhaps she was right.

We heard footsteps on the landing.

No sooner had Alma wiped the yolk from her chin with a lace hanky than there was a tap on the door.

Alma called, 'Come in!'

'Good morning, ladies.' Sergeant Garvin stepped in first, followed by Marcus. 'This is Chief Inspector Charles from Scotland Yard, Mrs Turner and her friend Mrs Shackleton.'

The sergeant, or was I imagining it, blushed when he looked at me. Perhaps he had recently had to account to Marcus for having detained me overnight.

I answered first, 'Good morning.'

Marcus came over to us. 'I just wanted to say, Mrs Turner, that we will do everything we can to locate your daughter. Mrs Shackleton has told me how worried you are.'

'Yes,' Alma said weakly. She was looking at him with undisguised admiration. It was clear that she thought him impressive. He was certainly good-looking, and at his most courteous.

Marcus continued, 'The sergeant will talk to you, but do rest assured that we will link the search for your daughter to our main and very tragic enquiry and will keep you informed.'

'Thank you, Chief Inspector.'

'It will mean that we need to look round the premises but we will keep disturbance to a minimum.'

187

What did he hope to find, I wondered.

Marcus gave me a quick look that gave nothing away. He nodded to both of us. 'Mrs Turner, I'll leave you with Sergeant Garvin. Good day.'

With that, he was gone, having given me the strong hint that he wanted the sergeant to speak to Alma alone.

Sergeant Garvin walked across the room, picking up a straight-back chair and bringing it with him to sit near Alma. 'Mrs Turner, I believe you have heard the sad news about Mr Philips.'

'Yes.'

'Because his was a sudden death, it must be looked into. We have additional officers here to investigate, but I have permission to speak to you myself, if that is all right?'

'I'd rather speak to you than some stranger, Sergeant Garvin.'

Anyone who knew Alma less well than I did would not have noticed her disappointment that the chief inspector had left.

'Good. And I would rather speak to you, Mrs Turner.' He turned to me. 'Mrs Shackleton...'

For a moment, Alma looked as if she might ask me to stay, but I moved quickly. 'Of course.' I went to the door. 'Alma, I'll find Mr Cricklethorpe, and I'll be here if you need me.'

I needed to ask shifty Mr Cricklethorpe some questions.

Twenty-One

Alma watched Kate leave the room. Fearing some terrible news, she wanted to call her back. 'Sergeant Garvin, are you really here about Mr Philips?'

'Is there some other reason why I would be here, Mrs Turner?'

'No ... only...'

He waited.

'...only I thought – this feeling of dread came over me, that you've already found Felicity, that something bad has happened to her and your Scotland Yard man didn't want to tell me.'

'You've no reason to think that. But I wish you'd told me yourself that Felicity is missing.'

'Yes, Kate, Mrs Shackleton said I should tell you, and give you this.' She went to the mantelpiece and picked up the note and pawn ticket. It made her feel ashamed that her daughter had run off. The nice little note did not change the way it must look.

'How upsetting for you,' the sergeant said, sounding not at all like a policeman. 'When did you last see Felicity?'

Alma was glad that Kate had already asked her this and that she could now give a correct answer. 'It was Thursday, after she finished at Botham's.'

Sergeant Garvin went to the sideboard. He picked up the framed photograph of Felicity, taken last year by the harbour. 'The last time I saw the

189

two of you together you were out at Saltwick gathering fossils, last Eastertime I think.'

'Yes.'

'When did you find the note?'

'Yesterday afternoon. It was in her room.'

'So, you didn't miss her on Friday night or Saturday morning?'

'No. She doesn't come home for tea on a Friday. She has something at work and goes to the pictures. I wash my hair on Friday night and go to bed early. We don't always see each other first thing Saturday.'

He took a blue linen bag from his pocket and put the note and pawn ticket inside. 'Don't worry. I'll ask you for some details. We'll find her, just see if we don't.' He glanced at the glass-fronted cabinet where they kept the fossils she and Felicity had collected. 'You have a fine collection, Mrs Turner.' He immediately cleared his throat as though to erase a comment that may have come involuntarily, like a belch.

Alma looked at the shells and fossils. It seemed suddenly impossible to her that the little girl with such curiosity for stones and shells, fearless in the face of waves and once so little as to be dwarfed by a swooping seagull, had deserted her and might be anywhere, lost, in danger. 'It's Felicity's collection. She wrote the labels. You might think that's a leaf but it's a reptile footprint.'

Sergeant Garvin walked over to the cabinet. 'So it is. Does she have a favourite?'

Alma joined him. She pointed to the second shelf. 'The starfish, that's her favourite. There's only one we can't identify.'

'Which one?'

'The little mound – that beige-coloured one with the dark markings.'

It was on the bottom shelf. He had to bob down to take a closer look. 'It's a dropping. It's dung.'

'Oh. Felicity said that. I thought she must be wrong, that dung would, you know, deteriorate. I don't know why.'

'It's not possible to know from what animal. You could make a guess at an extinct shark.'

'Felicity doesn't like to guess. She likes certainty.'

He straightened up. 'That's a good quality.'

'But one can never be certain. Life is all guesses, when one thinks about it. People expect me to be certain when I tell their fortunes. They remember the parts that are true, or come true, and forget the rest.'

'There's something in that, Mrs Turner, but here we are, like two philosophers seated on the mountain, and there are matters that must be looked into. Only I will just say this, if you don't mind...'

She waited.

'That frog fossil, you know, it's most unusual to find such a rare specimen. It should be kept under controlled conditions, or it will deteriorate. Believe me, it is something rather special.'

She began to cry.

He pulled out a large hanky. 'I am so sorry, and here I was thinking it would be better for me to talk to you rather than the man from Scotland Yard.'

'Oh it is. It is.' She would feel embarrassed to be thought a fool and a poor specimen of a mother by that good-looking man from Scotland Yard. Serge-

191

ant Garvin knew she had only ever done her best.

He led her to the table. 'Then let's sit down, eh?' They sat opposite each other. He took out his notebook. 'Tell me about the pawn ticket.'

'I didn't know that Felicity was going to pawn the watch-guard.'

'So she needed money. Do you have any inkling where she might have gone? A relative, a favourite place, a school friend?'

'I wish I did. We went to Lindisfarne a few years ago. She loved it there.'

She ought to tell him about the automatic writing, and about Turner, but since Sergeant Garvin had previously made remarks hinting at her bigamous situation, she decided against it.

'Is there anything else you can tell me?' He waited. 'Anything at all?'

'She may have gone in a boat with Brendan Webb.'

He looked down, so that she could not read his expression. 'What makes you think that?'

She was betraying a confidence now but felt she had no choice. 'Mrs Webb came to see me last night in the pepper pot.'

'What else did she tell you?'

'That Brendan helped Jack do up the boat. And she told me something that I'd rather not say.'

'Concerning Brendan?'

'Yes.'

He closed his notebook. 'His parentage?'

'Yes.'

He moved his mouth, making a funny shape. 'I've heard. It's an open secret.'

'Well I didn't know.'

192

'Just say it, Mrs Turner, so we both know what you are talking about.'

'Brendan is Jack's son.'

He nodded. 'It's one of those secrets people speak of behind their hands.'

'So it's true?'

'I couldn't possibly say, Mrs Turner. I'm just a simple policeman. But you know, Mr Webb was a hero at the time of the *Rohilla* disaster, fearless in the rescue attempts.'

'I heard that. I heard people say what a good man he was until he lost his ship, and then took to drink. I suppose the *Rohilla* disaster allowed him to redeem himself, for a time.'

'Yes.' The sergeant stroked his face from cheek to chin as though to ease his jaw. 'What I need to ask may sound a little intrusive, and believe me it is not meant to be, but only to help us have a clear picture of certain matters, you understand.'

She nodded, though she did not understand and wished he would get on with it.

There was a loud thumping on the stairs.

The sergeant stood. 'It's just some other officers, taking a look about. Excuse me. I'll tell them about Felicity.'

He went from the room and was gone for several minutes.

When he came back, Alma asked, 'Why are there so many of you here?'

'We have Mr Cricklethorpe's permission.'

'You should have asked my permission too.'

'Yes. I'm sorry.'

'What do you expect to find?'

'That I'm not at liberty to say, let's you and I

193

have our little chat.'

'Are you asking Mr Cricklethorpe about Felicity, or about something else?'

'Do you think we should ask Mr Cricklethorpe about Felicity?'

She wanted to say, 'You're the police, you tell me,' but she did not. Did they think Felicity was hiding somewhere in the house? What if Felicity's note was forged? Cricklethorpe. There was always something odd about Cricklethorpe. He had hidden Felicity in a trunk in one of those rooms they never used.

'I don't know what you should ask.' Her throat felt parched. 'Or what you want to know from me.'

What the constable began to ask her next was rude, intrusive and embarrassing. She could not believe such questioning. He had been working up to it, she guessed.

'How much money do you make from your publications, Mrs Turner?'

'What?'

'I'm sorry but there is a point to the question. You have several on sale to the public. I thought your *Yuletide Decorations from the Natural World* a most interesting little book. I intend to try out some of the suggestions myself.' When she did not answer, he added, 'The chief inspector from Scotland Yard needs to know.'

She rose and went to the sideboard, took her account book from the drawer. She had a note of what the printer charged, and how many sales she made, and the cost of postage. This was for her own satisfaction, to prove to herself that all the scribbling – which took its toll – was worth her while.

'Would you mind if I borrow this, just overnight?'

'Take it. Throw it on the bonfire for all I care, just find Felicity.'

He squeezed out the next words. 'I know what you charge for Tarot readings and so on, and you are popular with the mill girls and factory girls.'

'Yes.'

'How much money would you say you have earned from that, this year? I know you have your rent on the pepper pot. I'm sorry to ask, but our temporary boss is terribly thorough.'

'It's also in the notebook. Turn it upside down and look from the back.'

'You are very efficient, Mrs Turner. I admire that greatly.'

'What does this have to do with anything, with Felicity, or Jack Philips's death?'

'Our visiting chief inspector likes to delve into what he calls the underlying economics of a situation.'

'Why?'

'He is one of the few people in the investigation section who specially trained himself to deal with fraud. He spent time in America with their investigation bureau.'

The thought came to her that this inspector would put a feather in his cap if he pointed out that the coastguard and Customs and Excise had failed to find contraband, and the clever Scotland Yard man had succeeded while busy on a murder investigation. She hated the intrusion into her dismal business affairs. Handsome and courteous

195

as this Scotland Yard man was, she might just make it her business to put a hex on him.

Sergeant Garvin cleared his throat. 'To that end, and I'm sorry for this impertinence, I must ask you about Felicity's father. Does he provide for her?'

When Alma stared at him, speechless, he repeated the question.

The answer would be no, but not a simple no. Felicity's father did not provide for his daughter. He had bought them the house on Henrietta Street that slid into the sea, but kept it in his own name. He had then been hoodwinked by Crickle-thorpe into buying them half a share in Bagdale Hall, shortly before it flooded. This was in Alma's name, and therefore became the millstone around her neck, not Walter Turner's. All of this was done through a third party, a solicitor. She had signed on a dotted line thinking for once something wonderful had come her way. And then she stepped into Bagdale Hall.

But the sharp pain that pierced her heart was not at the question regarding maintenance for Felicity. The sharp pain that turned into a sick feeling at the pit of her stomach was in the phrasing of the question. Sergeant Garvin had not said, 'Your husband', but 'Felicity's father'. What did he know of her history? She tried to be private. All her life she tried to be private. Now suddenly she trusted no one. She had confided in Kate Hood, or Kate Shackleton as she now was. Surely Kate would not have betrayed her confidence about the bigamist? Of course bigamy was against the law, but she had not committed it. I am the innocent party, she thought. Innocent enough to be thought stupid. And yet she was suspected of something. That much was clear.

Sergeant Garvin turned a page of his notebook, looked at it and blushed. She felt suddenly sorry for him. He would be here long after his superior with the interest in underlying economics was gone. She and he would pass each other in the street. She would see him during his off-duty hours, walking the beach or on the cliffs. After today's exchange, he would stop and talk to her about fossils. He would ask had she done anything about the fossil frog that required special conditions.

Perhaps he would be too embarrassed to speak to her in future, about fossils or anything else. Or he might take against her, as people sometimes did when the fault was really theirs, not yours. He might become officious about the fossil frog and requisition it.

From somewhere deep inside came the courage to speak. 'It is several years since we heard from my husband. The climate in England does not suit him. He lives abroad.'

'Do you know where abroad?'

'He sent postcards, to Felicity. The last one was about three years ago, from Madeira. A bank transfer followed.'

'May I have his full name?'

He could have more than that, she decided. He could have her marriage lines – not that they meant anything, but it would let him know that she believed herself to be married. She went to the sideboard, opened the drawer and from a cigar box took out her marriage certificate, but not Felicity's birth certificate, there being a slight discrepancy in the dates. Of course, she could always say that Felicity was premature.

She handed the marriage certificate to Sergeant Garvin. He glanced at it and placed it in the blue linen bag with the notebook, Felicity's note and the pawn ticket. He had expected to take some things away with him, she realised, because he produced a receipt book. Slowly and carefully he wrote a receipt for the items in the bag.

That was not the end. 'I have to ask you about the late Mr Philips. You and he were friends.'

Alma felt like a person who walked on quicksand, first slithering into the sandy suspicions of bigamy and now accused of something close to adultery. Was she really and truly 'friends' with the late Mr Philips? Was his interest in her real, or a soft soaping out of which she blew a great bubble of hope? She had taken tea with him several times in public. On Boxing Day, she had invited him to call. Bringing out the best china, she served pork pie, pickled onions and cold meats. Felicity had made mince pies. He brought a bottle of port wine and they all took a taste, even Felicity. That was the day her hopes rose, only she did wonder, when he left at a little after five o'clock that evening, where he might go next. There had always been snide gossip about the man and the ladies he gathered, but she had the vanity to think she was different. Until now.

'We were friends,' she said, finally.

'Tell me about him.'

'I don't know what there is to tell. He was a most

198

amiable man, straightforward and gentlemanly.'

'How did you come to know him?'

Alma felt herself blush. 'I visited his shop on one occasion, regarding a set of pearl beads that needed re-threading.'

'And after you first met Mr Philips in his shop, did you see much of him? This is not to pry, Mrs Turner. I am merely trying to have a sense of what the late Mr Philips was like.'

'Don't you know?'

'I would like to know what you think.'

Alma sighed. She could not just now say what she thought, but only tell him what she remembered, and with such sadness. 'He was on the pier one day, just as I was locking up the pepper pot. He asked if I would care to take tea with him. We fell into the habit of having tea together, sometimes the two of us, sometimes with Felicity. He recommended her for the job at Botham's, because he knows the family.'

'Apart from taking tea, did you see much of him?'

'We went to the Spa to see a visiting orchestra. He called on Boxing Day.'

'So there was a strong friendship between you?'

'I found him sympathetic and good company.'

He picked up his pencil, though had not written anything down so far. 'Can you think of anyone who would have wished him harm?'

'No! He was the gentlest of men.'

'With Mr Philips and yourself being on such good terms, did you not think it odd that he would give your daughter thirty shillings without your knowledge?'

'No. I expect she must have said I sent her, although I would not have done that, not now.'

He leaned just a little closer towards her. 'Not now? Meaning?'

'Not now that Mr Philips and I are ... were on good terms, I would have felt embarrassed, and besides, I'm managing. It is a long time since I pawned the watch-guard.'

There was a tap on the door. Sergeant Garvin went to see. He exchanged a few words that she could not catch. When he came back, he said, 'Mrs Turner, we have additional officers drafted into Whitby.'

'I saw them this morning.'

'One of them, with your permission, is going to have a good look round this room. If there is any clue to Felicity's whereabouts, we shall find it.'

She felt her face grow hot. They would look through her underwear, touch her stockings, see the sentimental letters Turner had written to her in the early days, paw the photograph in the broken frame that she intended to mend.

He was still speaking. There was something she hadn't heard. He repeated it. 'Perhaps you and I might go into the kitchen while the officers do their job.'

She nodded, realising this was not a request. Perhaps they would find something she had missed, but what?

As she followed Sergeant Garvin down the stairs, she asked, 'How many men are here? Can't some be sent to search for Felicity?'

'We've a good complement of the best chaps, all as keen to find Felicity as I am, and that's very keen indeed, Mrs Turner, I assure you.'

'What do they hope to find in my room?'

He opened the kitchen door. 'We'll let them do their job, eh? The quicker they're satisfied the quicker they move on. Now will you let me mash a pot of tea, and have you eaten today?'

'I'm not hungry.' Alma sank into a chair. She was ashamed of this shabby kitchen.

He opened cupboard doors and brought out a paper bag. 'Ah, fig biscuits.'

She noticed that the bag was frayed at the corner. It should have been put in the tin. That was Mr Cricklethorpe for you. 'No biscuit for me.'

There was a scraping noise from the yard. 'What's that?'

The kettle was on the hob. He pushed it closer to the fire. 'Just one of our chaps.'

'Doing what? There's nothing there, only coal and logs.' She hoped that was true, and that Cricklethorpe had moved whatever he had put there a few days before, when the coal delivery came from Upgang.

'I know that and you know that, Mrs Turner, but this job has to be done by the book.' He took a cone of mint humbugs from his inside pocket and offered it.

She took one. 'Where is Mr Cricklethorpe?'

A flood of fear engulfed Alma. They were not looking for contraband whisky. Mr Cricklethorpe had always doted on Felicity, his little ray of sunshine. He wanted her company for the twalking. That note from Felicity that Sergeant Garvin had in his blue linen bag, she suddenly wanted to look at it again. Was it really Felicity's writing, or had Mr Cricklethorpe forged her hand? What if he had done away with her, in the way men did when they had accomplished a terrible deed? She always thought herself lucky on the day of the flag-selling. How fortunate that the bad thing had not been an even worse thing, a thing to cost her life. That man who had bought a flag and walked away somehow knew that Alma would not tell. Felicity was not one to keep quiet. If Cricklethorpe had done a bad thing, he would have had to silence her. But he wouldn't, would he? She knew him. Trusted him. But Cricklethorpe would never let her read his palm. He drew something around himself like a cloak of invisibility.

'What is it?' the sergeant asked. 'You look quite faint.' He was beside her now, his hand on her back, the other on her arm. 'Do you have smelling salts?'

She shook her head. 'You think Cricklethorpe has killed Felicity, that's it, isn't it?'

'We have no reason to suppose any such thing.'

The line of automatic writing came back to her, that cruel jibe that Jack Philips had not been interested in her, but in her daughter. That could not be so, could it?

'Sergeant Garvin, tell me the truth about Mr Philips. One hears rumours. Has he ever ... would he ... I don't know how to say this.'

Before Alma had time to bring the phrase to her lips, there was a tap on the kitchen door. Sergeant Garvin excused himself and went to see, stepping back into the hall and closing the door behind him.

None of them want to look me in the eye, Alma

told herself, because they know something bad has happened to Felicity. They make the sergeant stay with me because he is local and has no choice in the matter.

He came back into the kitchen. 'It's nothing terrible, Mrs Turner. The inspector has a question about the toffee.'

'Toffee?'

'In Felicity's room. Did she or you buy it?'

Alma couldn't remember any toffee.

Sergeant Garvin did not look at her, but warmed the teapot with the boiled water. 'Ah here's the caddy. Take your time. Try to remember.'

'What toffee?'

'A slab of cream toffee.'

She still could not remember, and then she did. 'Ah no, not Felicity. Mrs Shackleton brought it. For Felicity I suppose.'

'I see.' He spooned tea into the pot.

He might see, Alma didn't. 'Why do you want to know about toffee?'

'Sometimes toffee comes with a small hammer, a toffee hammer, only there isn't one in the packet.'

She blinked. The men who were searching, they wanted sweets and expected her to break the toffee for them.

'Do you remember whether there was a hammer with the toffee when Mrs Shackleton brought it to you?'

She stared at him. 'You think one of us killed Jack with a hammer. Well you're wrong. I'm not saying another word until some of you go out and find Felicity. I want her back.'

Twenty-Two

Leaving Alma alone with Sergeant Garvin, I walked along the landing to go down to the floor below in search of Mr Cricklethorpe. It must be the worst-kept secret in Whitby that Percival Cricklethorpe dealt in contraband whisky. That did not concern me. What I wanted to know was this: did he know where Felicity had gone, and why?

At the top of the stairs I paused, hearing the heavy tread of a policeman's boots on the stairs. I waited until the owner of the boots had reached the ground floor and tramped across the stone flags.

What I heard next must have been some echoing trick. The sound was of someone tripping lightly down the stairs, but there was no one to be seen as I descended. Either the staircase had re-adjusted itself to the absence of weight, or I was sharing the stairs with a curious ghost.

The landings of Bagdale Hall form a reverse letter L with the bottom of the L to the left as one enters the landing, forming a box shape with two doors on one side and a third door at the end. Earlier, all these doors were closed. Now they stood open. I tapped on the first door. No answer. I stepped inside.

In shape, this was a room like Alma's. It had the same heavy furniture, including a four-poster bed.

Sheets and blankets were strewn across the floor. I sneezed and then saw feathers and flocks. The mattress, bolster and pillows had been slashed. Every drawer had been pulled out and its contents tipped. Cupboard doors hung open. Items of linen lay spilled from a trunk in the corner.

The second room was bare of furniture. Only the walls were full. From just above skirting board level all the way to the ceiling, oil paintings ranged side by side creating a dizzying effect of being at sea. There were seascapes on stormy days, seascapes where smooth waves shimmered in a hazy light. As I entered the room to take a closer look, the strangest feeling came over me – the door might close behind me. There would be no way out. I would have to live forever inside one of these paintings, sailing smoothly or trapped on the ship that would in one more moment be tossed into an angry eternity.

From this part of the landing, I moved into the next area where there were also three rooms. One was so sparsely furnished that any search must have been perfunctory. The door to the next room had been forced. Perhaps the key to this chamber was lost. Here, too, were paintings. Although there were also ships at sea, these bobbed daintily and looked certain to reach safe harbour. There were theatre scenes, including a portrait of an actress and her attendant in a dressing room and a group of dancing children in bright costumes. There were figures in groups, and singly. A fisherman on the harbour smoked his pipe. A couple on the swing bridge leaned into each other, not a sliver of space between them. In a narrow yard, similar to the one where Mrs Webb and Hilda lived, a woman hung out washing. The signature on these paintings was 'P C' – Percival Cricklethorpe.

As I reached the last door, I heard a sound. Had I been mistaken, and was some officer still searching? The door was slightly ajar and so I peered round. There was so much to see that at first, I saw only him, Cricklethorpe, in his white shirt, dark trousers and red tie. He was alone, seated in the centre of the floor, surrounded by heaps of colourful clothing: embroidered dresses, velvet skirts, sequinned capes. Tears rolled down his cheeks. Women's shoes the size of small boats were strewn about the floor.

I stepped back, not wishing to embarrass him. Silently, I trod back along the landing, hoping he did not hear the creaks and groans of the complaining floorboards. After a couple of moments, I called out, and walked more noisily back towards the door. I tapped.

There was no answer.

I tapped again. 'Mr Cricklethorpe, it's Kate Shackleton. I need to speak to you.'

Silence.

'Mr Cricklethorpe?' Any decent person would have turned and walked away but when a pall of suspicion hangs in the air – suspicion of murder – and when one's goddaughter is missing, niceties may be spared. That is my view.

'Mr Cricklethorpe, I am sorry to see you so distressed.' He looked up slowly, blinking. My words bounced through a dark tunnel to reach him and when they did, he took out his handkerchief and blew his nose.

Slowly, he came to his feet and walked towards the door. He would have come onto the landing, to keep me out of the room, but I edged in, apologising for disturbing him but not meaning it in the least.

I had to say something to turn his sympathy outwards and engage his interest.

'I was locked in a cell all night. So whatever has happened to you, I sympathise.'

'You?'

'Yes. So may we talk?'

A row of straight-back velvet-upholstered chairs lined the wall as if to make space for a quadrille in the centre of the room. He moved two chairs slightly forward. We sat side by side, facing the jumbled pile of garments and, beyond them, clothing rails and empty hangers. A red dress and an orange cape gave the impression of an indoor bonfire.

He stared at the outfits. 'Believe it or not, these costumes were neatly arranged, and the shoes in rows.'

'The police?'

'Yes. Not the local men. They know I play the panto dame. It's the others, the outsiders, full of spite and knowing nothing. They see a man who has a liking for red shoes with a nice heel and they jump to conclusions.'

'Shall I help you hang them?' The outfits were so splendid that it would be a pleasure to take a closer look.

He wiped his nose. 'I haven't the heart. I'll have them taken away. Let someone else play the dame in future.'

He put the hanky in his pocket. 'You say you were arrested?' It had taken a while for my words to penetrate his misery but now he stared at me, wide-eyed.

'I'm sorry they made a mess of your things, Mr Cricklethorpe.'

'And a mess of their investigations. Why arrest you?'

'I'm not even sure I was arrested. Kept for my own safety as a witness, until Sergeant Garvin learned my parentage.'

'That's not like him.' Cricklethorpe frowned. 'He is a most courteous man.'

'He was courteous. But when murder is abroad people behave differently.'

Cricklethorpe didn't look at me but at his hands resting on his ample thighs. 'I can tell you now the most likely killer of Jack Philips. No mystery.'

'Who?'

'It wouldn't be fair to say.'

'That's an exasperating remark, Mr Cricklethorpe. You can't say you know who it is and then play dumb. What if you had to clear my name?'

'If you are charged I will come forward.'

'But if you know the killer...'

'The most likely, I said. There is a person to whom Philips owed an obligation. Don't ask me to say more.'

'All right. But will you promise me you'll mention this to the chief inspector? He won't jump to conclusions.'

'I'll think about it.' He rubbed a finger across his nostrils and then retrieved his hanky and wiped his nose. 'Don't think I'm upset about being under suspicion. The police have their work to do. If Jack Philips was murdered, I want justice for him.'

'Then tell the police what you know. But am I right in thinking you were annoyed with Mr Philips, or had a grudge?'

He sniffed. 'The man was foolishly leading Alma up the garden path. He doesn't – didn't – under-stand women, thought it possible to be friends.'

'You're friends with Alma, aren't you?'

'That's different. I'm different.'

'Perhaps he is too.'

'No! He's having his house in Sandsend done up because he has some plan, and Alma's not part of it.'

'You knew him well?'

'I suppose I did, one way or another. He was a great supporter of the Seamans Mission and a stalwart of the Whitby Players, gave a fine per-formance as Abanazar in *Aladdin*. I'm just sorry we parted on bad terms.'

'Because of Alma?'

'He was raising her hopes. We rowed about it after the Whitby Players' last meeting and I daresay we were overheard.'

'What was the row about?'

'I refused to sell Jack Philips a painting.'

'Why?'

'He wanted my painting of the wreck of the hos-pital ship *Rohilla*. We almost came to blows. The man thinks – thought – he was entitled to what-ever money can buy.'

'Did you tell the police that?'

'I most certainly did. I've seen him break the hearts of many a good Christian woman. He'd strike up a friendship, raise a female's expectations, and then show his true colours.'

'He was a charmer.'

'Indeed. Women of great intelligence and enormous insight can be taken in by charmers and bounders.'

'It's a pity Alma didn't develop a nose for deceivers.'

He stared glumly at the red dress by his feet. 'You're thinking of her history.'

So he knew about the bigamous marriage. Was this because Alma had confided in Percival Cricklethorpe, or because he knew Walter Turner of old? I waited, not wishing to fire questions. He continued.

'There was an unfortunate congruity of events. One quiet morning Mrs Turner dealt her own Tarot cards and learned of romantic prospects. That very afternoon she caught Jack Philips's eye and he asked her to tea.'

'Just like that?' I could picture the meeting.

Cricklethorpe sighed. 'That's how she tells it. Jack probably meant it kindly. He invited her and Felicity, treated them now and again. She helped the business along by wangling tickets to a concert and asking would he like to go. Now, here we are – suspects in his murder.'

'I wonder where you and I come in the list of suspects, Mr Cricklethorpe? Not in the first rank from what you say.'

'Speaking for myself, I expect to be high on the list. Being something of a misfit gives me a boost.'

'In what respect are you a misfit?'

He glared at the pile of costumes, said nothing

210

but then turned and gave me a most comical look. We both laughed.

I stood. 'Come on, let's hang these frocks.' He made no move. 'They are too good to be left on the floor.' I picked up a bright red and white polka dot dress the size of a tent and held it against myself.

He did not move, but said, 'That's for the kitchen scene, when Widow Twanky bakes a cake.' He reached for a white pinafore with ruched edging. 'This goes with it.'

Slowly, he joined me in picking up garments. As we placed the items on hangers and returned them to their rails, I asked him about the paintings. 'Are they all yours?'

'Some of them. Others belong to the previous owner, the man who left this house to me in his will.'

'I thought the house was jointly owned with Alma.'

'Oh, she told you?'

'Yes.'

'That absent husband of hers had an eye to the future. He bought half from me. I accepted the money so as to have necessary work done.'

'This must be an expensive house to keep up.'

'You sound a little like Chief Inspector Charles of Scotland Yard. He wants to know how I earn my living.'

'And did you tell him?'

'I mentioned selling paintings, occasionally. When I told him that I guide visitors about the town, that of course made him understand that I know all the nooks and crannies, all the twisting passages and hidden yards that would take me to the back door of Philips's jewellers and allow me to enter and kill the man.'

'What does the chief inspector have as your motive?'

'I am protective of my friend, Mrs Turner.'

'Not the strongest of motives given that you are not a blood relation or romantically involved. All the more reason to give him any information you can. What did Mr Charles have as your weapon?'

'His young constables have taken away a wand.'

'A wand?'

'A magic wand.'

Being in this man's company made me feel we were auditioning for the role of music hall double act, with me as the straight man. I picked up a tulle dress in green and pink that looked most forlorn. There were layers of stiff net between the green and pink tulle, created by a talented dressmaker. I waited for him to explain.

'I keep some of the pantomime props here, having so much space. The youngest constable became quite excited at the sight of a broken wand, used by the fairy godmother in *Sleeping Beauty*. I expect he intends to look at it under a microscope. Perhaps it will be smeared with blood and hairs from the unfortunate deceased, so as to firm up a case against me.'

His answer made me shudder as I remembered the small but deadly wound on the jeweller's skull. 'How do you know that's how Mr Philips died?'

'Aha, Mrs Turner said you had talents.'

'No, I mean it. You must tell me how you know. Perhaps I can eliminate you from enquiries.'

'You're not investigating.'

'Who said I'm not?'

Cricklethorpe gave a grim smile. 'I read the odd detective story. If Jack Philips was thought to be hit by a magic wand, it would have had to be a blow to the head. Some people have what are called egg shell skulls. It was mentioned in something or other I read. They are at greater risk of mortality because of thinness of the bone. It only takes a light blow with a heavy object or a heavy blow with a light object to kill them.'

'You ought to be recruited onto the chief inspector's team.'

'So ought you.'

'There's time yet. But you have local knowledge, and I don't.'

'What do you want to know? I'm not from here myself, but I've been here long enough to know Whitby inside out and upside down.'

'So where are you from?'

'Hull.'

'It's an achievement for an outsider to be accepted in a place like Whitby, I should think.'

'One finds ways.'

'How did you come to be here, and living in this house?'

'Do you really want to hear about me?' Cricklethorpe asked.

'Of course.' I wanted him to talk. It would be better than asking him outright about Walter Turner, and whether my guess that he knew Turner's whereabouts and Felicity's intentions was correct. Of course, it was also plausible that Cricklethorpe could be a suspect, not simply because he was pro-

tective towards Alma. He and she had a convenient arrangement, which Jack Philips threatened to
upset. If Philips was truly interested in Alma, she
would leave here. I had twice heard that Philips
had been doing up his house in Sandsend. Might
that be because he intended to marry?

In spite of my prompt, Cricklethorpe did not
begin to tell me his story. I tried again. 'Tell me
how you came to land in Whitby.'

He flung a dress on the floor. 'I've lost all heart
for this.'

'Then sit down. If I see to your costumes while
you talk, your heart may find its way home.'

I picked up a glittering gold satin gown and
placed it on a hanger. Its front was latticed in
silver and studded with gems. Next I gathered up
a red velvet dress, the seams sewn by hand. Its
heavy hem allowed it to fall in swirls. His eyes
narrowed as I felt the material between fingers
and thumb. 'Top quality, and beautifully made.'

'We have a wardrobe mistress. She's a busy
woman, a widow with a family and lodgers, but
she finds time each year to help at the pantomime.'

I suddenly thought that the wardrobe mistress
with a family and lodgers might be Mrs Webb
who had been making a skirt when Hilda took
me to see her.

'Whitby is lucky to have you. It's Hull's loss
that you came here. What was the prompt?'

As Percival Cricklethorpe told me his story, I
became engrossed, in both the story and the
costumes.

Perhaps he obliged in order to keep me from

paying too much attention to his extraordinary bejewelled garments. My mother and my aunt have a knack for telling real from fake gems. I wished they were here to confirm my hunch that Percival kept some of the proceeds of his smuggling sewn into his costumes.

Cricklethorpe took a seat and began to talk, as if telling a story to an audience whose attention must be held at all cost. 'When I was a boy, there were expectations of me. I won't say great expectations, but solid expectations. I felt them even as a little fellow. My father was a clerk in one of the great shipping companies in Hull. He forbad my mother to work, but she would slip out for a couple of hours each day and help in a dry cleaner's shop. She was also a good seamstress.'

'Like Mrs Webb?' I straightened a brocade jacket with gold buttons. It had some kind of cardboard stiffening in the back. Not that I could smell five-pound notes, but I wondered.

'Yes. Mrs Webb and Ma would have hit it off had they ever met. I wish she could see me now. I was supposed to rise mightily in some way no one was ever quite sure about, an only child until my sister the Little Nuisance came along. I tried. Good at sums, a neat hand, but something else was required. I never knew what. My love was art, my painting set. I liked to paint ships. I liked the dramatics, too. When my sister was recruited as a dancing babe in *Humpty Dumpty*, the dame fell sick with influenza. I was only seventeen and clerking at my father's place of employ but I stepped up. I did scene painting for them and made a few props, that kind of thing. I enjoyed it.

215

Father didn't like seeing me in a dress. I missed night school you see. I was supposed to be taking the languages further and immersing myself in the laws of shipping, so as to rise. But I didn't enjoy the laws of shipping. "You're not supposed to enjoy it," my father said. "You're supposed to rise in the world." All the while, I was painting, spending my money on art materials. It came to a head in the year of *Jack and the Beanstalk* because by then I'd flunked Shipping Law.'

I shook out a crumpled skirt made of organza and lined with unbleached linen. The skirt made a crinkling sound as I placed it over a hanger.

Some impulse prompted Cricklethorpe to lean down and pick up a stray pair of green pantaloons. He continued. 'The top and bottom of it was that I left home and came to Whitby, to try and be myself.'

As I listened to Percival Cricklethorpe, I gathered his pantomime shoes from where they had been flung across the room. There was a pair of enormous black boots, the laces tightly tied.

The dame continued his story.

'When I came to Whitby, I met real artists, here and in Robin Hood's Bay. That turned me dejected. It cast me down to see the real stuff. We'd an art gallery in Hull but I'd looked at that in a different way, not connecting it with myself. Coming here to Whitby, and taking a fresh look, I knew what I would have to live up to.

'Fortunately, it was summer. I took an hotel job, helping the chef, washing up, doing whatever had to be done. I went on painting because I couldn't help it. A habit you see. I painted on the

216

empty tins that had held baked beans, practised my drawing on wrappers and smoothed out sugar bags. They had me writing menus and adding little decorations. It was temporary, so I didn't mind. I had a feeling of mad self-confidence, alongside knowing I wasn't good enough. It would come. Something would come of all these thoughts in my head, this knowing that it would work out. Call it faith if you like. At the end of the season my services were no longer required. The chef told me to go and see old Mr Pearson at Bagdale Hall because he wasn't up to fending for himself and he might give me a room in exchange for a bit of help around the house.

'Mr Pearson was frail. He was ninety-two and a prickly old geezer. Suspicious. He let me in because the chef had told him I wasn't a bad lad, and could turn my hand, was willing.

'Mr Pearson had been an artist. He looked at what I'd done. He couldn't paint much himself, being blighted with arthritis and lumbago but he cheered me up. He said, "Have you had lessons?" I told him just the drawing at school. He said in that case I wasn't bad and should keep on painting. I could help him keep things straight. I suited him. He suited me. One day, he said, "If I leave you this house, will you live in it?"

'I said yes I would.

'He hobbled along to Flowergate the next day and made his will.'

Cricklethorpe paused in his story as I folded a pair of bloomers and then, as if he had always had a lady's maid who needed instruction, said, 'Just put underwear on the hangers.'

217

I picked up a pink corset, an underskirt and an enormously heavy bustle. 'I suppose being an artist didn't always pay very well. You needed an income and have a large house with lots of storage. Deliveries of fuel might easily include a barrel or two of whisky.'

Mr Cricklethorpe surveyed the costumes, gave a smile at the re-imposed order. 'An interesting theory, Mrs Shackleton.'

'And you are near the station and on good terms with some of the railway workers I would guess.'

One of the hangers was on the rail the wrong way round. He righted it. 'I trust you will never take a job with the coastguard.'

'Don't worry. I won't. But I would like a bottle of whisky for my assistant, Mr Sykes. He's on holiday with his family in Robin Hood's Bay.'

'You've helped me with my frocks, Mrs Shackleton. It's the least I can do.'

'The police did not find what they were looking for either in the yard or in any of the rooms.'

'As I say, they took the wand as a likely weapon.'

'They didn't look closely at the costumes.'

'Antagonism got the better of them. They were two young lads from Grosmont and Lythe, trying to outdo each other. Their overriding idea was to humiliate me. Let me watch as they threw my collection about the room, looking in the pockets of the garments and in the bag that the dame sometimes carries.'

'That was upsetting for you, but it could have been worse.'

'What can you possibly mean, dear lady?'

'The inspector, being a specialist in fraud, has a

great interest in incomes and expenditure. Young chaps with no experience wouldn't understand that what seems a tawdry costume may be of more value than one imagines.'

'This wardrobe would take some replacing, that's true.'

Was I right, I wondered? Had Mr Cricklethorpe and his partner in contraband, Walter Turner, made a great deal of money? What kind of whisky was he moving from the yard that night when I called with Hilda? Perhaps the source of the whisky would lead to the mysterious Walter Turner.

'This whisky I'm to have, what's its provenance?'

There was a long pause before he answered. Would he trust me? Did he know what I was really asking? He watched as I adjusted a red dress.

'The distillery is in Elgin.'

'Then I'm sure it will be excellent.' I let the moment pass and turned my attention to the dresses, adjusting a gown on a padded hanger. 'This is stunning.' It was made of scarlet satin, studded with rubies.

'It's one of my walk-down gowns for the wedding finale.'

'Pantomimes are so reliable. And what fine rubies! Don't let Chief Inspector Charles take a look at these, Mr Cricklethorpe.'

Cricklethorpe gave me a cautious look, and rubbed his chin. 'Want them for himself, would he?'

'He's a most discerning detective, just back from America and keen to make his mark. Go see him, and then he won't need to come here.'

These were not paste jewels, I felt sure of it.

Was it Jack Philips who had supplied the gems and paid the money into his own account so that there would be no suspicion about the proceeds of contraband goods?

Cricklethorpe was no one's fool. He was looking at me, his eyes narrowed. 'I might just go and see your chief inspector.'

'Good.' I smiled. 'I was just thinking.'

'I thought you might be.'

'Which was the painting that you wouldn't sell to Mr Philips?'

He was relieved to have a change of topic. 'It's over there. *The Wreck of the* Rohilla. She sank in 1914.'

There were paintings on the far wall that I had not paid much attention to. I went across to look and stood a few feet from the painting of the sinking of the hospital ship *Rohilla*.

The broke-back vessel, tossed onto its side in the stormy sea, seemed close enough to touch. Tiny figures clung to the deck side. Its mast pointed accusingly at the lowering clouds and mountainous waves.

It was so finely executed that looking at it made me shiver. 'I can't remember what happened exactly. Did the *Rohilla* strike a mine?'

'No. That's what the captain thought, that he had been grounded by a mine. He was sailing far in to shore so as to avoid mines and hit the scaur, near Saltwick Nab.'

In the foreground, an unlit lighthouse loomed, indifferent to the efforts of those tiny figures carrying swaying lanterns and the men attempting to launch a lifeboat against crashing waves.

'Why was the lighthouse unlit?'

'Wartime security.'

'Of course, I forgot.'

'One does,' Cricklethorpe said. 'The ship was so close, only a mile off shore. Some took their chance, jumped ship and swam. The lifeboats couldn't be launched in that tempest. The worst thing for the lifeboat crew was to be helpless in the face of such a tragedy. They wouldn't and couldn't give up. The rescue attempts lasted three days.'

'There are men walking out into the sea.'

'Some from the ship were drawn to safety. Others met their maker over those three days. More than eighty drowned.'

'Yet it's so close.'

'That was the worst part for the Whitby men, being unable to reach the ship. There were lifeboats from all along the coast but no chance of getting out of the harbour from seaward. With no motorboats, all depended on the power of oars. There was an attempt to launch the lifeboat from below the East Cliff where the rocks are treacherous. The boat was damaged, but they rowed on, making two trips, and saved thirty-five lives. Out of two hundred and twenty-nine souls on board, one hundred and forty-six were saved. But it's the lost ones, those who perished we mourn. I salute the brave folk of Whitby who did more than would be thought humanly possible. Some of those heroic chaps who went to the rescue are hard-pressed to feed their families now. So if I can do a little bit of good for this place and the people in it,

'I will.'

I admired the cheek and boldness of Percival Cricklethorpe. He regarded his illicit trading, in part, as a service to the community.

It would have been tactless for me to ask if he thought some little bit of good included despatching Philips to an early grave. What did Cricklethorpe really hold against Jack Philips that he refused to sell him a painting? Cricklethorpe's story of the *Rohilla* disaster touched me deeply. 'It's a fine painting. I'm not surprised you wouldn't part with it.'

'I wouldn't, but especially not to him.'

'Why especially would you not sell to Mr Philips?'

'I had previously sold him another painting – Sandsend at dawn.'

'Did he have a particular reason for wanting this one?'

Cricklethorpe crossed the room and came to stand beside me. He pointed to one of the tiny figures pushing a boat into the water. 'That's Webb, Cap'n Webb as we all called him. He was a fine man. Made one mistake and lost his master's licence. After that he turned to drink, but he'd brought up Brendan like his own son. Everyone could see the likeness to Jack Philips, and there was talk, but it quietened down, out of respect for Cap'n Webb.'

We were silent for a while, continuing to hang the costumes. When we had done, I began to look at the paintings that hung on either side of the window. There were theatrical scenes, and some by a much younger and inexperienced hand. I looked at the signature and was delighted to see that they were by Felicity.

'How lovely that Felicity paints! She sometimes did little drawings on her thank you notes but I didn't know she could paint too.'

Cricklethorpe smiled. 'She likes this room and the costumes. She used to help me sometimes, mixing paint and daubing a bit herself.'

'Would you say she has talent?'

'She brims with talent, but not for painting.'

'This one looks good.'

It was full of colour – a tropical island.

The painting next to it, also Felicity's, might have been copied from a school atlas. It was a map of the world, painted in a simple style with the British Isles dominating the Earth.

Capital cities were named, and ports. Dotted lines had been added between certain places, criss-crossing between Liverpool and Dublin; Whitby and Bordeaux; Bordeaux and Lisbon; Lisbon and Madeira; Dublin to Belfast; Belfast to points in Scotland and the Inner Hebrides.

I turned to Cricklethorpe. 'Sergeant Garvin asked me an odd question after he found me on the West Cliff. I was shining my torch, looking for Alma after you'd told me she sometimes walked there.'

'What did our fossil-collecting sergeant ask?'

'He wanted to know had I visited Northern Scotland or been to the Hebrides.'

'A good guess. And had you?'

'No.'

Cricklethorpe gave a little shake of the head. 'Well as far as I'm concerned, this painting was just something to help Felicity with her geography you know. Geography was her favourite subject.'

'And based on her father's travels?'

'He did send postcards.'

I looked at Felicity's painting of the map. 'Alma said that the postcards from Madeira stopped several years ago.' I traced the line above the routes, taking care not to touch the painting. 'He deals in wines and spirits?'

'How perceptive of you.'

'Not at all. It's what these places have in common. Bordeaux, Madeira, Lisbon, for wine and port, Dublin for Jameson's whiskey, Scotland for malt.'

'So, Mrs Shackleton, you didn't want whisky for your assistant. You want to know where Felicity has gone.'

He was right that I did not want whisky for Jim Sykes. If Sykes knew it was contraband, he would choke. 'You're right, Mr Cricklethorpe, but I would like some for myself. So Felicity has gone to Elgin to find her father?'

'She was desperate to see him. The longing came over her so strongly. Alma wouldn't have agreed to her going. With my hints and her postcards, she came up with her plan. She's a clever girl.'

'Why now?'

'Because very soon it will be too late. I've had word that Walter doesn't have long to live.'

Twenty-Three

They were here because that was the story Felicity had told the coastguard, who had a presence here on Lindisfarne.

You have to stick to your story.

When Felicity and her mother came here they had reached the Holy Island by walking across the causeway at low tide, along with pilgrims and visitors. There was a sense of excitement – the possibility of being cut off, the feeling that here was somewhere very special. Her mother recited a poem to her as they walked across the causeway. Walter Scott had written about the path. She remembered the words and repeated them to herself.

Dry-shod, o'er sands, twice every day,
The pilgrims to the shrine find way;
Twice every day, the waves efface
Of staves and sandall'd feet the trace.

Approaching by sea seemed strange, as if they had come from a long time ago and the visit must be special and significant. Previously, the lighthouses and the markers had been for other people, for seafarers. Now she was a seafarer, a voyager into a strange land.

There was only one place she wanted to go and that was the church, to pray for her father, to keep him alive by determination and faith. 'Are you coming with me?' she asked Brendan.

He shook his head. 'We're not here just to stick to the story.' He looked about. 'I need to talk to someone who knows this coast.' He nodded towards a bent old man who was mending a lobster pot, and surrounded by lobster pots. 'I reckon him.' With the toe of his boot, Brendan dug a pebble from the sand. 'Weather's changing. We need to know a safe harbour if it turns foul.'

She saw that two of the old fishing boats had been turned upside down and made into sheds. 'We could stop here, like the coastguard officer said.'

Brendan shook his head. 'I want to get us to Berwick. We've time.'

'Well then, you ask for that old man's help. I'll ask for God's.'

He nodded. 'I hope we won't need it.'

Twenty-Four

Cricklethorpe and I were interrupted by a tap on the door. It was Sergeant Garvin, wanting to talk to me. 'A word in private,' as he put it.

He led the way along the corridor into the room that held paintings.

'Would you like to sit down, Mrs Shackleton?' With a conjuror's flourish, he indicated the dusty chairs.

'I'll stand.'

'You brought an item of confectionery for Felicity.'

'Yes. A slab of toffee.'

He gave a surprised look as if I had confessed too easily and too soon. 'So you admit to having brought toffee?'

'Yes.'

'This toffee, when and where did you buy it?'

'At Dowzells newsagents, shortly after I arrived.'

'And where is the toffee hammer?'

'There was no toffee hammer. It wasn't the kind of toffee that comes with a hammer.'

Sergeant Garvin's eyes narrowed. 'We shall be enquiring further into this.'

'Sergeant, I didn't kill Mr Philips with a toffee hammer, or any other weapon.'

I decided against assuring him that the small hammer found by the constables searching the bins at the back of the Royal Hotel had nothing to do with me. Only the guilty protest too much. Besides, such a comment might lead to a question of why I was looking through binoculars from a window on a third floor back room at the Royal.

'Thank you. That will be all for now.' He held open the door for me.

Was he pondering his next move towards putting a noose around my neck as we parted at the top of the stairs?

I heard him leave the building as I went to find Alma.

The door to her room was wide open. She was sitting in the window, looking out onto Bagdale, a linen tablecloth, etched with flowers and leaves for embroidering, draped across her lap. She looked up from her needle-stabbing and cast a wan smile in my direction. 'There you are, Kate, I thought you'd abandoned me in my hour of need.'

'Not yet, but give me five minutes.'

'What do you mean?'

'Why didn't you tell Sergeant Garvin that I knew nothing about Jack Philips's interest in you, or yours in him, until after I found him dead? I'm his favourite suspect.'

'He didn't ask me about that.' She poked her needle into the cloth. 'I praised you. I said how protective you were of any girl at school who was upset or in bother.'

'He'll make an utter fool of himself if he goes on suspecting me.'

'He doesn't suspect you.' She withdrew her needle from a partially completed silvery leaf. 'I just happened to mention that you always brought toffee for Felicity, even though she doesn't like it any more.'

I felt deflated at hearing Felicity had gone off toffee. 'I hope she would have told me.'

'Oh, she would.' Alma reached for her hanky. 'I'm so worried that I feel sick.'

I took her hand.

'Felicity has gone to find Walter. You must know that.'

'But how? He's probably in Madeira with that woman.'

'He's in Scotland. There's a map in the costumes room with all his travels marked on it.'

'But we haven't had a postcard for ages.'

'You did say that Felicity had been picking up the post before you.'

'Yes, so she did.' The hope didn't stop her tears. 'If you're right, I'm such an idiot and a useless mother.'

She bent her head towards the embroidery. 'Felicity bought me this cloth and threads for Christmas. I thought it would be soothing, and that if I worked on it, her postcard would come but the postman passed us by and there's only one delivery on Sunday.'

Sitting down beside her, I remained calm and did not let myself become annoyed. 'Alma, dear, why do you prefer not to know things?'

She slotted her needle into the fabric. 'I might just as well ask you why you have to know everything. It was drilled into me by my old deaf aunt. A lady must be prepared to turn a blind eye. A lady must not enquire too deeply into things.'

'What do you call communing with the moon and the spirits?'

'Oh that's different,' she spoke with bright certainty and then blew her nose. 'Did everyone but me know? Brendan Webb is Jack's son.'

'What? Alma, you're confusing me.'

'Mrs Webb came to see me last night in the pepper pot. She told me that Jack Philips is Brendan's father. That explains why Brendan looks different to everyone else in that family. My automatic writing was correct. Turner came through in the writing. He said that Jack Philips didn't want me for myself, he wanted Felicity.'

'In what way did he want Felicity?'

'Not in that way, thank goodness. But you see, with Felicity being Brendan's sweetheart, having me and Felicity as friends would be a way for

Jack to see Brendan.'

'That would be a bit convoluted. If what you say is true...' Alma did not let me finish the sentence which was just as well as I didn't know where my own thought would lead.

'But don't you see it? Because I do. And how could he, Kate, how could he?'

'How could he what?'

'Have an affair with a married woman from the east side and give her a baby. I'm shocked, Kate.'

'I'm surprised Mrs Webb found the time.'

'Her husband was alive then.' Alma made an extravagant gesture that sent her embroidery silks scattering across the floor. 'But that was convenient for Jack I suppose, leaving his cuckoo in the nest.'

'Alma, concentrate on finding out about Felicity. Talk to Sergeant Garvin. You don't have to tell him about the contraband.'

'What contraband?'

'Oh never mind. Just say that you think the Doram is sailing up the coast.'

'But how do I know the Doram is sailing up the coast? And if I did say that, would I be getting Felicity into trouble?' She began to pick up her embroidery threads and I wondered if it was so that I would not see her face. How much did she really know?

'Is there time for them to have landed in Elgin? I've no idea how long such a voyage would take.'

'Neither have I, but if she has gone to see her father, I shouldn't stop her.'

'No, but it might be an idea to stop them coming back with a boat full of whisky and being caught by the coastguard.'

'How do I do that?' She closed the lid on her embroidery basket.

'Talk to Mr Cricklethorpe. He must have ways of communicating with Walter.'

I moved to leave the room.

She called me back. 'Wait! If what you say is true and Cricklethorpe and Walter Turner have been in cahoots all this time...'

'You must know they have.'

She carried the embroidery basket back to the sideboard. 'You're right. Do you know how I know you are right?'

'Do tell, Alma.'

'When Walter Turner was in Madeira and Portugal, crates of port came. It was very good.'

Alma was not stupid but was either self-deluded or so self-centred as to not see what was under her nose unless through a crystal ball. On the other hand, she could be leading me a merry dance. Perhaps there was a stronger motive for the jeweller's death than jealousy or greed. He may have been in a position to betray the lucrative trade in which Cricklethorpe took pride.

'I'm going now, Alma.'

'Where are you going? I don't want to be on my own.'

'I need some fresh air.'

Alma picked up her cape. 'What's it like out there? I'm coming with you.'

'Come on then. Let's go for a walk.'

The police had all left. A calm hush pervaded the atmosphere. I thought of the first occupants of the house, their optimism, their faith, their love, and of the quotation above the door. Come along with me, the best is yet to be.

At the turn in the stairs, we both saw him at the same moment, Percival Cricklethorpe, lying motionless on the floor in front of the fire.

Alma froze.

I hurried down the steps.

Cricklethorpe lay face down, his head by the fender, a nasty gash on the back of his head. He was unconscious but breathing. I took off my coat and made a pillow, raising his head a little.

Alma hovered behind me. 'Is he...?'

'He's alive. Give me your cape.'

She did so and I covered him. 'Run to the police station. Say we need a doctor and ambulance. Tell them Mr Cricklethorpe has been attacked.'

'Shall I go straight to the hospital?'

'The police will get help more quickly. Hurry!'

I sat with Percival Cricklethorpe, talking to him, trying to rouse him, hoping he could hear me. His pulse was slow and his breathing laboured but his eyes flickered.

It seemed an age that I sat on the floor, holding his hand, until Marcus arrived.

He bobbed down beside me. 'We'll have him in hospital shortly. Do you have your camera?'

'No.'

He took a small sketchpad from his pocket. 'Step back, Kate.'

With deft movements, he began to sketch Cricklethorpe and the area around him. He was still drawing when the doctor and two ambulance men arrived.

The doctor did a quick examination, raising

Percival Cricklethorpe's eyelids and checking his pulse. He took lint from his bag and applied it to the wound.

At his nod, the ambulance men manoeuvred their patient onto a stretcher.

The doctor took a brief look at me and then glanced at Marcus.

'I'm all right,' I said.

One of the ambulance men spoke. 'We'll cut through the back way, doctor, if the door's open.'

The doctor went ahead of them, opening the door into the corridor that led into the kitchen and the yard.

As they disappeared through the back, Sergeant Garvin arrived at the front. He and I stood back, watching as Marcus examined the scene. He carefully lifted the heavy poker from its place in the tidy with the brush and shovel. He carried it outside to examine it in the light, beckoning to the sergeant to go with him.

Marcus came back alone. 'That was the weapon.'

Poor Cricklethorpe. I did not have much hope for his chances of recovery if he had been hit with that.

Marcus continued his look around. I sat on the stairs, watching.

After several moments, he joined me. 'Did you hear anything?'

'No. Alma and I were in her room on the second floor. Mr Cricklethorpe's rooms are on the first floor.'

'Had you spoken to him?'

'Yes, earlier, after your men had made a mess of

his pantomime room. He was upset.'

'He had on his jacket. Did he give any indication where he was going or who he would be seeing?'

'I believe he may have been coming to the station to see you and give a statement. He knew something.'

'What?'

'He had a strong suspicion as to who killed the jeweller and why but he wouldn't tell me. I encouraged him to come and talk to you.'

'Did he give any hint?'

'No.'

'Pity. And it's a pity he cleared out all the whisky. You look as if you could do with a tipple.' He stood and offered his hand to haul me up from the stairs.

We walked through the shady courtyard into the bright light of day. 'Mrs Turner said she'd wait at the hospital, and stay with Cricklethorpe. If he regains consciousness it will be good for him to see a familiar face. There's nothing more you can do here, Kate.'

'I know.'

'Thank you.'

I shrugged. 'I did what anyone would do, which was not very much. I only hope he has a chance of pulling through.'

'Will you go to the hospital?'

'Not yet. I'll let the doctors do their work and call later.'

There was an odd awkwardness between us, a reluctance to turn away from each other.

Twenty-Five

As I walked the few yards to the railway station, I wondered was I doing the right thing. I needed to talk to someone, not Marcus. He was too busy, and there was still that awkwardness between us. After all that had happened since yesterday, I felt in need of moral support and a listening ear, as well as a brief escape from the tragic events in Whitby. There was just one person who would help me take the measure of all that had happened. That person was my assistant, Jim Sykes.

Reluctant as I was to butt into his holiday, I intended to do exactly that.

Sykes, his wife Rosie and their children were holidaying about eight miles away, in Robin Hood's Bay, a busy coastal village. Gerald and I had walked to the Bay and I had promised myself I would follow that route again. From the top of the West Cliff, a path wound onto the cliffs, giving superb views of the bay on what I remembered as that long-ago perfect day. Gerald had worried that the walk was too strenuous, but I just laughed, not finding it at all difficult. We took our cameras and photographed a ship that moved so slowly that it appeared to stand still. We made a detour down a steep and rocky path to Saltwick Bay. An aged man, who must have been sure-footed as a goat, provided tea from an urn. Would he be there still, as old as Methuselah? After climbing back up to the cliff path, the way led us beyond a lighthouse, and slightly inland. I tried to remember the point at which we dipped down into Robin's Hood Bay.

I would have loved to do that walk again, but not today. It would take too long. Nor did I feel inclined to drive to the Bay as I remembered the road into the village as being almost vertical. With the way my luck was going since arriving in Whitby, the car would scoot down the hill and into the sea.

The train would suit me better. It might even allow me to pretend to myself that the visit was a social call on the Sykes family. Trying to banish images of the dead Jack Philips, and Cricklethorpe lying so helpless by the fireplace, I thought about the Sykes family.

They had been spending their annual holiday in the cottage on Martins Row for several years now, since we made the acquaintance of Miss Horrocks, the Bradford owner, during an investigation regarding a missing person. The Horrocks family was glad of the rental income. For Sykes's eldest boy, his first visit to Robin Hood's Bay had marked a turning point. Thomas was keen on woodwork and the local cabinet maker took a liking to him and let him help in his workshop. This experience gained him an apprenticeship with a firm of carpenters and joiners in Leeds. Now, whenever the family visited the Bay, the cabinetmaker and his wife gave Thomas a room and made a fuss of him.

At least they would all be enjoying their holiday, I hoped, as would my housekeeper Mrs Sugden who was visiting her cousin just a few miles further south, in Scarborough.

At the station, I was pleased to arrive just in time for the next train to Robin Hood's Bay. This small triumph felt like a good omen. I boarded the train, along with others making this Sunday excursion. The experience of spending the night in a cell added to the sense of freedom that comes from a railway journey.

As I turned into Martins Row, I saw Rosie standing in the doorway, exchanging a few words with an elderly woman who carried a basket on her arm. Whatever remark Rosie made, it drew a smile.

The woman moved on.

Rosie shaded her eyes. 'Mrs Shackleton, how lovely to see you.'

Really? How lovely could it be that her husband's boss intruded even here? 'Hello, Rosie. How are you getting on?'

'Very well.'

'Where is everyone?'

'The girls are on the beach with a picnic. Thomas is over at the workshop, helping Mr Fosdyck. Jim is having a drink at the Bay Hotel. But come in. The kettle's on the boil.'

I had been in the cottage only once before. It was neat and clean, with distempered walls and a low fire in the grate.

Rosie poured water into the teapot, while giving me chapter and verse about her journey here. Sykes had driven through all the lanes and byways across the moors, stopping every now and then to check his compass and the road map.

'Thomas and the girls came by train. They're so independent now, not children any more. The time goes by so quickly.' She sighed. 'This could be our last family holiday.'

'Thomas is seventeen, isn't he?'

'Yes and thinks himself entirely grown up, and you know that Irene's been working in Schofields haberdashery these last two years, very steady she is and well-liked. It's all haberdashery with her now. She's highly critical of the little shop in Robin Hood's Bay, says it's entirely out of date and she wishes she could have three hours in there, sorting out the place.'

'Robin Hood's Bay better watch out!'

She laughed. 'Aye, it's no more buckets and spades on the beach for my little lot. But here I am chatting my head off. How is that school friend of yours?'

Rosie had been the gracious recipient of Alma's pamphlets and prophecies which I had purchased in quantities. 'Are you sure you want to know? It's a long story.'

'They're the best kind.'

Now that news of the jeweller's death had been broadcast from pulpits, with the clear implication of foul play, I gave her a brief account of finding the body. As briefly as I could, I told her about Alma and her worries about the missing Felicity. Somehow I could not bring myself to talk about the attack on Percival Cricklethorpe, not yet, not while he lay fighting for his life. That the outrage had happened when Alma and I were in her room unsettled me deeply. If we had gone downstairs a little sooner, our presence might have prevented

238

the attack.

Rosie was clearly shaken at the thought of a murder in a place so near by, and the disappearance of my goddaughter upset her greatly. 'If one of my girls took off, I'd be frantic. How is Mrs Turner coping?'

My own sigh surprised me. 'Not very well. Life hasn't been easy for her.' I took the Alma line of explanation regarding Walter Turner. 'Her husband has worked away for many years and I do believe that Felicity may have gone to find him.'

Rosie nodded. 'I see, and so perhaps Mrs Turner wouldn't be pleased at that. Do you know where she has gone?'

In spite of her chattiness, Rosie can be discreet. Even so, I decided against mentioning the likelihood that Felicity was sailing to Elgin to find her bigamist smuggler of a father. 'The police have informed the coastguard.'

'She's in a boat?'

'We think so.'

'I'm surprised the police have time, with a murder on their hands.'

'The thing is Felicity was in the jewellers shop, and may have been one of the last people to see Mr Philips alive.'

'Was he robbed?'

'I don't know what was taken. I suppose he kept inventories so the police may learn what the intruder was after.'

'Perhaps whoever did it didn't intend to kill him and became afraid, wanted to be gone before anyone saw them.'

'Perhaps.'

'Did anyone see a man going in there?'

'If it was a man. I don't know. I'm not privy to investigations.'

'Is Scotland Yard on the case?'

'Yes. It's Chief Inspector Marcus Charles.'

She tried to hide her surprise. 'You and he are friends, aren't you?'

'I wouldn't put it as strongly as that, though we do have some regard for each other.' That was putting it mildly. I had been rather bowled over by him, but also hugely irritated, and I sometimes wished we had kept each other at arms' length. I diverted the conversation. 'Felicity pawned a watch-guard with the jeweller and then left the pawn ticket for her mother to redeem so the police want to talk to her about that.'

'Thoughtful of her! Children these days. We'd never have dreamed of doing such a thing.'

'I might as well come clean, Rosie. I'm hoping Mr Sykes will find the time to ... well, pay a visit to Whitby with me and see how the land lies.'

'I'm sure Jim would want to help find the lass.'

'I don't want to spoil your holiday by dragging him away.'

'Well it's not for something little, is it? A murder, perhaps a jewel robbery. Could it be anything to do with smuggling?'

Was the woman a mind reader? She should be the one in the pepper pot, handing out fortunes. 'What makes you think that?'

'I've heard about diamonds being smuggled in from Amsterdam, stolen diamonds.'

'Really? That's news to me.'

'Well you and I wouldn't have thought of it but

smuggling is something of a tradition round here.' She stood. 'Have you been round this house?'

'No.'

'Well then, you'll find the cellar of interest.'

'Is there something special about it?'

She lit a candle. 'Come and see. Our Thomas noticed it when he was exploring, the first time we came.'

I followed her through the door at the back of the room. She led the way down twisting stone steps into the kind of cellar one sees everywhere: a stone slab; a cold press with a mesh door for keeping butter and cheese; a heap of coal in the corner and above it the grate where the coalman tipped the bags.

'But look at this.' She opened a small door that led onto a corridor too low and narrow for an adult to pass through. She ducked down, turned to her right and then held the candle aloft. 'See!'

I followed her and saw that a concealed turning led off into a hidden passage that widened into a tunnel. 'How extraordinary. Where does it lead?'

'To the shore line. Thomas and the girls insisted on walking it. Frightened me to death. I imagined the roof caving in on them.'

'But why is it here? What was the purpose?'

'It's a smugglers' passage. There are lots of them, according to Mr Fosdyck the cabinet maker. Smuggling was the way many poor people made their living.'

'It gives me the shudders. How long must this tunnel be?'

'Too long for me.' The candle flickered as she moved towards the opposite wall. 'See that blocked-up opening? That led to the next house along. This village is a warren of underground passages and bolt holes. It's said that a bale of silk could pass from the bottom of the village to the top without leaving the houses. If these walls could speak we'd hear some fine tales.'

We left the cellar and climbed up the worn stone steps. I was glad to be back on ground level. Moments ago, the ground floor room had seemed small and gloomy. After the shadows of the cellar it felt suddenly bright, light and airy.

Rosie paused at the top of the steps. 'I see why you want Jim to join you, with all that's going on up in Whitby.'

'I'm sorry to have come barging in on your holiday.'

'Don't be sorry. We've been here going on two days, he'll be glad of the diversion.' She looked at the clock on the mantelpiece. 'Come with me. I said I'd meet him for a sandwich in the Bay Hotel at one o'clock.'

Jim Sykes was seated on a bench outside the Bay Hotel, his hat on the table. It was reassuring to see him looking so relaxed, though he made no concessions to summer attire. He wore his usual weekday suit and a patterned tie. He smiled broadly, showing no surprise at seeing me. 'Hello! There isn't a seat to be had inside. Do you mind the bench?'

We didn't mind. One glance at the pub told us how crowded it was. People were spilling out of the doors.

To say Sykes had caught the sun would be an

understatement. His face had the hue of a well-boiled lobster.

He touched the back of his neck gingerly. 'I'm glad of a bit of shade. Take my trilby off and the back of my neck and forehead burn. Put it on and I roast.' He called the waiter, and we placed our order for sandwiches and drinks.

Sykes already knew about the murder of Mr Philips. News had travelled along the coast, gathering colourful details on the way. I gave him the more sober version of finding the body before telling him about Felicity Turner's sudden departure, and Alma's connection with the jeweller.

Sykes gave me a quick glance. He knew there was much I left unsaid and that both Alma and Felicity would need to be eliminated from police enquiries.

Rosie joined the conversation, sympathising and hoping Felicity would turn up soon.

Sykes fanned a wasp from his beer. 'Did you drive from Whitby?'

'I came on the train.'

'Well why don't we drive back together and you can show me the lie of the land.'

I glanced quickly at Rosie. 'I didn't intend this business to intrude on your holiday.'

Rosie bit into her sandwich. 'I hate bought sandwiches.'

'Don't eat it if you don't like it, love.'

'Well I'm not going to waste it, am I?' She chewed and swallowed. 'I don't know why I didn't make them myself.'

'Because you're on holiday,' Sykes said.

Rosie looked from him to me. 'You two aren't

on holiday, not any more.'

'It's just a precaution, Rosie.' I tried to sound unconcerned. 'You see, I know this will sound ridiculous but Alma, Felicity and I are at the eye of the storm – until something changes. The local sergeant suspected me of the murder.'

Rosie choked on a crumb, took a coughing fit and then a sip of lemonade. 'What?'

'I know. It's ludicrous. Now that Marcus has taken charge the sergeant will be bound to let his nonsense drop but I feel uneasy on all sorts of counts, and for Alma and Felicity.'

Sykes drained his pint of beer. 'Marcus? Chief Inspector Marcus Charles?'

'Yes. He arrived this morning.'

Rosie had not quite recovered from her choking fit. She gulped. 'Well he'll have it sorted soon enough, won't he?'

'I expect he will.'

The wasp now hovered over Rosie's lemonade. She flicked it away. 'If I was in Whitby on my own and found a body and some idiot thought I'd done it, I'd worry. Jim, you go back with Mrs Shackleton. Just do it.'

Sykes lit a cigarette. 'Right, as long as you don't choke on a crust while I'm gone.'

'It just sticks in my gullet to eat pub sandwiches. My mother would be horrified. Don't eat bought sandwiches and never eat in the street. And here I am.'

Sykes gave a cheerful grin. 'We're not exactly in the street.'

'What else would you call sitting outside on a bench?'

'I'd call it a holiday. Don't worry, love, Mrs Shackleton and I will have this Whitby business sorted out before you can say donkey rides on the sand.'

Rosie had stopped listening. She was looking up the hill. 'Hey up! Who's that then?'

Sykes and I followed her gaze.

'It is,' Sykes said. 'Well spotted, Rosie.'

She had seen us first and strode purposefully in our direction. She carried a carpet bag in one hand, a handbag and newspaper in the other, and wore that familiar tweed coat, far too heavy for August. From a distance one would think her older than she is because she dresses in the old-fashioned, pre-war way with clothes designed to last and to keep out the weather.

'It is, isn't it?' Rosie asked. 'It's her.'

Twenty-Six

The figure walking down the steep hill, tilted back by the gradient and the wind, was none other than my housekeeper, Mrs Sugden.

Rosie shaded her eyes. 'I thought she was staying in Scarborough with her cousin.'

'So did I.'

Sykes was already on his way up to meet her. They paused for a moment. He took her carpet bag. They walked a little way together and then Sykes turned off towards the cottage, taking Mrs Sugden's bag with him.

She continued down the hill without him, fanning herself with the newspaper as she came to join us. 'By heckerslike, it's hot.'

We budged up to make room for her. Neither Rosie nor I suggested that she take off her coat. That would have been presumptuous.

Mrs Sugden let out a sigh. 'Scarborough wasn't to my liking. Well, not Scarborough itself, I've no complaints there. It's that cousin of mine.'

'Are you here for the day?' Rosie asked.

'I'm not stopping. Mr Sykes just took my bag into your cottage to save me carrying it round. I'm off back to Leeds on the late afternoon train. I've had enough of our Deborah.'

The waiter passed, carrying a tray of empties back inside. He gave us a querying glance.

Mrs Sugden shook her head. 'I don't eat bought dinners and I don't eat outside, but I wouldn't mind an ice cream in a minute, and a deck chair to have a cool off. It was murder on that charabanc. I could have gone back direct from Scarborough to Leeds but I wanted to let you know I was off, Rosie, and to say cheerio. I didn't expect to find you here, Mrs Shackleton.'

Half an hour later, the four of us sat on deck chairs, looking out to sea. Rosie took out her knitting. Mrs Sugden reported on her attempt at a holiday.

'She was such a lively lass, my cousin Deborah. That feller she married, and he's no older than you, Mr Sykes, he's turned her into an old woman. They go to bed before nine o'clock. He's up and out at six for his constitutional. She does nowt,

246

absolutely nowt. He takes her a cup of tea when he comes back from the walk. She's not up till ten. She's one of these that's busy doing nothing. A little lass comes in and skivvies for her and the poor child can do nothing right in Deborah's book. Her only conversation is about her ailments and what the child does wrong. Well I couldn't be doing with it.'

'That's a shame!' Rosie rested her knitting in her lap. 'You had such high hopes of seeing your cousin.'

'Aye well, more fool me. I should have taken the hint of how she's changed from her letters, dripping with lumbago and ingrowing toenails.'

A good idea popped into my head. It would be a shame for Mrs Sugden to cut short her holiday, when she had been looking forward to it and all the arrangements were in place for the cat, the telephone and the post. 'Come to Whitby, Mrs Sugden.'

'I'm not staying at the Royal. Even if I could afford it, I wouldn't thoil it at them prices.'

'My friend Alma lives in a huge house, and she was disappointed that I wouldn't stay. They had a room ready for me.'

'Alma Turner, the prophetess?'

'Yes. You wouldn't object, would you?'

'I would not. I'd like to meet her.'

'That's settled then. We'll go back together.'

There would be time on the return journey to tell her more. She would need to know about the attack on Mr Cricklethorpe and we would have to make sure that Bagdale Hall was locked and secure.

Mrs Sugden had already taken to the idea. 'That would suit me very well but I'm not going in another charabanc today. It was that hot. I wouldn't be surprised if we have a storm.'

'We'll all squeeze in the motor,' Sykes said. 'It's not far. Do you want to come, Rosie?'

Rosie blew out her cheeks, giving her the appearance of a cherub. 'What, and sit on't car bonnet? I don't think so. I'll stop here where there's some comfort and I can keep an eye on my lassies.'

'You do right, Rosie,' Mrs Sugden agreed. 'I'd no notion of moving on myself. Thought I'd be settled for the duration.'

'You'll like Whitby, Mrs Sugden,' I said encouragingly.

'How much would your friend rush me for this room?'

'Not a penny. She owns the house jointly with a Mr Cricklethorpe who is in hospital at present. They'd welcome you there.'

She brightened considerably. 'That's nice.'

'Yes, only there is one thing you must promise me.'

'What's that?'

'The house is on the neglected side, to put it mildly. I don't want you to feel obliged to do anything different about that.'

'Count on it. As long as my own room is clean, and the kitchen, that will do.'

The kitchen. I would keep quiet about the kitchen.

Mrs Sugden was smiling now, a rare sight. 'I wasn't relishing going home this soon and telling Miss Merton her help is no longer needed. She

248

was quite excited at the thought of having your telephone calls passed on to their number, and minding Sookie. I would have felt a failure in the holiday-making department.'

Sykes stood. 'I'll fetch the ice creams.'

I moved to join him. 'I'll help you carry them.'

Rosie paused in her knitting and gave us an odd look.

As we walked towards the ice cream seller, Sykes said, 'Summat's up, eh? Are we on a job?'

'Possibly.'

'Go on,' he said. 'What's happened? These youngsters who've disappeared, is there some connection between them and the murder?'

'I'm not sure. But I've been drawn into this, because of Alma. I was out looking for her on Saturday night and ... well not to go into great details but I was picked up as a suspicious character and spent the night in the clink.' I have rarely stopped a person in their tracks, but Sykes skidded to a halt on the sand. 'Just keep walking, Mr Sykes. I'll tell you about it on the way back. Mrs Sugden will need to know too, and Rosie if you'd like to tell her.'

'Tell me now!'

'If Sergeant Garvin had his way there would be a warrant for my arrest on the grounds of an unsatisfactory explanation regarding a toffee hammer found in a bin at the back of the Royal Hotel.'

'Someone is trying to point the finger at you by planting the weapon at your hotel, if it is the weapon.'

'Or, the suspect is staying at the Royal Hotel, or lives nearby.'

'No. They would throw it in the sea.'

We joined the queue for ice cream, leaving a little distance between ourselves and the person in front and lowering our voices. 'Mr Crickle-thorpe, the joint owner of Bagdale Hall along with my friend Alma, he was attacked and is in hospital. That was just before I left to come here. I believe it's because he has a suspicion about the jeweller's killer.'

'Then I'm very glad you came. Is Alma safe?'

'I think so. She wears a cloak of naivety and that's a good protection. In some ways she's not of this world, though she knows a lot more than she lets on. I don't think it's occurred to Alma that she might be in danger.'

'Do you feel confident that she and Felicity are not involved?'

'At the moment I feel confident of nothing. I have this nagging worry that there's much more going on, and I don't know what. It'll be up to the police to get to the bottom of it, but I would like to know for sure that Alma and Felicity have someone to look out for their interests.'

'And yours!'

It was our turn. Sykes ordered four cornets, insisting, 'These are on me.'

The dark-haired Italian man scooped ice cream into the cones.

I took two, Sykes took two.

We made our way back along the beach. Much as I hated keeping something back, mentioning plentiful supplies of whisky might be a bad idea. Mr Sykes would take a harsh line on dealings in contraband, even though it might be the trade that provided much-needed income in a town that seemed to have so little work for its inhabitants.

'Rosie says she doesn't mind that I came to find you, but what do you think?'

'She might mind more if I'm under her feet for the fortnight and driving her mad.'

'My engagement and wedding rings came from the late Mr Philips's shop. He was such a charming man. I went back there and bought a hip flask for Gerald and had it engraved.'

'And you want to know who killed him?'

'Obviously it's being investigated. It's not up to me.'

'But...?'

He licked his hand where melting ice cream had trickled. 'I hate not having a clue what's going on. For obvious reasons I can't ask Marcus. He wouldn't tell me anyway.'

Suddenly I heard a familiar voice call my name. I looked round.

'What is it?' he asked.

'Someone just called Kate – obviously they didn't mean me because no one here knows me.'

'I didn't hear anyone call.'

I did not add that the voice sounded rather like Alma's, and that was why I looked all around the crowded beach, but she was not there. Either I had imagined it, or she really did have the power to send astral messages. If so, I wished she would keep that talent to herself and not use it on me.

Sykes took a lick of ice cream. 'About Chief Inspector Charles.'

'What about him?'

'Did that shipboard romance of his come to anything?'

'How do you know about that?'

'Didn't you tell me?'

'Certainly not, so how do you know?'

He took another lick. 'Good ice cream.'

'Don't be annoying. Who told you?'

'I happened to bump into your father. He'd heard something about it turning sour.'

I nearly tumbled over a sandcastle, destroying some child's carefully made parapet. Fortunately the child had left the beach. 'Are you and Dad discussing me?'

'No, of course not. We never mentioned you. I just happened to see him one day, near the Town Hall when he was attending a meeting. He took a shine to Marcus when he was up here.'

'So did I, for a while. But what's Dad's interest in Marcus's private business?'

'You'd have to ask him.'

Several thoughts flitted through my mind and I would have been better off without them. If Marcus was deeply unhappy and his shipboard romance really had turned sour, he might enjoy making me pay for turning down his proposal of marriage. The other thought was even more unsettling. Was Jim Sykes reporting to my dad on how I was getting on? In spite of everything I've achieved, there is nothing much to be done when men believe they have a woman's best interest at heart and collude behind her back.

Now I was really curious. Had Marcus come back married to the woman he met on board ship? Sykes knew something, I could tell. He was waiting for me to ask. I wouldn't give him the satisfaction.

The four of us went back to the cottage on Martins Row. Sykes, Mrs Sugden and I needed a strategy. Mrs Sugden seemed content with the idea of coming to Whitby, especially if there would be something useful to do, i.e. ensure that I was not arrested and that we safeguarded Alma the prophetess.

By tacit agreement, Rosie Sykes was taken into our confidence. The four of us sat round the kitchen table in the cottage and I told them everything that had happened since my arrival in Whitby, including the attack on Mr Cricklethorpe.

'And that's where I'll be staying, where this attack happened?' Mrs Sugden made a fist.

'Not if you don't want to,' I assured her. 'I'm sure we can find somewhere perfectly clean and tidy that provides good meals.'

Mrs Sugden's jaw tightened. 'No thug will put me off. I'm only sorry I don't have a lethal weapon to hand.'

Rosie had said she would keep quiet and just listen, but she was the first to speak. 'The police can't really imagine you murdered that man, and with a toffee hammer.'

'It would be a plausible weapon. The mark on his skull was small. If he had a thin skull, it would be enough to cause a haemorrhage.'

The room went quiet while Sykes, Rosie and Mrs Sugden all thought about toffee hammers in a new light.

253

Rosie broke the silence. 'But why? What motive?'

I shrugged. 'I was protecting my friend from a dishonourable association with Mr Philips?'

Mrs Sugden leaped in with her theory. 'I have great admiration for your friend Mrs Turner's writings, and especially her prophecies written as Madam Alma, but she could be guilty of killing Mr Philips, if he let her down.'

Sykes took out his pipe. 'Did Mr Philips never marry?'

'No.'

'Why would he change his spots now?'

'I don't know. But Alma had high hopes.'

'Based on?' Sykes asked.

'Having tea, outings.'

Sykes tapped tobacco into his pipe. 'Perhaps your friend read too much into it.'

'She did, according to Mr Cricklethorpe. I wish I'd prompted him to tell me more.'

'She'll be a suspect in the attack on Mr Cricklethorpe then.' Mrs Sugden took out her notebook. 'And since that's where I'm to be staying – if she agrees – then I should be on the look-out for any little slips, in relation to that and her movements at the time of the jeweller's death.'

'Could Mrs Turner have attacked Mr Cricklethorpe?' Sykes asked. 'The way you've described it, there were just the three of you in the house.'

I came to Alma's defence. 'I'm absolutely sure she's innocent.'

All three looked at me as though I were the innocent.

'And would Mrs Turner have had time to attack the jeweller?' Rosie chipped in. 'If she found out he wasn't serious, she may have resented having spent time on him.'

Mrs Sugden welcomed an ally in the Alma-could-just-possibly-be-guilty-of-everything camp. 'Of course there's Madam Alma's Prophecies for 1927. She did prophesy some rather strange events and was uncannily accurate. If I remember rightly, she prophesied a death that could have meant Mr Philips.'

'Well that can't be hard, can it?' Sykes was showing signs of impatience. 'We could all prophesy a death and then point to one.'

Mrs Sugden did not reply. She is dangerous when in a sulk. Needing her not to go silent, I had to think of something. The prophecies were written in rather tedious rhyme. I had read them very quickly, though not as quickly as they deserved. 'I can't remember the detail, Mrs Sugden. Remind me about this death.'

'Hang on!' Rosie went to the mantelpiece. 'I brought my copy, thinking Madam Alma might sign it for me. Here it is.'

Mrs Sugden took the pamphlet, regarding herself as the expert in this matter. 'Well you see what I wonder, Mrs Shackleton, is this. Does your friend know more than she realises?'

'What do you mean?'

'I'll give a few examples.'

Sykes glowered. Mrs Sugden made as if not to notice and continued. 'Listen to this. "Across oceans lone voices travel, The mystery of distance to unravel." What do you make of that?'

'I'm not sure. What do you make of it?'

Mrs Sugden had clearly already given the matter some thought. 'Wasn't there that telephonic conversation across the Atlantic ocean earlier this year? None of us saw that coming.'

Sykes pooh-poohed the idea. 'There are lots of people who keep up with developments in these sorts of things.'

'Is Madam Alma one such?' Mrs Sugden did not wait for an answer.

She opened the prophecies at another page. 'There was that big earthquake in Japan. Well, listen to this. "The world turns dark for all to wonder, Earth will quake without lightning or thunder."'

It had fallen to Sykes and Rosie to be Mrs Sugden's audience, Sykes impatient, Rosie in thrall. My role became devil's advocate. 'There's always an earthquake somewhere in the world.'

'True, but she wasn't to know what would happen in the diamond rush in South Africa. None of us knew what lengths big grabbers would go to. Don't you remember? Companies hired athletes to stake out claims? There was a picture in the *Sunday Pictorial*.'

'She mentions that?'

'She does. "Where gems sparkle feet will race, Wealth and wonder to embrace."'

'It does sound rather like that incident, but it could be metaphorical. There'll always be people chasing gold or diamonds.'

'Not all of them do it in plimsolls.'

Sykes's patience gave way. 'So, what is your point, Mrs Sugden? You've quoted a few of her rhymes but there are bound to be more that mean nothing. It's all to do with interpretation.'

Mrs Sugden produced her trump card. 'Whatever we call her, Mrs Turner or Madam Alma, your friend has a gift, Mrs Shackleton. If the police trouble to read her prophecies she'll have questions to answer. Listen to this. "For greed and envy a vicious smack Steals breath from life in fierce attack." If that doesn't foretell the jeweller's death, I don't know what does.'

Sykes made his bid for centre stage. 'I don't think the police take this kind of thing seriously.'

Mrs Sugden remained undaunted. 'Well I will take it seriously if I'm under Madam Alma Turner's roof. Believe you me, I will leave nothing unexamined. And here's one more for you. Because where do you say Felicity is? In a boat with her sweetheart. Well, listen to this. "In sailing boat to stow away, Longing for a wedding day". Now tell me the police won't be interested.'

It was time to bring some order to proceedings. 'Thank you, Mrs Sugden. Now, Rosie. Mr Sykes, what do you suggest?'

Sykes took a breath ready to speak. Mrs Sugden had not finished. 'Which officer suspected you of wielding a toffee hammer, Mrs Shackleton?'

'It's not something we should take seriously. He's the local sergeant, being over-keen. Before that the bee in his bonnet was the whereabouts of Alma's husband, whether they were still married, whether he was alive or dead.'

Sykes once more was about to speak but Mrs Sugden's eyes lit up. She leaned forward in her eagerness to make a point. 'Then it's obvious. This sergeant is in love with the prophetess. He's under her spell. Any little thing that will shift her out of the line of guilt and he will seize it.'

We all three stared at her, marvelling at this genius leap. She had something. When Sergeant Garvin had found me on the cliff, he expected to see Alma, not to arrest her, but to warn her, to protect her. 'I'm glad you'll be coming to stay at Bagdale Hall, Mrs Sugden.'

And now it was Sykes's turn, at last. 'I'll find out what kind of life the jeweller led when he wasn't selling his wares.'

'How will you do that?' Rosie asked.

At that moment, I remembered the tickets I had bought for the bazaar and sale of work. This would be a perfect way to include Rosie and an ideal time and place for Sykes to do some of his clever undercover investigating. I delved in my bag, took out the tickets and handed two to Rosie and one to Mrs Sugden. 'I know this event will go ahead because it's too late to let people in the outlying districts know.'

Rosie took the tickets eagerly. 'Oh yes! This would suit me. Look, Jim. It's a bazaar and sale of work in aid of seamen.' She had forgotten about saying she would stay in Robin Hood's Bay.

Sykes nodded. 'It'll be a useful mingling opportunity.'

Rosie stood. 'I'll write a note for the girls and leave them an egg salad.'

Sykes took out his notebook. 'Is there anyone in particular I should look for?'

'I'm not sure. I bought the tickets from the assistant in Dowzells newsagents, the shop next door to the jewellers. I don't know her name.'

'Someone from the shop next door sounds a

good place to start,' Sykes agreed. 'But you sound doubtful.'

'From her interest in selling the tickets, I'd have said she would certainly be there. I took the impression that she was one of the organisers.'

'But?'

'I saw her this morning as she was going to church and the change was remarkable. She looked utterly devastated.'

'What age is she? What does she look like?'

'Pushing forty, about five feet four, faded blonde curly hair.'

'Wedding ring?'

'No.'

'Any distinguishing features?'

'A few freckles and a mole on her cheek. She wore a Celtic cross on a gold chain.'

'And the newsagent himself, will he be there?'

'At a guess I'd say yes. He came to see me at the hotel yesterday, apologising that he hadn't realised how serious it was when I went into the shop and asked if he had a phone.'

'And he's Mr Dowzell?'

'So I assume.'

'What's he like?'

'Full of himself, hard to tell his age but forties, thinning hair, grey moustache, about five feet eight, portly.'

Rosie was listening intently. 'In what way was he full of himself?'

'Oh you know, a touch of the bombasts. He said he was an ex officio JP and on the Urban District Council. I suppose he's bound to be at this afternoon's event.'

'And the shop next door, on the other side?' Sykes looked at his watch. 'I suppose we should get a move on.'

'It's one of those seaside resort shops that sells knick-knacks, gifts to take home, little toys, that sort of thing. I didn't go in there.' I stood. 'You're right. We should get going. Come on, Mrs Sugden. You and I will catch the train back to Whitby. Mr Sykes, Rosie, let's meet up later at the Royal. I'll book a table for supper and we'll compare notes.'

Sykes picked up Mrs Sugden's bag. 'I'll take this in the car, save you carrying it.'

'No thank you.' She took it back from him. 'I'll keep it by me and then I know I have my necessaries.'

As we left the relative shelter of Martins Row, the wind whipped itself into a temper and brought with it a splattering of rain.

Mrs Sugden tucked her newspaper inside her coat. 'We had us ice creams just in time. I wouldn't want to be on the beach now.'

She was right. I felt a sudden pain around my heart as I thought of Felicity sailing in the cold North Sea. Had I been here just a few days sooner, I might have found out about her plan.

The steepness of the climb and the battering rain meant that we did not talk much as we battled our way up the hill to the station.

Not until we were on the train did Mrs Sugden ask, 'Is there something in particular you want me to look into while I'm staying with your friend?'

I thought for a moment. 'Well, she's in need of company, and reassurance.'

'I'm very good at that.'

260

'Yes you are. I'd like to think she'll be able to get a good night's sleep if you're along the landing.'

Mrs Sugden tucked her newspaper into her bag. 'There's something else, isn't there?'

There was something else and I felt almost treacherous in saying so. 'Alma is very good at "not knowing" and at pretending.'

'In what way, don't you trust her?'

'I'm not sure. At school she was almost too good at amateur dramatics, pretending to be something she wasn't.'

'And now?'

'She made out that her husband Walter is in Madeira and reckoned to be surprised when I said I knew he was in Scotland, and that he and Cricklethorpe had business dealings not entirely above board.'

'What, smuggling?'

'Yes. I haven't mentioned it to Mr Sykes, and won't unless it becomes important.'

'He wouldn't like it.'

'Normally, I wouldn't mind what secrets Alma wants to keep but it irks me that Felicity may have become involved. According to Mr Cricklethorpe, Walter Turner is a very sick man. If Alma doesn't know, she should be told, but I'm reluctant to add to her worries without more information.'

'Where is Mr Turner?'

'Unless Mr Cricklethorpe is also being slippery, Walter is in Elgin. Just out of interest, see if you can find out whether Alma knows.'

'Elgin? That's quite far up isn't it?'

'Yes, it's beyond Aberdeen.' I looked out of the carriage window. Lashing rain blurred the view. A fierce wind made trees shudder. A seaside August in England. God help those youngsters on the high seas in this weather.

Although it offended Mrs Sugden's sensibilities to eat while sitting outside an hotel that was also a public house, the railway station buffet was quite acceptable to her. She ordered tea and a scone with the contented air of a world traveller arriving at a desert oasis.

'You go off and enquire, Mrs Shackleton. Don't mind me.'

'I will, and I don't expect to be long. The hospital's a few minutes' walk away.'

As soon as I left the station for that short walk, my spirits flagged. I could not help but anticipate bad news after the terrible blow that some vicious person had inflicted on Percival Cricklethorpe. How I wished I had offered to go with him when I harped on that he should tell the police his suspicions as to who murdered the jeweller.

The rain had stopped, leaving glistening cobbles and damp pavements. A young family who had been caught in the downpour, hair flattened, coats soaked, went laughing past me unsubdued, the children singing. They were on holiday and nothing would come between them and gaiety.

My steps slowed as I entered the hospital, dreading the possibility that Cricklethorpe's life had ebbed away.

The porter at the desk looked up from his newspaper. He was a gaunt-faced man with thick dark hair greying at the temples.

'My name is Mrs Shackleton. I was with Mrs

262

Turner at Bagdale Hall when we found Percival Cricklethorpe. How is he, and is Mrs Turner still with him?'

'Mrs Turner has gone home, but I will enquire for you.' The porter moved so quickly from his cubby hole that I felt he must be keen to have the latest on Cricklethorpe himself.

So at least he was still alive.

In spite of what Marcus had said about Alma intending to stay with her friend so that he might hear a friendly voice, it did not surprise me that she had been sent home. Matrons do not like friends and relatives cluttering up their wards.

The porter was gone for several minutes. I had expected one of the stock answers, that he was very poorly, or critical, or dangerously ill.

The porter came back walking far more slowly, so slowly that I feared the worst.

He shook his head. 'The patient hasn't regained consciousness. A nurse is with him now.'

'Thank you. I'll call again tomorrow.'

'It must have been a shock for you and Mrs Turner to find him like that.'

'It was. Do you know Mr Cricklethorpe?'

'Not to speak to, but I take the grandkids to the panto every year. He plays a fine dame.'

The porter and I rather optimistically wished each other good day.

It was time for me to introduce Mrs Sugden to Alma. After that, I intended to take a walk to Sandsend. I would enjoy the walk. I had a strong feeling that there would be something for me to find out.

Twenty-Seven

Felicity's stomach churned as the boat tossed on a rip tide. The wind spoke quietly, half-stilled by heaviness in the air. The sea was almost black. Clouds darkened in sympathy, showing just a patch of blue the colour of her father's cravat. She saw the black conical bag flying high on a flag-staff beyond a coastal station, triangle pointing upwards, warning of a gale from the north.

She couldn't get to the side of the boat quickly enough and was sick in the pudding basin. Brendan took it from her, emptied it over the side and gave it back. 'I know. Feels as if you want to die. Stay still.'

She kept her lips tight shut. The least movement brought on a wave of nausea so strong that her body was no longer her own.

'Just drink a little.' Brendan offered her a sip of water. 'We'll make it to Berwick before storm.'

'And if we don't?' She wet her lips.

'Motor gives us a good chance.'

Felicity thought there must be nothing left in her stomach but it heaved again. She filled the basin with a horrible mixture and stumbled towards the side of the boat where she tipped the basin clumsily, spilling vomit on her life jacket.

And then the wind came, tilting the boat, tossing a wave the size of St Mary's church at them with the ease of a child's ball thrown against the wall of a house. There was a tearing sound as one of the sails ripped. An inky darkness blotted out the blue sliver of cravat, turning the sky entirely black. Sudden rain pelted her. She wanted to escape into the bunk even though a short time ago when she had lain there the movement, the shifting and tossing, had turned her innards inside out.

Brendan was speaking to her, handing her a torch. He wanted her to do something, shine a light. She couldn't make out his words but it was something to do with the torn sail and his blessed ropes that he took such pride in. He said the word shroud. She heard it clearly above the din of the wind that was suddenly entirely against them.

He had tethered himself to a safety line and wanted to do the same for her but she wouldn't let him. If the boat capsized and she was tied, she would be under it and no rescuer would help her.

Brendan crawled among ropes and what she loved about him was how much he had to say for himself in such a dire situation, calling out to her words she could barely catch. Jammed. Twisted. Don't worry.

Something changed. The engine had stopped. Under the bellowing of the wind she heard the familiar grating vibration that meant he was trying to coax the engine into life. 'It's flooded,' he called.

In the slowed-down moment before the wave crashed, she saw it bearing down on them and knew this must be how it would end – she and Brendan, clinging together, ready to face eternity.

He pulled apart from her. A bucket had rolled towards him. He began to bail water from the boat. Head throbbing, stomach churning, eyes burning, she began to bail with the pudding basin, wanting to cry, wanting to laugh when he gave her that smile.

And then the wave rose, like a mountain on the move.

Twenty-Eight

Mrs Sugden stood beside Alma Turner, who was showing her the room that Felicity had prepared for Mrs Shackleton. It was beautifully ordered, with a white candlewick counterpane on the four-poster bed, dark polished furniture, and the smell of beeswax.

Mrs Sugden set down her bag. She walked across to the casement window. It was utterly mad of Mrs Shackleton to prefer a stay in an hotel when she could be here. But that was Mrs Shackleton for you. She had brought Mrs Sugden to this astonishing house, introduced her to her friend and hurried off quick enough to shake the devil.

Mrs Sugden was delighted with the room, and impressed by the trouble Felicity had taken over it. She had even put a posy of anemones on the chest of drawers in a tiny blue vase. She took a quick peek in the top drawer and saw that it was lined with clean brown paper. 'It's lovely, Mrs Turner!'

'I'm glad you like it, Mrs Sugden. Thank goodness that it was Sergeant Garvin who searched this room and not one of those young constables who seem to delight in throwing one's stuff about the place. Now do you want to hang up your clothes or shall I show you the rest of the house?'

'Oh, I'd like to see round, please.'

'Then come this way.'

Alma Turner was everything Mrs Sugden had hoped for from the author of *Prophetic Tellings*. She was tall, with hair edging towards auburn, wore a flowing dress and an artificial flower in her hair. Her skin had a translucent quality and her eyes protruded just enough to suggest that she saw more than ordinary mortals. She had an enigmatic quality that might hide a multitude of sins. As Mrs Sugden followed her onto the landing, noting the quick, graceful movements, she could well imagine that this woman might feel quite entitled to hit a naughty man on the back of the head with a small hammer if he led her up the garden path.

The dismay crept up on Mrs Sugden gradually, as she began to notice the cobwebs and, in a corner at the foot of the stairs, a litter of dead beetles. Not all the windows had curtains. Even in the poor light it was obvious that the few curtains were not just dirty but filthy. Mrs Sugden, having agreed to stay, could not back out – at least not immediately – and she was more than grateful to the missing daughter for having cleaned her room. Now that she had begun to look around her with more attention, she saw that the floors had not been mopped since King Dick was a lad.

Mrs Sugden now suspected that Mrs Shackleton had dashed off with wings on her heels not because she was in a hurry to go somewhere but so that she, Mrs Sugden, would feel compelled to stay here and keep company with the grieving prophetess.

The only cheering aspect was that the rain had stopped. Mrs Turner led her into the little courtyard. 'Look, the sun's come out! Take the weight off your feet, Mrs Sugden. I'll make us a cup of tea.'

There was a small wrought iron table and chairs by the wall. The chairs had been tilted to keep off the rain. Mrs Sugden straightened two and sat down to wait. It was a pretty little yard, with a well and pot plants. Someone had kept it tidy. As Mrs Sugden sat waiting for a cup of tea and anticipating a slice of shop cake, she thought that perhaps it was too much to expect that a prophetess, fortune teller and writer of pamphlets would know how to handle a brush and dustpan or have the wherewithal to bring in a cleaner.

The shock of squalor had brushed from Mrs Sugden's memory what Mrs Shackleton had asked her to find out. Ah yes, something about how much Alma knew, about Scotland, about her husband's dealings, and whether that husband was seriously ill.

Mrs Turner emerged carrying a tray, teapot, cups and saucers, milk jug and a plate with three fig biscuits, two with corners missing. Mrs Sugden sniffed the milk from three feet away.

'I'll take my tea black, thank you, Mrs Turner.'

'Very well.' Mrs Turner pushed the plate of fig biscuits towards her.

'I couldn't,' Mrs Sugden made an attempt at showing how very full she was.

Mrs Turner seemed a little more relaxed now

that she knew she would have company. 'I was beginning to feel like a prisoner in there, sitting at the window, hoping for news, waiting to see Felicity stepping into view.'

'It's always good to come out,' Mrs Sugden agreed. 'Perhaps we could go for a walk later, if you feel up to it.'

'Possibly.'

As they drank their tea, Mrs Turner unburdened herself regarding the shock of finding Felicity's note. 'She has given up her job as a waitress in the tea rooms. What was she thinking of?'

Mrs Sugden shook her head. That was a mystery to her, too: at least as a waitress in tea rooms the girl would have had a decent bite to eat in clean surroundings.

When Mrs Turner drained her cup, she stared at her tea leaves in a most intense fashion. She seemed to have slipped off somewhere else in her thoughts. Mrs Sugden remembered that Mrs Shackleton's complaint had been that her school friend was slippery, couldn't be kept on track. She might not be guilty of murder. Having met the woman, Mrs Sugden was ready to give her the benefit of the doubt, but she must have an inkling about the smuggling business.

The best way would be to pretend ignorance about absolutely everything. Make conversation and see what came out.

'I'm sorry to ask this, because I don't know your circumstances, Mrs Turner, but are you a widow, like my boss, Mrs Shackleton?'

Mrs Turner looked up from her perusal of the tea leaves and laughed.

'What's so funny, Mrs Turner?'

'The idea of Kate Hood being your boss, and please call me Alma.'

Mrs Sugden would need to think about that. First names seemed a rather unwarranted intimacy. Mrs Sugden decided on a touch of flattery. 'I suppose it must seem a little odd, me sitting here with you and you a prophetess and a woman of property – this fine house.'

Mrs Turner left the table for a moment, to tip her tea leaves into a plant pot. Perhaps she had disliked their message. 'Kate was head girl, you know – at school.'

'I didn't know, but I'm not surprised.' Mrs Sugden wondered if she should copy her hostess and tip her tea leaves into a plant pot, but didn't.

'Well, joint head girl. A rather dull girl shared the honour because Kate wasn't entirely trusted. A lot of us girls boarded, including me and Kate. When we were in our second or third year, and we were the old hands, we'd see the younger girls, some of them so homesick they cried half the night. If they didn't get over their misery after a day or so, Kate would do a whip round for the fare, take them to the railway station and put them on a train home. Being Kate, she managed to talk her way out of trouble.'

'But she was made head girl.'

'To direct her talent for helping – or interfering as some might see it.'

Alma Turner had avoided the question about whether she was a widow.

The silence stretched.

Finally, Alma said, 'No. I'm not a widow.

Felicity's father and I have lived apart for a long time.' She fell back on what Mrs Sugden guessed was an old explanation. 'He is not a well man and preferred warmer climates.'

Mrs Sugden had always liked geography at school. She tried to remember whether the Gulf Stream made its way to Elgin, forming a mild oasis on the wild Scottish coast. She thought not. 'But he keeps in touch, does he?'

'Not regularly.' She twisted the ring on her finger. 'We haven't heard from him for a long time, so long in fact that I...'

She did not finish her thought. Mrs Sugden did that for her. 'If something had happened to him you would have heard, surely?'

'That's what I thought, and yet I did wonder. In fact, only yesterday I ... you will think this silly.'

Mrs Sugden would be disappointed to think it silly. She had so looked forward to meeting this friend, the talented Mrs Turner, or Madam Alma when in her prophetic guise. 'I'm sure I won't find it at all silly.' She suspected that she might.

'Yesterday, when I was in my pepper pot – that's my little place where I work on the pier – struggling to make sense of everything, I tried my automatic writing, and he came through. He is alive, though complaining about old age. Older than me, you see.'

'That's most interesting,' Mrs Sugden said truthfully. 'Did the police ask you about him when you reported Felicity missing?'

'Not in the same terms that you have asked. Sergeant Garvin is a sensitive man in many ways. But he had previously probed about Walter. Now he seems more concerned about my sources of income, under the instruction of some horrid chief inspector.'

Mrs Sugden tut-tutted sympathetically. 'A person's life isn't her own any more. There's always some busybody wanting to know this or that. Tell me, was Mr Turner in the habit of staying in touch with you and Felicity?'

'He would send a card to Felicity on her birthday. He put in a five pound note each time, no matter where in the world he was.'

Mrs Sugden was impressed by people who travelled for reasons other than making war. 'And where in the world was he?'

Mrs Turner smiled. 'Oh, Portugal at first, for a few years, and then Madeira. That's where the cards came from. That didn't seem so far away, but then it was somewhere in South Africa.'

'How extraordinary that he was able to find English five-pound notes in all those places.'

'Then it was Dublin and Belfast. I didn't tell Kate all this because I know she'd think me a fool for not cutting him off or knocking him into shape.'

'Goodness me, all that travelling and you living in an Elizabethan hall...' Lost for words, Mrs Sugden shook her head at the marvel of it all. 'And five-pound notes showering in every birthday, wherever he was in the world.'

Alma was in her stride now, distress temporarily forgotten. She leaned forward, she chuckled. 'Believe it or not, the only place from where he didn't send an English five pound note was Scotland. He sent a fiver drawn on a Scottish bank!'

'Never! That's the Scots for you. I expect it was one of their well-known banks or she might have had difficulty cashing it, the Bank of Scotland was it, or the Edinburgh Bank?'

'No it was not.' Alma laughed.

Mrs Sugden decided to invent some currency of her own. 'I once had a pound note from a little bank in the midlands and I can't tell you how many places turned it down.'

'You are right, Mrs Sugden, you are right. Crickly – that's Mr Cricklethorpe my co-owner of the house – changed this one for sovereigns. It was drawn on the Elgin Bank.'

'Well, well, well.' Mrs Sugden shook her head. 'I am so glad I came here. And I suppose that must be a wishing well.'

'It might well be. People do sometimes throw in the odd coin.'

'Well then I will too.' Mrs Sugden took out a penny. She threw the penny into the well and heartily wished that she had changed the subject quickly enough for Alma Turner not to notice she had admitted that Mr Turner was indeed in Elgin.

There were tea leaves in the bottom of Mrs Sugden's cup and to her untrained eye they took the shape of an elephant. 'What do you make of that?' Mrs Sugden pushed the cup towards Alma, waited, and listened patiently to talk of a letter that would come from a relative.

Mrs Sugden walked to the plant pot and tipped in the informative tea leaves. It must be time for a change of scene. She delved in her pocket and took out the tickets for the charity bazaar. 'Now do you fancy a walk up to this event in an hour or so, Mrs Turner?'

Mrs Turner put her hand to her mouth. 'Oh, no! I'd entirely forgotten.'

'What?'

'Crickly and I, poor Percival who lies between life and death in a hospital bed and the matron wouldn't let me stay...'

'Well they don't. They have to get on with their work.'

'We are meant to be doing a reading in the Captain's Room, a dramatised reading from Mrs Gaskell's *Sylvia's Lovers*.'

'Oh dear, I haven't heard of that one.'

'It's set in Whitby you see and it's not for general consumption. It's a special event for academic ladies from Leeds. What am I to do?'

Mrs Sugden could not at first think what to suggest. She watched as her companion went through various stages of distress, putting her head in her hands, biting her lip, pulling a face.

'You have great talents, Madam Alma. Mrs Shackleton told me you were a whiz at amateur dramatics in school. You are an authoress, a teller of fortunes and a writer of prophecies. Just think for a moment, and I'm sure the answer will come to you.'

Mrs Sugden watched the effects of her words. At the reference to amateur dramatics and fortunes, Alma Turner's shoulders softened and dropped a little.

Mrs Sugden waited. Surely in such exalted company the suggestions need not come from her.

'I'm at the end of my tether, Mrs Sugden. I can't think.'

'But you can recite, I'm sure, you can read. Do you have the novel to hand?'

'Yes. The passages are marked and I have slips of paper in the appropriate pages.'

'Then you can do it, or if you really cannot then the performance could be cancelled. People would be disappointed, but they would understand.'

Mrs Turner took a deep breath. 'You are right. The late and lamented Jack Philips made the Seamans Mission his charity. I can do no less than play my part, as a tribute to his friendship and his memory. Wait here!'

She went inside and returned moments later with a book. 'I will do a rehearsal. You may be my audience. If I can prevail upon your kindness, after the performance would you be so kind as to stand with a hat by the door?'

Mrs Turner took several deep breaths and did a chewing exercise, moving her lips and cheeks in a most rubbery manner, and then she began.

As she spoke, Mrs Sugden noticed a police sergeant come to the gate. He was about to step inside, but he paused, watching and listening, rapt with admiration.

At the end, he applauded.

Mrs Turner feigned surprise at seeing him. 'Sergeant, what is it? Do you have news for me?'

'No news yet, Mrs Turner. I came to make sure you are safe and sound and locking your doors.'

'That's kind. Mrs Sugden, this is Sergeant Garvin. Sergeant, my guest, Mrs Sugden.'

They exchanged how-do-you-dos.

'I am glad you have company, and I'll be keeping an eye. You are valiant, Mrs Turner, to go

275

ahead with the reading at a time like this.'

She gave a brave smile. 'Shall we go, Mrs Sugden?'

'Yes.'

'Not before you lock the door, ladies. I want to see you do it.'

Alma smiled. 'You are a tyrant, Sergeant Garvin.'

'I am a police officer, Mrs Turner.'

She locked the door.

He tipped his cap, and was gone.

The two women set off, Mrs Turner clutching the Gaskell novel. 'I suppose it will take my mind off things to do the reading.'

'Yes it will. I'm sure Felicity would be sorry to think of you worrying. When she comes back, you'll be able plan how to go on. It must be difficult, living in a place that could do with an army of staff.'

'*If* she comes back. For all I know she and Brendan have eloped.'

It was a pleasure to Mrs Sugden to walk towards the harbour and take in the view of the abbey. She was glad to be staying by the sea and not chugging back to Leeds on the train. 'I did notice there was an elopement in one of your prophecies.'

'Was there? I tend to forget what I've written. It doesn't always come from me you see. I am the instrument through which the prophecies come.'

'This prophecy concerned a boat.' It was no surprise when Mrs Sugden saw the harbour that Madam Alma would have at least one prophecy featuring a boat.

'Then I was more exact than I could have

276

imagined. For all I know she and Brendan have eloped and I'll never see her again.'

'Oh you will. She'll come back. There'll be no finer antidote to romantic illusions than being cooped up in a small boat privy to another person's bodily functions and irritating habits.'

'She is too young to be irritated by others' habits, except mine.'

'Mark my words, she'll be back quicker than she went.'

'Do you think so?'

'Well that's my own prophecy for what it's worth.'

'My powers desert me, what with the worry about Felicity and the attack on poor Mr Cricklethorpe. If only he were here now.'

'You'll do the reading wondrous well, I'm sure, and do him proud.'

'Then there's the shock of Mr Philips's death – I had such hopes of that gentleman you see.'

Mrs Sugden could not be doing with this. Things happened. Life was unfair. There was no point in moaning about it. 'You'll excuse me if I speak plainly, Mrs Turner.'

Alma Turner shot her a quick shrewd look, saying, 'You've spoken plainly so far, Mrs Sugden. I expect that's why you and Kate get on.'

'All I was going to say was this, Mrs Turner: women of a certain age, in which I include myself and Mrs Shackleton and you, we have to look to our own future.'

'I do.'

'Be sad for that poor man's death, but think of yourself and your daughter. You weren't engaged to be married to Mr Philips or any such thing. Look to your future, and your daughter's. That house of yours could be a palace. I'm under strict instructions from Mrs Shackleton not to clean, but there is nothing to stop you from bringing in a couple of strong-armed young women to give the place a bottoming.'

'They would want to be paid.'

'Then pay them, or offer accommodation in return.'

'We can't get help locally. The house is said to be haunted. The only time there were live-in servants was when girls with no say were shipped in from a Catholic orphanage. I couldn't be doing that.'

'Something must be done.'

'People always say that. I suppose human beings have said that since they were in the caves. Something must be done.'

'You can't wait for life to put itself right. You have to get on with it.'

'That's easy to say. I had such hopes. My fortune was so definite.'

'You must help the future along, nudge life in your direction.'

'How? I expected to be living in a bungalow at Sandsend.'

She glanced somewhere off to the north and as she did so, a thought struck Mrs Sugden. There were certain women who would always need a man to rely on, and here was one such who thought herself the half of a whole. Was she gazing north to Sandsend, or to Elgin? Wherever it was, no one would be gazing back. Here was a woman who would go on waiting. She would wait for her knight in shining armour to ride along the beach on his snow-white steed.

Mrs Sugden felt like telling her to pull up her socks and get on with it. She also felt a stirring of pity. Pity won, and then a thought struck her. 'That nice, attentive Sergeant Garvin, is he wed?'

Alma stopped still, as if she had come up against a brick wall. 'No. He lived with his mother, and she died.'

'Ah, I just wondered.' And then Mrs Sugden feared she may have said the wrong thing. Sergeant Garvin clearly had a soft spot for the prophetess but no member of the constabulary would be allowed openly to associate with a married woman, and a fortune teller.

They had turned off to the left. Lots of people were going in the same direction and just as great a number crossing the bridge. 'My pepper pot is along here. We have a little time before my reading and I would show you inside but there's Mr Dowzell and his wife. He's on the Urban District Council and might suspect me of flouting the by-laws regarding Sunday closure.'

Mrs Sugden looked at the couple that Mrs Turner had indicated. He was a round, pompous-looking man. She was done up like a dog's dinner in a fur coat that should only be worn when there was a letter r in the month.

I'm glad it's Mr Sykes who'll be dealing with that pair, Mrs Sugden thought to herself.

Twenty-Nine

It had not been the best of drives from Robin Hood's Bay to Whitby. Rain pelted against the windscreen, blown by a high wind. The rain eased off as Sykes drove down the main street, heading towards the centre.

Rosie sat beside him, finely turned out in the green dress and coat that had to be called aquamarine, the making of which had turned the house upside down for a week. She peered out of the window. 'This is Bagdale, look out for that house.'

'You look out for it!' Sykes's attention was on suicidal pedestrians dashing across the road.

'It's there, on our right.'

Sykes slowed down and turned his head. He saw more than an Elizabethan house, he saw money. It was as if every leaded window reflected sovereigns. True, it was in a shabby condition but that is what a crook would want people to see. 'I'm not a crook really. I can't afford to fix the roof.' Sykes, ready to suspect everyone, thought Mrs Shackleton had fallen in with a den of thieves.

At the bottom of the hill, Rosie instructed him to turn right. Since his wife had an unerring ability to make wrong guesses about direction, Sykes took the left turn.

Being with Rosie made finding the way through a strange place a simple business. He would simply do the opposite of whatever she suggested.

'You could be right,' Rosie said, as the crowd thickened.

'Well I'd better stop or I'll be mowing down the population.'

Sykes parked the motor. They climbed out. This was a strong-smelling spot that on weekdays must be the open-air fish market.

A gull perched on a covered stall watched them. 'It's Sunday,' Sykes told the bird. 'You'll have to do your own fishing today.'

In reply, the gull flew across to the car and left a message on the roof.

'Ask it where this sailors' hall is when it's at home,' Rosie advised. 'I thought it would be back where we've come from, and that it'd be a long low building. I pictured it in my mind.'

They walked behind an old woman in her long dress, a child on either hand. A younger man walked beside her, toddler perched on his shoulders. The little one wore the man's bowler hat which covered its face. A little further on, people were turning left.

Rosie nudged him. 'They're all off to our event.'

'You're uncanny, love. You have a sixth sense for people's intentions.'

'Don't rub it in that I fall down in the finding-my-way stakes.'

When they turned off the Pier Road, a fine brick Georgian-style building came into view with porch entrance, twin pillars and many windows.

They edged their way round the waiting crowd for a better view.

A placard outside announced:

Summer Bazaar and Sale of Work
In aid of Seamans Mission
2 o'clock Grand Opening

A smaller hand-written sheet drawing-pinned to the board read:

Leeds Ladies College Event
Dramatised reading from Mrs Gaskell
Captain's Room 3 pm

A length of red tape stretched across the entrance of the building. Four people on the steps of the building formed an official-looking welcoming party.

From left to right Sykes studied a man in naval uniform with the stripes of a commander, doubtless a person with a local connection. A couple in their more than Sunday best, he perhaps a Whitby worthy, fine of girth and good at throwing back his shoulders, she overdressed in a fur coat, interested Sykes. The man matched Mrs Shackleton's description of Dowzell, the newsagent. He was about five feet eight inches tall, with a small moustache, dressed in a navy striped suit and wearing a grand watch-guard that befitted his girth. His wife, she must be his wife, had suspiciously white-blonde hair and wore a small green hat. Her fur coat was open and revealed a green dress with some sort of lace.

Alongside this glossy pair hovered a faded female who gave the impression of wanting to be anywhere but here. Sykes came to the conclusion that she could be the shop assistant, described by

Mrs Shackleton. She wore a plain black mourning dress and a small black hat.

It was left to the naval man to begin proceedings. He consulted his watch and then addressed the waiting crowd.

'Good afternoon, ladies and gentlemen, boys and girls, and a particular welcome to all who are visiting our fair town. We are here today to raise money for the most worthy cause of the Mission that aids seafaring men and their families. Mr Dowzell will say a few words shortly. But first, some sad tidings. Many of you will have heard announcements from the pulpit this morning regarding the sudden and unexpected death of Mr Philips the jeweller. It is my duty to ask that we remember him now with a moment's silence.'

People bowed their heads as the moment's silence began. Sykes observed the woman in black. She looked as if she might collapse. The woman in the fur coat must have sensed that too because she unceremoniously nudged her into the corner so that she was jammed between the fur coat and the wall.

When the silence ended, Mr Dowzell took a deep breath. 'Good afternoon all. As the commander said, we are here today to raise money for those who risk their lives at sea. Thank you to the ladies and gentlemen on the committee, represented here today by my sister, Miss Dora Dowzell.' He glanced at the woman in black. 'They have worked tirelessly to provide an afternoon and evening that in its variety will satisfy all manner of tastes including a cornucopia of exciting goods followed by a special concert. This evening, the Whitby Quartet will provide music for dancing. To those who think dancing on the Sabbath should not be allowed, be assured we have a special dispensation.'

He waved his arm and summoned a trio of clergymen from their hovering spot. They said nothing, but stepped up and smiled in benign unison. The audience applauded.

Mr Dowzell continued. 'It now only remains for me to ask Commander Whitehorn to do the honours.'

The commander produced a large pair of scissors. 'I declare this most worthy of events open.'

He reached forward and cut the red tape.

The crowd applauded.

On the instant, two girls leaped from the crowd, each grabbing a piece of the tape before dodging round the dignitaries and through the door.

The commander stepped aside to let Mrs and Miss Dowzell lead the way.

Sykes took Rosie's hand. They nipped smartly up the steps and through the door. It was a grand building with several rooms off from the entrance hall and a wide staircase that led to a landing with a huge stained-glass window. Whitby took its obligation to seafarers very seriously.

'What do we do?' Rosie asked

'You keep an eye on Miss Dowzell. Talk to her. I'll flatter Mr Dowzell.'

'What do I say to her?' Rosie whispered.

'Anything at all. Find out who she's in mourning for. It's odd that the brother and sister-in-law aren't wearing black.'

'That's a bit of a sensitive point on a first meeting.'

'You'll think of something.'

Mr Dowzell had already disappeared. Sykes went into the large room that was given over to goods for sale. On trestle tables were laid out scarves and gloves, tea cosies, antimacassars, crocheted doyleys, costume jewellery, and rather a lot of Whitby jet.

Sykes caught sight of Mrs Dowzell fondling a pin cushion.

Just as he thought that this room packed with tempting items would be a magnet for shop-lifters, Sykes spotted a girl slipping a small ornament in her pocket. She was one of the kids who had snatched a length of the red tape to take as a ribbon. Sykes made a start towards her before reminding himself that he was not here to impose law and order. The girl was about twelve or thirteen. No, he was not here to police the room, but if he didn't, who would? He kept the child in view. She wore a primrose-coloured dress and a straw bonnet. As he came closer he saw that her dress had conveniently large pockets. Barely moving his lips, he spoke to the top of her head. 'Put it back and no more said.'

She froze.

'Do it now. And just remember, you've been spotted. Next time you'll be up before the magistrate.'

She did not turn to look at him and he wondered whether this was out of fear of showing her face or seeing his. Her hand went in her pocket. She walked back towards the table that held costume jewellery and knick-knacks. He stayed close until she had replaced the item.

Sykes spotted his prey. Mr Dowzell was roaming the room, nodding and smiling at the women, patting men on the back, shaking hands. Every inch the politician, Sykes thought. Mrs Sykes had said he was an ex officio justice of the peace, due to his position on the Urban District Council.

After several rounds of circulating the hall, Mr Dowzell left by another door. Sykes followed him into a back room that served as a bar. When Mr Dowzell made for the counter, Sykes took the opportunity to join him.

'A fine opening.' Sykes offered his hand. 'Congratulations on a splendid event. Jim Sykes, here from Leeds for a fortnight in Robin Hood's Bay. What's your poison?'

Mr Dowzell named his poison and Sykes ordered two pints.

The barman pulled their drinks. 'It's a cause close to our hearts, this Mission.' Dowzell watched as the barman tipped the glass and ensured a fine head of foam.

'I've no experience of being at sea,' Sykes admitted, 'but have a lot of respect for seamen.'

'My elder brother was a navy man, lost his life in the war.' Dowzell took a deep drink. 'That's why my sister has made this her charity. She and the womenfolk work year round to make this and the Christmas event a success.'

'She was with you on the steps, for the opening,' Sykes said. It was sometimes helpful to state the obvious, oil a conversation along.

'She was, along with my lady wife.'

286

Sykes could think of nothing to say regarding the lady wife that would not sound impertinent. He fell back on one of his many aunts. 'I had a spinster aunt who wore black all her life for a brother lost in the Boer War. Does she always wear black, your sister? Is she mourning your brother still?'

'Ah no.' Dowzell took another gulp at his drink. 'The minute's silence, I didn't stress this because ... well we are here for people to spend money, and enjoy their day, but...'

'But?' Sykes prompted.

'The man we held the minute's silence for, Mr Philips, he had the shop next door to my newsagents. Dora took it hard. You see if it was robbery, which the police suspect, then it could have been us, and she's in the shop on her own, insists on it, likes her routine of fetching in the papers each morning.'

Sykes let out his breath in a puffing sound. 'How shocking, and in a peaceful place like Whitby. It must have been a hard choice to go ahead with today's event.'

'We have great support locally. People come in from the outlying districts. We even have stalwarts from Middlesbrough, where my wife does her shopping. That's why it wasn't possible to cancel today.'

'It's one thing to have a tragedy off your shore and another for a man to be attacked in his own shop.'

'I'd rather not talk about it, Mr Sykes. The police don't want rumours spreading and they're still investigating, you see. Scotland Yard are here.'

'Really?' Sykes's eyes widened. 'Who would

have thought it, eh?'

Dowzell did some nodding, but said nothing.

'You're more than a newsagent, Mr Dowzell. You know Whitby inside out I should think.'

'I do. I'm on the Urban District Council and an ex officio JP.'

'Because of your council office?'

'Yes, not everyone understands that. Are you a council man yourself?'

'I'm thinking of standing next year.' Sykes drew on one of the histories that he kept for just such an occasion as this. 'I've moved from insurance into the motor trade. There'll be a time when every other man you meet will have a car. I want to be the one who sells them.'

They talked of cars and motorbikes while Sykes tried to get the measure of the man. It was hard to dig beneath the surface gloss. Sykes now saw the bottom of his glass. Dowzell had not offered a refill. It would be better to retreat and trade on the acquaintanceship at a later time. He could always pop into the shop tomorrow.

With a regretful sigh, Sykes placed his glass on the counter. 'Better go and find the wife before she accuses me of abandonment.'

'You won't let me buy you one?' the newsagent said, with certainty.

'Another time. And my condolences on the loss of your neighbour.'

They shook hands.

Mr Dowzell saw someone he knew in the corner and ordered a pint to be brought to him there.

Sykes went back to the main room where he had left Rosie.

There was no sign of her, or of the captain or of the commander, or the young girl with the nimble fingers and big pockets.

He wandered about the tables. There was a display of the famous Whitby jet, or at least black beads and brooches. He could not tell the difference.

'Is it jet?' he asked the woman behind the table.

'Oh yes. It's all been donated for the sale, and all genuine.'

He remembered hearing that some jet was better than others but since this woman may have been one of the givers and all the pieces were modestly priced, it seemed churlish to enquire about the quality. He chose a pendant for Rosie, and necklaces for the girls, feeling pleased at his thoughtfulness.

He put the pieces in his inside pocket and then went in search of Rosie.

He spotted her in the refreshment room, on the wrong side of the counter, selling cakes. She reached across the table to take money from a stout woman with several children in tow, the tiniest ones hanging onto her skirt.

Transaction completed, Rose spotted him and raised her hand. He walked over to her. 'Hello. Making yourself useful?'

'As soon as I got chatting to that poor woman, I knew she ought not to be here. She should be home in bed.'

'You're talking about Miss Dowzell?'

'Yes. I don't know how Mrs Shackleton ever saw her as vivacious. She's like a poorly ghost.'

'Where is she now?'

'Gone into that room marked Private for a glass of water and a sit down. She was unsteady on her feet. I told her she should go home and I'd mind this table while her helper turns up.'

'Did you have chance to say much to her?'

'No, but you will. I said I'd ask you to walk her back home. She lives above her shop. It's on Skinner Street, wherever that is.'

Sykes had to control his glee. He tried not to bounce with excitement as he thought about seeing the shop next door to the deceased jeweller's. 'What did you tell her about me?'

'I told her you'd been on the force, and that if anyone would see her safely back it would be you.'

'Did she mind the idea of being walked home by a stranger?'

'She preferred it to the idea of facing her brother. He would insist she stayed, this being her main charity.'

'Will you be all right till I get back, Rosie?'

'Of course I will. As long as you do get back.'

'And if it comes up again, let's get our story straight. I told her brother that I left insurance and I'm in car sales.'

He waited while Rosie took the money for three cream buns.

She gave change to her customer. 'Well then before you went from insurance to car sales, you were on the force. That's easy to remember.'

There was no one else in the room marked Private, only the woman with the lined face, faded blonde curls showing below the small black hat that was held in place with a jet hatpin. She had sunk deeply into a battered armchair. Her black dress was decorated with cat hairs. She sat with her knees apart, making a hollow of her dress between her thighs. In this hollow, she rested a half-empty glass of water, cupped between her hands. In the instant before she became aware of him, her whole being bore the marks of utter dejection.

She looked up.

She had not been crying, or at least her eyes were not red-rimmed but blue-grey pools of emptiness.

'Hello, Miss Dowzell. I'm Jim Sykes. You spoke to my wife.'

She pressed the empty water glass tightly enough to break it. 'I'm all right. It was kind of her to offer, but I'm quite capable of getting home.'

She looked capable of doing nothing.

'I'm sure you are, but I have my orders. Would you like more water?'

She released her hold on the glass. 'No, no thank you.'

He took the glass from her. 'I believe you organised this event.'

She looked at him as if he had come from somewhere far off and spoke a different language.

He tried again. 'Do we drive, or walk?'

She noticed fluff among the cat hairs on her skirt and attempted to stroke it away.

'I'll be all right. I just need to go home.'

A coat stand stood by the door. Sykes looked at it and picked up a black mac. 'Is this yours?'

She stared at the mac. 'It must be.'

He put the mac over his arm, waiting. She didn't move from the chair. 'It's fortunate for the

Mission that this is your choice of charity.'

'My brother was lost at sea. Choice doesn't come into it.'

Coming from the West Riding where people always said our brother, our mam, our sister, it was strange to hear both Mr and Miss Dowzell say 'my brother'. Sykes wondered whether this was the way of speaking here, or whether there was a rift between brother and sister that was marked in their speech.

'I'm sorry. It's hard to lose a brother or sister.'

She made a move as if to go but seemed to lack the strength to push herself out of the armchair that swallowed her.

He reached out to her, thinking she would shun contact. She let him take her hands in his and allowed him to draw her to her feet.

As she withdrew her hands, Miss Dowzell seemed for a moment unsteady. 'I'm not myself today. A slight dizziness.'

'What about a cup of tea and a bun?'

'I've drunk enough tea to launch a battleship. It's just the thought of... I have steps to climb or a longish walk round. It's really nothing, but today...'

'You don't feel up to it.' Sykes helped her into her coat. 'You must let me walk you home.'

She hesitated.

'Miss Dowzell, you will be doing me a favour. I could do with a breath of air.'

'Very well, if your wife won't mind.'

'It was her suggestion.' He smiled. 'Is there a side entrance?'

She nodded, but pulled her arm away from him

as he tried to steer her by the elbow. 'I don't want anyone to see that I'm under the weather.'

'Then you lead the way. I'll follow.'

Sykes stayed a few feet behind her as she moved towards the exit. He watched as she walked as steadily and determinedly as a drunk trying to prove herself sober. What did Philips's death mean to you, Sykes wondered? Was he more than the shopkeeper next door?

In the side hallway of the building, people stood about in small groups, chatting, smoking, standing with a cup of tea or a pint. No one turned to look at Miss Dowzell as she made her way to the door. It was as if she did not exist. Sykes drew one or two looks himself. It was because he was a stranger, he told himself, and certainly not because he looked like a policeman, or a former policeman. He was wearing a brown suit and brown brogues. That was not very policeman-like.

The outer door was open to let in air. What struck him was this: Miss Dowzell drew no attention to herself. People did not notice her. This could be because the crowd gathered near the door were holidaymakers, not locals, and had no reason to notice a middle-aged woman in a black mackintosh with a small and rather pathetic hat perched on dull curls. Or it could be that here was a woman people just did not notice. She could go into the jewellers shop as if invisible. The newsagent was next door to Philips's shop. There would be a back entrance. All she had to do was tap on the door. But why would she do that? What motive might she have for killing the jeweller? Perhaps she was entirely what she seemed, a blameless spinster who devoted her life to good works and her adopted charitable cause.

Or perhaps she was a murderess, engulfed with remorse.

Thirty

It was time for me to act like a person who is really and truly on holiday and take a walk along the beach. The newsagent's assistant had suggested I walk to Sandsend, and had recommended the Sandsend café.

Trying to clear my mind of everything that had happened since my arrival here, I made my solitary way to the beach, glad that the rain had cleared. Blue and grey fought for the sky.

It cheered me to see that I was not the only lone individual on the beach. An elderly woman sat in a deck chair, reading. A man, trousers rolled, carrying his shoes, paddled his way through the waves. A couple of solitary individuals walked dogs, which made them somehow more acceptable.

This was just the right sort of walk. I kept to the damp sand and the pebbles but told myself I would come back in the morning, take off my shoes, and feel the sand between my toes.

By the time I reached the hamlet of Sandsend, I felt so much better and could almost pretend, if briefly, that nothing bad had happened.

Passing the café that the shop assistant had

mentioned, I decided to walk on a little further. A shelter and a bus stop stood not far from the café, perhaps a stopping-off point for charabancs.

It was somewhere not far off that Jack Philips had his bungalow. It was sad to think of poor Alma looking through the windows, imagining herself mistress of an up-to-date house with modern conveniences. We all have our dreams.

A family of ducks waddled over from the stream on the left. They crossed and re-crossed the road in front of me, as if insisting upon their right of way. Perhaps the road had once been a stream, too, and they were instinctively acting out some ritual of their duck forbears.

On the other side of the stream were houses, and a couple of bungalows. I veered off and walked the path that ran parallel to the stream. There was a church on the right, so plain and simple in style that it was difficult to say how old it must be. Like so many churches roundabout, it was called St Mary's.

The car parked just ahead was an Alvis, the type used by some police forces. My father had something similar. This could be a coincidence, but it might also mean that Marcus or one of his men were nearby. That was not surprising. They would be bound to question Jack Philips's neighbours.

Just out of interest, I would take a look at the bungalow, and then make my way back to the café. A little bridge crossed the stream. As I walked along the bridge, I saw a uniformed policeman emerge from a bungalow. So that was the house that Mr Philips was having decorated.

Perhaps if he had been at home here instead of staying above the shop, he might still be alive.

All the gardens were beautifully kept. In the three that I passed, were similar flowers and bushes. This was the kind of place where people gave cuttings and seeds to their neighbours. There was forsythia, jasmine, buddleia, berberis and fuchsia. They had withstood the battering rain and now drew bees and butterflies.

The police constable who had emerged from the bungalow now stood at the front gate. How sad that Mr Philips wouldn't see his cottage garden again. It was in full bloom. The constable was watching me. He gave a nod. 'Lovely garden, eh miss?'

'Yes. Beautiful.'

There was a nameplate on the gate. *Doram*. The same name as Jack Philips's boat. Previously I hadn't thought about the significance of naming a boat. There must be some thought behind the choice.

'Do you know why the house is called *Doram*, constable? It seems an odd name.'

'You have me there, miss.'

It would not be random but named for a loved one, or a hope or a dream. *Doram*.

As we were speaking, a woman came from the direction of the back of the house. Both he and I were taken by surprise at the loud voice of the thin-as-a-stick young woman in dark dress and bonnet, announcing in a foghorn voice that broke the quiet of the overcast afternoon, 'Back door's locked!'

The constable looked concerned. 'You shouldn't

be trying doors. Chief Inspector is in there.'

She pushed by him to the gate. 'I must be let in.'

'You're not allowed.'

'I want to know what's happened to his cat. I've been all round Mulgrave Woods calling his name. Has he turned up?'

'I don't know about a cat, missis,' the policeman said.

'Well is he in there? Only he might be frightened and hiding.'

'There's no cat.'

She took a deep breath and drew herself to a greater height. 'Officer, I'm the cleaner and I ought to know. He comes and goes through the bathroom window so I can tell you for sure a cat lives here.'

I should have walked on, but didn't. It occurred to me that she might know why the house and boat were called *Doram*.

Marcus appeared in the doorway. He glanced at the man in uniform and the woman in the pinny and then looked at me.

How annoying! He would think me a ghoul and a gawper, a nosey parker. He would suspect me of investigating when I was doing nothing more than taking a stroll and admiring the gardens.

Should I stay, or go? To go would look like fleeing. Marcus gave a friendly nod as he came along the crazy paving path, as though seeing me at the dead man's bungalow was only to be expected. It then would have seemed rude to continue on my way so I loitered while he, the constable and the young woman exchanged words.

Marcus said, 'It's Mrs Bailey, isn't it? We have your statement.'

The woman looked pleased that he remembered her name. 'You do, and you have my fingerprints.'

'So what is it you want, Mrs Bailey?'

'I want to go in there and look for Mr Philips's cat. It might be frightened and hiding with all this going on.'

'There's no cat. The house has been searched and all the windows are closed.'

'Then where's he got to?' She launched into an account of where she had looked, and where her children had looked.

'Just a moment.' Marcus came across to me and drew me out of hearing distance. 'Do me a little favour, Kate?'

'What?'

'You're good on cats.'

'Am I?'

'You found that black one, didn't you? The one that belonged to the woman in Bridgestead.'

I was surprised that he knew, and that he remembered. 'Yes but...'

He smiled. 'Talk to her, reassure her. The cat's probably taken to the woods but I don't want her tramping about, distracting my officers and trying to get into the house. She's already asked me who's going to pay for the cleaning she did last week.'

'Well if you think it might help I'll talk to her.' I pretended a slight reluctance though secretly I relished the thought of finding out more about this bungalow and its occupant.

'Thanks, Kate. You must let me give you supper

when this is over.' He turned to walk back to Mrs Bailey.

Marcus went back into the garden. 'Mrs Bailey, this lady occasionally helps the police with their enquiries.' He paused so that I would pick up the humour of his reference to my having been kept in a cell overnight. He continued. 'Mrs Shackleton would be very happy to take details of the missing cat. The constable will let you into the garden, you two can sit on the bench and you can tell her all about it.'

The constable duly held open the gate and led us up the garden path. He gallantly dabbed at the wet bench with his large white hanky. Mrs Bailey showed much pleasure at having my personal attention. The rain had sharpened the scent of hollyhocks and wallflowers.

'Tell me about the cat, Mrs Bailey.'

'Mr Philips was very fond of that cat. Had him since a kitten. He's from my cat's litter you see so I don't want him to come to harm.'

'Of course not. Can you describe him?'

'He's a bonny fellow with tigerish markings, brown and black, dainty little prick-up ears and marmalade eyes.'

'What age?'

'Five years old, same as my little boy.'

'And what's his name?'

'Tiger.'

I did not need to write down this information but thought it would look better to do so and took out my notebook. 'Thank you. Let's hope it's not too long before we find him. And talking of names, do you happen to know why this bungalow and

Mr Philips's boat are both called *Doram?*'

'Do you know, I never gave that a thought. All the times I've stepped through the gate and not wondered, and here you are straight away wondering about the name of the house. I expect that's why you help the police with their enquiries.'

'And have you cleaned for Mr Philips long?'

'Oh about six years, coming in most days. I'll miss him, and I'll miss the work.'

'Mrs Bailey, I don't suppose you know of anyone who might be interested in doing some cleaning at Bagdale Hall? Only I know there's superstition locally about the place being haunted.'

She laughed. 'Haunted! What nonsense. If they pay a proper rate I'd clean it myself.'

'Would you? It's a big house.'

'Then I'd get my sister to come along.'

It was selfish of me, but the last thing I wanted was for Mrs Sugden to take a look at the Bagdale Hall kitchen and catch the next train back to Leeds, leaving me to cope with Alma.

'Well that's very good of you. Write down your address and what days you'd be free to come and we'll send word.' I handed her my notebook and pencil. When she had finished writing, I said, 'It must have been difficult cleaning in here with all the work, all the decorating.'

'Oh we managed. One room at a time you know.'

'Mr Philips had plans I believe.'

'He did, and it's a tragedy that his life was cut short.'

'I heard he might be taking a wife.'

She nodded. 'That's what folk were saying.

Don't ask me who. She wasn't from Sandsend I can tell you that. We all knew him, you see.'

The day had once more grown overcast. A dark stain spread across the sky with its threat or promise of rain. Well, let it rain. But as I walked back from the bungalow, the heavens opened and it was not just rain. As I crossed the little bridge, hailstones began to rattle down, pelting me in the face. Even the ducks had abandoned the road. I hurried back to the Sandsend café. It was closed.

Head down, I sought the roadside charabanc shelter. Rain I could bear, rain I could enjoy, but these hailstones must have been cast in iron for the torture of those foolish enough to take an English seaside walk without benefit of raincoat, galoshes and umbrella.

I was still sheltering, sitting on the bench, soaked to the skin, when the Alvis glided into view. Through the torrent, I could make out Marcus in the back. The car stopped. The last thing I wanted was to be transported like a lame duck back to Whitby, but it was that or catch pneumonia. Marcus got out. He unfurled an umbrella and crossed to the shelter.

'Care for a lift?'

'I won't say no.'

We crossed back. He opened the car door.

I slid in, dripping rain across the back seat. 'Thank you.'

'My pleasure, Kate. Ducks shake themselves, if that helps.'

'I'll spare you the shaking.'

'Not been your ideal holiday so far, has it?'

301

'At least try to keep the amusement out of your voice.'

He made a solemn face. 'Where are you heading?'

'Back to the hotel.'

'Wise choice.' He spoke to the driver, asking him to drop me at the Royal.

As we drove along the coast road, I cleared the misty window with my glove and looked out at the waves lashing the shore.

Marcus wanted to say something. I could hear his brain ticking.

'What is it, Chief Inspector? Are you going to ask me to keep my nose out of police business?'

'I don't entirely mind your nose.' He paused. 'I'm not sure... This is for your ears only, at present.'

'All right.'

'The coastguard boarded the *Doram*. Your god-daughter and her friend were heading for Lindisfarne. They stayed there an hour or so and then went on, in spite of being advised against it.'

'Couldn't they have been stopped?'

'Brendan Webb told an old fisherman they were going to Scotland to see Felicity's father.'

'That's what I thought.'

'There's no law against that. I only hope for her sake that's all she and the Webb boy are planning to do.'

I took off my wet hat and ran my hands through my hair. Rain drops slid down my back. 'I wish they'd been stopped. Look at it out there, Marcus! Two kids in a small boat in this.'

'Let's hope they know what they're doing.'

Thirty-One

The person in Felicity's skin didn't feel like herself at all. She was still alive, with the pudding basin in her hand. Brendan clung to her. The boat was flooded and sinking. She could feel it sinking. Instead of a quick blotting out of life it would be a slow freezing end. Every inch of her hurt. If she moved she would die. If she didn't move she would die.

He shoved a bucket into her hands. 'Keep bailing. Tide's taking us in.'

She tried but began to retch, and tried again. Somehow she filled the bucket and threw its contents overboard, and the wind threw it back.

Brendan bailed so hard that she could see the crack in the bottom where the water poured in.

Finally, the bottom of the boat began to scrape. The crack in the wood widened. Felicity felt too dazed to understand at first and then realised that they were almost ashore. Brendan undid his own tether to the safety line and turned to do the same for her. She had been too sick to notice that he had tied a rope to her when she refused. They half-stepped, half-fell into thigh-deep water.

The men who came spoke in broad Scots, like the men who brought their boats south. There was a dark-dressed woman, too, who looked like one of the girls who followed shoals of herring around the coast and came to Whitby and Scarborough in the summer, to gut and to salt. Their voices washed over Felicity. She felt sick and weak, waves and voices pounding her brain, not letting her take in the words.

When Felicity looked out of the cottage window, she saw her clothes hanging on the washing line. She was sitting in front of a fire, wearing a coarse blue dress and wrapped in a man's overcoat and a blanket, though she couldn't stop shivering. A young woman with black hair and red cheeks, who was able to do all sorts of jobs with one hand while holding a baby, gave her a basin of hot water to soak her feet and a cup of broth to warm her hands and belly. 'I'm Barbara,' she said when Felicity told her own name.

Felicity's money belt was on the fireguard, drying. 'Where are we?'

'By Scremerston. The men saved your stuff.'

After she had washed, Felicity brought out face cream from her knapsack. She rubbed the cream onto her face that was red raw from wind. She pushed it across to Barbara. 'Try it. My friend works in a hotel. Someone left it behind.'

'Where ye gannin'?'

'Elgin, to see my dad.'

'How will ye gang there noo?'

'I'll walk.'

Barbara laughed. She pointed to the money belt. 'Catch a train from Berwick.'

Felicity's brain came back to life. 'How far are we off Berwick?'

'No distance.' She set the sleeping baby in the cradle and sat down to examine the face cream.

'Who's yon laddie to you?'

'My intended.'

'He has it in mind to mend the boat.' She shook her head and tapped her forehead with her finger. 'It's salvage, pure salvage.'

Thirty-Two

Miss Dowzell clicked open her back gate. 'Thank you, Mr Sykes. It was good of you to see me home.' She took a breath, ready to wish him goodbye.

Sykes put his hand on the gate. 'My wife would give me gyp if I didn't see you safely in.'

'Very well.'

It struck Sykes that it would be a brave woman, or man, who would not be cautious after what had happened in the shop next door.

They took a few strides across the paved yard, passing the outside privy, the crate of empty pop bottles and a battered dustbin that smelled of ashes.

She fumbled for a key in her mackintosh pocket. 'There was a time when none of us locked our doors.' The key began to shake in her hand.

Sykes thought it best not to notice. 'Have habits changed with the influx of visitors?'

'Whitby isn't what it was when I was a girl.' She mastered the key and unlocked the door.

She was at least talking now, on her home ground. People are so trusting, Sykes thought. For all she knows my wife could be the bait and me the man who comes from behind with the hammer.

Suddenly she seemed to lose her nerve and stepped back giving the impression that she wanted him to go into the house first, perhaps to check that there were no intruders.

Sykes opened the door and stepped inside, holding it for her, looking about. She followed.

They were in a scullery kitchen, with a Belfast sink with single tap, cupboards and a gas ring. Once she was in, he put the chain on the latch. 'Will you let me put the kettle on?'

She had opened the door to the room between the scullery and the shop. This must be the mirror of the room where Mrs Shackleton found the body of the jeweller. Sykes noticed the dark oak sideboard, above which hung a print of Holman Hunt's *The Light of the World*. On the opposite side was the fireplace and oven, though no fire burned. Miss Dowzell had not answered his question about the kettle.

She spoke to a cat that sat in the rocking chair. It was a strange-looking creature with tiny pointed ears, a flat face and black and brown markings. As she stroked it, the cat stood, arching its back and tilting its head.

Everywhere there were signs of the newsagent business. Boxes of wine gums and boiled sweets stood on the sideboard alongside lollipops and cigarettes. Stacks of magazines and comics that must be ready for display or to be returned to the publisher unsold took up much of the table space. Sykes glanced at bills from wholesalers.

He asked again. 'Shall I put the kettle on?'

'Something stronger for me, I think.' She opened the sideboard door. 'Will you join me?'

'Yes. Thank you.' He had not expected to be offered alcohol. It would be sweet sherry.

The cat watched as she took two glasses from the cupboard. A woman of surprises. It was brandy. Here was someone who shared Mrs Shackleton's philosophy. In time of need, reach for the brandy.

'Medicinal.' She handed him a brandy balloon. 'Won't you sit down, Mr Sykes?'

She sat in the rocking chair, lifting the cat onto her lap. It jumped down and strode away. Sykes took the chair opposite. It was low with a padded seat and a straight back that tilted when he leaned against it. 'You have it cosy here.'

'I'm used to it. We lived here with my parents.'

'Are they still alive?'

'No. Just my brother and me left now, and his wife of course. You will have seen him at the opening ceremony.'

'Yes, he and I met.' There was a long silence. He decided not to mention that he had bought her brother a drink. 'I expect you are on good terms with the other shopkeepers along the row, Miss Dowzell.'

It was the wrong thing to say. She gave him a sharp look. 'Who are you really?'

'I'm Jim Sykes.'

'And were you a policeman?'

'Yes.'

'Are you still? Are you one of the men from Scotland Yard?'

'No, on both counts.'

'Do you write for the newspapers?'

'No, and I'm not here to pry.'

'I think you are, but I would like to know why, if you are not with the police.'

There was something about her, so direct and candid that it disarmed him. In the force, he had often had to break bad news and see the shattering depths of grief but there was something else in this woman, a kind of despair that made his skin itch. She should be wrapped in a blanket and given a hot water bottle. Rosie should be sitting with her, or Mrs Shackleton. She would be more likely to talk to them.

He felt the awkwardness of his situation, investigating but not officially. For once, no glib story came to mind. The truth would have to do.

'I'm here on holiday, at Robin Hood's Bay. When not on holiday, I work with an enquiry agent or private detective called Mrs Shackleton. She had the misfortune to find Mr Philips yesterday.'

'I see.' Miss Dowzell rocked her chair. 'She came into the shop afterwards but said nothing to my brother. I had gone out for air.'

He could not read the expression on Miss Dowzell's face but her hand gripped the glass more tightly. 'Is she the lady who bought postcards?'

'I don't know. She bought tickets for the sale of work.'

'I remember her. Tim, my brother, said she acted oddly.'

'It's absurd but she briefly fell under suspicion.'

She put down her glass. 'As did I, and am under suspicion still for all I know.'

Sykes could well understand why this woman would come under suspicion. He must tread carefully. Strike a wrong note and she would clam up. He took a sip of brandy. 'I think Mr Philips's death touches you more than most.'

'You are right.'

'You called him Jack earlier.'

She closed her eyes, tightly enough to fight off tears. 'We understood each other. He and I were born in the same year, the same month, two days apart. The midwife who attended his mother on the 15th of April came to my mother the following evening. We knew each other, through and through.'

'You loved each other.' Sykes surprised himself. It was as if the words had come from someone else, from Rosie, or Mrs Shackleton.

'Sometimes I blame myself for how Jack's life turned out.'

'In what way?'

'Oh, that he thought marrying someone else might hurt me. Something came between us, something huge. I sometimes wondered whether he dallied with other women and disappointed them only because I had refused him. Ever after that, he was the one to leave some woman mystified. He made a fine art of it.'

'Why did you refuse him?'

She stared into her glass and something changed. She did not look at him. 'My parents needed me. This business needed me. It was their income, and mine.'

For the first time, Sykes thought she was not being truthful. Marrying a jeweller might have been a reasonably safe financial course of action. A jeweller's wife might provide for her elderly parents. Other difficulties would easily be resolved. 'But you have a brother. You run the shop together I believe.'

'The business came to me. My brother was away at the time. And now my brother has a wife and a son. The business keeps us all.'

'The business came to you, the daughter. That's unusual.'

'All families are unusual in their different ways.' She stood. 'Your wife will think you've got lost. Thank you, and give her my regards.'

As Sykes stood, the bundle of last month's magazines on the table caught his eye.

'Is there anything I can do for you before I go? Are these returns to go outside?'

'Yes. There's a cover to keep them dry. You could carry them into the shop doorway for me.'

They walked through into the shop, Sykes carrying the magazines. She unshot bolts and turned a key.

He set down the magazines in the doorway. 'What time do the papers come in the morning?'

'Five o'clock.'

'Will anyone be here to help you?'

'I'm used to it.'

'But your brother...'

'He comes in later in the day, usually in the afternoon, for an hour or so.'

They went back through the shop to her living room, the little scullery and then into the yard. She looked such a lonely figure, standing at the gate. He still could not make up his mind. Had

310

she carried a torch for Jack Philips all these years, regretted her decision to refuse him, resented his women, and finally taken revenge?

Thirty-Three

As I thanked Marcus for the lift back to my hotel, and got out of the car, the doorman came to meet me with his sheltering umbrella.

Discreetly, he pretended not to notice that I resembled a drowned rat. 'There is a party of persons waiting for you in the library, madam.'

'Would you do something for me please?'

'Of course.'

'Enquire at the hospital whether there has been any change in Mr Cricklethorpe's condition.'

He gave me a look that struggled to be neutral. 'I will, madam.'

I would be garnering a fine reputation here. I find a body. I befriend, or am befriended by, a chambermaid who then changes floors to avoid me. I stay out all night helping police with their enquiries. I enter Bagdale Hall where no one has come to harm in the past several hundred years and Mr Cricklethorpe is severely attacked. Now I come in dripping and have a reception committee of Mrs Sugden, Sykes and Rosie.

I had arranged to meet them in the library at five and it was past five. I popped my head around the door. There the three were, along with a heavily whiskered old gentleman who nodded over the pages of a newspaper.

My three were engaged with a jigsaw puzzle, a country scene with one of those idyllic thatched-roof cottages that in real life would be both plagued by damp and easily ignited. I apologised for keeping them waiting. 'I won't be long. I'll just go upstairs and change.'

Sykes thoughtfully offered to order me a hot toddy.

Within twenty minutes I was back in the library, having booked a table in the restaurant. The elderly gentleman had departed so the library was ours. We were free to compare notes as to what we had uncovered during the afternoon.

Mrs Sugden did not wait to see who should go first. 'That friend of yours, Alma Turner, she knows very well where that husband of hers is. He's in Scotland. She gave it away without realising, saying how wherever he was in the world he always sent an English five pound note to Felicity and the only time he didn't was when it was a Scottish five pound note. And I know it was recent because she came to that part of her tale last and the note was drawn on the Elgin Bank.'

'So why would she keep quiet about that?' Rosie asked.

I gave a quick glance at Sykes. Mrs Sugden, Rosie and I might be willing to turn a blind eye to the Turner and Cricklethorpe connection with contraband whisky. Sykes was a different matter. For now I would keep to myself the suspicion that Cricklethorpe at least had made a great deal of money from the connection, and that Jack Philips may have been helpful in ensuring that not too

312

much ready money was kept in Bagdale Hall by providing precious gems in exchange for cash. At some future date, Cricklethorpe might travel to another town and sell the jewels that Mrs Webb had sewn into the pantomime costumes.

Perhaps I would need to tell Sykes about this, but not yet.

I answered Rosie's question. 'Alma kept quiet about her husband because she doesn't want to think about him. I believe there's no doubt that Felicity has gone to find her father, but why now? I can only think it's because she and Brendan had access to the boat, the *Doram*. That's also the name Jack Philips gave to his bungalow.'

'What does the name mean?' Mrs Sugden asked.

'I don't know. But I'm worried sick about them being in that boat. The coastguard had them in their sights, and now they haven't.'

Rosie touched her hand to her heart. 'And that storm today. It doesn't bear thinking about.'

Sykes attempted nonchalance, picking up a jigsaw piece and slotting it in. 'Why is the coastguard keeping them in sight? If it was to do with the suspicion of stealing a boat, or knowing something about the murder, they'd bring them in.'

'For safety reasons,' I suggested. 'They're young and inexperienced. Nobody would want to see them come to grief.'

Rosie chipped in. 'Why didn't Felicity just tell her mother? Just say, "I'm off to see my dad."'

I hesitated. Would Sykes also feel obliged to denounce the wayward Walter Turner as a bigamist? Doubtful, but I decided not to take the chance. 'Perhaps Felicity wanted a quiet life and Alma

313

might have objected. She has reason to be angry with her husband. I was a witness at their wedding. I won't go into details but she should never have married him.'

This piqued interest from Mrs Sugden and Rosie. I could see that each of them had instantly come up with a catalogue of sins committed by Walter Turner.

There was that slight flicker of Sykes's eyelashes that indicated he would from now on be alert to any tiny detail that would allow him to find out the reason for Alma's anger, and the interest of the coastguard. I could see by the look in his eyes he knew that I was putting them off some scent.

'Anything else, Mrs Sugden?' I asked.

'Your friend Alma Turner is most definitely after a husband. Now that the poor jeweller has gone to meet his maker, she'll be on the look-out. She's one of them women who has to have a man at her side.'

Sykes's jaw did not exactly drop but his mouth opened long before he spoke. 'How can she be looking for a husband when she's married? What about Mr Turner? Whatever he's done, they're still wed.'

There was a pause, a long pause. No one commented on Sykes's question.

Rosie broke the silence. 'The husband is well out of the picture. But here's the question, did Alma Turner end up disappointed in love? So disappointed by Jack Philips that she did him in? Might she have slipped up to the shop?'

Mrs Sugden thought not. 'She wouldn't have

314

given up hope so quickly. She's more likely to have cast a spell, or despatched a rival, than kill the man.'

It was my turn. 'What about the assistant from the newsagents? From the way she looked this morning, I don't suppose she turned up for the sale of work.'

Sykes and Rosie exchanged a look. Rosie was a picture of sympathy. 'That poor woman, and she's not just the assistant. She's Miss Dowzell. She did come. Jim walked her home. She has taken Mr Philips's death very hard.'

Sykes was slow to speak. 'She's one of the few who will miss him. There was a minute's silence for him this afternoon, and no one shed a tear or said a word of regret.'

I felt annoyed with myself. 'Why did I jump to the conclusion that she was the assistant?'

Sykes tried not to look superior. 'You'd no reason to ask her name and rank when you bought postcards. She's Dora Margaret, the owner. I saw her name on some correspondence.'

Rosie touched her husband's arm. 'You took a bit of a shine to her, Jim.'

'I did not. I pity her. She looked exhausted. That brother of hers swans into the shop in the afternoon. The rest of the time, as far as I can gather, he goes about being self-important, the councillor and ex officio justice of the peace, too tight to buy a pint for a chap who buys one for him. Miss Dowzell is up every morning to take in the newspapers and there she is, all alone, only a cat for company, in a shop next to where her friend was murdered.'

Something in Sykes's words was niggling, some connection, but what? 'You say they were friends?'

Sykes took out a cigarette. 'She's not an unattractive woman. There was a moment when she was nursing the cat. It stood and turned itself around to adopt a more comfortable position. She tilted her head and gave the brightest of smiles. She and Jack Philips had been close all their lives. She turned him down when he proposed because something came between them. She said it was something huge.'

'What?' Rosie and Mrs Sugden both spoke at once.

Sykes lit his cigarette. 'I've no idea. Some other woman probably. I daresay Dora Dowzell was well out of it.'

It was one of those moments when we came to a full stop. I was tired and could not quite pull together the various strands that were emerging. Sykes knew that Miss Dowzell must be a suspect and yet was reluctant to acknowledge that fact.

Mrs Sugden had no such hesitation. 'This puts a different slant on the business. If the jeweller wronged Miss Dowzell, perhaps she's simmered for years. She might just have had enough and done away with him.'

'Why now?' Rosie asked.

'Because Alma Turner cast her spell on him.' Mrs Sugden waited to be contradicted by Mr Sykes. He said nothing. Mrs Sugden continued. 'Alma Turner might be a good fortune teller and prophetess, and she certainly put on a fine performance reading from a novel this afternoon, but there's not a bite of food in that house. I don't know what she lives on. I'm not surprised her daughter has taken to the high seas.'

'What is the relevance of that contribution?' Sykes spoke sharply.

'I'm only saying that I don't know what Jack Philips saw in Mrs Turner.'

It was time for me to help us focus, if I could. 'We are not here to judge anyone, or even to find who did the murder. I just want to know that Alma and Felicity aren't involved, and try to work out how to find Felicity. We all seem flummoxed so let's hope that Chief Inspector Charles does a reasonable job.'

'Have you spoken to him?' Sykes asked.

'I walked along to Sandsend to take a look at the bungalow. Marcus Charles was there. He was friendly enough, though in retrospect perhaps a touch sniffy.'

Sykes surprised me by speaking his mind about Marcus. He had never shown any feelings about him before. 'I never liked that man.'

'How was he sniffy?' Rosie asked.

'There's a cat missing. Mr Philips's cleaner came while I was there, enquiring whether anyone had seen it. Marcus very smartly said she should describe it to me.'

'And did she?' Sykes asked.

'Yes.'

'Is anyone else hungry?' Mrs Sugden gave a sigh. 'Only I haven't eaten since that scone in the railway buffet.'

'Well I've booked a table in the restaurant so we can go in if we're all ready.'

Mrs Sugden and Rosie decided they would go

to the ladies room.

Sykes pondered the jigsaw puzzle for a moment. 'This missing cat of Jack Philips, how did the cleaner describe it?'

'Black and brown, flat face, little pointy ears.'

'Did she say its name?'

'Tiger.'

'Miss Dowzell has it.'

'That's strange. It couldn't have found its own way to Skinner Street from Sandsend.'

Sykes agreed. 'So either he took it to her, or she went to fetch it when she knew he was dead.'

That was when it struck me, and Sykes too. He spoke first. 'Dora and Jack. Dora Margaret. *Doram*. He named his boat for her.'

'And his bungalow.'

Sykes stubbed out his cigarette. 'So what was the "something huge" that came between them?'

The age of the bungalow, the age of the boat, the age of the boy, all pointed in the same direction. 'The "something huge" was that when Jack was courting Dora, he got someone else pregnant.'

'That's a bit of a leap, Mrs Shackleton.'

'Brendan Webb, Felicity's boyfriend, is Jack Philips's son. Miss Dowzell must have known that. It might have been a last straw for her that Jack let his son take the boat that was named for her.'

'Miss Dowzell did it,' Sykes said. 'That's what you're thinking.'

'I don't know. When I saw her on Saturday, she didn't look like a woman who had just committed murder.'

'She may have been pretending it didn't happen. After you found the body, she had to face up

318

to what she'd done.'

'Do you believe that, Mr Sykes, or are you putting the case for the prosecution so that I'll knock it down?'

'I don't know. But I'll find out. I'm seeing her in the morning.'

We walked towards the dining room. The doorman spotted me and came across. 'Sorry to say there is no change. Mr Cricklethorpe is still unconscious.'

Thirty-Four

Jim Sykes took Rosie a cup of tea at half past four. She turned over, pulled up the eiderdown and declined his invitation to go with him to the newsagents in Whitby.

'Jim, I'm on my holidays and it's the middle of the night. Go away!'

'I'm going to give Miss Dowzell a hand with the morning papers.'

'Don't be sticking your sneck in where it's not wanted. She'll have her own friends.'

Jim wasn't so sure about that. There were no friends in evidence yesterday. 'Well don't let your tea go cold.'

She would. He could see that by the slant of her shoulder.

He looked in on the girls. Sleeping. Sleep was an enviable state but Sykes would rather be up and doing.

319

Dora Dowzell was a damsel in distress. His emotions puzzled him. He did not normally feel such pity, but there was something about the woman that touched him. His aunt Harriet had kept a shop, all on her own, day after day, year in, year out. It was only after her death that he realised what courage it must have taken, what energy and staying power. They had all thought her wealthy when she left one hundred and twelve pounds between her nieces and nephews. Now he understood how she must have striven to keep up those habits of hard work and thrift.

If Miss Dowzell had murdered Jack Philips, he must have driven her beyond endurance.

When he arrived at Skinner Street, the shutters were down and the door still bore its Closed sign. The Monday morning newspapers, tied with string, had been left in the doorway.

He glanced up and saw that the curtains were drawn. Sykes found his way round the back and entered the yard.

There was no chink in the curtains at the downstairs window. He felt a sense of panic. The woman had been so distressed that he feared for her, yet she was made of stern stuff. It was not that he imagined she would harm herself, more that she might turn her face to the wall. But there was the cat.

If she had gone to the trouble of visiting the bungalow and bringing back the cat, how had she done it, he wondered? Was it the kind of cat that would drape itself around her neck, or be carried under her arm? Perhaps she took a carton. Carrying a cardboard box with a cat would be heavy and awkward for her. She was thin from overwork yet must be strong from heaving parcels of newspapers about.

If he made too much noise, the neighbours would be alerted and it would be difficult to explain what he was up to. They might be suspicious if he said, 'I'm a total stranger, here to help Miss Dowzell because I think no one else will.'

Whatever had been between Dora Dowzell and Jack Philips, they had kept quiet about it. Quiet enough for Mrs Turner to think he might be her very special gentleman friend.

Just as Sykes wondered what to do next, the cat appeared in the window, looking out at him. Feeling rather stupid, he tapped on the pane. The cat stared.

He went back round to the front of the shop. The papers were still there, untouched in the doorway.

This is silly, he told himself, and walked back round to the yard.

Now the cat was sitting on the outside wall. Either it had found a way out, or Miss Dowzell had opened the door for it. He knocked on the back door.

A voice called, 'Who is it?'

'It's me. Jim Sykes, from yesterday. I'm here to help as I said I would.'

'I'm not opening the shop today.'

'Then at least don't leave the papers where they are, otherwise someone will be calling the police, or your brother.'

A long silence ensued.

Sykes did not want to alarm her by knocking

again, but he sensed that she was behind the door. 'Miss Dowzell, just bring the papers in and add something to the Closed sign. Closed due to bereavement. People will understand. They'll respect you for it. They won't interfere.'

No answer.

Sykes tried again. 'I was a newspaper boy. You'll have a lad coming to take out deliveries. If he doesn't, people will be round asking for their morning paper.'

No answer.

'I'll fill the newspaper lad's satchel for you, Miss Dowzell. Do you have one lad or two?'

She came to the window, hair undone, wearing a dressing gown. She pointed, and mouthed, 'Go round to the front.'

He did her bidding and then waited in the shop doorway so long that he thought she must have changed her mind. It took ten more minutes before she opened the door.

She was wearing the same plain black dress from yesterday, her hair uncombed.

Twenty minutes later, Sykes had set the kettle to boil on the gas ring, set and lit the fire, and was filling satchels with morning papers. There were two satchels. Both boys would come at seven. She had told him that they knew their own rounds but the papers had to be put in the bags in order.

Having told him what to do, Miss Dowzell watched for a while. 'I'll have to dress.'

'You can leave this to me, Miss Dowzell. I won't make a mistake.'

'Why did you come?'

'A little help is worth a lot of sympathy.'

She tilted her head and gave that sudden smile that so far only the cat had merited. 'I have a lot to do. There'll be arrangements to make.'

'Arrangements?'

She did not expand on her remark but went upstairs. He heard her begin to cry. She was in no fit state to make arrangements, whatever she had in mind.

At seven o'clock when the boys came for the papers, she was again downstairs. Her eyes were red and her cheeks blotchy. He thought she must have been crying half the night.

She poured two mugs of tea from the pot. He had sliced bread from a stale loaf and found the toasting fork. 'You must eat something.'

She did not look at him when she said, 'I'll wait for the boys to come back with their bags and then I'll put the Closed sign on the door.'

He nodded. 'I would offer to mind the shop but you'd have to tell me every price. I suppose you can leave the papers in their rack outside and people will pay you later, or put out an honesty box for visitors.'

The idea seemed too much for her.

'I'll make you a box from cardboard, with a slot. Might your brother come earlier to help? Does he have a telephone?'

'No.' She spoke so adamantly that Sykes did not pursue the question.

'Is there anyone else? Do you have an assistant who could come in?'

'Yes, there is someone. Mrs Broomfield.'

She hadn't thought of this, Sykes realised. That

323

happened when a person was in shock, the simplest ideas, the simplest possibilities, did not occur, like being in a fog or a blinding storm, not able to see the way forward. There was something in her eyes, a kind of blank puzzlement.

He took out his notebook.

'What's your assistant's address?' It was not that he thought the shop should remain open. He simply wanted someone to be with her.

'She lives in Haydocks Place, off Flowergate.'

He handed her the notebook. 'Write it for me.'

Writing and thinking might nudge her back into the land of the living. She should not be nudged. She should be left to mourn, to sleep if she could, or to stare into the fire. But as long as she was alone it seemed to Sykes better that she should do something, come slowly into the day ahead.

It did not take him long to find his way to Flowergate and turn into the yard that was Haydocks Place. Mrs Broomfield answered the door. Her sleeves were rolled above her elbows. There was a smell of soap and her pinny was wet. She pushed back a strand of hair with a chapped hand.

He explained. 'Miss Dowzell is unwell and needs help. She'd be grateful if you would come.'

'I'm washing. I'll come as soon as it's hung out.'

'Isn't there anyone else...'

She cut him short. 'I have a key. I can let myself in if Miss Dowzell needs to lie down.'

Sykes walked back to Skinner Street. He would stay until Mrs Broomfield came. Later, the brother would arrive. When he told Miss Dowzell his plan to stay with her for the time being, she seemed not to be listening.

The cat was back and sat on her lap. Woman and cat stared at the fire.

He repeated his words. 'I'll wait with you until your assistant comes, Miss Dowzell.'

'There's no need.'

He saw that she had dropped a cup. He picked up the pieces and mopped up spilt tea.

She watched him. 'Jack sent me a guardian angel.'

When he came back from putting the broken crockery in the dustbin, he asked, 'Will Tiger be all right here? It would be a shame if he strayed, being used to the bungalow.'

'How do you know he was at the bungalow?'

'The cleaner was worried. Mrs Shackleton said she was asking the police about Tiger.'

'I'll have to let Mrs Bailey know. Tiger won't stray from me.' She stroked the cat. 'Who's Mrs Shackleton?'

She had forgotten that he mentioned her yesterday. 'She came in here on Saturday and bought postcards.'

'Ah, you told me.' She hesitated. 'She found Jack.'

'Yes. She came back here but when your brother told her there was no telephone, she went to the police.'

'My brother said she might have had a hand in Jack's death.'

'Then he was wrong.'

This did not seem to surprise her. 'I had to have my fingerprints taken.'

'It's routine, you being his neighbour.'

'That's what Sergeant Garvin said. Routine.'

They lapsed into silence. There were many questions Sykes would have liked to ask, but she would have been interviewed. It was not up to him to stick his oar into this investigation. Much as he had taken a dislike to Chief Inspector Charles, the man must be left to do his job.

Sykes told himself he ought to leave now.

He didn't.

Nothing happened. The clock ticked. The fire crackled. When the clapper rang as someone entered the shop, it made Sykes jump.

Miss Dowzell stood and walked into the shop. People came, and went. Something in Miss Dowzell's manner subdued even the chatty customers. When someone spoke of the death, or the bazaar or the weather, she said nothing. They went away.

In a lull between customers, she said, 'This Mrs Shackleton, you said you work together.'

'Yes, on investigations.'

'And is she a friend of yours?'

'I like to think so.'

'I can't remember what else you said. I know, you used to be a policeman. You don't look like a policeman.'

Sykes was so happy to hear her say so that he could have kissed her, but didn't.

When the clapper sounded, it was Sykes who went into the shop. He took payment from an elderly man for a morning paper and five Woodbines. It was not hard. He knew the price of cigarettes. Sweet jars were marked. He could get the hang of this.

When the clock ticked towards nine, Miss Dowzell said, 'Your wife must wonder where you are. Mrs. Broomfield will be here soon.'

'I'll stay until she comes.' Sykes chatted to her now and then, telling her where he was staying in Robin Hood's Bay, telling her about Mrs Shackleton at the Royal. He did not mention Alma Turner and her fortune telling, or her designs on Jack Philips.

It took both Sykes and Miss Dowzell by surprise when the brother arrived, hours earlier than his usual time. Bustling in, walking like a crowd. He did not have his elbows out but somehow he seemed to take up a great deal of space.

Sykes expected to be asked to leave.

Miss Dowzell looked at her brother in surprise. 'What are you doing here so early?'

The brother stared at Sykes. 'Who's this?'

Sykes came to his feet. 'Morning, Mr Dowzell. We met at the Mission yesterday.'

'So we did. Why are you here?'

Miss Dowzell's answer surprised Sykes. She did not move from the chair. The cat still sat on her lap. It glanced at the new person in the room, and then half-closed its eyes. 'I asked Mr Sykes to help me with the morning papers.'

'Why didn't you ask me?'

Sykes wanted to say that the brother should not have needed to be asked, but he bit his tongue.

Miss Dowzell did not answer the question. 'Mr Sykes is staying until Mrs Broomfield arrives. After that I have things to do.'

'What things? Where's that cat from?'

'It's Jack's cat, from the bungalow. It's living here now.'

The brother came and stood over his sister, but

he looked at Sykes. 'You can go now.'

Sykes didn't move.

'You need a rest,' the brother, the ex officio JP, said to his sister. 'I'm arranging for you to have some convalescence. I'll take over now.'

'I'm all right.'

'No. You're not. Everyone said yesterday how poorly you look. I've sent for the doctor. You can come back with me and stay with us, and then we'll see. I've found somewhere quiet for you to stay, somewhere restful.'

'Go away. Go home. Nothing has changed as far as we're concerned.'

Sykes felt uncomfortable. He was glad when the clapper sounded and he had the excuse to go back into the shop. The customer wanted a *Yorkshire Post* and twenty Capstan.

When Sykes returned to the back room, he saw that the brother was still standing over Miss Dowzell. The cat stared at the man.

She gazed ahead, and spoke to the air. 'I have to stay here. There's Tiger to think of. And you don't know about the paper deliveries, the lists. You wouldn't be here on time.'

'You're ill.'

'No. I'm sick and tired. Jack's death changes everything and it changes nothing.'

'You're making no sense.'

'I'm making the only sense there is.'

Mr Dowzell became aware of Sykes behind him and turned. He leaned forward, clenching his fists, his mouth forming a snarl. 'Time for you to go.'

Miss Dowzell rose. 'No, Timothy. It's time for you to go. It's over. Everything is over. Don't come back.'

Mr Dowzell rocked to and fro like a man impatient to hear the starting pistol. He looked from Sykes to his sister and back again. For a moment it seemed to Sykes that he would lash out.

He barked at his sister. 'I'll be back. I'll be back with a doctor. I'll be back with two doctors. They'll sign you off and they'll sign you into a nursing home.'

She did not look at him but simply said, in a quiet voice, 'I'd go to no place you would pick.'

'Then we'll see. I'll be back with the police. They'll know who had it in for Jack Philips and I'll tell them why. I'm looking after you. The doctors will say diminished responsibility.'

'Out!' She stood and took a step towards him.

The stalemate broke when the clapper sounded. One of the returning newspaper boys called through from the shop.

'I'll be back!' Timothy Dowzell marched out.

Sykes watched as Miss Dowzell went calmly into the shop and took the satchel back from the newspaper boy.

She was shaking when she returned to the room and stood before the fire.

'What do you want me to do?' Sykes asked.

'I don't know. I don't know what to do.'

'Start by changing the locks. I saw a locksmith on Flowergate.'

She nodded.

'Is your brother trying to have you committed?'

'I think so.'

'Why?'

'This shop is mine, and it's over. Jack and I

decided I'd done enough. Tim won't let go. He could never let go.'

'You need a solicitor.'

'I have a solicitor.'

'Would your brother find doctors to have you sent away?'

'Oh yes. He knows all sorts of convenient people. He knows the police superintendent too. If they don't find someone for killing Jack, they could pick on me. That would suit him.'

'Why would it suit him?'

She shook her head. 'I can't say it. I can't say what I fear.'

She did not need to. Sykes just wished that woman would come, that Mrs Broomfield, that she would leave her washing in the set pot and bustle herself up here.

'Come on, Miss Dowzell. Let's drop the latch and go. You're not up to being bullied by your brother and mistreated by doctors.'

At least she smiled. 'No I'm not. But where can I go?'

'Where do you want to go?'

'To the bungalow, but the police had it cordoned off when I went to find Tiger.'

'Would you like to spend a little time in the Royal Hotel with Mrs Shackleton?'

'I want to be out of my brother Tim's way. I need to think, and I can't.'

'Then come with me. After that I'll go to the locksmith, and your solicitor, and whatever other errand you want me to run.'

'There is one thing.'

'Yes?'

She hesitated. When she spoke, it was with difficulty, squeezing out the words. 'That storm. Jack's boat, the *Doram,* he let Brendan take it. I want to know if Brendan is safe.'

'Where was he going?'

'Up the coast. He didn't say where. What with the storm…'

Sykes almost did not say it, but then he did. 'Brendan is Jack's son?'

She looked at him steadily. 'And mine, though not a word. We haven't told him yet.'

'I'll make enquiries.'

'I'll go mad if we've lost him too.'

First, Sykes went to the locksmith who said he would call within the hour. Next, he went to see the solicitor on Silver Street. The man was in a meeting with a client. Sykes left a note asking him to visit Miss Dowzell, urgently.

He had seen the coastguard station and walked there as rapidly as he could, once more passing the shop, relieved to see that the brother had not returned.

The uniformed coastguard officer was in the back room in shirt sleeves. When he saw Sykes at the desk, he put on his jacket and walked through. Sykes wished him good morning.

'What can I do for you, sir?' There was a practised patience in his voice that told him the man was used to townies arriving and wanting to know this or that just because some grandfather had been at sea or a cousin was in the navy.

'It's about Mr Philips's boat the *Doram.* I'm enquiring on behalf of Miss Dowzell, Mr Philips's neighbour and friend. She's concerned about the young people aboard and whether they've reached their destination.'

'Well then you can put her mind at rest as regards the youngsters. They're unharmed. The boat came aground at Scremerston.'

'Thank you. I'll tell her.'

'You're the second person to ask today.'

'Mrs Webb I suppose?'

'Someone on the east side took word to Mrs Webb.'

'Does Mrs Turner know?'

'She'll know by now. A Mrs Shackleton, Felicity's godmother, was here enquiring earlier.'

Sykes had never met Alma Turner, but he took an instant dislike to her on the grounds that she was the one who should have been here, asking about her daughter. 'Well thank you again. Miss Dowzell will be relieved.' He was relieved himself. 'You chaps do a grand job.'

'Aye, so they say. Good day to you.'

From there, Sykes went back to the newsagents.

His first impression on opening the door was of the number of people present and the thought that it must be a busy time. Then the figures registered. There was the self-important Mr Dowzell, standing to the right by the jars of sweets, arms folded across his chest. Beside him was the assistant, Mrs Broomfield, smelling of soap and washing day.

It had been years since Sykes clapped eyes on Chief Inspector Marcus Charles, but he knew him at once. The uniformed sergeant was unfamiliar to Sykes, but he recognised him from Mrs Shackleton's description as the pleasant man with a collection of fossils. He had a hand on Miss Dowzell's elbow, urging her to come quietly.

She had the wild-eyed-look of a hunted fox.

As she was taken past her brother she gave him a look of contempt. 'What else can you do?'

The brother made an attempt at concern. 'I'll make sure you are seen by the doctor. I'll do everything. You'll have the best defence.'

His eyes told a different story. The eyes shone with triumph.

Miss Dowzell glanced at Sykes as she was led away, half-beseeching but also defeated.

'I'll go straight back to your solicitor, Miss Dowzell.' He risked coming closer and whispered, 'Brendan is safe.'

The chief inspector spared Sykes a cursory glance. 'Mr Sykes, will you go quietly or do I have to arrest you for obstruction?'

It gave Sykes a quiet satisfaction to realise that the animosity and dislike between him and Chief Inspector Charles was mutual.

Any doubt he had as to Miss Dowzell's innocence vanished as he watched her being led away. Marcus Charles had yet again arrested the wrong person.

Thirty-Five

Felicity decided that there was no better place to be than in a train. Going somewhere. Arriving in Aberdeen. Departing Aberdeen. When the carriage emptied, she hung Brendan's gansey and her cardigan from the luggage rack because they were still damp and giving off the smell of wet sheep.

Brendan hadn't smiled once, and looked so pale. Every so often he would repeat his laments in a quiet voice that other passengers had pretended not to hear. Now that they were alone, he could be louder.

'If we'd stayed on Lindisfarne... If I'd asked our Ian to come... How will I tell Mr Philips?... What will he say when I tell him *Doram* is beached at Scremerston?... If I'd been at home I might have mended her...'

'No you wouldn't, love. The Scremerston men were right. It's salvage.'

'How will I pay him back for the boat?'

'We both will.' Felicity felt cheerful now that she had decided never again to go to sea. 'I'll offer to work in his shop, on commission. I'll sell jewellery. I'd like that. I'd be good at it.'

'And what am I supposed to do?' He spoke as if she had already sold several diamond tiaras and he was tramping for work. 'I'll be paying Mr Philips back when I'm ninety.'

'Stop feeling sorry for yourself. What's done is

334

done. We're alive. We're together.'

At last, he smiled. Sort of.

Felicity thought about the three telegrams they had sent from Berwick. She should have asked how long they would take to arrive.

She went over the wording, wondering if it was clear enough and tactful enough. Her mother's first.

Safe and well visiting WT in Hopeman

No need for a name, or a STOP to add to the word count. There was only one WT in the world: Walter Turner.

At Felicity's insistence, Brendan had sent a telegram to his mother, although he knew that by now the mothers would have spoken to each other. Hilda, who had been trying to find out their plans, would have seen to that. His message cost the least.

Am alright Mam

The one that gave most trouble, and almost made them miss the train, concerned the *Doram*. Felicity thought it best that they should break the news to Mr Philips gradually.

Regret storm damage Doram *STOP*
Explanation follows STOP Brendan

Thirty-Six

My breakfast table was by the window. The old black Jowett hurtled into view as if in a race. It came to a stop at the front of the hotel. Sykes leaped out as if the motor was on fire and hurried towards the hotel entrance. Straight away I knew he was not out for a morning constitutional or calling to pass the time of day. I called the waitress and asked her to let the reception desk know that I was here and to send in my visitor, Mr Sykes. I also asked for another cup to be brought and whether the chef might rustle up an additional breakfast. From my quick glance, Sykes looked as though he needed something.

I was breakfasting later than usual because I had visited the coastguard, and then called to tell Alma the good news that Felicity and Brendan had landed (if that was the right word) in Scremerston. We looked it up in the atlas. 'So she is on her way to see Walter,' Alma had said. 'I wish I could ask Crickly what to do about it.'

But Mr Cricklethorpe had still not regained consciousness. We had taken enormous comfort from hearing that he was 'stable', but who knew what unseen damage that blow had inflicted?

I left Alma and Mrs Sugden to the breakfast that Mrs Sugden had made.

Sykes came into the dining room. He was agitated. Rarely did I see Sykes upset. He came

336

across and sat down. I poured tea and pushed the cup towards him. He seemed to relax a little. I recognised the feeling. Sometimes we just need another person to talk to, and something normal to happen. He tonged sugar lumps into his cup, spilling tea onto the tablecloth.

'Have you eaten, Mr Sykes?'

'A slice of toast with Miss Dowzell. I called to help her with the morning papers.'

'Then you must have some breakfast.'

He stirred the tea. 'She's been taken into custody, Miss Dowzell I mean.'

'Has she been charged?'

'Not charged, no, but it looks bad. Whatever else she may have done, I'm sure she didn't kill Jack Philips.'

'Then she'll be released.' It was not like him to be so affected. I tried to say something encouraging. 'So was I taken into custody and kept overnight. Perhaps they make a habit of pointless detentions in Whitby.'

'It's not funny.'

'I'm not laughing.'

'Your good friend Chief Inspector Marcus Charles has taken her in.'

I did not trouble to correct him on the 'good friend' department. My stomach suddenly took against the bacon and eggs and did a small churn. Marcus could be as single-minded, and wrong, as anyone else. But was it possible that Dora Dowzell could be guilty of the murder of Jack Philips? From Marcus's point of view, there would be motive. Naming a bungalow and a boat for the beloved was a fairly definite way of pledging troth. Dora Dowzell then had to watch as Jack spent decades flaunting other women under her nose.

Sykes read my thoughts, or imagined he did. 'She didn't do it, Mrs Shackleton. That boy, Brendan, your goddaughter's sweetheart, he's their child, Philips's and Miss Dowzell's child.'

'How do you know?'

'She told me.'

'I wonder whether that's really so.' It seemed unlikely.

Sykes took a gulp of tea. 'It's true, I'm sure of it. She was concerned about him, saying about the storm and whether he would be safe.'

'His mother is Mrs Webb.'

'That's what the world thinks. But what if that was a convenient lie? Dowzell, the brother, was round there this morning, threatening to fetch a doctor. He was trying to have his sister committed.'

'To keep her from being charged?'

'I don't know. When she stood up to him, he returned with the police.'

'Then he must think she killed the jeweller. He doesn't want her to face the death penalty.'

'She loved Jack Philips. She didn't kill him.'

Love can so quickly turn to its opposite, but now was not the time to say so. It was not like Sykes to be so wholeheartedly on the side of the underdog when the underdog was under suspicion. Miss Dowzell had more reason than most to feel anger and distress, as she watched Philips court Alma Turner.

I began to speak. 'Miss Dowzell could have

done it.' He was about to interrupt me. I held up my hand. 'Just listen to me. We must make sure the police notify her solicitor.'

He rapped his fingers on the table.

'I went to her solicitor, twice. The first time he was engaged and the second time he seemed too casual about the whole business. She needs our help.'

'I don't see what we can do until we know more. We're not investigating the murder.'

'Then we should be. Miss Dowzell wouldn't have bludgeoned Jack Philips and then gone to find his cat.'

'That's exactly the kind of thing a woman on the edge might do. She might also convince herself that Jack Philips's child is hers.'

'I hope you're simply playing devil's advocate, Mrs Shackleton.'

'I'm saying let Marcus Charles do his job. We'll keep our distance.'

'From him? Because it makes it difficult for you?'

'No!' Sykes's remark hit home. Was that why, as long as I was safe, and Alma and Felicity free from suspicion, I wanted nothing to do with the business? But I couldn't let Sykes believe that.

'If Brendan really is her child, that could make it worse for Miss Dowzell.'

'Because a jury would judge her on her morals.'

'Yes. But he's Brendan *Webb*.'

Sykes would not give up. 'King George calls himself George Windsor but everyone knows his name is George Saxe-Coburg Gotha. It's just that folk aren't tactless enough to mention it.'

'Did Miss Dowzell say that Mrs Webb adopted Brendan?'

'No. But you could talk to Mrs Webb. You've met her.'

'Yes I've met her.'

'She's the only person who knows the truth.'

Silence reigned while we glared at each other. He was right that I wanted to avoid tangling with Marcus as he did his job. 'I could try speaking to Mrs Webb. She'll probably tell me to sling my hook.'

Sykes seized on this suggestion. 'Miss Dowzell won't talk to Marcus Charles. He'll be no good at interviewing a woman, especially one as upset as she is.'

He had a point there.

I stood.

'Do you want me to come with you?'

The waitress was bringing a plate towards our table. 'You stay here. I ordered breakfast for you, and don't send it away or you'll put me in the chef's bad books.'

He made the effort of smiling at the waitress and making space for the plate.

'Enjoy your bacon and egg. See that bench across the road?'

'Yes.'

'I'll meet you there after I've spoken to Mrs Webb.' I picked up my key. 'It's possible that Marcus simply wanted to question Miss Dowzell at the station so as to have control over the interview. He could hardly speak to her in the shop with people coming in and out to buy the morning paper and an ounce of baccy.'

'Then why didn't he say so?'

'Because he's a chief inspector and doesn't have to explain himself.'

'You mean because he's arrogant.'

In Clark's Yard, Mrs Webb was pegging out washing, and agreeing with two neighbours that this was not a good drying day.

I had not thought of a good excuse for coming and might have known it would be difficult to speak to her alone. The other women looked from me to her when I said good morning, and then I hit on an idea. 'Mrs Webb, I'm sorry to barge in but Hilda told me you might recommend a good place for me to buy fabric.' It was not the best of stories, but she humoured me.

She pegged a towel onto the line. 'Just along by the old Town Hall. You'll see a stall there.'

'I'll take a look, thank you.'

The towel divided us from her nearest neighbour. I mouthed, 'I need to talk to you. It's important.'

She raised her voice. 'You might want to go up to Middlesbrough if you want a bigger selection.'

'That's a thought.'

'There's a good train service.'

'I'll take a look at the stall first.'

'I'll be along there myself soon. I have shopping to do.'

I left the yard and turned along Church Street where I wandered about the stalls and shops, not seeing, not paying attention.

It was less than half an hour before Mrs Webb appeared. The black shawl covering her head and shoulders made her look older than her years. She carried a basket over her arm and had already made some purchases. A woman called to her. She returned the greeting.

When she reached me, she said quietly, 'All along Henrietta Street.'

She set off. I followed at a distance, passing jet workshops, little alehouses and then the street of cottages. The smell of smoking herrings wafted from the kipper house.

By the time I caught up with her, she stood on the cobbled landing looking out to sea. This part of the beach was quiet. A man, trousers rolled, led his little boy into the waves, the little boy laughing.

Mrs Webb turned to me. 'How is Mr Cricklethorpe, have you heard?'

I gave her the latest bulletin. 'Poor man. I hope and pray he'll come through.'

Usually I am good at phrasing the right question but this morning I somehow could not get my tongue around the words.

Mrs Webb prompted, in a not entirely friendly manner, 'Well, what is it you want this time?'

I must now come to the point, and this felt very awkward. She might just turn and go back the way we had come.

'I'm sorry to ask and wouldn't unless it were necessary.'

'If it's about Brendan and Felicity, they're safe. Sergeant Garvin has called asking about them, and did I know if they had permission to take the *Doram*.'

'It's Brendan I want to ask you about. I'm sorry if my question upsets or offends you, but Miss

342

Dowzell has been taken to the police station for questioning.'

'About whether Jack Philips gave permission for them to take the boat?'

'No. As I understand, she is being questioned about Mr Philips's death.'

She laughed, and it turned into a groan. 'Then she'll have nothing to fear. How can they be so stupid, at a time like this? The woman's grieving.'

I thought carefully about how to phrase my next question. The little boy who was paddling stumbled. His father picked him up and whirled him round. Come to the point, Kate, I told myself. Just say it.

'It must have been difficult for you, as Brendan grew and the likeness to Mr Philips became clear.'

For a moment she watched the father and son walk along the shore, and the boy try to chase a gull, and then she spoke. 'It happens in families. There was a red-haired uncle on my side. No one who wasn't looking for mischief thought anything of it.'

'Your husband accepted Brendan as his own son.'

'I didn't give him a choice. He was a fine man, Vincent, when I married him. But he lost his master's licence. Our income vanished overnight.'

'That was tragic for him, losing his licence.'

'He made a split-second decision. A ship was written off. He never recovered from that episode.' She looked across the bay. 'I thought he'd pulled round. When the *Rohilla* ran aground, he was a hero. He went back and back to bring survivors from the wreckage. I thought he had

343

won back his self-respect. For a week, that held true, then the nightmares came back, all the old nightmares and some new ones too. He drank himself to death in the finish.'

I could not think what to say that would not sound trite and we had moved away from the subject I wanted to discuss. 'I'm very sorry to hear it. Your husband must have been a fine man before he had such bad luck.'

'He was. Strange how lives can turn, just as the tide ebbs and flows.'

I drew us back to the here and now. 'Like Miss Dowzell's life.'

'Yes.'

'My friend and colleague, Mr Sykes, helped Miss Dowzell with the papers this morning.'

'She could do with help, proper help. Mrs Broomfield is a dab hand at weighing out pear drops but not much else.'

'You go to Dowzells newsagents?'

'Yes.'

'There must be a nearer shop.'

'There is a nearer shop.' She spoke so quietly that the noise of the waves and gulls threatened to drown her words. 'I don't go all the time, just sometimes, and just over the last year or so.'

'To let Miss Dowzell know how Brendan is getting on?'

'How did you guess?' Mrs Webb's shawl had slipped from her head. She clutched at it and held it tightly around her shoulders. She turned and walked away. At first I thought she had decided to end our conversation but she said, 'Let's sit on the wall. I've been on my feet all morning.'

We crossed the sand to where a wall ran down towards the sea.

She heaved herself onto the wall. 'I promised. I promised never to speak of it.'

I copied her and sat on the wall. 'Promised Miss Dowzell?'

'No. I promised old Mrs Dowzell, Dora's mother, and the old fellow, her father.' She swung her legs back and forth, touching her heels against the wall. 'It's been a strange business. If I'd known truth from start we wouldn't have agreed, my man and me.'

'Please tell me. It might help Miss Dowzell.'

'Once Jack Philips worked it out, I couldn't deny it. Jack came to me. He'd seen Brendan at Sandsend and he asked his age and his birthday. I've been mother to Brendan in all ways that matter, but I didn't give birth to him.'

'How did you get away with passing him off as your own?'

'I never showed much when I was carrying.' She smiled. 'When I produced him, my neighbour said, "By, you're a sly one!" I told her people fussed too much. Have it and get on, that was what I said.'

'But what about Miss Dowzell, and Mr Philips? They must have wondered what had happened to their baby.'

'Jack Philips didn't know there was a baby. He was in Amsterdam, training with a diamond merchant. Dora, she didn't know she was pregnant until it came on, either that or she shut her mind to it. She had baby in bath. Her mother must have been blind not to see it coming. Perhaps she did.

345

Afterwards, a fever set in. Parents sent Dora to a sanatorium. She was under various doctors. When she asked about her baby, first she was told she'd dreamed it. When she wouldn't shut up, they said baby died. They brought him to me. I hadn't weaned Ian, so I had milk. I was given money to keep quiet.'

'And you did.'

'By the time Jack Philips came to see me, old Mr and Mrs Dowzell had long swallowed the anchor but a secret doesn't die at the grave. First I denied it, put Jack Philips off. But it was no use. Brendan had gravitated towards Sandsend while he was still at school, hung about, messing with boats, calling it helping. He was always up there. I tried to keep him away. Last year, he started to help Jack do up the *Doram*. He'd come back and tell me. There was nothing I could do, except try and keep him busy with something else.'

'What made Jack so sure that Brendan was his child?'

'It wasn't just the likeness, though that was strong. It wasn't just dates of birth, though that tied in with Dora being packed off to sanatorium. What made him sure was a gesture of Brendan's, a mannerism. I'd thought nothing of it. He has this way of tilting his head, and then he'll give a big smile. Jack wasn't to be put off. He said, "That's Dora in him. That's how Dora smiles."' Mrs Webb adjusted her shawl, covering her head again. 'To tell you truth, I resented it, resented Jack Philips and his insistence. All them years I'd looked after Brendan, long after money ran out, and now that Brendan was working age and able to tip up a wage, in stepped Jack Philips.'

'And then what happened, Mrs Webb?'

'Jack asked me all about it. I hadn't known what tale Mr and Mrs Dowzell had fed to Dora and Jack. I really hadn't. When he came back from Holland, Dora was in sanatorium. He visited her. She told him about baby and that he died. Jack felt helpless. He presented her with mourning jewellery, wanted to know where baby was buried.'

'What a terrible lie they were told.'

She nodded. 'And I was part of it.'

'When did Dora Dowzell learn the truth?'

'I couldn't speak of it, not at first. And then six months ago, Jack and I went together to tell Dora.'

'What did she say?'

'Nothing. She just cried.'

'And Brendan?'

'I haven't told him yet. We were waiting for the right moment to tell him. Three weeks ago, Jack came to tell me that he and Dora were going to marry. She would give up the newsagents and they'd live at bungalow. He was having it done up.'

'Would you tell this to the police?'

'Why should I? What does it have to do with anyone else, except me and my kids?'

'Miss Dowzell could be accused of murdering Jack Philips.'

'That's crackers. They wanted to make up for lost time. They've set a wedding date at St Mary's in Sandsend.'

'Does Brendan have any inkling about his true parentage?'

'He always had an idea of being cuckoo in nest. I told him when he first asked me why he looked

347

different from his brothers and sisters. I told him that he had other parents but that I was the one who wanted him. It seemed best thing to say.'

'And now?'

'Jack and Dora promised not to do anything rash, anything to upset me, or to make Brendan take fright.'

'Yet Mrs Turner believed Jack was interested in her.'

'Lots of women did. Once he said good afternoon and smiled at her, Madam Alma Turner was all over him like a bad case of ringworm. He tried to shake her off, refuse her invitations. She was very persistent. I suppose Jack found out my Brendan was friends with Felicity Turner, and Jack didn't want a queer pitch.'

'I wonder why Jack and Dora kept their plans secret?'

She sighed. 'They were about to try again. Perhaps they didn't dare tempt fate by making too much of it.'

'If what you say is correct, someone found out and put a stop to it, but who?'

'I've said enough. I've said too much already.'

Thirty-Seven

Sykes was waiting for me on the bench that gave a wide view of the sea, the West Cliff, the church and ruined abbey. I sat down beside him.

Enforced inactivity and sea air had turned him

348

philosophical. He looked towards the estuary. 'I've never known a seaside with two piers. It's a bit like our situation. There's the estuary between the piers, like the big gap between what we know and what we need to know.'

'The gap narrows, Mr Sykes. I saw Mrs Webb.'

'You were gone a long time.'

'But worth it. According to Mrs Webb, Dora and Jack Philips had planned their wedding at the little church in Sandsend. They had thought their baby dead. When Jack realised that Brendan was their child, the rift between them was mended.'

Ever the practical man, wanting facts and figures, Sykes asked, 'Had they set a date?'

'I believe so.'

Sykes rocked forward on the bench as if about to spring into action. 'That's something to go on. I can drive there, talk to the clergyman, or a verger. She wouldn't murder the man she was about to marry.'

'Wait.' I put my hand on his arm. 'First, don't imagine that Marcus Charles doesn't know this. Second, think about it. Jack was doing up the house in preparation for Dora moving in, and buttering up his son by lending him the boat. What if something went wrong? Say Alma Turner became a fly in the ointment, an irritation to Dora, or a threat, Dora and Jack might have fought about it. Dora could have hit out.'

'Oh no.' Sykes was more adamant than I had ever seen him. 'If that were the case, it's not Jack Dora would have walloped, it's your friend Alma. The rival. If she really was a rival.'

'Mrs Webb thinks not. She believes Alma was

349

pushy and trying her luck. That could have caused Jack and Dora to fall out.'

We lapsed into silence. In other circumstances we might have felt inspired by the view and the freshness of the breeze. But not today.

Sykes spoke first. 'It's a pity you're not on better terms with Marcus Charles.'

'We are on good terms but he won't tell me about the investigation, so forget that.'

We stared out to sea. Sykes tried again.

'He threatened to have me taken in for obstruction, but you could charm him into an indiscretion.'

I had to laugh. 'Me? Do you think Whitby has turned me into some kind of Mata Hari? I don't want to charm him.'

Sykes smiled. 'I know! You could tell him you've located Tiger.'

'What is the matter with you? I shouldn't have interrupted your holiday. Your brain needs a rest. Go back and blissfully wander around Robin Hood's Bay.'

He took out another cigarette. 'There's nothing the matter with me.'

'Of course not. You just don't trust anyone else to do the job.' I kicked at the mound of tab ends strewn around the bench. 'What a mess you've made for someone to sweep.'

He lit his cigarette. 'They'll be glad of the employment.'

'There is no point in sitting here and talking in circles.'

'What then?'

I stood. 'Come on. Mrs Sugden has been abandoned at Bagdale Hall for long enough. And I want to know how poor old Cricklethorpe is doing.'

Sykes began to walk towards his car. 'Cricklethorpe must know something or he wouldn't have been attacked. He only needs to regain consciousness long enough to make a statement.'

'I hope for more than that, Mr Sykes. I liked him.' Straight away it worried me that I had spoken of the dame in the past tense.

Sykes drove the short distance back to Bagdale. 'I'll drop you off, Mrs Shackleton. I'll just call in on Miss Dowzell's solicitor, and see whether he has news.'

Mrs Sugden was sitting in the courtyard at Bagdale Hall, knitting. I was pleased to see that she looked happy and settled.

I sat down. 'Where is Alma?'

'The hospital must have agreed to let her see Mr Cricklethorpe. She went with that intention and hasn't come back.'

'That's a good sign.'

We chatted for a while. She was cheered by the news that a woman from Sandsend was willing to clean Bagdale Hall.

Sykes arrived, looking glum. 'That solicitor is worse than useless. Miss Dowzell said she had no objection to being questioned and he left her to it. I can't credit it. Do you think he's the brother's solicitor as well – some crony?'

'He could be. Mr Dowzell will know lots of people and move in the inner circles.'

Sykes looked at me rather pointedly. 'I can't go to the station. There's no point in me asking to

351

talk to Mrs Dowzell. She wanted to meet you, Mrs Shackleton. She asked about the person who found Jack Philips.'

Mrs Sugden picked up her knitting, maintaining an unusually meaningful silence that signified agreement with Sykes.

They both waited for me to speak. There was nothing else for it. I would fail, but at least I must try.

'I'll go to the station.'

With a bit of luck I might see the sympathetic sergeant and learn how things stood with Miss Dowzell and whether she was charged or simply providing information. Without a bit of luck, I would see Marcus and be appointed to find another cat.

Thirty-Eight

Sergeant Garvin came from the back office to the counter. He greeted me warmly before asking, 'How is Mrs Turner this morning?'

'She's feeling much better and relieved to know that Felicity is safe.'

The sergeant smiled. 'A great relief to us all. Mrs Turner is a plucky lady. She's in her pepper pot I suppose?'

'Well no, I believe she is at the hospital by Mr Cricklethorpe's bedside. The hope is that if he hears a familiar voice it might help his recovery.'

Sergeant Garvin's eyes widened with surprise

and pleasure. 'If anyone can bring him back into the world, she will.' He glanced at his paperwork. 'Now, was there something, Mrs Shackleton?'

'Yes.' It was thoughtful of him to think that I might have come in for a reason other than to sing Alma's praises. 'I believe that you have Miss Dowzell in custody.'

'And you'll understand I can't comment on that.'

'Has she been seen by a policewoman, or a doctor?'

'I can't comment, of course.'

'Of course. Only I believe Miss Dowzell wanted to speak to me and I should very much like to see her.'

'As it happens that lady's sister-in-law is in the station now, with female necessaries.'

That put me in my place. Mrs Dowzell could visit but I couldn't.

He gave a sigh and looked again at his paper-work before relenting and saying in a whisper, 'She won't speak to anyone. Miss Dowzell hasn't said a word.'

The screech came from along the corridor. 'Get her out of here!'

Sergeant Garvin hurried from behind the counter in the direction of the small cell where I had enjoyed a night's rest.

Moments later, a woman in a mauve coat and hat came hurrying into the reception area, clutching her throat. 'She attacked me!'

A young constable tried to detain her. 'Mrs Dowzell, please, wait a moment!'

She fled the premises, calling to anyone who

would listen. 'The woman's mad. Demented.'

It was at this moment Marcus Charles came into the building, hat in hand. The constable with him had intercepted the woman in mauve and now spoke soothingly, asking her if she would just wait a moment. They would give her a cup of tea and she could say what was the matter.

He led her away.

Marcus took off his hat. 'Kate.'

'Marcus.'

'What are you doing here?'

Where should I begin? That I wanted to see Miss Dowzell, that I wanted to know what was going on. There might be some way of phrasing a sentence that would ensure he did not show me the door within fifteen polite seconds.

'I'd like to talk to you.'

'About?'

'Miss Dowzell.'

'This isn't a good time. No need to meddle.'

He waited.

I waited.

He waved his hat in the direction of the counter. We walked through to the room at the back. There was just one constable seated at a table. Marcus spoke to him.

'Find out from the sergeant what's going on.'

'Yes, sir.'

Marcus pulled out a chair.

We sat across from each other.

He placed his hands on the table. So did I. 'Marcus, Miss Dowzell didn't kill Jack Philips. They were to be married at St Mary's in Sandsend.'

He showed no surprise. 'On the first Monday

of September at noon.'

Well that was a relief. He knew. 'When I saw Miss Dowzell on Saturday, right before I found Jack Philips's body, she was so happy, so full of life and hope. It shone out of her. She didn't know he was dead.'

'Anything else?'

'She has asked to see me. I think she wants to know the circumstances surrounding my finding Jack. Also, she'll be concerned about their cat while she's locked up here.'

'The cat?'

'Jack's cat, Tiger – the one that Mrs Bailey asked about yesterday. Miss Dowzell took him home. Someone will have to look in on him.'

'I can't spare a constable for the cat but I'll look into it carefully. Was there anything else?' He pushed back his chair.

I hate it when people say that they will look into something carefully. Such words are rarely truthful.

He stood. 'Well thank you, Kate. I won't keep you.'

I didn't budge when Sergeant Garvin came hurrying in. 'The councillor's wife was near hysterical, sir. We've calmed her down but she's claiming that her sister-in-law, Miss Dowzell, tried to choke her, pulled the beads from her neck. I went to ask Miss Dowzell what was going on. She says the necklace came from the safe. I think she means the jeweller's safe.'

At the door, Marcus turned to me. 'Wait here.'

He was gone for several minutes. When he returned, his mouth was set tight. 'In your statement to Sergeant Garvin, you said that there were jet beads across the floor of the deceased's living room.'

'Yes.'

'You can speak to Miss Dowzell. Don't mention that the safe was open. Don't say anything about beads on the floor. Sergeant Garvin will be listening. Let Miss Dowzell talk to you. Say as little as possible.'

Sergeant Garvin trod softly as he led me back to the familiar cell.

Dora Dowzell was sitting on the narrow bed, knees pulled up against her chest. She clutched a broken necklace in her hand. Some beads had fallen onto the bed. They were Whitby jet beads carved in the classic rose flower shape. The ones that remained threaded were in ascending order of size. A jet pendant, also carved with a rose, hung from the centre of the necklace.

'Dora.'

She raised her head.

'I'm Kate. We met, briefly, on Saturday. I bought postcards, toffee, tickets, and the *Gazette*.' She stared, not really seeing.

'I'm so sorry about Jack's death. I went in his shop to buy a bracelet. It was I who found him.'

She lowered her head onto her knees. A few more beads dropped from the snapped thread of the necklace onto the bed.

She watched me pick them up.

I did not know where to begin. Say as little as possible, Marcus had instructed. Yet one of us must speak.

'May I sit down?' She did not say no. I perched

356

on the end of the bed. 'Jim Sykes and I are friends. He walked you back from the Mission yesterday. He helped you with the papers this morning. He told me you asked to speak to me.'

It was a small brainwave to open my bag where I carried the 'lucky pebbles' that Felicity gave me when she was about four years old. Not that I am superstitious but it had seemed a good idea to bring them with me. The pebbles were in a velvet pouch. I took it out and dropped the pebbles into my bag. I put the spilled beads into the pouch and offered it to Dora. 'Keep your necklace in this for now, until it can be re-threaded.'

She took it from me. Her hands shook. She could not do it.

'Let me.' She allowed me to take the necklace from her and place it in the pouch. I looked for more beads and found two on the floor. 'We have them all I think. It's beautiful.'

'It's mine.'

'Did Jack buy it for you?'

She nodded. 'He had it made. He had all sorts made for me in the jet workshop, when we thought...'

'When you thought your baby had died.'

'You know.'

'I talked to Mrs Webb. Brendan is safe.'

There was the slightest sound from beyond the open door.

'How do you come to have the necklace in here?'

'She was wearing it. My sister-in-law. It was in the safe, Jack's safe, along with a mourning collar and a brooch. She must have taken it.'

'I have a mourning collar. My mother-in-law bought it for me when they held a service for my husband.' I never wore it. 'What was yours like?'

She looked up. 'A triple row, carved, faceted, too fancy to wear.' Her hand went to her throat. 'Yet it was the kind of piece you like to touch.'

'He had them specially made at the jet workshop?'

'Yes, on Church Street, as if that would make up for my baby. It was no good. That was always between us, like a great fall of rock. They lied you see. My parents. They said my baby had died.'

'Where was Jack when you had the baby?'

'In Amsterdam. I stopped writing. When he came back, he didn't understand what had gone wrong. I had to tell him, and that it was all over.'

'And then you found out the truth, that Brendan was alive.'

'I wouldn't have called him Brendan, but I don't mind the name.' She sat so still that I feared she could become comatose. I waited, expecting Marcus or Sergeant Garvin to come in.

Nothing happened.

I waited.

After a long time, Dora looked up. Something in her had come back to life. 'Jack ... tell me about how you found him. Was he still alive? Did he speak?'

'He had been dead for a little while. I'm not sure how long.'

'How did he look?'

'He looked pale, but himself.'

Two large tears came to her eyes. 'When Mother told me my baby was a boy, and he died,

I always wondered would he have looked like Jack, or perhaps he would have taken after my side. I'm glad he looks like Jack.'

'Dora, where did you keep the jewellery that you no longer needed when you knew that Brendan was alive?'

'I stopped wearing it.'

'And where did you put the mourning collar and the necklace?'

'I gave it to Jack. He put it in the safe. He was already looking after the jewellery I had from my mother, because she was always after it.'

'She?'

'My sister-in-law. She'll have that too, but not for long. It will go like everything else, on the horses, on the dogs, on some scheme.'

'If it's been taken, you must have it back. Can you describe the jewellery to me?'

She stared at me. 'Why do you want to know?'

'It's yours. Your mother gave it to you. I think she must have been sorry for what she did, for the lies. Perhaps she knew you would eventually find out the truth. Brendan might marry, might have a daughter. You could pass something on.'

'I want to get out of here. I left Tiger in the house. And it's up to me to make the arrangements for Jack. Why am I here?'

I took out my notebook. 'You'll be home before you know it. Start with your mother's rings. I want to know what was taken from Jack's safe. Tell me. You're helping to make sure there is justice for Jack.'

A constable sat with Dora Dowzell.

In the office, Marcus looked through my notes at the description of Dora's jewellery – the pieces she had from her mother.

'May I take these pages, Kate?'

'Keep the notebook. There's little else in it.'

'Thank you.' Marcus had that nervous impatience to be off. 'I need to get to the brother's house and do a search. If he was stupid enough to let his wife wear a necklace taken from Jack Philips's safe then we have a good chance of finding the other jewellery too.'

'He could say that Dora was lying.'

Marcus temporarily lost his hard edge. He was still in a hurry but found time to explain. 'He could accuse her of lying, but we have his fingerprints from the safe.'

'Is that enough to go on?'

'We have sightings of Timothy Dowzell at the back of the Royal Hotel, near where we found the toffee hammer with blood on the head. He was seen by one of the porters.'

'Why? He could have wiped it clean or thrown it in the sea.'

'I think he knew there needed to be a suspect, and he kindly chose you, Kate. He chose the wrong woman.'

'And he did it twice. When I turned out to be a bad bet, he pointed a finger at his own sister.'

Perhaps I had misjudged Marcus. There was no animosity when he said, 'Nice man, eh, Kate?'

'Did he take the hammer with him into the jewellers? That would be a strange thing to do.'

Marcus picked up his hat, ready to go. 'Jack Philips had a sweet tooth. He had toffee on the sideboard. Dowzell picked up the little hammer and used it. Philips had a thin skull, sadly for him. But if it hadn't been the toffee hammer it would have been some other weapon.'

'Why? Not just for the jewellery?'

'The marriage. If Dora married Jack Philips, she would have sold up, and felt no obligation to provide for her brother. He'd run through his share of their legacy and been leeching on her for years.'

'The underlying economics, eh?'

'Exactly.' He put on his hat. 'If you'll excuse me, I have an arrest to make.'

He and I walked together into the waiting area. He left with a constable. I sat down. They must let Miss Dowzell out soon and I wanted to be sure she did not have to walk home alone.

Moments later, Sergeant Garvin came out from the back room. He was beaming. 'Good news. I have just taken a telephone call that Mr Cricklethorpe has regained consciousness. A nurse and a constable are with him now. Mrs Turner has returned home.'

'How wonderful. That's a great relief. And what about Miss Dowzell, sergeant?'

'Well, Mrs Shackleton, I'm about to escort Miss Dowzell home.' He lowered his voice. 'Would you care to come along? It would be helpful to have a lady present.'

'Yes I'll come.'

He glanced about. 'If we go straight away, we won't pass a certain person in the street when he is brought in for questioning...'

'You mean Timothy Dowzell?'

'It might be a good idea to call at Bagdale Hall

361

for a few moments, until the coast is clear.'

It staggered me that the sergeant thought this a good idea. If I were Dora Dowzell, the last person I would want to see would be Alma Turner who had tried her best to snaffle the ill-fated Jack Philips and his bungalow.

'Sergeant, isn't it up to Miss Dowzell to say where she wants to go? I'm guessing it will be home.'

Mrs Sugden was right. The man was besotted with Alma. He was searching for a reason to see her. 'Mrs Turner may have returned to Bagdale and I simply thought...'

'Of course. You'll want to call on her later. Mr Cricklethorpe may have said something significant to Alma as he was regaining consciousness.'

Thirty-Nine

It was almost dark by the time Felicity and Brendan reached Hopeman. A few bracket lamps were lit on Harbour Street. They walked the length of the street, assuming that the 'first house' meant the one nearest the harbour.

Felicity had expected her dad to live somewhere grand. Perhaps he had lived in a great house in Elgin.

Brendan must have been thinking along similar lines. 'He'll need to be by the harbour in his line of work.'

'Don't even consider it. We'll both need jobs,

362

but not that.'

She knocked on the door of the first house and stepped back.

A dog barked.

Someone spoke.

After a moment or two, the door opened. The woman who peered at Felicity wore a black dress and flowered pinny. She was old, probably fifty, with grey hair and a worn face. She looked at Felicity as if at a puzzle she could not make out, searching her face for something significant.

Felicity remembered her manners. 'I'm sorry to call so late. I'm here to see Mr Turner.' The woman stared at her. Felicity tried again. 'Am I at the right house for Mr Walter Turner?'

Now that she looked at this person, Felicity remembered that her mother once mentioned a countess in the same breath as Felicity's father. This woman was no countess. She was someone you might see along Church Street, shopping at the market. Felicity thought she had better give her name. Perhaps she was being mistaken for a debt collector.

'I'm Felicity, Walter Turner's daughter. I'm here to see my father. This is Brendan.'

The woman opened the door wider. 'Come in, lassie. Sorry to keep you on the step. I was no expecting callers at this hour.'

The doorway was so low that Brendan had to stoop.

The dog that had barked was old and thin, a black and white border collie. It pounded its tail on the rag rug but made no attempt to move. Felicity went up to it and stroked its head. The dog was tired, and so, suddenly, was she.

The woman took her knapsack. 'Sit yerself doon.' There was a rocking chair, a straight-back chair and a tall stool.

Felicity and Brendan exchanged a look. He moved towards the stool. She sat down in the straight-back chair. 'We're at the right house then?'

'Indeed you are. Your father is sleeping.' She pointed to the ceiling. So when Felicity had stood outside and heard someone speaking, it had been the woman talking to the dog.

The woman put a pan of milk and water on the fire. She buttered pieces of seed cake as the pan heated. 'You must be fair frozen and clemmed to have come all this way.'

So she knows about me, Felicity thought. Who is she? The woman did not think to give her name and Felicity could not ask. Perhaps she was supposed to know.

She made cocoa for them and put it on the square lino-covered table with the buttered slices of cake. 'I see the likeness to Walter. I do, I do.' She watched Felicity eat and drink. 'You'd like to see your da.'

I would.

The woman nodded. 'Aye, aye, that you would.' She lit a candle. 'Are the pair of you wed?'

'Not yet,' Brendan answered.

'Then I'll take you next door, Brendan.' She turned to Felicity. 'You can sleep on the trundle bed.'

Felicity followed her up the stairs.

The iron bedstead with its frail occupant dominated the room. It was placed so as to give a view through the window. A low fire burned in the grate. A scent of herbs came from a great bowlful of greenery on the chest of drawers. The woman set a straight-back chair near the bed and motioned Felicity to sit.

At first, Felicity thought there must be some mistake. This man was old and thin, his eyes bright with something like fever. His face was hollow, cheekbones taut against the skin, but there was a little cleft below his nose, and the memory of a dimple in his chin.

'Dad. It's Felicity. I've come to see you.'

His face did not change. Only his Adam's apple moved and he gulped as if for air. The movement seemed to pain him and send a shudder through the body under the blankets. His hand appeared. More claw than hand. His fingers stretched towards hers. He squeezed her hand. His lips moved in something like a smile. She had never before seen a man cry. It was a very small set of tears. The voice in her head said, Don't cry, Felicity. Smile.

'How did I know you'd come, Felicity? I just did. I wished it.'

She took out the small fruitcake she had brought from Botham's, wrapped and re-wrapped to keep it dry. 'I brought you a cake.'

His words came out as a croak. 'Did you bake it?'

'No. It's from Botham's.'

It was a small smile. His teeth were black, and missing. 'Good lass. You get nothing done standing over a stove.'

'That's what Mam says.'

'How is she?'

'She thinks of you.' Felicity had meant to say that her mother wanted him back, but now she could not say it, especially since the woman downstairs might be listening.

'Tell her I think of her.'

'She knows.'

They sat for a long time. She held his hand, which as she grew used to the candlelight she saw was blue with lines, the skin almost transparent. 'What's that woman's name, and who is she?'

'She is Morag McAndrew. Say you brought the cake for her.' He shut his eyes.

Perhaps he was asleep, perhaps not.

She took the cake downstairs. The woman sat in the rocking chair, knitting, the dog lying by her feet. 'I've taken your laddie round to a neighbour.'

'Thank you.' Felicity took out the cake. She saw now that it was not fit to offer. 'I brought something, but it's no good. My knapsack went overboard.'

Morag McAndrew set aside her knitting and took the cake from her. 'A drop of seawater won't hurt. Now come on, you can help me make up that bed. I'll sleep down here the night and be the better for it.'

Her dad had fallen asleep. Mrs McAndrew pulled out the bed. 'I'm not changing sheets at this hour. No one's slept on it but me and I'm clean.'

She produced a nightgown for Felicity. It was freshly laundered and smelled of lavender. Whoever she was, Felicity felt glad that her dad had someone to take care of him. But why hadn't he come home? Would she ever ask him, would he ever say, ever admit that her mother sent him away? Perhaps that wasn't true. He was a wanderer, her mother had said. Wanderers can't help it.

As she settled down on the narrow bed, she was aware that he was awake, and listening. She felt snug and glad. 'Did you ever come back to Whitby in the night and come to see me?'

'I did. You were always sleeping. Sleep now.' He blew her a kiss, and it was as if he cast a spell because she closed her eyes and slept.

When she woke it was the early hours and the fire almost out. She put on a few coals and poked at the ashes. As the fire burned more brightly, shadows danced on the ceiling. She sensed that he was awake too.

'Do you remember, Dad, when the sea took our house?'

'We'll never see anything like that again.'

The next morning, he was already sitting up when she woke. He looked so much better that she felt full of hope. Morag McAndrew was beside him, watching him drink tea.

'There's tea in the pot down there and some hot water and a basin in the scullery. I'll be up here a wee while so have yourself a wash. There's soap and towel.'

When she had washed and drunk a cup of tea and eaten a slice of cake, Felicity felt revived. Her plan had worked, though not in the way she imagined. She could not think what must come next.

She went out to look about and was drawn to the harbour. Hopeman was a pretty spot. If there had been fishing boats, they were all gone out. Only an upturned rowing boat and something under tarpaulin remained. The white sand was strewn with seaweed thrown up during the sea's fierce tantrums. Kelp, egg wrack and wig wrack.

It would do her dad good to come outside, catch the sunshine and breathe fresh air after being cooped up in that little bedroom.

She went back to the house, with this new plan in mind.

It was only then that she gave him the money belt, after taking out what remained of her own savings.

He handed the five-pound notes to Morag McAndrew. 'To pass on,' he said. He looked at Felicity and winked. 'There's been a change of management. I'm retired from the fray.'

Felicity expected to see Brendan. Morag told her that Brendan had gone out fishing with the man from next door.

She and Morag helped her dad downstairs. A rickety wheelchair that she had noticed the night before stood in the street, braked with a brick to keep it from running away. Her dad edged himself into it, brushing away their attempts to help.

Together, they pushed him down to the harbour. Morag came back with a chair for Felicity and then left them together.

His breathing was so slow and laboured that Felicity feared it might shudder to a stop.

After a long time, his body relaxed a little and he found the energy to speak. 'Sea air does me good.' He began to cough, screwing up his face and closing his eyes. He made light of it. 'It's a cough

368

that'll carry me off, but not yet, not now you're here.'

Felicity wanted to hear about Madeira, about South Africa, about how you hypnotise a person. He wanted to know about Brendan, about Botham's, the Spa ballroom, and how Alma taught herself to be a fortune teller.

They talked, on and off, until late afternoon, with long rests between while he concentrated very hard on breathing, or dozed a little.

The fishing boats came back. Brendan joined them.

That was when Morag came hurrying down, a telegram in the pocket of her apron, as though it must be kept secret until handed to its recipient: Felicity.

Felicity had never received a telegram before. She opened it.

Arrange nuptials STOP Birth certificates follow STOP Notify date STOP Alma Turner Mary Webb

'Is there a reply?' Morag asked. 'The telegram lad's waiting.'

Felicity stared at the words. 'I don't know what Mam means.'

Morag took it back from her and read. She passed it to Walter, who read it and passed it to Brendan.

It was Morag who interpreted. 'It means you two don't go back to Whitby till you're wed.'

'No reply,' Walter said. 'Your mothers have spoken. Just do it.'

Forty

Alma sat beside Percy Cricklethorpe's bed. He had been allowed home on condition that he engage a nurse to take care of him. His brush with death had led to a loosening of the purse strings. Crickly no longer voiced objections to parting with cash. He was more than willing to pay for cleaners, and the professional nurse who came highly recommended.

When the nurse was at her dinner, Alma came to sit with him. She had harboured a specific question for several days but had waited until he was sufficiently recovered before interrogating him. She feared he might slip into unconsciousness, real or pretended, if challenged.

After disarming him with harmless chitchat, she came to her point in a teasing way. 'It was you, Crickly. You sent Felicity chasing after Walter. Now don't deny it.'

He looked shifty, which she took as an admission of guilt.

'Why did you do that behind my back?'

He puffed out his cheeks, and ran his tongue around the inside of his mouth, looking for the right words. 'I knew Walter was ill.'

'Well so did I.'

'You don't know how poorly he is. He's given up on everything. Our Walter doesn't have long to live.'

Alma felt a deep spasm of regret. She supposed that she knew that all along, without having let herself fully acknowledge the truth. Turner turned cold, Turner turned old.

'You should have consulted me.'

'Anyway, I didn't send Felicity. I merely gave hints, led the way. She's wanted to see him for years. You knew that.'

'Felicity could have died in that boat. They both could.'

Cricklethorpe pushed himself up against the pillows. 'I never imagined Brendan Webb would be so foolish as to think himself capable of sailing the *Doram* without a more experienced hand beside him.'

'Of course he's foolish. He's eighteen years old. Weren't you foolish at eighteen?'

'I suppose so.' Cricklethorpe looked uncomfortable and cast about for an explanation, looking at the ceiling for help. 'It was the words of the old song you know, when I thought about Felicity and her longing to see Walter.'

'What old song?'

He gave a tuneful rendition of the wartime number 'I don't want to lose you, but I think you ought to go'.

Alma sighed. 'Lean forward.' She plumped up his pillows. 'Well as it happens, it's turned out for the best. We have a date for the wedding.'

'What wedding?'

'Felicity and Brendan in Hopeman Kirk.'

'What kind of church is that?'

'The United Free Church of Scotland.'

'They won't accept Felicity and Brendan.'

'It's arranged. The father will give away the bride, even if he has to be carried to the church and propped up.'

For the first time since his recovery, Cricklethorpe could find no words.

Alma helped him out by continuing. 'Of course it will be after Jack's funeral. People will understand that the wedding was already arranged.'

'And was it?'

'Of course not, but don't you dare say otherwise.'

Cricklethorpe frowned. 'Felicity is marrying Brendan Webb, after he nearly got her killed?'

'The nearly getting her killed, that was you.'

'I thought he was just the brother, Hilda's brother. Felicity can do better than that. He's a long streak of whitewash. Sails up and down the coast on a pleasure boat, looking for tips.'

'He's a long streak of whitewash who may be in line for a legacy. Mrs Webb and I have discussed it. At the very least we believe we might see Felicity and Brendan running the newsagents on Skinner Street.'

'With Miss Dowzell?'

'She will be moving into the bungalow at Sandsend, with her cat and a small dog she found in Mulgrave Woods.' Alma allowed herself a sigh. Being carried over the threshold of that bungalow would have been an entry into dreamland.

Cricklethorpe stared at his glass of water. Alma did not help him. He leaned over, but couldn't quite reach it. 'Can't they marry here, in Whitby?'

'After they've been up to Scotland and back unaccompanied? Don't be silly.'

'But you'll want to see Felicity married.'

Alma smiled serenely. 'And so I shall, with Kate, Mrs Webb and Miss Dowzell. We intend to make sure of this business. There's been more than enough scandal, speculation and tittletattle in this town. We'll take the train from York. First class. We're booked into a highly superior hotel in Elgin, recommended by the management at the Royal.'

Cricklethorpe made a small choking sound. 'Miss Dowzell and Mrs Webb, and you?'

Alma passed him the glass of water. 'Miss Dowzell and Mrs Webb have a lot in common.'

'Since when, and what?'

'They're both great supporters of the Mission.'

The afternoon was hot. Alma was sitting in the courtyard, with a jug of lemonade. She had brought out an extra glass. When Sergeant Garvin put in an appearance, she was able to pour him a drink. He was out of uniform and therefore off duty.

'I thought I'd call on my way home, and return your property.' He produced the bag in which he had taken away her marriage lines and the record of her fortune-telling earnings.

'Thank you. Do you need the bag now?' She did not wish to put everything on the small table and be reminded of that awful day. Nor did she wish to risk spilling lemonade on her papers.

'No. Keep the bag for now.' He was cheerful, and she saw what he must be thinking. Once emptied, the hessian bag would give them a reason to see each other again.

She smiled.

He sipped his lemonade. 'I'm very happy to hear the news of the wedding, Mrs Turner. An excellent match, your Felicity and young Brendan.'

'A summer wedding is always a treat, though it is distressing that it should be so close to poor Jack Philips's funeral.'

They maintained a respectful silence. A butterfly landed on the camellias.

As the scent of camellias and lavender drifted across the courtyard, she knew that it must be time to speak, to give him some little encouragement.

'You may be wondering why the wedding is to be held in Scotland.'

He shook his head. 'I'm sure there is a good reason.'

'My husband' – these were two words she avoided saying whenever possible – 'My husband Walter is in Scotland. He is not well enough to travel and that is the reason we go there.'

'I see. I'm sorry to hear it.'

She hoped he was not really sorry. 'Walter's sojourns in warmer climes did not help in the long run. He has given up his search for health.'

'Oh.'

'He lived in foreign lands. He says he wishes to die in his own language.' Walter had said no such thing but she was glad to have thought of it. 'Warmer climes carry their own dangers. I'm afraid the doctors do not give him long.'

He reached across the table and squeezed her hand.

After a sorrowful moment, she spoke again.

'There was something I hoped you might help me with, Sergeant Garvin.'

'Anything at all, Mrs Turner.'

'I need to be absent from my fortune-telling duties for at least a week, to attend Felicity's wedding. I know the Urban District Council has more important matters in hand, what with a new election to replace the man whose name I won't speak. You know everyone. Would you guide me towards finding a replacement who will take over the pepper pot?'

'Of course.' He put on his thoughtful look. 'It would be a disappointment for visitors not to have a consultation in your pepper pot, but it would have to be just the right person to fill your shoes.' He thought for a moment. 'There are two competent ladies who might be willing to step in. One of them is a genuine Romany, but with no connection to Madam Rosa.'

'A genuine Romany would be perfect.' Alma was taking a chance. A genuine Romany might show her up as something of a fraud. Still, one door closes and another opens.

The sergeant finished his lemonade. It was now or never for Alma. She disliked the thought that one of these competent fortune-telling women could cast a spell on Sergeant Garvin.

'You are not on duty today, Mr Garvin?'

He put down his glass. 'No, not today.'

'I know you sometimes take a walk on your free afternoons. Today I intend to take a walk myself.'

'Then perhaps we might walk together, Mrs Turner?'

'I'd like that, Mr Garvin.'

375

'Do you think you might call me Rodney, when we're alone?'

She fixed him with her most melting stare. 'If you'll call me Alma.'

They walked along the front, which Alma knew was quite a risk for the sergeant – for Rodney – to take. People might talk. No. People would certainly talk.

They made their way along the West Cliff and stood to admire the colourful row of bathing huts. Someone emerged from one of the huts. Alma stared. Rodney Garvin was looking in the other direction and did not recognise Kate Shackleton in her bathing costume. She raced towards the sea with Chief Inspector Marcus Charles, similarly clad, beside her.

Forty-One

We took a chance, Marcus and I, on not being noticed on the sands. It was not the done thing for a man who had just escorted a prisoner to York, and completed paperwork for a murder trial, to be seen bathing in the North Sea on a sunny afternoon.

The sea was so icy it made me screw up my eyes. We ran until the water reached my waist, and then began to swim. Marcus is a strong swimmer. He ought to be, given that he lives near Hampstead Heath and goes swimming in the pond there almost every day summer and winter. I wished I had a pool so close.

It was wonderful to let the sea wash away the horror and uncertainty of the past days.

Marcus turned, swam underwater and came up beside me. 'I wish we were here on holiday together, for another fortnight or a month.'

'Well we're not, so make the most of it.'

'I intend to.'

'And you wouldn't wish it if the weather turned and we had another downpour.'

'Oh yes I would.'

When we had swum, we sat by our hired bathing hut, drinking tea from a flask. I unwrapped the sandwiches made in the hotel kitchen.

'I missed you when I was away in America.' Marcus bit into an egg and cress.

'Did you?' This was not what I wanted to hear.

'You know I did.'

If he had missed me during his shipboard romance, then no wonder it failed. But to say that would sound teasing, and only lovers tease.

I could not honestly say that I had missed him, though I might miss him, after today.

We both pulled a face at the same time. Sand had found its way into the sandwiches, as sand always does.

'What time is your train, Marcus?'

'Why?'

'I was thinking you could do with a meal before you go back. If there's time, we could go somewhere else – away from the hotel.'

He nodded. 'I'd like that. We could take the train to Scarborough and find somewhere to eat there.'

I had a better idea. 'I'll bring my car round to the Crescent. I know somewhere we can go. Bring your case if you like. I'll drop you off at the station after we've eaten.'

Forty-Two

Felicity's wedding would be in three days. This seemed hard to believe. I would have to stop myself thinking of her as a child. My trunk had gone ahead to Elgin, containing the black and white dress I had bought for her, along with something she might borrow. Alma would bring something blue.

The plan was that we would meet in the ladies waiting room of York railway station: Alma, Mrs Webb, Hilda Webb, Miss Dowzell and me. Hilda was to be bridesmaid. Ian Webb, Brendan's brother and best man, would follow the next day.

I stepped from the Leeds train into the noise, smoke and steam of York station, carrying the rather large bag of provisions Mrs Sugden had prepared. She does not trust railway food.

Alma was already in the waiting room, by the fire, looking beautiful in silk and velvet. She smiled a welcome. 'The others won't be long. Hilda is buying chocolate. Miss Dowzell and Mrs Webb are in search of something to read on the train.'

I put down my bag. 'I've brought a couple of novels too, and a pack of cards.'

Alma gave a slightly tragic smile as if to indicate

378

that novels and playing cards would not be required by her. 'It will be strange to see Walter again after all this time. Felicity wrote to say I must prepare myself for a shock.'

'Poor Walter.'

'Yes, poor Walter. Only the thought of Felicity's wedding keeps him going. He won't last the winter, especially not up there on that coast.'

'Then I'm glad for Felicity's sake that she found him.'

Alma budged up to make room for me. 'So am I.'

'It's brave of Miss Dowzell to come.'

Alma looked about, to make sure no one was listening. 'Brendan doesn't know his parentage but he might one of these days, and then he'll be glad to have had his natural mother witness his marriage.'

'How complicated it sounds when you say it, but here we are, and it doesn't seem difficult at all.'

'There is something I wanted to say, Kate, before the others come back.'

'Oh?'

'If I don't say it now I may forget and then in a year or so, you might say, "Well, Alma never told me that".'

'What is it?'

She took out her powder compact, looked at herself in the mirror and was satisfied. 'Say I were to marry in a year's time. When that day comes, would you mind very much if I don't ask you to be maid of honour?'

'No of course not.'

'Only you didn't bring me much luck last time.'

'I'm sorry.'

'Oh it's not entirely your fault, but I must be careful how I do things, and you did spend that night in custody.'

It was thoughtful of her to remind me of that, not that I would ever forget it.

She continued. 'A police officer can't marry just anyone. Rodney – Sergeant Garvin – believes I will have to be interviewed by the superintendent. We've already decided what to say regarding my fortune telling.'

'What will you say?'

'Why, just the truth of course. I only ever took on fortune telling to oblige the Urban District Council after Madam Rosa treacherously decamped to Scarborough for better pickings.'

'And if you are asked about your Madam Alma prophecies?'

'Oh, so few copies were sold that people will forget all about it. After all, my prophecies were for 1927. As soon as 1927 is history, who will care? We should all look forward, look to the future, even you, Kate.'

Acknowledgments

Thanks to the many people in Whitby who talked to me about their town.

I'm grateful to Geoff Wilson (Mr Whitby) for his guided tour; John Cattaneo of Bagdale Hall Hotel; Pat Welch; Yvonne Barlett; Joy Peach; Jo Botham; Libby Thompson; Jim and Mary Hebden; Lynn Runskill; Fiona Duncan; Cheryl Killey; Deb Gill Anders; George and Susan Dawson; Noel Stokoe; staff at Whitby Library and the Whitby Literary and Philosophical Society; Kieran and Margaret for the lift from Sandsend, and John Jackson for calculating nautical miles.

The publishers hope that this book has given you enjoyable reading. Large Print Books are especially designed to be as easy to see and hold as possible. If you wish a complete list of our books please ask at your local library or write directly to:

Magna Large Print Books
Magna House, Long Preston,
Skipton, North Yorkshire.
BD23 4ND

This Large Print Book for the partially sighted, who cannot read normal print, is published under the auspices of

THE ULVERSCROFT FOUNDATION

THE ULVERSCROFT FOUNDATION

... we hope that you have enjoyed this Large Print Book. Please think for a moment about those people who have worse eyesight problems than you ... and are unable to even read or enjoy Large Print, without great difficulty.

You can help them by sending a donation, large or small to:

**The Ulverscroft Foundation,
1, The Green, Bradgate Road,
Anstey, Leicestershire, LE7 7FU,
England.**
or request a copy of our brochure for more details.

The Foundation will use all your help to assist those people who are handicapped by various sight problems and need special attention.

Thank you very much for your help.